**Praise for Jim Butcher and the #1 *New York Times*
bestselling Dresden Files**

"What would you get if you crossed Spenser with Merlin? Probably you would come up with someone very like Harry Dresden."
—*The Washington Times*

"Harry Dresden is perhaps the best-written supernatural detective working today."
—SFRevu

"Superlative."
—*Publishers Weekly* (starred review)

"The Dresden Files is still one of the most consistently well-written urban fantasy series in existence."
—LoveVampires

"An edge-of-your-seat thriller."
—*Locus*

"Butcher . . . spins an excellent noirish detective yarn in a well-crafted, supernaturally charged setting."
—*Booklist* (starred review)

"Dynamic and complex and utterly fascinating."
—Huntress Book Reviews

"A great series . . . one of the most enjoyable marriages of the fantasy and mystery genres on the shelves."
—*Cinescape*

"This stunning, exciting series entry with its heart-stopping action will shock and thrill Butcher fans."
—*Library Journal*

# JIM BUTCHER

# BRIEF CASES

## MORE STORIES FROM THE DRESDEN FILES

ACE
NEW YORK

ACE
Published by Berkley
An imprint of Penguin Random House LLC
1745 Broadway, New York, NY 10019

Copyright © 2018 by Jim Butcher
"A Fistful of Warlocks" copyright © 2017 by Jim Butcher. First published in *Straight Outta Tombstone*,
edited by David Boop (Baen Books). Reprinted by permission of the author.
"B is for Bigfoot" copyright © 2012 by Jim Butcher. First published in *Under My Hat:*
*Tales from the Cauldron*, edited by Jonathan Strahan (Random House Books for Young Readers).
Reprinted by permission of the author.
"AAAA Wizardry" copyright © 2010 by Jim Butcher. First published in The Dresden
Files Roleplaying Game, Volume Two: Our World, edited by Amanda Valentine
(Evil Hat Productions, LLC). Reprinted by permission of the author.
"I Was a Teenage Bigfoot" copyright © 2012 by Jim Butcher.
First published in *Blood Lite III: Aftertaste*, edited by Kevin J. Anderson
(Pocket Books / Simon and Schuster). Reprinted by permission of the author.
"Curses" copyright © 2011 by Jim Butcher. First published in *Naked City: Tales of Urban Fantasy*,
edited by Ellen Datlow (St. Martin's Griffin). Reprinted by permission of the author.
"Even Hand" copyright © 2010 by Jim Butcher. First published in *Dark and Stormy Knights*, edited by
P. N. Elrod (St. Martin's Griffin). Reprinted by permission of the author.
"Bigfoot on Campus" copyright © 2012 by Jim Butcher. First published in *Hex Appeal*, edited by
P. N. Elrod (St. Martin's Griffin). Reprinted by permission of the author.
"Bombshells" copyright © 2013 by Jim Butcher. First published in *Dangerous Women*,
edited by George R. R. Martin and Gardner Dozois
(Tor Books). Reprinted by permission of the author.
"Cold Case" copyright © 2016 by Jim Butcher. First published in *Shadowed Souls*,
edited by Jim Butcher and Kerrie L. Hughes (Roc). Reprinted by permission of the author.
"Jury Duty" copyright © 2015 by Jim Butcher. First published in *Unbound*, edited by Shawn
Speakman (Grim Oak Press). Reprinted by permission of the author.
"Day One" copyright © 2016 by Jim Butcher. First published in *Unfettered II*, edited by Shawn
Speakman (Grim Oak Press). Reprinted by permission of the author.
"Zoo Day" copyright © 2018 by Jim Butcher. Published here for the first time in
any form by permission of the author.
Penguin Random House supports copyright. Copyright fuels creativity, encourages diverse voices,
promotes free speech, and creates a vibrant culture. Thank you for buying an authorized edition of
this book and for complying with copyright laws by not reproducing, scanning, or distributing any
part of it in any form without permission. You are supporting writers and allowing Penguin Random
House to continue to publish books for every reader.

ACE is a registered trademark and the A colophon is a trademark of
Penguin Random House LLC.

ISBN: 9780451492111

The Library of Congress cataloged the hardcover edition as follows:

Names: Butcher, Jim, 1971– author.
Title: Brief cases / Jim Butcher.
Description: First edition. | New York: Ace, 2018. | Series: Dresden files
Identifiers: LCCN 2017058794 | ISBN 9780451492104 (hardcover) |
ISBN 9780451492128 (ebook)
Subjects: | BISAC: FICTION/Fantasy/Urban Life. | FICTION/Short Stories
(single author). | GSAFD: Fantasy fiction.
Classification: LCC PS3602.U85 A6 2018 | DDC 813/.6—dc23
LC record available at https://lccn.loc.gov/2017058794

Ace hardcover edition / June 2018
Ace trade paperback edition / June 2019

Printed in the United States of America
1   3   5   7   9   10   8   6   4   2

Cover art by Chris McGrath

This is a work of fiction. Names, characters, places, and incidents either are the product
of the author's imagination or are used fictitiously, and any resemblance to actual persons, living or
dead, business establishments, events, or locales is entirely coincidental.

# TABLE OF CONTENTS

# BRIEF CASES

# A FISTFUL OF WARLOCKS

Some stories happen because a writer gets inspired by some wild idea that needs expression. Some stories are carefully put together as part of a greater whole.

And some stories you write because a professional friend asks you if you want to contribute to an anthology, and it sounds like a really fun idea. This is how the next tale was born—I needed a weird, weird West story so that I could contribute to *Straight Outta Tombstone*.

The upside of putting this project together is that the late-nineteenth century was largely a blank slate in the universe of the Dresden Files, so I was able to do whatever I wanted without being restricted by the 1.5 million words of story that had already been written. The downside was that the late-nineteenth century in the universe of the Dresden Files was largely a blank slate, so I had to start figuring out how to braid this story thread in particular into the greater story.

One of my go-to concepts when writing earlier eras of any story is to focus on characters who are the passionate young hotheads in any given setting—those are the people who generally provide me with the most interesting choices and stories. So, for this story, Anastasia Luccio fit the bill perfectly, and I've always loved the character and wished she could have more stage time. I worked out her early history as a young Warden and decided that she had been instrumental in the White Council's decades-long war with, and victory over, the greatest necromancer of the previous millennium.

This is the start of what is now in my head a four- or five-book story all its own. I don't know that I'll ever get to write that tale of dark old Western supernatural horror, featuring Anastasia as the magical and gun-fighting protagonist, flanked by such figures as Wyatt Earp and Doc Holliday of the Venatori Umbrorum, but it's a hell of a good movie in my head.

So maybe imagine as you read this next piece that the movie begins here. . . .

The American West was not the most miserable land I had ever traveled, but it came quite near to it. It was the scenery, more than anything, that drove the spirit out of the body—endless empty plains that did not so much roll as slump with varying degrees of hopelessness, with barely a proper tree to be seen. The late-summer sun beat the ground into something like the bottom of an oven.

"I grow weary of Kansas," said my not-horse. "The rivers here are scarcely enough to keep me alive."

"Hush, Karl," I said to the *näcken*. "We are near to town, and to the warlock. I would prefer if we did not announce our presence."

The *näcken* sighed with a great, exaggerated motion that set the saddle to creaking, and stomped one hoof on the ground. With a pure white coat and standing at a lean and powerful seventeen hands, he made a magnificent mount—as fast as the swiftest mortal horse and far more tireless. "As you wish, Anastasia."

"Warden Luccio," I reprimanded him tartly. "And the sooner we catch this creature and his master, the sooner you will have served your probation, and the sooner you may return to your homeland."

The *näcken* flattened his ears at this reminder of his servitude.

"Do not you become angry with me," I told him. "You promised to serve as my loyal mount if I could ride you for the space of an hour without being thrown. It is hardly my fault if you assumed I could not survive such a ride under the surface of the water."

"Hmph," said the *näcken*, and he gave me an evil glare. "Wizards." But he subsided. Murderous monsters, the *näcken*, but they were good to their word.

It was then that we crested what could only quite generously be called a rise, and I found myself staring down at a long, shallow valley that positively swarmed with life. Powdery dust covered the entire thing in a vast cloud, revealing a hive of tarred wooden buildings that looked as if they'd been slapped together over the course of an evening by drunken teamsters. Then there was a set of gleaming railroad tracks used so often that they shone even through the dust. On the northern side of the tracks stood a whitewashed mirror image of those buildings, neat streets and rows of solidly built homes and businesses. Corrals that could have girdled the feet of some mountains were filled with a small sea of cattle being herded and driven by men who could scarcely be distinguished from their horses beneath their mutual coating of dust. To one side of the town, a lonely little hill was crowned with a small collection of grave markers.

And the people. The sheer number of people bustling about this gathering of buildings in the middle of nothing was enough to boggle the mind. I sat for a moment, stunned at the energetic enormity of the place, which looked like the setting of some obscure passage from Dante, perhaps a circle of hell that had been edited from the original text.

The warlock I pursued could take full advantage of a crowd like that, making my job many times more difficult than it had been a moment before.

"So," said the *näcken* sourly, "that is Dodge City."

THE WARLOCK WOULD hide in the rough part of town—his kind could rarely find sanctuary among stolid, sober townsfolk. The unease warlocks created around them, combined with the frequent occurrence of the bizarre as a result of their talents, made them stand out like mounds of manure in a field of flowers. But the same talents that made them pariahs in normal mortal society benefited them in its shadows.

I rode for the south side of the tracks and stopped at the first sizable building.

"Do not allow yourself to be stolen," I advised Karl as I dismounted.

The *näcken* flattened his ears and snorted.

I smiled at him, patted his neck, and tossed his reins over a post and beam set up for the purpose outside of the first building that looked likely to support human beings in better condition than vermin. I removed the light duster that had done the best it could to protect my dress from the elements, draped it neatly over the saddle, and belted on my sword and gun.

I went into the building, and found it to be a bathhouse and brothel. A few moments of conversation with the woman in charge of it resulted in a job offer, which I declined politely; a bath, which I could not enjoy nearly thoroughly enough to satisfy me; and directions to the seediest dens of ruffians in town.

The warlock wasn't in the first location or the second, but by the time I reached the Long Branch Dance Hall and Saloon near sundown, I was fairly sure I'd found my man.

I entered the place to the sound of only moderately rhythmic stomping as a dozen women performed something like a dance together on a wooden stage, to the music of several nimble-fingered violinists playing in the style of folk music. The bar was already beginning to fill with a crowd of raucous men. Some of them were freshly bathed, but others were still wearing more dust than cloth, their purses heavy with new coin.

But, more important, the air of the place practically thrummed with tension. It was hardly noticeable at first glance—but eyes glanced toward the doors a little too quickly when I came in, and at least half of the men in the place were standing far too stiffly and warily to be drunkenly celebrating their payday and their lives.

"Pardon me, ma'am," said a voice to my right as I came in.

I turned to find a very tall, lean fellow whose wrists stuck out from the bottom of his coat's sleeves. He had a thick, drooping mustache, a flat-brimmed hat, and a deputy's star pinned to his coat, and wore his gun as if it had been given to him upon the occasion of his birth.

His demeanor was calm, his voice polite and friendly—and he had the eyes of a raptor, sharp and clear and ready to deliver sudden violence at a moment's notice.

"Yes?" I asked.

"City ordinance against carrying sidearms, ma'am," he said. His voice was deep and musically resonant in his lean chest. I liked it immediately. "If you're not a peace officer, you'll need to turn in your gun for as long as you're in town."

"I find this ordinance irksome," I said.

The corners of his eyes wrinkled and his cheeks tightened slightly. The mustache made it difficult to see his mouth. "If I was a woman as good-looking as you in a place like this, I'd find it powerful irksome, too," he said, "but the law is the law."

"And what does the ordinance say about swords?" I asked.

"Can't recall that it says anything 'bout that," the deputy said.

I unfastened my belt and slid the gun from it, still in its holster. I offered it to him. "I assume I can turn it over to you, Deputy?"

He touched the brim of his hat and took the gun. "Thank you, ma'am. Might I know your name so I can be sure your weapon gets safe back to you?"

I smiled at him. "Anastasia Luccio."

"Charmed, Anastasia," said the deputy. He squinted at my sidearm and said, "Webley. Lot of gun."

He was not so very much taller than me. I arched an eyebrow at him and smiled. "I am a lot of woman. I assure you, Deputy, that I am more than capable of handling it."

His eyes glinted, relaxed and amused. "Well. People say a lot of things, ma'am."

"When my business here is done, perhaps we shall go outside the town limits and wager twenty dollars on which of us is the better marksman."

He let his head fall back and barked out a quick laugh. "Ma'am, losing that bet would be a singular pleasure."

I looked around the saloon again. "It seems that tensions are running high at the moment," I said. "Might I ask why that is?"

The lawman pursed his lips thoughtfully and then said, "Well, there's some fellas on one side of the tracks upset at some other fellas on the other, ma'am, is the short of it." He smiled as he said it, as if enjoying some private jest. "Shouldn't be of much concern to you, ma'am. This is a rough place, but we don't much take kindly to a man who'd lift his hand to a woman." A pair of cowboys entered the saloon, laughing loudly and clearly already drunk. His calm eyes tracked them. He slid my holstered gun around beneath his stool and touched his finger to the brim of his hat again. "You have a good time, now."

"Thank you, Deputy," I said. Then I walked to the exact center of the room.

As a Warden of the White Council of Wizardry, I traveled a great deal and dealt with dangerous men. I was comfortable in places like this one and worse, though I had noted that they rarely seemed to be comfortable with me. The only women in sight were those working behind the bar, in the kitchen, and on the stage, so I rather stuck out. There was little sense in attempting anything like subtlety, so I donned my bottle green spectacles, focused my supernatural senses, and began a slow survey of the entire place.

The energy known as magic exists on a broad spectrum, much like light. Just as light can be split into its colors by a sufficient prism, magical energy can be more clearly distinguished by using the proper tools. The spectacles gave me a chance to view the energy swirling around the crowded room. It was strongly influenced by the presence of human emotion, and various colors had gathered around individuals according to their current humor.

Angry red tension tinted many auras, while lighter shades of pink surrounded the more merrily inebriated. Workers, including the dancers and dealers at the tables, evinced the steady green of those focused on task, while the deputy and a shotgun-wielding man seated on a tall stool at the end of the bar pulsed with the protective azure of guardians.

The warlock sat in the little balcony overlooking the stage, at a table with three other men, playing cards. Through the spectacles, shadows had gathered so thickly over their game that it almost seemed they had doused their lanterns and were playing in the dark.

I drew a breath. One warlock was typically not a threat to a cautious, well-trained, and properly equipped Warden. Two could be a serious challenge. The current Captain of the Wardens, a man named McCoy, a man with a great deal more power and experience than me, had once brought down three.

But as I watched through the spectacles, I realized that the warlock hadn't simply been running. He'd been running to more of his kind.

There were four of them.

I took off the spectacles and moved into an open space at the bar, where I would hopefully be overlooked for a few moments longer, and thought furiously.

My options had just become much more limited. In a direct confrontation with that many opponents, I would have little chance of victory. Which was not to say that I could not attack them. They were involved in their card game, and I had seen no evidence of magical defenses. An overwhelming strike might take them all at once.

Of course, fire magic was the only thing that would do for that kind of work—and it would leave the crowded building aflame. Tarred wood exposed to a blast of supernatural fire would become an inferno in seconds. Not only that, but such an action would violate one of the Council's unspoken laws: Wizards were expected to minimize the use of their abilities in the presence of magic-ignorant mortals. It had not been so long since our kind had been burned at stakes by frightened mobs.

While I could not simply attack them, neither could I remain here, waiting. A warlock would have fewer compunctions about exposing his abilities in public. The wisest option would have been to report in to the captain, send for reinforcements, veil myself, and follow them.

I had never been a particularly cautious person. Even the extended life of a wizard was too brief a time, and the world full of too much pleasure and joy to waste that life by hiding safely away.

I was not, however, stupid.

I turned to begin walking decisively toward the door and practically slammed my nose into that of a handsome man in his mid-forties, beard neatly shaved, dressed in an impeccable suit. His eyes were green and hard, his teeth far too white for his age.

And he was pressing a tiny derringer pistol to my chest, just beneath my left breast.

"Timely," he said to me in a fine German accent. "We knew a Warden would arrive, but we thought you would be another week at least."

"I don't know what you're talking about," I said.

"Please," he said, his eyes shading over with something ugly. "If you attempt to resist me, I will kill you here and now." He moved smoothly, stepping beside me and tucking my left arm into the crook of his right, positioning the tiny gun in his left hand atop my arm, keeping it artfully concealed while trained steadily on my heart. He nodded once at the balcony, and the four men on it immediately put their cards down and descended, heading out the door without so much as glancing back.

"You're making a mistake," I said to him tightly. "To my knowledge, you and your companions are not wanted by the Council. I'm not here for you today. I've only come for Alexander Page."

"Is that a fact?" he asked.

"He is a murderer. By sheltering him, you have become complicit in his crimes," I said. "If you kill me, you will only draw down the full wrath of the Wardens. But if you let me go immediately and disassociate yourself from Page, I will not prosecute a warrant for your capture."

"That is most generous, Warden," said the German. "But I am afraid I have plans. You will accompany me quietly outside."

"And if I do not?"

"Then I will be mildly disappointed, and you will be dead."

"You'll be more than disappointed when my death curse falls upon you," I said.

"Should you live long enough to level it, perhaps," he said. "But I am willing to take that risk."

I flicked my eyes around the room, looking for options, but they seemed few. The fellow on the high stool had his eyes on a man dealing cards at a nearby table. The cowboys were far more interested in drinking and making merry than in what, to them, must have appeared to be a domestic squabble between a wife come to drag her husband from a den of iniquity. Even the deputy at the door was gone, his chair standing empty.

*Ah.*

I turned to the German and said, "Very well. Let us take this discussion elsewhere."

"I do not think you realize your position, Warden," the German said, as we began walking. "I am not asking for your consent. I am merely informing you of your options."

I flinched slightly at the words and let the fear I was feeling show on my face. "What do you mean to do with me?" I asked.

"Nothing good," he said, and his eyes glinted with something manic and hungry. Then he frowned, noticing that his last words had fallen into a silence absent of music or stomping feet.

Into that silence came what seemed like a singularly significant mechanical click.

"Mister," the lanky deputy said. "You pass over that belly gun, or your next hat is going to be a couple of sizes smaller."

The deputy had moved in silently behind him and now held his revolver less than a foot from the back of the German's skull.

I let the fear drop off my face and smiled sweetly up at my captor.

The German froze, his eyes suddenly hot with rage as he realized that I had distracted him, just as his fellows had distracted me. The derringer pressed harder against my ribs as he turned his head slightly toward the deputy. "Do you have any idea who I am?"

"Mmmm," the deputy said calmly. "You're the fella who's about to come quietly or have lead on his mind."

The German narrowed his eyes and ground his teeth.

"He's not asking for your consent," I said. "He's merely informing you of your options."

The German spat an oath in his native tongue. Then he slipped the little pistol away from my side and slowly held it up.

The deputy took the weapon, his own gun steady.

"You will regret this action," said the German. "Who do you think you are?"

"My name is Wyatt Earp," said the deputy. "And I think I'm the law."

EARP TOOK THE German to the town marshal's office, which was on the southern side of the tracks and contained a pair of iron jail cells. I led Karl along, and the *näcken* was mercifully well behaved for once, playing the role of a horse to perfection when I tied him to the post outside the office.

"Deputy," I said, as we entered the building. "I do not think you understand the threat."

Earp passed me his lantern and nodded toward a hanging hook on the wall. I put it there, as he walked the German into the cell, gun steady on the man all the while. He made the man lean against a wall with both hands and patted him down for weaponry, removing a small knife—and calmly taking a charm hanging from a leather necklace around his neck.

"What?" he said evenly. "On account of he's a sorcerer? Is that what you mean?"

I felt both of my eyebrows lift. Typically, and increasingly, authority figures had very little truck with the world of the supernatural.

"Yes," I said. "That is precisely what I mean."

Earp walked over to me and held out the necklace and its simple, round copper charm. A familiar symbol was carved onto its surface: a skull, twisted and horrifically stretched, marked on its forehead with a single slanted, asymmetric cross.

"Thule Society," I murmured.

"Hngh," he said, as if my recognition of the symbol confirmed his suspicions rather than surprising him. "Guess that makes you White Council."

I tilted my head at him. "A Warden. Goodness, you are well-informed. I must ask, how do you know of the Council, sir?"

"Venator," he said simply. "Lost my necklace in a card game. You can take it or leave it that I'm telling the truth."

The Venatori Umbrorum were a secret society of their own, steeped in the occult, quietly working against supernatural forces that threatened humanity. They boasted a few modestly gifted practitioners, but had a great many members, which translated to a great many eyes and ears. The society was a longtime ally, more or less, of the White Council—just as the Thule Society was more or less a longtime foe, using their resources to attempt to employ supernatural powers for their own benefit.

I regarded Earp thoughtfully. It was, I supposed, possible that he could be in league with the German, playing some sort of deceitful game. But it seemed improbable. Had he and the German wanted me dead, Earp could simply have watched him walk me out without taking note of it.

"I believe you," I told him simply.

"That cell's warded," Earp said. "From the inside, he's not going to be doing much." He glanced over at the German and gave him a cold smile. "Makes a lot of noise if you try, though. Figure I'll shoot you five or six times before you get done whipping up enough magic to hurt anybody."

The German stared at Earp through narrowed eyes and then abruptly smiled and appeared to relax. He unbuttoned his collar, removed his tie, and sat down on the cell's lumpy bunk.

"Nnnngh," Earp said, a look of mild disgust on his face. He squinted around the room at the building's windows. Then he looked back at me and said, "Warden, huh? You're a lawm—" He pursed his lips. "You carry a badge."

"Something like that," I said.

"What I mean to say is, you can fight," Earp said.

"I can fight," I said.

He leaned his lanky body back against the wall beside the desk and tilted his chin toward the German. "What do you think?"

"I think he has four friends," I said. "All of them gifted. Do your windows have shutters?"

"Yep."

"Then we should shutter them," I said. "They will come for him."

"Damn," he drawled. "That's what I think, too. Before dawn?"

The hours of darkness were the best time for amateurs to practice the dark arts, for both practical and purely psychological reasons. "Almost certainly."

"What do you think about that?"

I narrowed my eyes and said, "I object."

Earp nodded his head and said, "Only so much I can do about someone bringing spells at me. Can you fight that?"

"I can."

Earp studied me for a moment, those dark eyes assessing. Then he seemed to come to a decision. "How about I'll put up the shutters?" he said. "Unless you'd rather me make the coffee, which I don't recommend."

I shuddered at the American notion of coffee. "I'll do that part," I said.

"Good," he said. "We got ourselves a plan."

"Well," Earp said a few hours later. "I don't much care for all the waiting. But this is some damned fine coffee, Miss Anastasia."

I had, of course, used magic to help it. The beans had not been properly roasted, and the grinder they had been through had been considerably too coarse in its work. Some other Wardens thought my coffee-making spells to be a frivolous waste of time in the face of all the darkness in the world, but what good is magic if it cannot be used to make a delicious cup of a fine beverage?

"Just be glad you did not ask me to cook," I said. "It is not one of my gifts."

Earp huffed out a breath through his nose. "You ain't got much femaleness to you, ma'am, if you pardon my saying so."

I smiled at him sweetly. "I'm on the job at the moment."

He grunted. "That Page fella you mentioned?"

I nodded.

"What's he wanted for?"

"He murdered three people in Liverpool," I said. "A girl he favored and her parents."

"Guess she didn't favor him back," Earp said. "He shoot 'em?"

I shook my head and suppressed a shudder at the memory of the crime scene. "He ripped out their eyes and tongues," I said. "While they lay blind and bleeding, he did other things."

Earp's eyes flickered. "I've seen the type before." He glanced at the German.

The German sat in exactly the same place he'd settled hours before. The man had his eyes closed—but he smiled faintly, as if aware of Earp's gaze on him.

Earp turned back to me. "What happens to Mr. Page when you catch him?"

"He will be fairly tried, and then, I expect, beheaded for his crimes."

Earp examined the fingernails of his right hand. "A real fair trial?"

"The evidence against him is damning," I said. "But fair enough."

Earp lowered his hand again. It fell very naturally to the grip of his gun. "I'd never want me one of those, if I could avoid it," he said.

I knew what he meant. There were times I didn't care for the sorts of things it had been necessary to do to deal with various monsters, human or otherwise. I expect Earp had faced his own terrors, and the dirty labor required to remove them.

Such deeds left their weight behind.

"I wouldn't care for one myself," I said.

He nodded, and we both sipped coffee for a while. Then he said, "Once this is wrapped up, I think I'd like to buy you a nice dinner. When you aren't on the job."

I found myself smiling at that.

I was an attractive woman, which was simply a statement of truth and not one of ego. I dressed well, kept myself well, and frequently had the attention of men and women who wished to enjoy my company. That had been a source of great enjoyment and amusement when I was younger, though these days I had little patience for it.

But Earp was interesting, and there was a tremendous appeal in his lean, soft-spoken confidence.

"Perhaps," I said. "If business allows for it."

Earp seemed pleased and sipped his coffee.


THE TOWN HAD gone black and silent, even the saloons, as the night stretched to the quiet, cool hours of darkness and stillness that came before the first hint of dawn.

The witching hour.

We both heard the footsteps approaching the front door of the marshal's office. Earp had belted on a second revolver, had a third within easy reach on the desk, and rose from his chair to take up a shotgun in his hands, its barrels cut down to less than a foot long.

My own weapons were just as ready, if less easily observable than Earp's. I'd marked a quick circle in chalk on the floor, ready to be imbued with energy as a bulwark against hostile magic. The sword at my side was tingling with power I'd invested in it over the course of the evening, ready to slice apart the threads binding enemy spells together, and I held ready a shield in my mind to prevent attacks on my thoughts and emotions.

And, of course, I had a hand on my revolver. Magic is well and good, but bullets are often swifter.

The footsteps stopped just outside the door. And then there was a polite knock.

Earp's face twisted with distaste. He crossed to the door and opened a tiny speaking window in it, without actually showing himself to whoever was outside. In addition, he leveled the shotgun at the door, approximately at the midsection of whomever would be standing outside.

"Evening," Earp said.

"Good evening," said a man's voice from outside. This accent was British, quite well-to-do, its tenor pleasant. "Might I speak with Mr. Wyatt Earp, please?"

"Speaking," Earp drawled.

"Mr. Earp," the Briton said, "I have come to make you a proposal that will avoid any unpleasantness in the immediate future. Are you willing to hear me out?"

Earp looked at me.

I shrugged. On the one hand, it was always worth exploring ways not to fight. On the other, I had no confidence that a member of the Thule Society would negotiate in good faith. In fact, I took a few steps back toward the rear of the building, so that I might hear something if this was some sort of attempt at a distraction.

Earp nodded his approval.

"Tell you what," he said to the Briton. "I'm going to stand in here and count quietly to twenty before I start pulling triggers. You say something interesting before then, could be we can make medicine."

There was a baffled second's silence, and the Briton said, "How quickly are you counting?"

"I done started," Earp said. "And you ain't doing yourself any favors right now."

The Briton hesitated an instant more before speaking in an even, if slightly rushed, tone. "With respect, this is not a fight you can win, Mr. Earp. If the Warden were not present, this conversation would not be happening. Her presence means we may have to contend with you to get what we want, rather than simply taking it—but it would surely garner a great deal of attention of the sort that her kind prefer to avoid, as well as placing countless innocents in danger."

As the man spoke, Earp listened intently, adjusting the aim of his shotgun by a few precise degrees.

"To avoid this outcome, you will release our companion unharmed. We will depart Dodge City immediately. You and the Warden will remain within the marshal's office until dawn. As an additional incentive, we will arrange for the new ordinances against your friend Mr. Short's establishment to be struck from the city's legal code."

At that, Earp grunted.

I lifted an eyebrow at him. He held up a hand and gave his head a slight shake that asked me to wait until later.

"Well, Mr. Earp?" asked the Briton. "Can we, as you so pithily put it, make medicine?"

Something hard flickered in Earp's eyes. He glanced at me.

I drew my revolver.

That action engendered a grin big enough to show some of his teeth, even through the mustache. He lifted his head and said, "Eighteen. Nineteen . . ."

The Briton spoke in a hard voice, meant to be menacing, though it was somewhat undermined by the way he hurried away from the door. "Decide in the next half an hour. You will have no second chance."

I waited a moment before arching an eyebrow at Earp. "I take it these terms he offered were good ones?"

Earp lowered and uncocked the shotgun and squinted thoughtfully. "Well. Maybe and maybe not. But they sound pretty good, and I reckon that's what he was trying for."

"What was he offering, precisely?"

"Bill Short went and got himself into some trouble with the folks north of the tracks. They want to clean up Dodge City. Make it all respectable. Which, I figure, ain't a bad thing all by itself. They got kids to think about. Well, Bill's partner run for mayor and lost. Fella that won passed some laws against Bill's place, arrested some of his girls—that kind of thing. Bill objected, and some shooting got done, but nobody died or anything. Then a mob rounded up Bill and some other folks the proper folk figured was rapscallions and ran them out of town."

"I see," I said. "How do you come into this?"

"Well, Bill got himself a train to Kansas City, and he rounded up some friends. Me, Bat, Doc, a few others."

I glanced at the lean man and his casually worn guns. "Men like you?"

"Well," Earp said, and a quiet smile flickered at the edges of his mustache. "I'd not care to cross them over a matter of nothing, if you take my meaning, Miss Anastasia."

"I do."

"So, we been coming into town to talk things over with this mayor without a mob deciding how things should go," Earp continued. "Little at a time, so as not to make too much noise." He opened the peephole in the office door and squinted out of it. "Got myself redeputized so I can go heeled. Been over at the Long Branch with Bat."

"The saloon the mayor passed a law against?"

"Well, it ain't like it's a state law," Earp said. "More of a misunderstandin'. See, as much as the good folks north of the tracks don't want to admit it, cattle and these cowboys are what keeps this town alive. And those boys don't want to come in at the end of a three-month trail ride and have a nice bath and a cup of tea. Kind of country they're going through can be a little tough. So they drop their money here, blowing off steam." He rubbed at his mustache. "Hell, sin is the currency around this place. Don't take a genius to see that. Those good folk are going to righteous themselves right out of a home." He sighed. "Dammit, Doc. Why ain't you here yet?"

"Friend of yours?" I asked.

"Holliday," Earp confirmed. "Good fella to have with you when it's rough. Plus he's got two of them Venator pendants around his neck. Took one from some fool in a faro game."

"I need to know," I said, "if you mean to take the Thule Society's offer seriously."

"Can't do that, Miss Anastasia," Earp said. "They're only offering me something I can get for myself just as well."

I found myself smiling at that. "You're willing to challenge an entire town to a fight? For the sake of your friend's saloon?"

"It ain't the saloon, ma'am," Earp drawled. "It's the principle of the thing. Man can't let himself get run out of town by a mob, or pretty soon everyone will be doing it."

"If a mob is responsible," I said, smiling, "is not something close to everyone already doing it?"

Earp's eyes wrinkled at that, and he tapped the brim of his cap.

"Idiot," said the German from the cell, contempt in his voice.

"Sometimes," Earp allowed. He shut the peephole and said, "Those Thule bastards ain't going to wait half an hour. Snakes like that will come early."

"I agree," I said. "But going out shooting seems an unlikely plan."

"Can't disagree," Earp said. "Course, maybe it's just a man's pride talkin', but it seems like it ain't much of an idea for them to try to come in here, either."

It was then that the drum began beating, a slow, steady cadence in the darkness.

I felt my breath catch.

The German smiled.

Earp looked at me sharply and asked, "What's that mean?"

"Trouble," I said. I shot a hard glance at the German. "We've made a mistake."

The German's smile widened. His eyes closed beatifically.

"Who are you?" I demanded.

He said nothing.

"What the hell is going on?" Earp said, not in an unpleasant tone.

"This man is no mere member of the Thule Society," I said. I turned my attention toward the outside of the jailhouse, where I could already feel dark, cold, slithering energy beginning to gather. "We are dealing with necromancers. They're calling out the dead. Is there a cemetery nearby?"

"Yep," Earp said. "Boot Hill."

"Deputy," I said. "We need to plan."

"Shoot," Earp said a quarter of an hour later, staring out the peephole. "I didn't much like these fellas the first time I shot them." He had added another revolver to his belt, and had traded in his shotgun for a repeating rifle. "And time ain't been kind. I make it over thirty."

I stepped up next to Earp and stood on my tiptoes to peer out the peephole. We had dimmed the lights to almost nothing, and there was just enough moon to let me see grim, silent figures limping and shambling down the street toward the jailhouse. They were corpses, mostly gone to bone and gruesome scraps of leathery skin with occasional patches of stringy, brittle hair.

"There's some more, coming up on that side," Earp said. "Forty. Maybe forty-five."

"Properly used, a dozen would be enough to kill us both," I said to him. I took a brief chance and opened my third eye, examining the flow of energies around the oncoming horrors. "We are fortunate. These are not fully realized undead. Whoever called them up is not yet an adept at doing so. These things are scarcely more than constructs—merely deadly and mostly invulnerable."

He eyed me obliquely. "Miss Anastasia, that ain't what a reasonable man would call comfortin'."

I felt my lips compress into a smile. "After a certain point, the numbers hardly matter. The drum beats for their hearts—it both controls the constructs and animates them. Stop that and we stop them all, even if there were a thousand."

"And until then?"

"Until then, aim for the head. That should disrupt the spell controlling them."

Earp looked over his shoulder at the German. The man looked considerably less smug or comfortable than he had throughout the evening. At my direction, Earp had hog-tied him to one of the wooden pillars supporting the roof and gagged him thoroughly. I had chalked a circle of power around him and infused it with enough energy to prevent him from reaching outside of it for any magical power. They were crude precautions, but we could not afford to give the German an opportunity to strike at us while we were distracted. Such measures would hinder any particularly dangerous attack—and would not stop Earp's bullet from finding the German's skull, should he attempt anything that was not instantly lethal.

I stepped back from the window, closed my eyes, and invoked the communication spell I had established with the *näcken*.

*Karl*, I murmured with my thoughts, *are you ready?*

*Obviously*, the *näcken* replied.

*Have you located the Thule Society?*

There was an amused tint to the dark faerie's reply. *On the roof of a building three doors down and across the street. They seem to think that they have warded themselves from sight.*

*Excellent*, I replied. *Then we will begin shortly.*

*Four warlocks*, Karl mused. *You realize that your death releases me from our contract?*

I ground my teeth without replying. Then I cocked my revolver, turned to Earp, and nodded.

"Seems like a bad hand, Miss Anastasia," Earp said. "But let's play it out."

And with no more fanfare than that, Wyatt Earp calmly opened the door to the jailhouse, raised his rifle to his shoulder, and walked out shooting, and I went out behind him.

Earp was a professional. He did not shoot rapidly. He lined the rifle's sights upon the nearest shambling figure and dropped a heavy round through its skull. Before the corpse's knees began to buckle, he had ejected the shell and taken aim at the next nearest. That shot bellowed out, and as the sound of it faded, the crowd of corpses let out a terrifying wave of dry, dusty howls and began launching themselves forward in a frenzied lurch.

I raised my Webley, took aim, and dropped a corpse of my own—

though in the time it took me to do it, Earp had felled three more without ever seeming to rush.

"Karl!" I screamed.

There was a thunder of hooves striking the earthen street and the enormous white horse appeared like a specter out of the night. The *näcken* simply ran down half a dozen corpses, shouldered two more out of the way, and kicked another in the chest with such force that it flew backward across the street and exploded into a cloud of spinning, shattered bone.

I swung up onto the *näcken*'s back, as summer lightning flickered and showed me the dead moving forward like an inevitable tide. Two more of the things reached for me, bony fingers clawing. I kicked one away and shot the other through the skull with the Webley, and then Karl surged forward.

I cast a glance back over one shoulder to see Earp grip the emptied rifle's barrel and smash a corpse's skull with the stock. That bought him enough time to back toward the jailhouse door, drawing a revolver into each hand. Shots began to ring out in steady, metronomic time.

"To the roof!" I snarled to the *näcken*.

And the dark fae let go of his disguise.

White horseflesh swelled and split as it darkened to a sickly, drowned blue-grey. A hideous stench filled the air, and the *näcken*'s body bloated to nearly impossible dimensions. The smell of fetid water and rotten meat rose from Karl's body in a smothering miasma, and with a surge of power that threatened to throw me from his back entirely, despite the saddle, the *näcken* leapt from the street to the balcony of a nearby building, bounding to the lower roof of the building next to it, then reversed direction and flung itself onto the roof of the original.

The Thule Society awaited us.

The roof was a flat space and not overly large. Much of it had been filled with a painted pentacle, the points of its star lapping outside of the binding circle around it—a symbol of chaos and entropy, unbounded by the circle of will and restraint. That same cold and horrible energy I'd felt earlier shuddered thick in the air. Torches burned green at each point of the star—and at the center knelt my quarry, the warlock Alexander Page, a plump, lemon-faced young man, beating steady time on a drum that looked like something of Indian manufacture.

The Briton and the other two Thules stood in a protective triangle around Page, outside the circle. The Briton's eyes widened as the savage *näcken* landed on the roof, shaking the boards beneath everyone's feet with his weight and power.

"Kill the Warden!" the Briton shouted.

He flung out his hand, and a greenish flicker of lightning lashed across the space between us. I stood ready to parry the spell, but it was poorly aimed and flew well wide of me—though it struck Karl along his rear legs.

The *näcken* bucked in agony and screamed in rage. I flew clear, barely controlling my dismount enough to land on the building rather than being flung to the street below. I landed on my feet and rolled to one side, avoiding a cloud of evil-looking spiders marked with a red hourglass, which one of the other Thule sorcerers summoned and flung at me.

I regained my feet and shot twice at him with the Webley—but the first shot was hurried, and the second wavered off course as the third Thule sorcerer called something like a small violet comet out of nowhere and sent it screaming toward my head. I lifted my left hand in a defensive gesture, shouting the word of a warding spell, and the thing shattered against an invisible barrier a foot from my head, exploding into white-hot shards that went hissing in every direction.

Page took one of them in the arm and let out a small shriek of startled agony, dropping the drumstick he held in his hand.

"No!" shrieked the Briton. "The Master is all that matters! Keep the beat!"

Page, his face twisted in agony, reached for the drumstick and resumed the rhythm—just as the *näcken* thundered furiously toward Page.

The three on their feet rushed to interpose themselves—even as the *näcken* crashed into the mordant power of the evil circle they'd infused, as helpless to cross into it as any fae would be.

But in the time it took them to realize that, I had caught my breath and my balance, aimed the Webley, and sent several ounces of lead thundering through the chest and, a heartbeat later, through the skull of the second Thule sorcerer.

Page screamed in terror. The third Thule spun to me and sent multiple comets shrieking toward me, howling curses with each throw. I discarded the emptied revolver and drew my blade. The enchanted silversteel shone brightly even in the dimness of the night, and with several swift cuts I sliced through the energies holding the attack spells together, disrupting them and changing them from dangerous explosives into exploding, dissipating clouds of violet sparks of light.

The Briton, meanwhile, dove out of the circle, spoke a thundering word of power, and sent Karl flying back through the air like a kicked kitten. The *näcken* screamed furiously and vanished into the darkness.

I had no time. I surged forward, striking down one deadly comet after another, and with a long lunge, rammed my slender blade into the third Thule's mouth.

The blade bit deep, back through the palate and into the skull, and I could suddenly feel the man writhing and spasming through my grip on the sword, a sensation oddly like that of a fish hooking itself to an angler's line. I twisted the blade and ripped it back in a swirling S motion, and as it came free of the sorcerer's mouth it was followed by a fountain of gore.

I whirled, raising a shield with my left hand, and barely intercepted another strike of sickly green lightning. It exploded into a glowing cobweb pattern just in front of my outstretched hand, little streaks leaping out to scorch and burn the roof, starting half a dozen tiny fires.

"Grevane!" screamed Page.

"Drum!" thundered the Briton, even as he raised his hands above his head, his face twisting into a rictus.

And as swiftly as that, I heard the dry, clicking, rasping sound of the dead beginning to scale the building toward us.

Terror filled me. My allies were gone, and I was outnumbered two to one, even before one counted the coming terrors. Further, I'd felt the power of Grevane the Briton's strike firsthand—and the man was no half-trained warlock, or even a senior sorcerer of the Thule Society. Strength like his could only come from one place.

He was a Wizard of the White Council.

And then, swift on the heels of my fear came another emotion. Rage, pure and undiluted, rage that this man, this *creature*, would spurn his responsibility to humanity and distort the power that created the universe itself into something so obscene, so foul.

He was a *warlock*. A traitor.

I flicked my sword into my left hand, then hurled my right hand forward, and a bolt of searing fire no thicker than my pinky finger lashed out at him, blinding in the night. Grevane parried the blow on a shield of his own and countered with more lightning. I caught part of it on the sword, but what got through was enough to drive me down to one knee and send agony racing back and forth through my nerve endings.

Even as I fought through the pain, I saw movement in the corner of my eye: the dead, swarming up the building and beginning to haul themselves onto the roof. In seconds, they would tear me apart.

I gritted my teeth, staggered back to my feet, and rushed forward, sword leading the way.

Grevane gathered more power, but held his strike until the last second as I closed on him—and then he bellowed something and smashed down at the roof beneath us with pure kinetic energy, opening an enormous gap just in front of me.

I dove to one side, a bound as light and graceful as any I had ever made, rolled, and felt the horrible, tingling, invasive presence of necromantic energy course over me as I crossed into their summoning circle—and drove my blade straight out to one side and into the heart of Alexander Page.

The warlock let out a short, croaking gasp. The drumstick fell from his suddenly nerveless hands, and, seconds later, silence reigned, marred only by the dry clatter of bones falling two stories down to the streets of Dodge City.

I stared at Grevane, crouched, as Page quivered on my sword. My left hand was lifted, a shield of pale blue energy already glowing, ready for the necromancer's next attack.

But instead, Grevane tilted his head to one side, his eyes distant. He smiled faintly. Then, without a further word, he simply stepped backward and fell over the edge of the building, dropping silently into the darkness below.

I ripped the sword free of Page and sprinted to follow him—but by the time I got to the edge and looked down, I saw nothing. Nothing at all but bones in an empty street.

I was so focused on Grevane that I didn't sense the attack coming at my back until it was nearly too late to survive it.

Pain, simple *pain*, suddenly fell upon me as if my entire body had suddenly been thrust into a raging fire. I let out a strangled scream, my back arching, and fought to simply keep from plummeting from the roof myself.

"Bitch," Page panted. He staggered across the roof, one hand desperately trying to stem a steady pulse of blood from what would be, in a few moments, a fatal wound. "Warden bitch. *Dolor igni!*"

Pain wiped everything else from my mind for the space of several seconds. By the time I could see again, I was sprawled back over the edge of the roof, about to fall, and a deathly pale Page stood over me, holding my own sword to my throat.

"You've killed me, bitch," he gasped. "But I won't go to hell alone."

I tried to thrash aside, to push the blade, but my body simply did not respond to me. Pure, frenzied, helpless terror, the kind I had previously known only in terrible dreams of running through quicksand, surged through me.

Page let out a frenzied little giggle and leaned on the sword.

And with a crack of thunder, his head snapped back into a cloud of misty gore. My sword fell from his fingers, and his body dropped limply down onto his legs, collapsing into an awkward pile.

I turned my head slowly.

Wyatt Earp stood on the street below, a trail of nearly headless dis-animated corpses strewn behind him, along with all but the last of the revolvers he'd been carrying.

He lowered the gun, and touched a finger to the brim of his hat in solemn salute.

"You sure you can't stay, Miss Anastasia?" Earp asked.

I shook my head. Karl, now back in his disguise, stamped an angry hoof onto the dirt of Dodge City's streets as I loaded his saddlebags with fresh supplies. "I'm afraid I can't. Not with those two still out there."

Earp grunted. "I never seen someone so determined to skin himself out of some ropes," he said. "Who was that German?"

I felt my mouth twist with distaste, even as a sour taste of fear touched my tongue. "If our information at the White Council is accurate, his name is Kemmler," I said. "That Briton was one of his apprentices, Grevane."

"Bad men?"

"Some of the most dangerous alive," I said. "I have to get onto their trail while I still can."

He nodded. "I hear you. Shame about that dinner, though."

I winked down at him and said, "Perhaps another time."

He smiled and tipped his hat slightly. Then he offered me his hand.

I shook it.

"Ma'am," he said. "Think maybe I'd have won that twenty dollars off you."

Instead of answering him, I opened my purse, fished out a golden coin, and flicked it to him. He caught it, grinning openly. "Have a drink for me, Deputy."

"Think maybe I'll do that," he said. "Good hunting."

"Thank you," I said.

KARL AND I headed out of town as the sun began to rise.

"I'm tired," the *näcken* said.

"As am I, Karl," I replied.

"Kemmler," said the *näcken* contemptuously. "You only found him to spite me. To keep me in this horrible place."

"Do not be tiresome," I said with a sigh. I checked the little leather medicine bag dangling from a thong. Earp had been quite right about Kemmler's skinning out of ropes with which he'd been bound. The man had left enough skin behind for me to lock onto him with a tracking spell. The bag swung back and forth gently in the direction in which the greatest necromancer in the history of man had gone. "We only do our duty."

"Duty," Karl said, disgusted. "I hate this land."

"I am not overly fond of it myself," I replied. "Come. Pick up the pace."

Karl broke into a weary jog, and I settled my hat more firmly on my head. The sun began to rise behind us, golden and warm, as we traveled deeper into the West.

# B IS FOR BIGFOOT

It is a source of considerable personal pride to me that I can honestly and without reservation type the next sentence: It came to me as a great shock and professional failure when one day I realized that I had made insufficient allowance in my work life for Bigfoot.

I mean, the Dresden Files was built from the ground up to embrace every creature of folklore and legend that I could dig up, regardless of where I might find them. I had made very careful plans for the roles of faeries, vampires, werewolves, angels, demons, and dozens of other beings at play in the story world. Imagine my shock when, several years into my entirely too-ambitious project, I realized that I hadn't even considered where Sasquatch fit in.

(This may or may not have happened the same year *Finding Bigfoot* debuted. I have no specific information on the exact chronology. But it might well have been that year. I'm just saying.)

This was a travesty! An outrage! It had to be addressed decisively, and at once! Oh, and also, I had promised three short stories to three different lovely people, and they were already weeks late, so hadn't I better get to work on them?

The result of my outrage at the oversight and time desperation was the trio of Bigfoot short stories, the first of which is in the following pages, and set just between the events of *Fool Moon* and *Grave Peril*.

**W**hen people come to the only professional wizard in the Chicago phone book for help, they're one of two things: desperate or smart. Very rarely are they both.

The smart ones come to me because they know I can help; the desperate come because they don't know anyone else who can. With a smart client, the meeting is brief and pleasant. Someone has lost the ring that was a family heirloom, and has been told I'm a man who can find lost things. Such people engage my services (preferably with cash), I do the job, and everyone's happy.

Desperate clients, on the other hand, can pull all sorts of ridiculous nonsense. They lie to me about what kind of trouble they've gotten themselves into, or try to pass me a check I'm sure will bounce like a basketball. Occasionally they demand that I prove my powers by telling them what their problem is before they even shake my hand—in which case, the problem is that they're idiots.

My newest client wanted something different, though. He wanted me to meet him in the woods.

This did not make me feel optimistic that he would be one of the smart ones.

Woods being in short supply in Chicago, I had to drive all the way up to the northern half of Wisconsin to get to decent timber. That took me about six hours, given that my car, while valiant and bold, is also a Volkswagen Beetle made around the same time flower children were big. By the time I got there and had hiked a mile or two out into the woods, to the appointed location, dark was coming on.

I'm not a moron, usually. I've made enemies during my stint as a professional wizard. So when I settled down to wait for the client, I did so with my staff in one hand, my blasting rod in the other, and a .38 revolver in the pocket of my black leather duster. I blew out a small crater in the earth with an effort of will, using my staff to direct the energy, and built a modest campfire in it.

Then I stepped out of the light of the campfire; found a comfortable, shadowy spot; and waited to see who was going to show up.

The whole PI gig is mostly about patience. You have to talk to a lot of people who don't know anything to find the one who does. You have to sit around waiting a lot, watching for someone to do something before you catch them doing it. You have to do a lot of searching through useless information to get to one piece of really good information. Impatient PIs rarely conclude an investigation successfully, and never remain in the business for long. So when an hour went by without anything happening, I wasn't too worried.

By two hours, though, my legs were cramping and I had a little bit of a headache, and apparently the mosquitoes had decided to hold a convention about ten feet away, because I was covered with bites. Given that I hadn't been paid a dime yet, this client was getting annoying fast.

The fire had died down to almost nothing, so I almost didn't see the creature emerge from the forest and crouch down beside the embers.

The thing was huge. I mean, just saying that it was nine feet tall wasn't enough. It was mostly human shaped, but it was built more heavily than any human, covered in layers and layers of ropy muscle that were visible even through a coat of long, dark brown hair or fur that covered its whole body. It had a brow ridge like a mountain crag, with dark, glittering eyes that reflected the red-orange light of the fire.

I did not move. Not even a little. If that thing wanted to hurt me, I would have one hell of a time stopping it from doing so, even with magic, and unless I got lucky, something with that much mass would find my .38 about as deadly as a pricing gun.

Then it turned its head and part of its upper body toward me and said, in a rich, mellifluous Native American accent, "You done over there? Don't mean to be rude, and I didn't want to interrupt you, wizard, but there's business to be done."

My jaw dropped open. I mean it literally dropped open.

I stood up slowly, and my muscles twitched and ached. It's hard to stretch out a cramp while you remain in a stance, prepared to run away at an instant's notice, but I tried.

"You're . . . ," I said. "You're a . . ."

"Bigfoot," he said. "Sasquatch. Yowie. Yeti. Buncha names. Yep."

"And you . . . you called me?" I felt a little stunned. "Um . . . Did you use a pay phone?"

I instantly imagined him trying to punch little phone buttons with those huge fingers. No, of course he hadn't done that.

"Nah," he said, and waved a huge, hairy arm to the north. "Fellas at the reservation help us make calls sometimes. They're a good bunch."

I shook myself and took a deep breath. For Pete's sake, I was a wizard. I dealt with the supernatural all the time. I shouldn't be this rattled by one little unexpected encounter. I shoved my nerves and my discomfort down and replaced them with iron professionalism—or at least the semblance of calm.

I emerged from my hidey-hole and went over to the fire. I settled down across from the Bigfoot, noting as I did that I was uncomfortably close to being within reach of his long arms. "Um, welcome. I'm Harry Dresden."

The Bigfoot nodded and looked at me expectantly. After a moment of that, he said, as if prompting a child, "This is your fire."

I blinked. Honoring the obligations of hospitality is a huge factor in the supernatural communities around the world—and as it was my campfire, I was the de facto host and the Bigfoot my guest. I said, "Yes. I'll be right back."

I hurried to my car and came back to the campfire with two cans of warm Coke and half a tin of salt-and-vinegar Pringles chips. I opened both cans and offered the Bigfoot one of them.

Then I opened the Pringles and divided them into two stacks, offering him his choice of either.

The Bigfoot accepted them and sipped almost delicately at the Coke, handling the comparatively tiny can with far more grace than I would have believed. The chips didn't get the careful treatment. He popped them all into his mouth and chomped down on them enthusiastically. I emulated him. I got a lot of crumbs on the front of my coat.

The Bigfoot nodded at me. "Hey, got any smokes?"

"No," I said. "Sorry. It's not a habit."

"Maybe next time," he said. "Now. You have given me your name, but I have not given you mine. I am called Strength of a River in His Shoulders, of the Three Stars Forest People. And there is a problem with my son."

"What kind of problem?" I asked.

"His mother can tell you in greater detail than I can," River Shoulders said.

"His mother?" I rubbernecked. "Is she around?"

"No," he said. "She lives in Chicago."

I blinked. "His mother . . ."

"Human," River Shoulders said. "The heart wants what the heart wants, yeah?"

Then I got it. "Oh. He's a scion."

That made more sense. A lot of supernatural folk can and do interbreed with humanity. The resulting children, half-mortal, half-supernatural, are called scions. Being a scion means different things to different children, depending on their parentage, but they rarely have an easy time of it in life.

River Shoulders nodded. "Forgive my ignorance of the issues. Your society is . . . not one of my areas of expertise."

I know, right? A Bigfoot saying *expertise*.

I shook my head a little. "If you can't tell me anything, why did you call me here? You could have told me all of this on the phone."

"Because I wanted you to know that I thought the problem supernatural in origin, and that I would have good reason to recognize it. And because I brought your retainer." He rummaged in a buckskin pouch that he wore slung across the front of his body. It had been all but invisible amid his thick pelt. He reached a hand in and tossed something at me.

I caught it on reflex and nearly yelped as it hit my hand. It was the size of a golf ball and extraordinarily heavy. I held it closer to the fire and then whistled in surprise.

Gold. I was holding a nugget of pure gold. It must have been worth . . . uh, well, a lot.

"We knew all the good spots a long time before the Europeans came across the sea," River Shoulders said calmly. "There's another, just as large, when the work is done."

"What if I don't take your case?" I asked him.

He shrugged. "I try to find someone else. But word is that you can be trusted. I would prefer you."

I regarded River Shoulders for a moment. He wasn't trying to intimidate me. It was a mark in his favor, because it wouldn't have been difficult. In fact, I realized, he was going out of his way to avoid that very thing.

"He's your son," I asked. "Why don't you help him?"

He gestured at himself and smiled slightly. "Maybe I would stand out a little in Chicago."

I snorted and nodded. "Maybe you would."

"So, wizard," River Shoulders said, "will you help my son?"

I pocketed the gold nugget and said, "One of these is enough. And yes. I will."

———

THE NEXT DAY I went to see the boy's mother at a coffee shop on the north side of town.

Dr. Helena Pounder was an impressive woman. She stood maybe six-four, and looked as though she might be able to bench-press more than I could. She wasn't really pretty, but her square, open face looked honest, and her eyes were a sparkling shade of springtime green.

When I came in, she rose to greet me and shook my hand. Her hands were an odd mix of soft skin and calluses—whatever she did for a living, she did it with tools in her hand.

"River told me he'd hired you," Dr. Pounder said. She gestured for me to sit, and we did.

"Yeah," I said. "He's a persuasive guy."

Pounder let out a rueful chuckle and her eyes gleamed. "I suppose he is."

"Look," I said. "I don't want to get too personal, but . . ."

"But how did I hook up with a Bigfoot?" she asked.

I shrugged and tried to look pleasant.

"I was at a dig site in Ontario—I'm an archaeologist—and I stayed a little too long in the autumn. The snows caught me there, a series of storms that lasted for more than a month. No one could get in to rescue me, and I couldn't even call out on the radio to let them know I was still at the site." She shook her head. "I fell sick and had no food. I might have died if someone hadn't started leaving rabbits and fish in the night."

I smiled. "River Shoulders?"

She nodded. "I started watching, every night. One night the storm cleared up at just the right moment, and I saw him there." She shrugged. "We started talking. Things sort of went from there."

"So the two of you aren't actually married, or . . . ?"

"Why does that matter?" she asked.

I spread my hands in an apologetic gesture. "He paid me. You didn't. It might have an effect on my decision process."

"Honest enough, aren't you?" Pounder said. She eyed me for a moment and then nodded in something like approval. "We aren't married. But suitors aren't exactly knocking down my door—and I never saw much use for a husband, anyway. River and I are comfortable with things as they are."

"Good for you," I said. "Tell me about your son."

She reached into a messenger bag that hung on the back of her diner chair and passed me a five-by-seven photograph of a kid, maybe eight or nine years old. He wasn't pretty, either, but his features had a kind of juvenile appeal, and his grin was as real and warm as sunlight.

"His name is Irwin," Pounder said, smiling down at the picture. "My angel."

Even tough, bouncer-looking supermoms have a soft spot for their kids, I guess. I nodded. "What seems to be the problem?"

"Earlier this year," she said, "he started coming home with injuries. Nothing serious—abrasions and bruises and scratches. But I suspect that the injuries were likely worse before the boy came home. Irwin heals very rapidly, and he's never been sick—literally never, not a day in his life."

"You think someone is abusing him," I said. "What did he say about it?"

"He made excuses," Pounder said. "They were obviously fictions, but that boy is at least as stubborn as his father, and he wouldn't tell me where or how he'd been hurt."

"Ah," I said.

She frowned. "Ah?"

"It's another kid."

Pounder blinked. "How . . . ?"

"I have the advantage over you and your husband, inasmuch as I have actually been a grade-school boy before," I said. "If he snitches about it to the teachers or to you, he'll probably have to deal with retributive friction from his classmates. He won't be cool. He'll be a snitching, tattling pariah."

Pounder sat back in her seat, frowning. "I'm . . . hardly a master of social skills. I hadn't thought of it that way."

I shrugged. "On the other hand, you clearly aren't the sort to sit around wringing her hands, either."

Pounder snorted and gave me a brief, real smile.

"So," I went on, "when he started coming home hurt, what did you do about it?"

"I started escorting him to school and picking him up the moment class let out. That's been for the past two months. He hasn't had any more injuries. But I have to go to a conference tomorrow morning and—"

"You want someone to keep an eye on him."

"That, yes," she said. "But I also want you to find out who has been trying to hurt him."

I arched an eyebrow. "How am I supposed to do that?"

"I used River's financial advisor to pull some strings. You're expected to arrive at the school tomorrow morning to begin work as the school janitor."

I blinked. "Wait. Bigfoot has a financial advisor? Who? Like, Nessie?"

"Don't be a child," she said. "The human tribes assist the Forest People by providing an interface. River's folk give financial, medical, and educational aid in return. It works."

My imagination provided me with an image of River Shoulders standing in front of a children's music class, his huge fingers waving a baton that had been reduced to a matchstick by his enormity.

Sometimes my head is like an Etch A Sketch. I shook it a little, and the image went away.

"Right," I said. "It might be difficult to get you something actionable."

Pounder's eyes almost seemed to turn a green-tinged shade of gold, and her voice became quiet and hard. "I am not interested in courts," she said. "I only care about my son."

Yikes.

Bigfoot Irwin had himself one formidable mama bear. If it turned out that I was right and he was having issues with another child, that could cause problems. People can overreact to things when their kids get involved. I might have to be careful with how much truth got doled out to Dr. Pounder.

Nothing's ever simple, is it?

THE SCHOOL WAS called the Madison Academy, and it was a private elementary and middle school on the north side of town. Whatever strings River Shoulders had pulled, they were good ones. I ambled in the next morning, went into the administrative office, and was greeted with the enthusiasm of a cloister of diabetics meeting their insulin-delivery truck. Their sanitation engineer had abruptly departed for a Hawaiian vacation, and they needed a temporary replacement.

So I wound up wearing a pair of coveralls that were too short in the arms, too short in the legs, and too short in the crotch, with the name NORM stenciled on the left breast. I was shown to my office, which was a closet with a tiny desk and several shelves stacked with cleaning supplies of the usual sort.

It could have been worse. The stencil could have read FREDDIE.

So I started engineering sanitation. One kid threw up, and another started a paint fight with his friend in the art room. The office paged me on an old intercom system that ran throughout the halls and had an outlet in the closet when they needed something in particular, but by ten I was clear of the child-created havoc and dealing with the standard human havoc, emptying trash cans, sweeping floors and halls, and generally cleaning up. As I did, going from classroom to classroom to take care of any full trash cans, I kept an eye out for Bigfoot Irwin.

I spotted him by lunchtime, and I took my meal at a table set aside for faculty and staff in one corner of the cafeteria as the kids ate.

Bigfoot Irwin was one of the tallest boys in sight, and he hadn't even hit puberty yet. He was all skin and bones—and I recognized something else about him at once. He was a loner.

He didn't look like an unpleasant kid or anything, but he carried himself in a fashion that suggested that he was apart from the other children; not aloof, simply separate. His expression was distracted, and his mind was clearly a million miles away. He had a double-sized lunch and a paperback book crowding his tray, and he headed for one end of a lunch table. He sat down, opened the book with one hand, and started eating with the other, reading as he went.

The trouble seemed obvious. A group of five or six boys occupied the other end of his lunch table, and they leaned their heads closer together and started muttering to one another and casting covert glances at Irwin.

I winced. I knew where this was going. I'd seen it before, when it had been me with the book and the lunch tray.

Two of the boys stood up, and they looked enough alike to make me think that they either had been born very close together or else were fraternal twins. They both had messy, sandy brown hair, long, narrow faces, and pointed chins. They might have been a year or two ahead of Irwin, though they were both shorter than the lanky boy.

They split, moving down either side of the table toward Irwin, their footsteps silent. I hunched my shoulders and watched them out of the corner of my eye. Whatever they were up to, it wouldn't be lethal, not right here in front of half the school, and it might be possible to learn something about the pair by watching them in action.

They moved together, though not perfectly in sync. It reminded me of a movie I'd seen in high school about juvenile lions learning to hunt together. One of the kids, wearing a black baseball cap, leaned over the table and casually swatted the book out of Irwin's hands. Irwin started and turned toward him, lifting his hands into a vague, confused-looking defensive posture.

As he did, the second kid, in a red sweatshirt, casually drove a finger down onto the edge of Irwin's dining tray. It flipped up, spilling food and drink all over Irwin.

A bowl broke, silverware rattled, and the whole tray clattered down. Irwin sat there looking stunned while the two bullies cruised right on by, as casual as can be. They were already fifteen feet away when the other children in the dining hall had zeroed in on the sound and reacted to the mess with a round of applause and catcalls.

"Pounder!" snarled a voice, and I looked up to see a man in a white visor, sweatpants, and a T-shirt come marching in from the hallway outside the cafeteria. "Pounder, what is this mess?"

Irwin blinked owlishly at the barrel-chested man and shook his head. "I . . ." He glanced after the two retreating bullies and then around the cafeteria. "I guess . . . I accidentally knocked my tray over, Coach Pete."

Coach Pete scowled and folded his arms. "If this was the first time this had happened, I wouldn't think anything of it. But how many times has your tray ended up on the floor, Pounder?"

Irwin looked down. "This would be five, sir."

"Yes, it would," said Coach Pete. He picked up the paperback Irwin had been reading. "If your head wasn't in these trashy science fiction books all the time, maybe you'd be able to feed yourself without making a mess."

"Yes, sir," Irwin said.

"*Hitchhiker's Guide to the Galaxy*," Coach Pete said, looking at the book. "That's stupid. You can't hitchhike onto a spaceship."

"No, sir," Irwin said.

"Detention," Coach Pete said. "Report to me after school."

"Yes, sir."

Coach Pete slapped the paperback against his leg, scowled at Irwin, and then abruptly looked up at me. "What?" he demanded.

"I was just wondering. You don't, by any chance, have a Vogon in your family tree?"

Coach Pete eyed me, his chest swelling in what an anthropologist might call a threat display. It might have been impressive if I hadn't been talking to River Shoulders the night before. "That a joke?"

"That depends on how much poetry you write," I said.

At this Coach Pete looked confused. He clearly didn't like feeling that way, which seemed a shame, since I suspected he spent a lot of time doing it. Irwin's eyes widened and he darted a quick look at me. His mouth twitched, but the kid kept himself from smiling or laughing—which was fairly impressive in a boy his age.

Coach Pete glowered at me, pointed a finger as if it might have been a gun, and said, "You tend to your own business."

I held up both hands in a gesture of mild acceptance. I rolled my eyes as soon as Coach Pete turned his back, drawing another quiver of restraint from Irwin.

"Pick this up," Coach Pete said to Irwin, and gestured at the spilled lunch on the floor. Then he turned and stomped away, taking Irwin's paperback with him. The two kids who had been giving Irwin grief had made their way back to their original seats, meanwhile, and were at the far end of the table, looking smug.

I pushed my lunch away and got up from the table. I went over to Irwin's side and knelt down to help him clean up his mess. I picked up the tray, slid it to a point between us, and said, "Just stack it up here."

Irwin gave me a quick, shy glance from beneath his mussed hair and started plucking up fallen bits of lunch. His hands were almost comically large compared to the rest of him, but his fingers were quick and dexterous. After a few seconds he asked, "You've read the *Hitch-hiker's Guide*?"

"Forty-two times," I said.

He smiled and then ducked his head again. "No one else here likes it."

"Well, it's not for everyone, is it?" I asked. "Personally, I've always wondered if Adams might not be a front man for a particularly talented dolphin. Which I think would make the book loads funnier."

Irwin let out a quick bark of laughter and then hunched his shoulders and kept cleaning up. His shoulders shook.

"Those two boys give you trouble a lot?" I asked.

Irwin's hands stopped moving for a second. Then he started up again. "What do you mean?"

"I mean I've been you before," I said. "The kid who liked reading books about aliens and goblins and knights and explorers at lunch and in class and during recess. I didn't care much about sports. And I got picked on a lot."

"They don't pick on me," Irwin said quickly. "It's just . . . just what guys do. They give me a hard time. It's in fun."

"And it doesn't make you angry," I said. "Not even a little."

His hands slowed down and his face turned thoughtful. "Sometimes," he said quietly. "When they spoil my broccoli."

I blinked. "Broccoli?"

"I love broccoli," Irwin said, looking up at me, his expression serious.

"Kid," I said, smiling, "no one loves broccoli. No one even likes broccoli. All the grown-ups just agree to lie about it so that we can make kids eat it, in vengeance for what our parents did to us."

"Well, I love broccoli," Irwin said, his jaw set.

"Hunh," I said. "Guess I've seen something new today." We finished, and I said, "Go get some more lunch. I'll take care of this."

"Thank you," he said soberly. "Um, Norm."

I grunted, nodded to him, tossed the dropped food, and returned the tray. Then I sat back down at the corner table with my lunch and watched Irwin and his tormentors from the corner of my eye. The two bullies never took their eyes off Irwin, even while talking and joking with their group.

I recognized that behavior, though I'd never seen it in a child before; only in hunting cats, vampires, and sundry monsters.

The two kids were predators.

Young and inexperienced, maybe. But predators.

For the first time, I thought that Bigfoot Irwin might be in real trouble.

I went back to my own tray and wolfed down the "food" on it. I wanted to keep a closer eye on Irwin.


BEING A WIZARD is all about being prepared. Well, that and magic, obviously. While I could do a few things in a hurry, most magic takes long moments or hours to arrange, and that means you have to know what's coming. I'd brought a few things with me, but I needed more information before I could act decisively on the kid's behalf.

I kept track of Irwin after he left the cafeteria. It wasn't hard. His face was down, his eyes on his book, and even though he was one of the younger kids in the school, he stood out, tall and gangly. I contrived to go past his classroom several times in the next hour. It was trig, which I knew, except I'd been doing it in high school instead of when I was nine.

Irwin was the youngest kid in the class. He was also evidently the smartest. He never looked up from his book. Several times the teacher tried to catch him out, asking him questions. Irwin put his finger on the place in his book, glanced up at the blackboard, and answered them with barely a pause. I found myself grinning.

Next I tracked down Irwin's tormentors. They weren't hard to find, either, since they both sat in the chairs closest to the exit, as though they couldn't wait to go off and be delinquent the instant school was out. They sat in class with impatient, sullen expressions. They looked like they were in the grip of agonizing boredom, but they didn't seem to be preparing to murder a teacher or anything.

I had a hunch that something about Irwin was drawing a predatory reaction from those two kids. And Coach Vogon had arrived on the scene pretty damned quickly—too much so for coincidence, maybe.

"Maybe Bigfoot Irwin isn't the only scion at this school," I muttered to myself.

And maybe I wasn't the only one looking out for the interests of a child born with one foot in this world and one in another.


I WAS STANDING outside the gymnasium as the last class of the day let out, leaning against the wall on my elbows, my feet crossed at the heels, my head hanging down, my wheeled bucket and mop standing unused a good seven feet away—pretty much the picture of an industrious janitor. The kids went hurrying by in a rowdy herd, with Irwin's tormentors being the last to leave the gym. I felt their eyes on me as they went past, but I didn't react to them.

Coach Vogon came out last, flicking out the banks of fluorescent lights as he went, his footsteps brisk and heavy. He came to a dead stop as he appeared and found me waiting for him.

There was a long moment of silence while he sized me up. I let him. I wasn't looking for a fight, and I had taken the deliberately relaxed and nonconfrontational stance I was in to convey that concept to him. I figured he was connected to the supernatural world, but I didn't know how connected he might be. Hell, I didn't even know if he was human.

Yet.

"Don't you have work to do?" he demanded.

"Doing it," I said. "I mean, obviously."

I couldn't actually hear his eyes narrow, but I was pretty sure they did. "You got a lot of nerve, buddy, talking to an instructor like that."

"If there weren't all these kids around, I might have said another syllable or two," I drawled. "Coach Vogon."

"You're about to lose your job, buddy. Get to work or I'll report you for malingering."

"Malingering," I said. "Four whole syllables. You're good."

He rolled another step toward me and jabbed a finger into my chest. "Buddy, you're about to buy a lot of trouble. Who do you think you are?"

"Harry Dresden," I said. "Wizard."

And I looked at him as I opened my Sight.

A wizard's Sight is an extra sense, one that allows him to perceive the patterns of energy and magic that suffuse the universe—energy that includes every conceivable form of magic. It doesn't actually open a third eye in your forehead or anything, but the brain translates the perceptions into the visual spectrum. In the circles I run in, the Sight shows you things as they truly are, cutting through every known form of veiling magic, illusion, and other mystic chicanery.

In this case, it showed me that the thing standing in front of me wasn't human.

Beneath its illusion, the spindly humanoid creature stood a little more than five feet high, and it might have weighed a hundred pounds soaking wet. It was naked, and anatomically it resembled a Ken doll. Its skin was dark grey, its eyes absolutely huge, bulbous, and midnight black. It had a rounded, high-crowned head and long, delicately pointed ears. I could still see the illusion of Coach Pete around the creature, a vague and hazy outline.

It lowered the lids of its bulbous eyes, the gesture somehow exceptionally lazy, and then nodded slowly. It inclined its head the smallest measurable amount possible and murmured, in a melodious and surprisingly deep voice, "Wizard."

I blinked a few times and waved my Sight away, so that I was facing Coach Pete again. "We should talk," I said.

The apparent man stared at me unblinkingly, his expression as blank as a discarded puppet's. It was probably my imagination that made his eyes look suddenly darker. "Regarding?"

"Irwin Pounder," I said. "I would prefer to avoid a conflict with Svartalfheim."

He inhaled and exhaled slowly through his nose. "You recognized me."

In fact, I'd been making an educated guess, but the svartalf didn't need to know that. I knew precious little about the creatures. They were extremely gifted craftsmen, and were responsible for creating most of the really cool artifacts of Norse myth. They weren't wicked, exactly, but they were ruthless, proud, stubborn, and greedy, which often added up to similar results. They were known to be sticklers for keeping their word, and God help you if you broke yours to them. Most important, they were a small supernatural nation unto themselves: one that protected its citizens with maniacal zeal.

"I had a good teacher," I said. "I want your boys to lay off Irwin Pounder."

"Point of order," he said. "They are not mine. I am not their progenitor. I am a guardian only."

"Be that as it may," I said, "my concern is for Irwin, not the brothers."

"He is a whetstone," he said. "They sharpen their instincts upon him. He is good for them."

"They aren't good for him," I said. "Fix it."

"It is not my place to interfere with them," Coach Pete said. "Only to offer indirect guidance and to protect them from anyone who would interfere with their growth."

The last phrase was as emotionless as the first, but it somehow carried an ugly ring of a threat—a polite threat, but a threat nonetheless.

Sometimes I react badly to being threatened. I might have glared a little.

"Hypothetically," I said, "let's suppose that I saw those boys giving Irwin a hard time again and I made it my business to stop them. What would you do?"

"Slay you," Coach Pete said. His tone was utterly absent of any doubt.

"Awfully sure of yourself, aren't you?"

He spoke as if reciting a single-digit arithmetic problem. "You are young. I am not."

I felt my jaw clench and forced myself to take a slow breath, to stay calm. "They're hurting him."

"Be that as it may," he said calmly, "my concern is for the brothers, not for Irwin Pounder."

I ground my teeth and wished I could pick my words out of them before continuing the conversation. "We've both stated our positions," I said. "How do we resolve the conflict?"

"That also is not my concern," he said. "I will not dissuade the brothers. I will slay you should you attempt to do so yourself. There is nothing else to discuss."

He shivered a little, and suddenly the illusion of Coach Pete seemed to gain a measure of life, of definition, like an empty glove abruptly filled by the flesh of a hand.

"If you will excuse me," he said, in Coach Pete's annoying tone of voice, walking past me, "I have a detention over which to preside."

"To preside over," I said, and snorted at his back. "*Over which to preside.* No one actually talks like that."

He turned his head and gave me a flat-eyed look. Then he rounded a corner and was gone.

I rubbed at the spot on my forehead between my eyebrows and tried to think.

I had a bad feeling that fighting this guy was going to be a losing proposition. In my experience, when someone gets their kids a super-natural supernanny, they don't pick pushovers. Among wizards, I'm pretty buff, but the world is full of bigger fish than me. More to the point, even if I fought the svartalf and won, it might drag the White Council of Wizardry into a violent clash with Svartalfheim. I wouldn't want to have something like that on my conscience.

I wanted to protect the Pounder kid, and I wasn't going to back away from that. But how was I supposed to protect him from the Bully Brothers if they had a heavyweight on deck, ready to charge in swinging? That kind of brawl could spill over onto any nearby kids, and fast. I didn't want this to turn into a slugfest. That wouldn't help Irwin Pounder.

But what could I do? What options did I have? How could I act without dragging the svartalf into a confrontation?

I couldn't.

"Ah," I said to no one, lifting a finger in the air. "Aha!"

I grabbed my mop bucket and hurried toward the cafeteria.

THE SCHOOL EMPTIED out fast, making the same transition every school does every day, changing from a place full of life and energy, of move-ment and noise, into a series of echoing chambers and empty halls. Teachers and staff seemed as eager to be gone as the students. Good. It was still possible that things would get ugly, and if they did, the fewer people around, the better.

By the time I went by the janitor's closet to pick up the few tools I'd brought with me and went to the cafeteria, my bucket's squeaking wheels were the loudest sound I could hear. I turned the corner at almost exactly the same time as the Bully Brothers appeared from the opposite end of the hall. They drew up short, and I could feel the weight of their eyes as they assessed me. I ignored them and went on inside.

Bigfoot Irwin was already inside the cafeteria, seated at a table, writing on a piece of paper. I recognized the kid's rigid, resigned posture, and it made my wrist ache just to see it: Coach Pete had him writing a sentence repetitively, probably something about being more careful with his lunch tray. The monster.

Coach Pete stood leaning against a wall, reading a sports magazine of some sort. Or at least that was what he appeared to be doing. I had to wonder how much genuine interest a svartalf might have in the NBA. His eyes flicked up as I entered; I saw them go flat.

I set my mop and bucket aside and started sweeping the floors with a large dust broom. My janitorial form was perfect. I saw Coach Pete's jaw clench a couple of times, and then he walked over to me.

"What are you doing?" he asked.

"Sweeping the floor," I replied, guileless as a newborn.

"This is not a matter for levity," he said. "No amount of it will save your life."

"You grossly underestimate the power of laughter," I said. "But if there's some kind of violent altercation between students, any janitor in the world would find it his honor-bound duty to report it to the administration."

Coach Pete made a growling sound.

"Go ahead," I said. "Let your kids loose on him. I saw how they behaved in their classrooms. They're problem cases. Irwin's obviously a brilliant student and a good kid. When the administration finds out the three of them were involved in a fight, what do you think happens to the Troublemaker Twins? This is a private school. Out they go. Irwin is protected—and I won't have to lift a finger to interfere."

Coach Pete rolled up the magazine and tapped it against his leg a couple of times. Then he relaxed, and a small smile appeared upon his lips. "You are correct, of course, except for one thing."

"Yeah? What's that?"

"They will not be exiled. Their parents donate more funds to the school than any ten other families—and a great deal more than Irwin's mother could ever afford." He gave me a very small, very Gallic shrug. "This is a private school. The boys' parents paid for the cafeteria within which we stand."

I found myself gritting my teeth. "First of all, you have got to get over this fetish for grammatically correct prepositions. It makes you sound like a prissy twit. And second of all, money isn't everything."

"Money is power," he replied.

"Power isn't everything."

"No," he said, and his smile became smug. "It is the only thing."

I looked back out into the hallway through the open glass wall separating it from the cafeteria. The Bully Brothers were standing in the hall, staring at Irwin the way hungry lions stare at gazelles.

Coach Pete nodded pleasantly to me and returned to his original place by the wall, unrolling his magazine and opening it again.

"Dammit," I whispered. The svartalf might well be right. At an upper-class institution such as this, money and politics would have a ridiculous amount of influence. Whether aristocracies were hereditary or economic, they'd been successfully buying their children out of trouble for centuries. The Bully Brothers might well come out of this squeaky clean, and they'd be able to continue to persecute Bigfoot Irwin.

Maybe this would turn out to be a slugfest after all.

I swept my way over to Irwin's table and came to a stop. Then I sat down across from him.

He looked up from his page of scrawled sentences, and his face was pale. He wouldn't meet my eyes.

"How you doing, kid?" I asked him. When I spoke, he actually flinched a little.

"Fine," he mumbled.

Hell's bells. He was afraid of me. "Irwin," I said, keeping my voice gentle, "relax. I'm not going to hurt you."

"Okay," he said, without relaxing a bit.

"They've been doing this for a while now, haven't they?" I asked him.

"Um," he said.

"The Bully Brothers. The ones staring at you right now."

Irwin shivered and glanced aside without actually turning his head toward the window. "It's not a big deal."

"It kind of is," I said. "They've been giving you grief for a long time, haven't they? Only lately it's been getting worse. They've been scarier. More violent. Bothering you more and more often."

He said nothing, but something in his lack of reaction told me that I'd hit the nail on the head.

I sighed. "Irwin, my name is Harry Dresden. Your father sent me to help you."

That made his eyes snap up to me, and his mouth opened. "M-my . . . my dad?"

"Yeah," I said. "He can't be here to help you. So he asked me to do it for him."

"My dad," Irwin said, and I heard the ache in his voice, so poignant that my own chest tightened in empathy. I'd never known my mother, and my father died before I started going to school. I knew what it was like to have holes in my life in the shape of people who should have been there.

His eyes flicked toward the Bully Brothers again, though he didn't turn his head. "Sometimes," he said quietly, "if I ignore them, they go away." He stared down at his paper. "My dad . . . I mean, I never . . . You met him?"

"Yeah."

His voice was very small. "Is . . . is he nice?"

"Seems to be," I said gently.

"And . . . and he knows about me?"

"Yeah," I said. "He wants to be here for you. But he can't."

"Why not?" Irwin asked.

"It's complicated."

Irwin nodded and looked down. "Every Christmas there's a present from him. But I think maybe Mom is just writing his name on the tag."

"Maybe not," I said quietly. "He sent me. And I'm way more expensive than a present."

Irwin frowned at that and said, "What are you going to do?"

"That isn't the question you should be asking," I said.

"What is, then?"

I put my elbows on the table and leaned toward him. "The question, Irwin, is what are you going to do?"

"Get beat up, probably," he said.

"You can't keep hoping they'll just go away, kid," I said. "There are people out there who enjoy hurting and scaring others. They're going to keep doing it until you make them stop."

"I'm not going to fight anyone," Irwin all but whispered. "I'm not going to hurt anyone. I . . . I can't. And besides, if they're picking on me, they're not picking on anyone else."

I leaned back and took a deep breath, studying his hunched shoulders, his bowed head. The kid was frightened, the kind of fear that is planted and nurtured and which grows over the course of months and years. But there was also a kind of gentle, immovable resolve in the boy's skinny body. He wasn't afraid of facing the Bully Brothers. He just dreaded going through the pain that the encounter would bring.

Courage, like fear, comes in multiple varieties.

"Damn," I said quietly. "You got some heart, kiddo."

"Can you stay with me?" he asked. "If . . . if you're here, maybe they'll leave me alone."

"Today," I said quietly. "What about tomorrow?"

"I don't know," he said. "Are you going away?"

"Can't stay here forever," I replied. "Sooner or later you're going to be on your own."

"I won't fight," he said. A droplet of water fell from his bowed head to smear part of a sentence on his paper. "I won't be like them."

"Irwin," I said. "Look at me."

He lifted his eyes. They were full. He was blinking to keep more tears from falling.

"Fighting isn't always a bad thing."

"That's not what the school says."

I smiled briefly. "The school has liability to worry about. I only have to worry about you."

He frowned, his expression intent, pensive. "When isn't it a bad thing?"

"When you're protecting yourself, or someone else, from harm," I said. "When someone wants to hurt you or someone who can't defend themselves—and when the rightful authority can't or won't protect you."

"But you have to hurt people to win a fight. And that isn't right."

"No," I said. "It isn't. But sometimes it is necessary."

"It isn't necessary right now," he said. "I'll be fine. It'll hurt, but I'll be fine."

"Maybe you will," I said. "But what about when they're done with you? What happens when they decide that it was so much fun to hurt you, they go pick on someone else, too?"

"Do you think they'll do that?"

"Yes," I said. "That's how bullies work. They keep hurting people until someone makes them stop."

He fiddled with the pencil in his fingers. "I don't like fighting. I don't even like playing Street Fighter."

"This isn't really about fighting," I said. "It's about communication."

He frowned. "Huh?"

"They're doing something wrong," I said. "You need to communicate with them. Tell them that what they're doing isn't acceptable, and that they need to stop doing it."

"I've said that," he said. "I tried that a long time ago. It didn't work."

"You talked to them," I said. "It didn't get through. You need to find another way to get your message through. You have to show them."

"You mean hurt them."

"Not necessarily," I said quietly. "But guys like those two jokers only respect strength. If you show them that you have it, they'll get the idea."

Irwin frowned harder. "No one ever talked to me about it like that before."

"I guess not," I said.

"I'm . . . I'm scared of doing that."

"Who wouldn't be?" I asked him. "But the only way to beat your fears is to face them. If you don't, they're going to keep on doing this to you, and then others, and someday someone is going to get hurt bad. It might even be those two jackasses who get hurt—if someone doesn't make them realize that they can't go through life acting like that."

"They aren't really bad guys," Irwin said slowly. "I mean, to anyone but me. They're okay to other people."

"Then I'd say that you'd be helping them as well as yourself, Irwin."

He nodded slowly and took a deep breath. "I'll . . . I'll think about it."

"Good," I said. "Thinking for yourself is the most valuable skill you'll ever learn."

"Thank you, Harry," he said.

I rose and picked up my broom. "You bet."

I went back to sweeping one end of the cafeteria. Coach Pete stood at the other end. Irwin returned to his writing, and the Bully Brothers came in.

They approached as before, moving between the tables, splitting up to come at Irwin from two sides. They ignored me and Coach Pete, closing in on Irwin with impatient eagerness.

Irwin's pencil stopped scratching when they both were about five feet away from him, and without looking up he said in a sharp, firm voice, "Stop."

They did. I could see the face of only one of them, but the bully was blinking in surprise.

"This is not cool," Irwin said. "And I'm not going to let you do it anymore."

The brothers eyed him, traded rather feral smiles, and then each of them lunged at Irwin and grabbed an arm. They hauled him back with surprising speed and power, slamming his back onto the floor. One of them started slapping at his eyes and face while the other produced a short length of heavy rubber tubing, jerked Irwin's shirt up, and started hitting him on the stomach with the hose.

I gritted my teeth and reached for the handle of my mop—except it wasn't a mop that was poking up out of the bucket. It was my staff, a six-foot length of oak as thick as my circled thumb and forefinger. If this was how the Bully Brothers started the beating, I didn't even want to think about what they'd do for a finale. Svartalf or not, I couldn't allow things to go any further before I stepped in.

Coach Pete's dark eyes glittered at me from behind his sports magazine, and he crooked a couple of fingers on one hand in a way that no human being could have. I don't know what kind of magical energy the svartalf was using, but he was good with it. There was a sharp crackling sound, and the water in the mop bucket froze solid in an instant, trapping my staff in place.

My heart sped up. That kind of magical control was a bad, bad sign. It meant that the svartalf was better than me—probably a lot better. He hadn't used a focus of any kind to help him out, the way my staff would help me focus and control my own power. If we'd been fighting with swords, that move would have been the same as him clipping off the tips of my eyelashes without drawing blood. This guy would kill me if I fought him.

I set my jaw, grabbed the staff in both hands, and sent a surge of my will and power rushing down its rune-carved length into the entrapping ice. I muttered, *"Forzare,"* as I twisted the staff, and pure energy lashed out into the ice, pulverizing it into chunks the size of gravel.

Coach Pete leaned forward slightly, eager, and I saw his eyes gleam. Svartalves were old-school, and their culture had been born in the time of the Vikings. They thought mortal combat was at least as fun as it was scary, and their idea of mercy embraced killing you quickly as opposed to killing you slowly. If I started up with this svartalf, it wouldn't be over until one of us was dead. Probably me. I was afraid.

The sound of the rubber hose hitting Irwin's stomach and the harsh breathing of the struggling children echoed in the large room.

I took a deep breath, grabbed my staff in two hands, and began drawing in my will once more.

And then Bigfoot Irwin roared, "I said no!"

The kid twisted his shoulders in an abrupt motion and tossed one of the brothers away as if he weighed no more than a soccer ball. The bully flew ten feet before his butt hit the ground. The second brother was still staring in shock when Bigfoot Irwin sat up, grabbed him by the front of his shirt, and rose. He lifted the second brother's feet off the floor and simply held him there, scowling furiously up at him.

The Bully Brothers had inherited their predatory instinct from their supernatural parent.

Bigfoot Irwin had gotten something else.

The second brother stared down at the younger boy and struggled to wriggle free, his face pale and frantic. Irwin didn't let him go.

"Hey, look at me," Irwin snarled. "This is not okay. You were mean to me. You kept hurting me. For no reason. That's over. Now. I'm not going to let you do it anymore. Okay?"

The first brother sat up shakily from the floor and stared agog at his former victim, now holding his brother effortlessly off the floor.

"Did you hear me?" Irwin asked, giving the kid a little shake. I heard his teeth clack together.

"Y-yeah," stammered the dangling brother, nodding emphatically. "I hear you. I hear you. We hear you."

Irwin scowled for a moment. Then he gave the second brother a push before releasing him. The bully fell to the floor three feet away and scrambled quickly back from Irwin. The pair of them started a slow retreat.

"I mean it," Irwin said. "What you've been doing isn't cool. We'll figure out something else for you to do for fun. Okay?"

The Bully Brothers mumbled something vaguely affirmative and then hurried out of the cafeteria.

Bigfoot Irwin watched them go. Then he looked down at his hands, turning them over and back as if he'd never seen them before.

I kept my grip on my staff and looked down the length of the cafeteria at Coach Pete. I arched an eyebrow at him. "It seems like the boys sorted this out on their own."

Coach Pete lowered his magazine slowly. The air was thick with tension, and the silence was its hard surface.

Then the svartalf said, "Your sentences, Mr. Pounder."

"Yessir, Coach Pete," Irwin said. He turned back to the table and sat down, and his pencil started scratching at the paper again.

Coach Pete nodded at him, then came over to me. He stood facing me for a moment, his expression blank.

"I didn't intervene," I said. "I didn't try to dissuade your boys from following their natures. Irwin did that."

The svartalf pursed his lips thoughtfully and then nodded slowly. "Technically accurate. And yet you still had a hand in what just happened. Why should I not exact retribution for your interference?"

"Because I just helped your boys."

"In what way?"

"Irwin and I taught them caution—that some prey is too much for them to handle. And we didn't even hurt them to make it happen."

Coach Pete considered that for a moment and then gave me a faint smile. "A lesson best learned early rather than late." He turned and started to walk away.

"Hey," I said in a sharp, firm voice.

He paused.

"You took the kid's book today," I said. "Please return it."

Irwin's pencil scratched along the page, suddenly loud.

Coach Pete turned. Then he pulled the paperback in question out of his pocket and flicked it through the air. I caught it in one hand, which probably made me look a lot cooler and more collected than I felt at the time.

Coach Pete inclined his head to me, a little more deeply than before. "Wizard."

I mirrored the gesture. "Svartalf."

He left the cafeteria, shaking his head. What sounded suspiciously like a chuckle bubbled in his wake.

I WAITED UNTIL Irwin was done with his sentences, and then I walked him to the front of the building, where his maternal grandmother was waiting to pick him up.

"Was that okay?" he asked me. "I mean, did I do right?"

"Asking me if I thought you did right isn't the question," I said.

Irwin suddenly smiled at me. "Do I think I did right?" He nodded slowly. "I think . . . I think I do."

"How's it feel?" I asked him.

"It feels good. I feel . . . not happy. Satisfied. Whole."

"That's how it's supposed to feel," I said. "Whenever you've got a choice, do good, kiddo. It isn't always fun or easy, but in the long run it makes your life better."

He nodded, frowning thoughtfully. "I'll remember."

"Cool," I said.

He offered me his hand very seriously, and I shook it. He had a strong grip for a kid. "Thank you, Harry. Could . . . could I ask you a favor?"

"Sure."

"If you see my dad again . . . could you tell him . . . could you tell him I did good?"

"Of course," I said. "I think what you did will make him very proud."

That all but made the kid glow. "And . . . and tell him that . . . that I'd like to meet him. You know. Someday."

"Will do," I said quietly.

Bigfoot Irwin nodded at me. Then he turned and made his gangly way over to the waiting car and slid into it. I stood and watched until the car was out of sight. Then I rolled my bucket of ice back into the school so that I could go home.

# AAAA WIZARDRY

This next story is set just after the events, I believe, of *Proven Guilty*, where Harry Dresden has become impressed with the need to instruct the younger wizards around him. I can just barely remember the actual writing of this tale, which probably means it happened around a move. I find moving homes to be among the more hideous experiences in life, and I tend to block out several days around the experience, just to be safe. If I was writing during that window, then I imagine that the story was likely late as well and absolutely needed to be finished. So once again, I met with Inspiration at the corner of Late and Hurry Up.

I wanted to write a story that began to show Dresden in his role as a teacher and mentor to the younger wizards, showing him taking on more responsibility in his community and becoming more of a leader as he grew as a wizard and as a person. He had added responsibilities now, including an apprentice of his own, and wasn't ever really going to be able to go back to the carefree days of being a roaming knight errant. So here he's trying to impress upon the younger wizards the danger of arrogance—something, let's face it, that Dresden has flirted with upon multiple occasions, often to his chagrin.

But this is a story in which we see Dresden beginning to grow into new roles and new responsibilities, while simultaneously catching a glimpse of his past.

The first thing I thought, looking at the roomful of baby Wardens, was, *They all look so darned young.* The close second was, *My God, am I getting old?*

"Okay, children," I said, closing the door behind me. I had rented an alleged conference center in a little Chicago hotel not too far from the airport, which amounted to a couple of rooms big enough for twenty or thirty people—if they were friendly—plus a few dozen chairs and several rickety old folding tables.

They didn't even provide a cooler of water—just directions to their vending machines.

After my fellow Warden-Commander in the United States, Warden Ramirez, and I had gotten done learning the little Warden-kind up on their mayhem, for the sake of getting them killed in a war as quickly as possible, we thought it might be nice to give them a little instruction in other things, too. Ramirez was going to cover the course on relations with mortal authorities, which made sense; Ramirez got on just fine with the cops in LA, and hadn't been shot by nearly as many law-enforcement personnel as I had.

The kids had all come to Chicago to learn about independent investigation of supernatural threats from me, which also made sense, because I'd done more of that, relative to my tender years, than any other wizard on the planet.

"Okay, okay," I said to the room. The young Wardens became silent and attentive at once. No shock there—the disruptive ones who didn't pay attention during lessons had mostly been killed and maimed in the war with the Red Court. Darwin always thought that it paid to be a quick learner. The war had simply made the penalty for not learning quite a bit steeper.

"You're here," I said, "to learn about investigating supernatural threats on your own. You'll learn about finding and hunting warlocks from Captain Luccio, whenever the Reds give us enough time for it. Warlocks, our own kind gone bad, aren't the most common opponent you'll find yourself facing. Far more often, you're going to run up against other threats."

Ilyana, a young woman with extremely pale skin and ice-blue, nearly white eyes, raised her hand and spoke in a clipped Russian accent when I nodded to her. "What kinds of threats?" she asked. "In the practical sense. What foes have you faced?"

I held up my hands and flipped up a finger for each foe. "Demons, werewolves, ghosts, faeries, fallen angels, Black Court vampires, Red Court vampires, White Court vampires, cultists, necromancers"—I paused to waggle one foot, standing with three limbs in the air—"zombies, specters, phobophages, half-blood scions, jann . . ." I waved my hands and foot around a bit more. "I'd need to borrow a few people to do the whole list. Get the picture?" A few smiles had erupted at my antics, but they sobered up after a moment's consideration.

I nodded and stuck my hands into my pockets. "Knowledge is quite literally power and will save your life. When you know what you're facing, you can deal with it. Walk into a confrontation blind, and you're begging to get your families added to the Wardens' death-benefits list." I let that sink in for a few seconds before continuing. "You can't ever be sure what you're going to come up against. But you can be sure about how to approach the investigation."

I turned to the old blackboard on the wall behind me and scribbled on it with the stub of a piece of chalk. "I call it the Four As," I said, and wrote four As down the left side of the board. "Granted, it doesn't translate as neatly to other languages, but you can make up your own native-tongue mnemonic devices later." I used the first A to spell *ascertain*.

"Ascertain," I said, firmly. "Before you can deal with the threat, you've got to know that it exists, and you've got to know who the threat's intended target is. A lot of times, that target is going to cry out for help. Whatever city you're based in, it's going to be your responsibility to work out how best to hear that scream. But sometimes there's no outcry. So keep your eyes and ears open, kids. Ascertain the threat. Become aware of the problem."

MY CAR DIDN'T make it all the way to Kansas City. It broke down about thirty miles short of town, and I had to call a wrecker. I had planned on being there before dark, but between walking eleven miles to find an increasingly rare pay phone, dumping most of my cash into a tow-truck driver's pocket, and the collapse of an office computer network that delayed picking up a rental car for an extra hour and a half, I wound up pulling to the curb of a residential address a couple of minutes before nine in the evening.

I'd gotten the address from a contact on the Paranet—the organization made up mostly of men and women who didn't have enough magical power to be accepted into the ranks of the White Council or to protect themselves from major predators, but who had more than enough mojo to make them juicy targets. For the past year, I and others like me had been working hard to teach them how to defend themselves—and one of the first things they were to do was notify someone upstream in the Paranet's organization that they were in trouble.

One such call had been bucked up to me, and here I was, answering. Before I had closed the door of the car, a spare, tense-looking man in his forties came out of the house and walked quickly toward me.

"Harry Dresden?" he called.

"Yeah," I said.

"You're late."

"Car trouble," I said. "Are you Yardly?" He stopped across the hood of the car from me, frowning severely. He was average height, and wore most of a business suit, including the tie. His black hair was cut into a short brush. He looked like the kind of guy who solved his problems through ferocious focus and mulish determination, and who tolerated no nonsense along the way.

"I'm Yardly," he said. "Can you show me some ID?"

I almost smiled. "You want to see my American Association of Wizards card?"

Yardly didn't smile. "Your driver's license will do."

"If I were a shapeshifter," I said, passing him the license, "this wouldn't help."

Yardly produced a little UV flashlight and shone it onto the license. "I'm more concerned about a simple con man." He passed me the license back. "I'm not really into my sister's group. Whatever they are. But she's had it rough lately and I'm not going to see her hurt anymore. Do you understand?"

"Most big brothers stop making threats about their little sisters after high school."

"I must be remedial," Yardly said. "If you abuse Megan in any way, you'll answer to me."

I felt my mouth lift up on one side. "You're a cop."

"Detective Lieutenant," he said. "I asked Chicago PD for their file on you. They think you're a fraud."

"And you don't?"

He grunted. "Megan doesn't. I learned a long time ago that a smart man doesn't discount her opinion out of hand."

He stared at me with hard and opaque eyes, and I realized, in a flash of insight, that the man was tense because he was operating on unfamiliar ground. You couldn't read it in his face, but it was there if you knew what to look for. A certain set of the shoulders, a twitch along the jawline, as if some part of him was ready to whirl around and sink his teeth into a threat that he could feel creeping up behind him.

Yardly was afraid. Not for himself, maybe, but the man was terrified.

"Megan says shrinks can't help with this one," he said quietly. "She says maybe you can."

"Let's find out," I said.

"SECOND A," I said to the Wardenlets, writing on the chalkboard as I did. "Analysis."

"How do you get an ogre to lie down on the couch, Harry?" called a young man with the rounded vowels of a Northern accent in his speech. The room quivered with the laughter of young people.

"That's enough out of you, there, McKenzie, you hoser," I shot back, in a parody of the same accent. "Give me a break here, eh?"

I got a bigger laugh than the heckler. Which is how you make sure the heckler doesn't steal the show from you. "Pipe down," I said, and waited for them to settle. "Thank you. Your second step is always analysis. Even when you know what you're dealing with, you've got to know why it's happening. If you've got an angry ghost, it's generally angry for a reason. If a new pack of ghouls has moved in down the block, they've generally picked their spot for a reason."

Ilyana raised her hand again and I pointed at her. "What does it matter?" she asked. "Ghost or ghoul is causing problem, still we are dealing with them, yes?" She pointed her finger like a gun and dropped her thumb like the weapon's hammer on the word *dealing*.

"If you're stupid, yeah," I said.

She didn't look pleased at my response.

"I used to have a similar attitude," I said. I held up my left hand. It was a mass of old scars, and not the pretty kind. It had been burned, and badly, several years before. Wizards heal up better than regular folks, over the long term. I could move it again, and I had feeling back in parts of all the fingers. But it still wasn't a pretty picture. "An hour or two of work would have told me enough about the situation I was walking into to let me avoid this," I told them. It was the truth. Pretty much. "Learn everything you possibly can."

Ilyana frowned at me.

McKenzie raised his hand, frowning soberly, and I nodded at him. "Learn more. Okay. How?"

I spread my hands. "Never let yourself think you know all the ways to learn," I said. "Expand your own knowledge base. Read. Talk to other wizards. Hell, you might even go to school."

That got me another laugh. I went on before it gathered much momentum.

"Warden Canuck there was onto something earlier, too. People are people. Learn about what makes them tick. Monsters are the same way. Find ways to emulate their thinking"—I wasn't even going to try a phrase like *Get into their heads*, thank you—"and you'll have insight into their actions and their probable intentions.

"Information-gathering spells can be darned handy," I continued, "but if you'll forgive the expression, they aren't magic. The information you get from them can be easily misread, and it will almost never let you see past one of your own blind spots. You can seek answers from other planes, but if you go bargaining with supernatural beings for knowledge, things can get dangerous fast. Sometimes what you get from them is invaluable. Most of the time, it could be had another way. Approach that particular well with extreme caution."

To emphasize those last two words, I stared slowly around the room in pure challenge, daring anyone to disagree with me. The young people dropped their eyes from mine. Eye contact with a wizard is tricky—it can trigger a soulgaze, and that isn't the kind of thing you want happening to you casually.

"Honestly," I said into the silence, letting my voice become gentler, more conversational, "the best thing you can do is communicate. Talk to the people involved. Your victims, if they can speak to you. Their family. Witnesses. Friends. Most of the time, everything you need is something they already know. Most of the time, that's the fastest, safest, easiest way to get it."

McKenzie raised his hand again, and I nodded. "Most of the time?" he asked.

"That's the thing about people," I said quietly, so they would pay attention. "Whether it's to you or to everyone or just to themselves, people lie."

MEGAN YARDLY WAS a single mother of three. She was in her early thirties and looked it, had gorgeous red hair and bright green eyes. She and her children lived in a suburb that was more sub than urb, southeast of KC, named Peculiar. Peculiar, Missouri. You can't make these things up. Megan opened the door, nodded to her brother, looked up at me, and said, "You're him. You're the wizard." Her eyes narrowed. "Your . . . your car broke down. And you think the name of our town is a bad joke." She nodded, like a musician who has picked up on a beat and a chord progression. "And you think this probably isn't a supernatural problem."

I lifted my eyebrows. "You're one hell of a sensitive."

She nodded. "You were expecting someone who was good at cold reading."

"A lot of professional psychics are," I said. I smiled. "So are you."

She arched an eyebrow at me.

"There's at least a fair chance that, if someone is late to what is perceived as an important appointment, that car trouble is to blame, particularly if they show up in a rental car. Most people who hadn't grown up around a town named Peculiar would think the name was odd." I grinned at her. "And gosh. A lot of professional investigators are just a tad cynical."

Her expression broke and she laughed. "Apparently." She turned from me and kissed her brother on the cheek.

"Ben."

"Meg."

"Child services was here again today," she said, her tone neutral.

"Dammit," Yardly said. "How's Kat?"

She waggled a hand in the air, but her face suddenly aged ten years. "The same."

"Meg, the doctors—"

"Not again, Ben," she said, closing her eyes briefly. She shook her head once, and Yardly shut his jaws with an audible click. Megan looked down at the ground for a moment and then up at me. "So. Harry Dresden. High Mucketymuck of the White Council."

"Actually," I said, "I'm a fairly low mucketymuck. Or maybe a mucketymuck militant. High mucketymucks—"

"Wouldn't come to Peculiar?"

"You're really into interruption, aren't you?" I said, smiling. "I was going to say, they wouldn't have a problem with their car."

"Oh, God," she said. "I think I like you."

"Give it time," I said.

She nodded slowly. Then she said, with gentle emphasis, "Please come into my home." She stepped back, and I came into the little house, crossing over the threshold, the curtain of gentle, powerful energy that surrounds every home. Her invitation meant that the curtain parted for me, letting me bring my power with me. I exhaled slowly, tightening my metaphysical muscles and feeling my power put a silent, invisible strain on the air around me. Megan inhaled suddenly, sharply, and took a step back from me.

"Ah," I said. "You are a sensitive."

She shook her head once, and then held up her hand to forestall her brother. "Ben, it's fine. He's . . ." She looked at me again, her expression pensive, fragile. "He's the real deal."

We sat down in the little living room. It was littered with children's toys. The place didn't look like an animal pit—just busy and well-loved. I sat in a comfy chair. Megan perched at the edge of her couch. Yardly hovered, evidently unable to bring himself to sit.

"So," I said quietly. "You think something is tormenting your daughters."

She nodded.

"How old are they?"

"Kat is twelve. Tamara is four."

"Uh-huh," I said. "Tell me about what happens."

Sometimes I seem to have the damnedest sense of timing. No sooner had I asked the question than a high-pitched scream cut the air, joined an instant later by another one.

"Oh, God," Megan said, and flew up to her feet and out of the room.

I followed her, but more slowly, as the screaming continued. She hurried down a short hallway to a room with a trio of large cartoon girl figures I didn't recognize. They had freaking huge eyes, though. Megan emerged a moment later, carrying a dark-haired moppet in pink-and-white-striped footie pajamas. The little girl was clinging to her mother with all four limbs and kept screaming, her eyes squeezed tight shut.

The sound was heart wrenching. She was terrified. I had to stop short as Megan immediately took two quick steps toward me and plunged through the next doorway. This one had a poster of a band of young men on it I didn't recognize. One looked rebellious and sullen, one wacky and lighthearted, one sober and stable, and one handsomely vogue. Another Monkees reincarnation, basically.

I went to the door and saw Megan, with her clinging moppet, sit down on the bed and start gently shaking the shoulder of a girl with hair like her mother's—presumably Kat. She was screaming, too, but she broke out of it a moment later, the instant her eyes fluttered open.

The moppet, presumably Tamara, stopped screaming, too, and at exactly the same time. Then they both burst into less-hysterical tears and clung to their mother.

Megan's face was anguished, but her voice and her hands were gentle as she touched them, spoke to them, reassured them. If she was an empath as sensitive as her file and her reaction to my test suggested, then she had to be in terrible psychic pain. She pushed enough of it aside to be there for her kids, though.

"Dammit," I heard Yardly breathe from the hall behind me. It was a tired oath.

"Interesting," I said. "Excuse me."

I turned and paced down the hallway to the younger child's room, and nearly tripped over a dark-haired child, a boy who might have been eight. He was wearing underwear and a T-shirt with a cartoon Jedi Knight on it, which raised my opinion of his mother immediately. The kid's eyes weren't even open, and he raised his arms blindly. I picked him up and carried him with me into the little bedroom.

It wasn't large—nothing about Megan's house was. One of the beds was pink and festooned with the same three big-eyed girls. The other was surrounded in the plastic shell of a *Star Wars* landspeeder. I plopped the young Jedi back into it, and he promptly curled into a ball and went to sleep.

I covered him up with a blanket and turned to examine the rest of the room. Not much to it. A lot of toys, most of them more or less put away; a dresser the two younger kids evidently shared; a little table and chairs; and a closet.

A nice, shadowy closet.

I grunted and got on the floor to peer beneath the little pink bed. Then I squinted at the closet. If I were four and lying on the girl's bed, the closet would be looming right past the ends of my toes.

I closed my eyes for a moment and reached out with my wizard's senses, feeling the flow and ebb of energy through the house. Within the defensive wall of the threshold, other energy pulsed and moved— emotions from the house's inhabitants, random energies sifting in from outdoors—the usual.

But not in the closet. There wasn't anything at all in that closet.

"Aha," I said.

"THIRD A," I said, writing on the board. "Assemble."

"Avengers," said McKenzie.

"Assemble!" crowed the young Wardens in unison. They're good kids.

"That is, in fact, one potential part of this phase of the investigation," I said, taking the conversation back in hand as I nodded my approval. "Sometimes, once you've figured out what's going on, you go and round up reinforcements. But what assembling really means, for our purposes, is putting everything together. You've got your information. Now you need to decide what to do with it. You plan what steps you need to take. You work out the possible consequences of your actions."

"Here's where you use your brain. If the foe has a weakness, you figure out how to exploit it. If you've got an advantage of terrain, you figure out how to use it. If you need specialized gear or equipment to help, here's where you get it." I started passing a stack of papers around the room. "There's recipes on these handouts for a couple of the most common things you'll use: an antidote for Red Court venom, which you're familiar with, and an ointment for your eyes that'll let you see through most faerie glamour, which you may not know about. Get used to making these."

I took a deep breath. "This is also the stage where sometimes you do some math."

The room was very quiet for a moment.

"Yeah," I said. "Here's where you decide whose life to risk, or whose isn't worth risking. Here's where you decide who you can save and who is already gone past saving. I've been doing this sort of thing for a while. Some of my seniors in the Council would call me foolish or arrogant, and they could be right—but I've never met anyone who was breathing who I thought was too far gone to help."

"You've got a boogeyman," I told Megan an hour later.

Megan frowned at me. "A-a . . . ?"

"A boogeyman," I said. "Sometimes known as a boggle or a boggart. It's a weak form of phobophage—a fear-eater, mostly insubstantial. This one is pretty common. Feeds on a child's fear."

Yardly's eyebrows tried to climb into his hair.

"That isn't possible," Megan said. "I'd . . . I'd sense something like that. I'd feel it. I've felt things like that before. Several ghosts. Once, a poltergeist."

"Not this one," I said. "You're too old."

She cocked an eyebrow at me. "Excuse me?"

"Ahem. I mean, you're an adult."

"I don't understand," she said.

"Only kids can sense them," I said. "Part of their nature conceals them from older awarenesses."

"The threshold," Meg said. "It should keep such things out."

"Sometimes they ride in with someone in the family. Sometimes if a child has a vivid enough dream, it can open up a window in the Nevernever that the boggart uses to skip in. They can use mirrors sometimes, too."

"Nevernever?" Yardly asked.

"The spirit world," I clarified.

"Oh, what bullshit, Meg—" Yardly said.

Megan stood up, her eyes blazing. "Benjamin." The tension between them crackled silently in the air for several seconds.

"Crap," he snarled finally, and stalked out the front door. He let it slam behind him.

Megan stared at the door, her lips tight. Then she turned back to me. "If what you say is true, then how can you sense it?" she asked.

"I can't," I said. "That was the giveaway. The rest of your house feels normal. The closet in the younger kids' room is a black hole."

"Jesus," Megan said, turning. "Tamara and Joey are asleep in there."

"Relax," I said. "They're safe for now. It already ate tonight. It isn't going to do it again. And it can't physically hurt them. All it can do is scare them."

"All it can do?" Megan asked. "Do you have any idea what they've

gone through? She says she never even remembers waking up screaming, but Kat's grades are down from straight As to Cs. She hasn't slept
a solid night in six months. Tamara has stopped talking. She doesn't
say more than a dozen words a day." Her eyes shone, but she was too
proud to let me see tears fall. "Don't tell me that my children aren't
being hurt."

I winced and held up my hands placatingly. "You're right. Okay?
I'm sorry. I picked the wrong words." I took a deep breath and exhaled.
"The point is that now that we know about it, we can do something."

"We?"

"It will be better if someone in the family helps with the exorcism,
yeah."

"Exorcism?" she asked. She stared at the doorway Yardly had
gone out.

"Sure," I said. "It's your house, not the boogeyman's. If I show you
how, are you willing to kick that thing's ass?"

"Yes," she said. Her voice was hard.

"Might be dangerous," I said. "I've got your back, but there's always a risk. You sure?"

Megan turned to face me and her eyes blazed.

"Yeah," I said. "That's what I thought."


"Last A," I said, writing. "Act."

"That seems obvious," Ilyana said.

"Sure," I said. "But it's where everything gets decided. And it's always a gamble. You're betting that you've seen everything clearly, that
you know everything that's going on."

"Yes," Ilyana said, her tone somewhat exasperated. "That is the
purpose of the first three ahs."

"Ays," McKenzie corrected her absently. "Eh?"

Ilyana speared him with an icy gaze. "Whatever. Already we are
discovering what is happening. That was the point of the method-
ology."

"Ah," I said, lifting a finger. "But do you know everything? Are you so sure you know exactly what's happening? Especially when you're about to put the safety of yourself or others on the line?"

Ilyana looked confused. "Why would I not be sure?"

I smiled faintly.

THE NEXT EVENING, the children went to bed at nine. They stopped asking for drinks, searching for the next day's clothing, waving glow-in-the-dark light sabers in the air, and otherwise acting like children by nine thirty. They were all sleeping by nine thirty-five.

Megan, a surly Yardly, and I immediately got ready to ambush the boogeyman.

While Megan collected clipped hairs from her childrens' heads, Yardly and I cleared off enough carpet for me to take a container of salt and pour it out into a circle. You can use just about anything to make a magic circle, but salt is often the most practical. It's a symbol of the earth and of purity, and it doesn't draw ants. You use sugar to make a circle on the carpet only once. Let me tell you.

Meg returned and I nodded toward the circle. "In there."

She went over to the circle, being careful not to disturb it, and dropped the locks of hair from her children, bound together by long strands of her own coppery curls, into the center. "Right," I said. "Meg, stand in the circle with them." She took a deep breath and then did it, turning to face the open, darkened closet. Her breathing was slow but not steady. She was smart enough to be scared. "Remember what I said," I told her quietly. "When you feel it on you, close that circle and think of your children." She nodded tightly.

"I'm right here," I told her. "It gets bad, I'll step in. You can do this."

"Right," she said, in a very thin voice.

I nodded to her, trying to look calm and confident. She needed that. Then I stepped back out into the hallway. Yardly came with me and closed the door behind him, leaving Megan and her children in the dark.

"I don't get it," he said in a low, quiet voice. "How's it supposed to help the kids if they're asleep?"

I gave him a look. "By destroying the creature that's attacking them?"

His lips twisted sourly. "It's a prophylactic-effect thing, right?"

"Placebo effect," I sighed. "And no, it isn't."

"Because there's a real monster," he said.

I nodded. "Sure."

He eyed me for a while. "You're serious. You believe it."

"Yep."

Yardly looked like he wanted to sidle a few more feet away from me. He didn't.

"How's this supposed to work?" he asked.

"The kids' hair is going to substitute for them," I said. "As far as the boogeyman is concerned, the hairs are the children. Like using a set of clothes you've worn to leave a false trail for something following your scent."

Yardly frowned. "Okay."

"Your sister's hair is bound around them," I said. "Binding her to the kids. She's close to them, obviously loves them. That's got a kind of power in it. She's going to be indistinguishable from the children to the boogeyman."

"She's a decoy?"

"She's a damned land mine," I said. "Boogeymen go after children because they're weak. Too weak to stand up to an adult mind and will. So once this thing gets into the circle, she closes it and tears it to shreds."

"Then why is she afraid?" he asked.

"Because the boogeyman has power. It's going to tear at her mind. It'll hurt. If she falters, it might be able to hurt her bad."

Yardly just stared at me for a long, silent moment. Then he said, "You aren't a con man. You believe it."

"Yeah," I said, and leaned back against the wall. It might be a long wait.

"I don't know what's scarier," Yardly said. "If you're crazy. Or if you're not."

"Kids are sensitive," I said. "They'll take the lead from their mom. If Mom is scared and worried, they will be, too. If it helps, think of this as my way of giving the kids a magic feather."

Yardly frowned and then nodded. "Like Dumbo."

"Yep," I said. "Couple months from now, that will be the easiest way to understand it."

He let out a short, bitter bark of laughter. "Yeah?"

"Definitely."

"You do this a lot."

"Yep."

We waited in silence for about half an hour. Then Yardly said, "I work violent crimes."

I turned my head to look at him.

"I helped my sister set up out here in Peculiar to get her away from the city. Make sure her kids are safe. You know?"

"I hear you."

"I've seen bad things," Yardly said quietly. "I don't . . . It scares the hell out of me to think of my nieces, my nephew, becoming another one of the pictures in my head."

I nodded and listened.

"I worked this case last week," Yardly said a moment later. "Wife and kids got beaten a lot. Our hands were tied. Couldn't put this guy away. One night he goes too far with a knife. Kills the wife, one of the kids. Leaves the other one with scars all over her face . . ." His own face turned pale. "And now this is happening. The kids are falling apart. Child Protective Services is going to take them away if something doesn't change."

I grunted. "I grew up in the system," I said. "Orphan."

He nodded.

"Something's going to change," I said.

He nodded again, and we went silent once more. Sometime between eleven thirty and midnight, a scream erupted from the older child's room. Yardly and I both looked up, blinking.

"Kat," he said.

"What the hell," I muttered.

A few seconds later, the little girl started screaming, that same painfully high-pitched tone I'd heard the night before.

And then Megan started screaming, too.

"Dammit!" Yardly said. He drew his gun and was a step behind me as I pushed open the door to Joey and Tamara's room.

Megan was crouched in the circle of salt, swaying. The lights were flickering on and off. As I came in, Joey sat up with a wail, obviously tired and frightened.

I could see something in the circle with Megan, a shadow that fled an instant after the lights came up, slower than the rest. It was about the size of a chimpanzee and it clung to her shoulders and waist with indistinct limbs, its head moving as if ripping with fangs at her face.

Megan's expression was twisted in pain and fear. I didn't blame her. Holy crap, that was the biggest boogeyman I'd ever seen. They usually weren't much bigger than a raccoon.

"Meg!" Yardly screamed, and started forward.

I caught his arm. "Don't break the circle!" I shouted. "Get the kids out of here! Get the kids!"

He hesitated for only a second before he seized Tamara and Joey and hauled them out of the room, one under each arm.

I went to the edge of the circle and debated what to do. Dammit, what had this thing been eating? If I broke the circle, it would be free to escape—and it was freaking supercharged on the dark-spiritual equivalent of adrenaline. It would fight like hell to escape and come back the next night, bigger and hungrier than ever.

Nasty as the thing was, Megan still ought to be able to beat it. She was a sensitive, feeling the emotions and pieces of the thoughts of others thanks to a naturally developed talent, something that would manifest as simple intuition. It would mean that she would have developed a certain amount of defensive ability, just to keep from going nuts in a crowd.

"Megan!" I said. "You can beat this thing! Think of your kids!"

"They're hurting!" she screamed. "I can feel them!"

"Your brother has them—they're fine!" I called back. "That's a lie it's trying to push on you! Don't let it trick you!"

Megan glanced up at me, desperate, and I saw her face harden. She turned her face back into the shadowy assault of the flailing boggart and her lips peeled back from her teeth with a snarl.

"They're mine," she spat, the words sizzling with vitriol. "My babies. And you can't touch them anymore!"

"Begone!" I called to her. "Tell it to begone!"

"Begone!" Megan screamed. "Begone! BEGONE!"

There was a surge of sound, a thunderous nonexplosion, as if all the air in the room had suddenly rushed into a ball just in front of Megan's pain-twisted face. Then there was a flash of light and a hollow-sounding scream, and a shock wave lashed out, scattering the salt of the circle, rattling toys, and pushing against my chest. I staggered back against the wall and turned my face away as a fine cloud of salt blasted out and rattled against the walls with a hiss.

Megan fell to her knees and started sobbing. I reached out around me with my senses, but felt no inexplicable absence in the aura of the house. The boogeyman was gone.

I went to Megan's side at once and crouched down to touch her shoulder. She flung herself against me, still sobbing.

Ben Yardly appeared in the doorway to the room a few moments later. He had Joey in one arm and Tamara in the other. Kat stood so close she was practically in his pocket, holding on to the hem of his jacket as if he was her own personal teddy bear.

"Okay," I said quietly. "It's okay. The thing is gone. Your mom stopped it."

Kat stared at me for a moment, tears in her eyes, and then ran to Megan and flung herself against her mother. That drove Joey and Tamara into motion, and they both squirmed out of Yardly's arms and ran to their mother. "Thank you," Megan said. She freed one hand from her children long enough to touch my arm. "Wizard. Thank you."

I felt a little bit sick. But I gave her my best modest smile.


I FINISHED THE recounting for the young Wardens and let the silence fall.

"What was my mistake?" I asked.

No one said anything.

"I trusted the process too much," I said. "I thought I had already analyzed the whole situation. Found the problem. Identified the source of the danger. But I was wrong. You all know what I did. What happened?" No one said anything

The boggart I'd identified wasn't the source of the attacks. It was just feeding on the fear they generated in the kids. It hadn't needed to expend any energy at all to generate nightmares and fear in them. All it had to do was feed. That's why it was so large.

"The source of the attacks wasn't an attack at all," I said. "Ben Yardly's job had exposed him to some pretty bad things—memories and images that wouldn't go away. Some of you who fought in the war know what I'm talking about."

McKenzie, Ilyana, and a few others gave me sober nods. "Kat Yardly was the eldest daughter of her mother, a fairly gifted sensitive. She was twelve years old."

"Damn," McKenzie said, his eyes widening in realization.

"Yes, of course," Ilyana said. The other students turned to look at her. "The eldest daughter was a sensitive, too—perhaps a skilled one. She had picked up on those images in her uncle's mind and was having nightmares about them."

"What about the little girl?" I asked.

McKenzie took over. "Kat must have been a pusher, too," he said, using the slang for someone who could broadcast thoughts or emotions to others. "She was old enough to be a surrogate mother to the younger daughter. They were probably linked somehow."

"Exactly, Warden McKenzie," I said quietly. "All the pieces were in front of me, and I just didn't put them together. I figured the situation for a simple boogeyman infestation. I set up Megan to do the heavy lifting because I thought it would be relatively safe and would work out the best for the family. I was wrong."

"But it did work out," Ilyana said, something tentative in her voice for the first time that day.

"You kidding?" I asked. "That big boggart inflicted mental trauma on Megan that took her most of a year to recover from. She had her own nightmares for a while." I sighed. "I went back to her and gave her and her daughter some exercises to do that would help insulate them both. Kat's problems improved, and everything worked out fine—but it almost didn't. If Yardly had panicked and used his gun, if someone had broken the circle, or if Megan Yardly hadn't bought my lie about the boggart pushing a falsehood on her, it might have ripped out her sanity altogether. I might have put three kids into the foster care system.

"Arrogance," I said quietly, and wrote it on the board, beneath the rest. "That's the fifth A. We carry it around with us. It's natural. We know a lot more than most people. We can do a lot more than most people. There's a natural and understandable pride in that. But when we let that pride get in the way and take the place of truly seeing what is around us, there can be horrible consequences. Watch out for that fifth A, children. The Yardlys turned out all right mostly out of pure luck. They deserve better from me. And from you.

"Always keep your eyes open. Learn all that you can—and then try to learn some more."

I took a deep breath and then nodded. "Okay. We'll break for lunch, and then we'll look at another case I didn't screw up quite as badly. Back here in an hour. Dismissed." The young Wardens got up and dispersed—except for McKenzie and Ilyana. The two came down to stand beside me.

"Commander," McKenzie said. "This girl, Kat. Most of the talented mortals only demonstrate a single talent. She demonstrated at least two."

"I'm aware," I said.

"This girl," Ilyana said. "Her talents were born in trauma and fear. This is one of the warning signs of a potential warlock."

"Yeah," I said. My talents had started in a similar fashion. "I heard that once."

"So . . . She is under surveillance?" Ilyana asked.

"I drop in on her once in a while," I said.

"That poor kid," McKenzie said. "What do we do?"

I spread my hands. "It's an imperfect world, Wardens. We do what we always do." I smiled at them lopsidedly. "Whatever we can."

They both looked down, frowning, concerned—concerned for a little girl who had no idea of what might be waiting for her.

*Excellent.*

The lesson hadn't been wasted. "Okay, guys," I said. "Burger King?" That perked them both up, though Ilyana, benighted soul that she was, didn't react with joy at the utterance of the holy name of the Mount Olympus of fast food. We left together.

You do whatever you can.

# I WAS A TEENAGE BIGFOOT

This next story, set around the same time as *Dead Beat* in the main Dresden Files story line, was written as part of correcting the injustice of not having considered Bigfoot sufficiently in my previous world building. For that reason alone, it was a totally necessary story.

But I also wanted to try a tale that was a little less smash-action-figures-together-y, which is a fair assessment of several of my short stories. So I plotted out this one, where the motives are perhaps a little less sinister and a little bit more dangerously human than a simple case of attacker versus defender, and to force Dresden to deal with a situation other than directly confronting some brand of bully.

Also, I wanted to show Irwin growing up as well—and particularly the effect Dresden had had on his life. The idea of the consequences of your actions coming back to you in the future is ingrained into the fabric of the Dresden Files—and both your terrible choices and your more inspired ones engender consequences that will eventually come home to roost.

There are times when, as a professional wizard, my vocation calls me to the great outdoors, and that night I was in the north woods of Wisconsin with a mixed pack of researchers, enthusiasts, and, well, nerds.

"I don't know, man," said a skinny kid named Nash. "What's his name again?"

With a stick I poked the small campfire I'd set up earlier and pretended that they weren't standing less than ten feet away from me. The forest made forest sounds like it was supposed to. Full dark had fallen about half an hour before.

"Harry Dresden," said Gary, a plump kid with a cell phone, a GPS unit, and some kind of video-game device on his belt. "Supposed to be a psychic or something." He was twiddling deft fingers over the surface of what they call a smartphone, these days. Hell, the damned things are probably smarter than me. "Supposed to have helped Chicago PD a bunch of times. I'd pull up the Internet references, but I can't get reception out here."

"A psychic?" Nash said. "How is anyone ever supposed to take our research seriously if we keep showing up with fruitcakes like that?"

Gary shrugged. "Dr. Sinor knows him or something."

Dr. Sinor had nearly been devoured by an ogre in a suburban park one fine summer evening, and I'd gotten her out in one piece. Like

most people who have a brush with the supernatural, she'd rational-
ized the truth away as rapidly as possible—which had led her to participate in such fine activities as tonight's Bigfoot expedition in her
spare time.

"Gentlemen," Sinor said impatiently. She was a blocky, no-nonsense
type, grey-haired and straight-backed. "If you could help me with these
speakers, we might actually manage to blast a call or two before dawn."

Gary and Nash both hustled over to the edge of the firelight to
start messing about with the equipment the troop of researchers had
packed in. There were half a dozen of them altogether, all of them
busy with trail cameras and call-blasting speakers and scent markers
and audio recorders.

I pulled a sandwich out of my pocket and started eating it. I took
my time about it. I was in no hurry.

For those of you who don't know it, a forest at night is dark. Sometimes pitch-black. There was no moon to speak of in the sky, and the
light of the stars doesn't make it more than a few inches into a mixed
canopy of deciduous trees and evergreens. The light from my little
campfire and the handheld flashlights of the researchers soon gave
the woods all the light there was.

Their equipment wasn't working very well—my bad, probably.
Modern technology doesn't get on well with the magically gifted.
For about an hour, nothing much happened beyond the slapping of
mosquitoes and a lot of electronic noises squawking from the loud-
speakers.

Then the researchers got everything online and went through
their routine. They played primate calls over the speakers and then
dutifully recorded the forest afterward. Everything broke down again.
The researchers soldiered on, repairing things, and eventually Gary
tried wood knocking, which meant banging on trees with fallen limbs
and waiting to hear if there was a response.

I liked Dr. Sinor, but I had asked to come strictly as a ride-along
and I didn't pitch in with her team's efforts.

The whole "let's find Bigfoot" thing seems a little ill planned to me, personally. Granted, my perspective is different from that of nonwizards, but marching out into the woods, looking for a very large and very powerful creature by blasting out what you're pretty sure are territorial challenges to fight (or else mating calls) seems . . . somewhat unwise.

I mean, if there's no Bigfoot, no problem. But what if you're standing there, screaming, "Bring it on!" and find a Bigfoot?

Worse yet, what if he finds you?

Even worse, what if you were screaming, "Do me, baby!" and he finds you then?

Is it me? Am I crazy? Or does the whole thing just seem like a recipe for trouble?

So, anyway, while I kept my little fire going, the Questionably Wise Research Variety Act continued until after midnight. That's when I looked up to see a massive form standing at the edge of the trees, in the very outskirts of the light of my dying fire.

I'm in the ninety-ninth percentile for height, but this guy was tall. My head might have come up to his collarbone, barely, assuming I had correctly estimated where his collarbone was under the long, shaggy, dark brown hair covering him. It wasn't long enough to hide the massive weight of muscle he carried on that enormous frame or the simple, disturbing, very slightly inhuman proportions of his body. His face was broad and blunt, with a heavy brow ridge that turned his eyes into mere gleams of reflected light.

Most of all, there was a sense of awesome power granted to his presence by his size alone, chilling even to someone who had seen big things in action before. There's a reaction to something that much bigger than you, an automatic assumption of menace that is built into the human brain: Big equals dangerous.

It took about fifteen seconds before the first researcher—Gary, I think—noticed and let out a short gasp. In my peripheral vision, I saw the entire group turn toward the massive form by the fire and freeze into place. The silence was brittle crystal.

I broke it by bolting up from my seat and letting out a high-pitched shriek.

Half a dozen other screams joined it, and I whirled as if to flee, only to see Dr. Sinor and crew hotfooting it down the path we'd followed into the woods, back toward the cars.

I held it in for as long as I could, and only after I was sure that they wouldn't hear it did I let loose the laughter bubbling in my chest. I sank back onto my log by the fire, laughing, and beckoning the large form forward.

"Harry," rumbled the figure in a very, very deep voice, the words marked with the almost indefinable clippings of a Native American accent. "You have an unsophisticated sense of humor."

"I can't help it," I said, wiping at tears of laughter. "It never gets old." I waved to the open ground across the fire from me. "Sit, sit. Be welcome, big brother."

"Appreciate it," rumbled the giant, and he squatted down across the fire from me, touching fingers the size of cucumbers to his heart in greeting. His broad, blunt face was amused. "So. Got any smokes?"

It wasn't the first time I'd done business with the Forest People. They're old-school. There's a certain way one goes about business with someone considered a peer, and Strength of a River in His Shoulders was an old-school kind of guy. There were proprieties to be observed.

So we shared a thirty-dollar cigar, which I'd brought, had some s'mores, which I made, and sipped from identical plastic bottles of Coca-Cola, which I had purchased. By the time we were done, the fire had burned down to glowing embers, which suited me fine—and I knew that River Shoulders would be more comfortable in the near-dark, too. I didn't mind being the one to provide everything. It would have been a hassle for River Shoulders to do it, and we'd probably be smoking, eating, and drinking raw and unpleasant things if he had.

Besides, it was worth it. The Forest People had been around long before the great gold rushes of the nineteenth century, and they were loaded. River Shoulders had paid my retainer with a gold nugget the size of a golf ball the last time I'd done business with him.

"Your friends," he said, nodding toward the disappeared researchers. "They going to come back?"

"Not before dawn," I said. "For all they know, you got me."

River Shoulders's chest rumbled with a sound that was both amused and not entirely pleased. "Like my people don't have enough stigmas already."

"You want to clear things up, I can get you on the Larry Fowler show anytime you want."

River Shoulders shuddered—given his size, it was a lot of shuddering. "TV rots the brains of people who see it. Don't even want to know what it does to the people who make it."

I snorted. "I got your message," I said. "I am here."

"And so you are," he said. He frowned, an expression that was really sort of terrifying on his features. I didn't say anything. You just don't rush the Forest People. They're patient on an almost alien level, compared to human beings, and I knew that our meeting was already being conducted with unseemly haste by River Shoulders's standards. Finally, he swigged a bit more Coke, the bottle looking tiny in his vast hands, and sighed. "There is a problem with my son. Again."

I sipped some Coke and nodded, letting a little time pass before I answered. "Irwin was a fine, strong boy when I last saw him."

The conversation continued with contemplative pauses between each bit of speech. "He is sick."

"Children sometimes grow sick."

"Not children of the Forest People."

"What, never?"

"No, never. And I will not quote Gilbert and Sullivan."

"Their music was silly and fine."

River Shoulders nodded agreement. "Indeed."

"What can you tell me of your son's sickness?"

"His mother tells me the school's doctor says he has something called mah-no."

"Mono," I said. "It is a common illness. It is not dangerous."

"An illness could not touch one born of the Forest People," River Shoulders rumbled.

"Not even one with only one parent of your folk?" I asked.

"Indeed," he said. "Something else must therefore be happening. I am concerned for Irwin's safety."

The fire let out a last crackle and a brief, gentle flare of light, showing me River Shoulders clearly. His rough features were touched with the same quiet worry I'd seen on dozens and dozens of my clients' faces.

"He still doesn't know who you are, does he?"

The giant shifted his weight slightly, as if uncomfortable. "Your society is, to me, irrational and bewildering. Which is good. Can't have everyone the same, or the earth would get boring."

I thought about it for a moment and then said, "You feel he has problems enough to deal with already."

River Shoulders spread his hands, as if my own words had spotlighted the truth.

I nodded, thought about it, and said, "We aren't that different. Even among my people, a boy misses his father."

"A voice on a telephone is not a father," he said.

"But it is more than nothing," I said. "I have lived with a father and without a father. With one was better."

The silence stretched extra long.

"In time," the giant responded very quietly. "For now, my concern is his physical safety. I cannot go to him. I spoke to his mother. We ask someone we trust to help us learn what is happening."

I didn't agree with River Shoulders about talking to his kid, but that didn't matter. He wasn't hiring me to get parenting advice, about which I had no experience to call upon, anyway. He needed help looking out for the kid. So I'd do what I could to help him. "Where can I find Irwin?"

"Chicago," he said. "St. Mark's Academy for the Gifted and Talented."

"Boarding school. I know the place." I finished the Coke and rose. "It will be my pleasure to help the Forest People once again."

The giant echoed my actions, standing. "Already had your retainer sent to your account. By morning, his mother will have granted you the power of a turnkey."

It took me a second to translate River Shoulders's imperfect understanding of mortal society. "Power of attorney," I corrected him.

"That," he agreed.

"Give her my best."

"Will," he said, and touched his thick fingertips to his massive chest.

I put my fingertips to my heart in reply and nodded up to my client. "I'll start in the morning."

IT TOOK ME most of the rest of the night to get back down to Chicago, go to my apartment, and put on my suit. I'm not a suit guy. For one thing, when you're NBA sized, you don't exactly get to buy them off the rack. For another, I just don't like them. But sometimes they're a really handy disguise, when I want people to mistake me for someone grave and responsible. So I put on the grey suit with a crisp white shirt and a clip-on tie, and headed down to St. Mark's.

The academy was an upper-end place in the suburbs north of Chicago, and was filled with the offspring of the city's luminaries. They had their own small, private security force. They had wrought-iron gates and brick walls and ancient trees and ivy. They had multiple buildings on the grounds, like a miniature university campus, and, inevitably, they had an administration building. I started there.

It took me a polite quarter of an hour to get the lady in the front office to pick up the fax granting me power of attorney from Irwin's mom, the archaeologist, who was in the field somewhere in Canada. It included a description of me, and I produced both my ID and my investigator's license. It took me another half an hour of waiting to be admitted to the office of the dean, Dr. Fabio.

"Dr. Fabio," I said. I fought valiantly not to titter when I did.

Fabio did not offer me a seat. He was a good-looking man of sober middle age, and his eyes told me that he did not approve of me in the least, even though I was wearing the suit.

"Ms. Pounder's son is in our infirmary, receiving care from a highly experienced nurse practitioner and a physician who visits three days a week," Dr. Fabio told me, when I had explained my purpose. "I assure you he is well cared for."

"I'm not the one who needs to be assured of anything," I replied. "His mother is."

"Then your job here is finished," said Fabio.

I shook my head. "I kinda need to see him, Doctor."

"I see no need to disrupt either Irwin's recovery or our academic routine, Mr. Dresden," Fabio replied. "Our students receive some of the most intensive instruction in the world. It demands a great deal of focus and drive."

"Kids are resilient," I said. "And I'll be quiet like a mouse. They'll never know I was there."

"I'm sorry," he replied, "but I am not amenable to random investigators wandering the grounds."

I nodded seriously. "Okay. In that case, I'll report to Dr. Pounder that you refused to allow her duly appointed representative to see her son, and that I cannot confirm his well-being. At which point I am confident that she will either radio for a plane to pick her up from her dig site, or else backpack her way out. I think the good doctor will view this with alarm and engage considerable maternal protective instinct." I squinted at Fabio. "Have you actually met Dr. Pounder?"

He scowled at me.

"She's about yay tall," I said, putting a hand at the level of my temples. "And she works outdoors for a living. She looks like she could wrestle a Sasquatch." *Heh. Among other things.*

"Are you threatening me?" Dr. Fabio asked.

I smiled. "I'm telling you that I'm way less of a disruption than

Mama Bear will be. She'll be a headache for weeks. Give me half an hour, and then I'm gone."

Fabio glowered at me.

ST. MARK'S INFIRMARY was a spotless, well-ordered place, located immediately adjacent to its athletics building. I was walked there by a young man named Steve, who wore a spotless, well-ordered security uniform.

Steve rapped his knuckles on the frame of the open doorway and said, "Visitor to see Mr. Pounder."

A young woman who looked entirely too nice for the likes of Dr. Fabio and Steve glanced up from a crossword puzzle. She had chestnut-colored hair, rimless glasses, and a body that could be readily appreciated even through her cheerfully patterned scrubs.

"Well," I said. "Hello, Nurse."

"I can't think of a sexier first impression than a man quoting Yakko and Wakko Warner," she said, her tone dry.

I sauntered in and offered her my hand. "Me neither. Harry Dresden, PI."

"Jen Gerard. There are some letters that go after, but I used them all on the crossword." She shook my hand and eyed Steve. "Everyone calls me Nurse Jen. The flying monkeys let you in, eh?"

Steve looked professionally neutral. He folded his arms.

Nurse Jen flipped her wrists at him. "Shoo, shoo. If I'm suddenly attacked, I'll scream like a girl."

"No visitors without a security presence," Steve said firmly.

"Unless they're richer than a guy in a cheap suit," Nurse Jen said archly. She smiled sweetly at Steve and shut the infirmary door. It all but bumped the end of his nose. She turned back to me and said, "Dr. Pounder sent you?"

"She's at a remote location," I said. "She wanted someone to get eyes on her son and make sure he was okay. And, for the record, it wasn't cheap."

Nurse Jen snorted and said, "Yeah, I guess a guy your height doesn't get to shop off the rack, does he?" She led me across the first room of the infirmary, which had a first-aid station and an examination table, neither of which looked as though they got a lot of use. There were a couple of rooms attached. One was a bathroom. The other held what looked like the full gear of a hospital's intensive-care ward, including an automated bed.

Bigfoot Irwin lay asleep on the bed. It had been a few years since I'd seen him, but I recognized him. He was fourteen years old and over six feet tall, filling the length of the bed, and he had the scrawny look of young things that aren't done growing.

Nurse Jen went to his side and shook his shoulder gently. The kid blinked his eyes open and muttered something. Then he looked at me.

"Harry," he said. "What are you doing here?"

"'Sup, kid," I said. "I heard you were sick. Your mom asked me to stop by."

He smiled faintly. "Yeah. This is what I get for staying in Chicago instead of going up to British Columbia with her."

"And think of all the Spam you missed eating."

Irwin snorted, closed his eyes, and said, "Tell her I'm fine. Just need to rest." Then he apparently started doing exactly that.

Nurse Jen eased silently out of the room and herded me gently away. Then she spread her hands. "He's been like that. Sleeping maybe twenty hours a day."

"Is that normal for mono?" I asked.

"Not so much," Nurse Jen said. She shook her head. "Though it's not completely unheard-of. That's just a preliminary diagnosis based on his symptoms. He needs some lab work to be sure."

"Fabio isn't allowing it," I said.

She waggled a hand. "He isn't paying for it. The state of the economy, the school's earnings last quarter, et cetera. And the doctor was sure it was mono."

"You didn't tell his mom about that?" I asked.

"I never spoke to her. Dr. Fabio handles all of the communication with the parents. Gives it that personal touch. Besides, I'm just the nurse practitioner. The official physician said mono, so, behold, it is mono."

I grunted. "Is the boy in danger?"

She shook her head. "If I thought that, to hell with Fabio and the winged monkeys. I'd drive the kid to a hospital myself. But just because he isn't in danger now doesn't mean he won't be if nothing is done. It's probably mono. But."

"But you don't take chances with a kid's health," I said.

She folded her arms. "Exactly. Especially when his mother is so far away. There's an issue of trust here."

I nodded. Then I said, "How invasive are the tests?"

"Blood samples. Fairly straightforward."

I chewed that one over for a moment. Irwin's blood was unlikely to be exactly the same as human blood, though who knew how intensively they would have to test it to realize that. Scions of mortal and supernatural pairings had created no enormous splash in the scientific community, and they'd been around for as long as humanity itself, which suggested that any differences weren't easy to spot. It seemed like a reasonable risk to take, all things considered, especially if River Shoulders was maybe wrong about Irwin's immunity to disease.

And besides. I needed some time alone to work.

"Do the tests, on my authority. Assuming the kid is willing, I mean."

Nurse Jen frowned as I began to speak, then nodded at the second sentence. "Okay."

NURSE JEN woke up Irwin long enough to explain the tests, make sure he was okay with them, and take a couple of little vials of blood from his arm. She left to take the vials to a nearby lab and left me sitting with Irwin.

"How's life, kid?" I asked him. "Any more bully problems?"

Irwin snorted weakly. "No, not really. Though they don't use their fists for that here. And there's a lot more of them."

"That's what they call civilization," I said. "It's still better than the other way."

"One thing's the same. You show them you aren't afraid, they leave you alone."

"They do," I said. "Coward's a coward, whether he's throwing punches or words."

Irwin smiled and closed his eyes again.

I gave the kid a few minutes to be sound asleep before I got to work.

River Shoulders hadn't asked for my help because I was the only decent person in Chicago. The last time Irwin had problems, they'd had their roots in the supernatural side of reality. Clearly, the giant thought that this problem was similar, and he was smarter than the vast majority of human beings, including me. I'd be a fool to discount his concerns. I didn't think there was anything more troublesome than a childhood illness at hand, but I was going to cover my bases. That's what being professional means.

I'd brought what I needed in the pockets of my suit. I took out a small baggie of powdered quartz crystal and a piece of paper inscribed with runes written in ink infused with the same powder and folded into a fan. I stood over Irwin and took a moment to focus my thoughts, both on the spell I was about to work and on the physical coordination it would require.

I took a deep breath, then flicked the packet of quartz dust into the air at the same time I swept the rune-inscribed fan through a strong arc, released my will, and murmured, "Optio."

Light kindled in the spreading cloud of fine dust, a flickering glow that spread with the cloud, sparkling through the full spectrum of visible colors in steady, pulsing waves. It was beautiful magic, which was rare for me. I mean, explosions and lightning bolts and so on were pretty standard fare. This kind of gentle, interrogative spell? It was a treat to have a reason to use it.

As the cloud of dust settled gently over the sleeping boy, the colors began to swirl as the spell interacted with his aura, the energy of life that surrounds all living things. Irwin's aura was bloody strong, standing out several inches farther from his body than on most humans. I was a full-blown wizard and a strong one, and my aura wasn't any more powerful. That would be his father's blood, then. The Forest People were in possession of potent magic, which was one reason no one ever seemed to get a decent look at one of them. Irwin had begun to develop a reservoir of energy to rival that of anyone on the White Council of Wizardry.

That was likely the explanation for Irwin's supposed immunity to disease: The aura of life around him was simply too strong to be overwhelmed by a mundane germ or virus. Supported by that kind of energy, his body's immune system would simply whale on any invaders. It probably also explained Irwin's size, his growing body drawing on the raw power of his aura to optimize whatever growth potential was in his mixed genes. Thinking about it, it might even explain the length of River Shoulders's body hair, which just goes to show that no supernatural ability is perfect.

Oh, and as the dust settled against Irwin's body, it revealed threads of black sorcery laced throughout his aura, pulsing and throbbing with a disturbing, seething energy.

I nearly fell out of my chair in sheer surprise.

"Oh no," I muttered. "The kid couldn't just have gotten mono. That would be way too easy."

I called up a short, gentle wind to scatter the quartz dust from Bigfoot Irwin's covers and pajamas, and then sat back for a moment to think.

The kid had been hit with black magic. Not only that, but it had been done often enough that it had left track marks in his aura. Some of those threads of dark sorcery were fresh ones, probably inflicted at some point during the previous night.

Most actions of magic aren't any more terribly mysterious or complicated than physical actions. In fact, a lot of what happens in magic can be described by basic concepts of physics. Energy can neither be created nor destroyed, for example, but it can be moved. The seething aura of life around the young scion represented a significant force of energy.

A very significant source.

Someone had been siphoning energy off of Bigfoot Irwin. The incredible vital aura around the kid now was, I realized, only a fraction of what it should have been. Someone had been draining the kid of that energy and using it for something else. A vampire of some kind? Maybe. The White Court of vampires drained the life energy from their victims, though they mostly did it through physical contact, mostly sexual congress, and there would be really limited opportunity for that sort of thing in a strictly monitored coed boarding school. Irwin had been attacked both frequently and regularly, to have his aura be so mangled.

I could sweep the place for a vampire. Maybe. They were not easy to spot. I couldn't discount a vamp completely, because they were definitely one of the usual suspects, but had it been one of the White Court after the kid, his aura would have been more damaged in certain areas than others. Instead, his aura had been equally diminished all around. That would indicate, if not conclusively prove, some kind of attack that was entirely nonphysical.

I settled back in my chair to wait, watching Bigfoot Irwin sleep. I'd stay alert for any further attack, at least until Nurse Jen got back.

River Shoulders was right. This wasn't illness. Someone was killing the kid very, very slowly.

I wasn't going to leave him alone.

Nurse Jen came back in a little less than two hours. She looked at me with her eyebrows raised and said, "You're still here."

"Looks like," I said. "What was I supposed to do?"

"Leave me a number to call with the results," she said.

I winked at her. "If it makes you feel any better, I can still do that."

"I'm taking a break from dating cartoon characters and the children who love them." She held up the envelope and said, "It's mono."

I blinked. "It is?"

She nodded and sighed. "Definitely. An acute case, apparently, but it's mono."

I nodded slowly, thinking. It might make sense, if Irwin's immune system had come to rely on the energy of his aura. The attacks had diminished his aura, which had in turn diminished his body's capacity to resist disease. Instead of fighting off an illness when exposed, his weakened condition had resulted in an infection—and it was entirely possible that his body had never had any practice in fighting off something that had taken hold.

Nurse Jen tilted her head to one side and said, "What are you thinking?"

"How bad is it?" I asked her. "Does he need to go to a hospital?"

"He's in one," she said. "Small, but we have everything here that you'd find at a hospital, short of a ventilator. As long as his condition doesn't get any worse, he'll be fine."

Except that he wouldn't be fine. If the drain on his life energy kept up, he might never have the strength he'd need to fight off this disease—and every other germ that happened to wander by.

I was thinking that the boy was defenseless—and I was the only one standing between Bigfoot Irwin and whatever was killing him.

I looked at Nurse Jen and said, "I need to use a phone."

"How SERIOUS?" Dr. Pounder asked. Her voice was scratchy. She was speaking to me over a ham radio from somewhere in the wilds of un-settled Canada, and was shouting to make herself heard over the static and the patch between the radio and the phone.

"Potentially very serious," I half shouted back. "I think you need to come here immediately!"

"He's that ill?" she asked.

"Yeah, Doc," I replied. "There could be complications, and I don't think he should be alone."

"I'm on the way. There's weather coming in. It might be tomorrow or the next day."

"Understood," I said. "I'll stay with him until then."

"You're a good man, Dresden," she said. "Thank you. I'll move as fast as I can. Pounder, out."

I hung up the phone, and Nurse Jen stared at me with her mouth open. "What the hell are you doing?"

"My job," I replied calmly.

"The boy is going to be fine," Jen said. "He's not feeling great, but he'll be better soon enough. I told you, it's mono."

"There's more going on than that," I said.

"Oh?" Jen asked. "Like what?"

Explaining would just convince her I was a lunatic. "I'm not entirely at liberty to say. Dr. Pounder can explain when she arrives."

"If there's a health concern, I need to know about it now." She folded her arms. "Otherwise, maybe I should let the winged monkeys know that you're a problem."

"I told his mother I would stay with him."

"You told his mother a lot of things."

"What happened to not taking chances?"

"I'm thinking I'll start with you."

I felt tired. I needed sleep. I inhaled and exhaled slowly.

"Nurse," I said. "I care about the kid, too. I don't dispute your medical knowledge or authority over him. I just want to stay close to him until his mom gets here. That's why I was hired."

Nurse Jen eyed me askance. "What do you mean, it's more than mono?"

I folded my arms. "Um. Irwin is a nice guy. Would you agree with that?"

"Sure, he's a great kid. A real sweetheart. Thoughtful."

I nodded. "And he has a tendency to attract the attention of . . . How do I put this?"

"Complete assholes?" Nurse Jen suggested.

"Exactly," I said. "People who mistake kindness for weakness."

She frowned. "Are you suggesting that his sickness is the result of a deliberate action?"

"I'm saying that I don't know that it isn't," I said. "And until I know, one way or another, I'm sticking close to the kid until the doc gets here."

She continued looking skeptical. "You won't if I don't think you should. I don't care how much paperwork you have supporting you. If I start yelling, the winged monkeys will carry you right out to the street."

"They'd try," I said calmly.

She blinked at me. "You're a big guy. But you aren't that big."

"You might be surprised," I said. I leaned forward and said very quietly, "I'm not. Leaving. The kid."

Nurse Jen's expression changed slowly, from skepticism to something very thoughtful. "You mean that, don't you?"

"Every word."

She nodded. Then she called, "Steve."

The security guard lumbered into the room from the hall outside.

"Mr. Dresden will be staying with Mr. Pounder for a little while. Could you please ask the cafeteria to send over two dinner plates instead of one?"

Steve frowned, maybe trying to remember how to count all the way to two. Then he glowered at me, muttered a surly affirmative, and left, speaking quietly into his radio as he went.

"Thank you," I said. "For the food."

"You're lying to me," she said levelly. "Aren't you?"

"I'm not telling you the whole truth," I said. "Subtle difference."

"Semantic difference," she said.

"But you're letting me stay anyway," I noted. "Why?"

She studied my face for a moment. Then she said, "I believe that you want to take care of Irwin."


THE FOOD WAS very good—nothing like the school cafeterias I remembered. Of course, I went to public school. Irwin woke up long enough to devour a trayful of food and some of mine. He went to the bathroom, walking unsteadily, and then dropped back into an exhausted slumber. Nurse Jen stayed near, checking him frequently, taking his temperature in his ear every hour so that she didn't need to wake him.

I wanted to sleep, but I didn't need it yet. I might not have had the greatest academic experience in childhood, but the other things I'd been required to learn had made me more ready for the eat-or-be-eaten portions of life than just about anyone. My record for going without sleep was just under six days, but I was pretty sure I could go longer if I had to. I could have napped in my chair, but I didn't want to take the chance that some kind of attack might happen while I was being lazy.

So I sat by Bigfoot Irwin and watched the shadows lengthen and swell into night.

The attack came just after nine o'clock.

Nurse Jen was taking Irwin's temperature again when I felt the sudden surge of cold, somehow oily energy flood the room.

Irwin took a sudden, shallow breath, and his face became very pale. Nurse Jen frowned at the digital thermometer she had in his ear. It suddenly emitted a series of beeping, wailing noises, and she jerked it free of Irwin just as a bunch of sparks drizzled from its battery casing. She dropped it to the floor, where it lay trailing a thin wisp of smoke.

"What the hell?" Nurse Jen demanded.

I rose to my feet, looking around the room. "Use a mercury thermometer next time," I said. I didn't have much in the way of magical gear on me, but I wasn't going to need any for this. I could feel the presence of the dark, dangerous magic radiating through the room like the heat from a nearby fire.

Nurse Jen had pressed a stethoscope against Irwin's chest, listening for a moment, while I went to the opposite side of the bed and waved my hand through the air over the bed with my eyes closed, trying to orient the spell attacking Irwin's aura, so that I could backtrack it to its source.

"What are you doing?" Nurse Jen demanded.

"Inexplicable stuff," I said. "How is he?"

"Something isn't right," she said. "I don't think he's getting enough air. It's like an asthma attack." She put the stethoscope down, turned to a nearby closet, and ripped out a small oxygen tank. She immediately began hooking up a line to it, attached to one of those nose-and-mouth-covering things, opened the valve, and pressed the cup down over Irwin's nose and mouth.

"Excuse me," I said, squeezing past her in order to wave my hand through the air over that side of the bed. I got a fix on the direction of the spell and jabbed my forefinger in that direction. "What's that way?"

She blinked and stared at me incredulously. "What?"

"That way," I said, thrusting my finger in the indicated direction several times. "What is over that way?"

She frowned, shook her head a little, and said, "Uh, uh, the cafeteria and administration."

"Administration, eh?" I said. "Not the dorms?"

"No. They're the opposite way."

"You got any lunch ladies that hate Irwin?"

Nurse Jen looked at me like I was a lunatic. "What the hell are you talking about? No, of course not!"

I grunted. This attack clearly wasn't the work of a vampire, and the destruction of the electronic thermometer indicated the presence of mortal magic. The kids were required to be back in their dorms at this time, so presumably it wasn't one of them. And if it wasn't someone in the cafeteria, then it had to be someone in the administration building.

Dr. Fabio had been way too interested in making sure I wasn't around. If it was Fabio behind the attacks on Irwin, then I could probably expect some interference to be arriving—

The door to the infirmary opened, and Steve and two of his fellow security guards clomped into the room.

—anytime now.

"You," Steve said, pointing a thick finger at me. "It's after free hours. No visitors on the grounds after nine. You're gonna have to go."

I eased back around Nurse Jen and out of the room Irwin was in. "Um," I said, "let me think about that."

Steve scowled. He had a very thick neck. So did his two buddies.

"Second warning, sir. You are now trespassing on private property. If you do not leave immediately, the police will be summoned and you will be detained until their arrival."

"Shouldn't you be out making sure the boys aren't sneaking over to the girls' dorms and vice versa? 'Cause I'm thinking that's really more your speed, Steve."

Steve's face got red. "That's it," he said. "You are being detained until the police arrive, smart-ass."

"Let's don't do this," I said. "Seriously. You guys don't want to ride this train."

In answer, Steve snapped his hand out to one side, and one of those collapsible fighting batons extended to its full length and locked. His two friends followed suit.

"Wow," I said. "Straight to the weapons? Really? Completely inappropriate escalation." I held up my right hand, palm out. "I'm telling you, fellas. Don't try it."

Steve took two quick steps toward me and raised the baton.

I unleashed the will I had been gathering and murmured, "*Forzare.*"

Invisible force lashed out and slammed into Steve like a runaway car made of foam rubber. It lifted him off his feet and tossed him back, between his two buddies, and out the door of the infirmary. He hit the floor and lost a lot of his velocity before fetching up against the opposite wall with an explosion of expelled breath.

"Wah," I said, Bruce Lee style, and looked at the other two goons. "You boys want a choo-choo ride, too?"

The pair of them looked at me and then at each other, gripping their batons until their knuckles turned white. They hadn't had a clear view of exactly what had happened to Steve, since his body would have blocked them from it. For all they knew, I'd used some kind of judo on him. The pair of them came to a conclusion somewhere in there that whatever I had pulled on Steve wouldn't work on both of them, and they began to rush me.

They thought wrong. I repeated the spell, only with twice the energy.

One of them went out the door, crashing into Steve, who had just been about to regain his feet. My control wasn't so good without any of my magical implements, though. The second man hit the side of the doorway squarely, and his head made the metal frame ring as it bounced off. The man's legs went rubbery and he staggered, bleeding copiously from a wound that was above his hairline.

The second spell was more than the lights could handle, and the fluorescents in the infirmary exploded in showers of sparks and went out. Red-tinged emergency lights clicked on a few seconds later.

I checked around me. Nurse Jen was staring at me with her eyes wide. The wounded guard was on his back, rocking back and forth in obvious pain. The two who had been knocked into the hallway were still on the ground, staring at me in much the same way as Jen, except that Steve was clearly trying to get his radio to work. It wouldn't. It had folded when the lights did.

I spread my hands and said to Nurse Jen, "I told them, didn't I? You heard me. Better take care of that guy."

Then I scowled, shook my head, and stalked off along the spell's back trail, toward the administration building.

THE DOORS TO the building were locked, which was more the academy's problem than mine. I exercised restraint. I didn't take the doors off their hinges. I only ripped them off their locks.

The door to Dr. Fabio's office was locked, and though I tried to hold back, I've always had issues with controlling my power—especially when I'm angry. This time I tore the door off its hinges, slamming it down flat to the floor inside the office as if smashed in by a medieval battering ram.

Dr. Fabio jerked and whirled to face the door with a look of utter astonishment on his face. A cabinet behind his desk that had been closed during my first visit was now open. It was a small, gaudy, but functional shrine, a platform for the working of spells. At the moment, it was illuminated by half a dozen candles spaced out around a

Seal of Solomon containing two photos: one of Irwin, and one of Dr. Fabio, bound together with a loop of what looked like dark grey yarn.

I could feel the energy stolen from Irwin coursing into the room, into the shrine. From there, I had no doubt, it was being funneled into Dr. Fabio himself. I could sense the intensity of his personality much more sharply than I had that morning, as if he had somehow become more metaphysically massive, filling up more of the room with his presence.

"Hiya, Doc," I said. "You know, it's a pity this place isn't St. Mark's Academy for the Resourceful and Talented."

He blinked at me. "Uh. What?"

"Because then the place would be SMART. Instead, you're just SMAGT."

"What?" he said, clearly confused, outraged, and terrified.

"Let me demonstrate," I said, extending my hand. I funneled my will into it and said, "Smagt!"

The exact words you use for a spell aren't important, except that they can't be from a language you're too familiar with. Nonsense words are best, generally speaking. Using *smagt* for a combination of naked force and air magic worked just as well as any other word would have. The energy rushed out of me, into the cabinet shrine, and exploded in a blast of kinetic energy and wind. Candles and other decorative objects flew everywhere. Shelves cracked and collapsed.

The spell had been linked to the shrine. It unraveled as I disrupted all the precisely aligned objects that had helped direct and focus its energy. One of the objects had been a small glass bottle of black ink. Most of it wound up splattered on the side of Dr. Fabio's face.

He stood with his jaw slack, half of his face covered in black ink, the other half gone so pale that he resembled a Renaissance Venetian masque.

"Y-you . . . you . . ."

"Wizard," I said quietly. "White Council. Heck, Doctor, I'm even a Warden these days."

His face became absolutely bloodless.

"Yeah," I said quietly. "You know us. I'm going to suggest that you answer my questions with extreme cooperation, Doctor. Because we frown on the use of black magic."

"Please," he said, "anything."

"How do you know us?" I asked. The White Council was hardly a secret, but considering that most of the world didn't believe in magic, much less wizards, and that the supernatural crowd in general is cautious about sharing information, it was a given that your average Joe would have no idea that the Council even existed—much less that they executed anyone guilty of breaking one of the Laws of Magic.

"V-v-venator," he said. "I was a Venator. One of the Venatori Umbrorum. Retired."

The Hunters in the Shadows. Or of the Shadows, depending on how you read it. They were a boys' club made up of the guys who had the savvy to be clued in to the supernatural world, but without the talent it took to be a true wizard. Mostly academic types. They'd been invaluable assets in the White Council's war with the Red Court, gathering information and interfering with our enemy's lines of supply and support. They were old allies of the Council—and any Venator would know the price of violating the Laws.

"A Venator should know better than to dabble in this kind of thing," I said in a very quiet voice. "The answer to this next question could save your life—or end it."

Dr. Fabio licked his lips and nodded, a jerky little motion.

"Why?" I asked him quietly. "Why were you taking essence from the boy?"

"H-he . . . He had so much. I didn't think it would hurt him, and I . . ." He cringed back from me as he spoke the last words. "I . . . needed to grow some hair."

I blinked my eyes slowly. Twice. "Did you say . . . hair?"

"Rogaine didn't work!" he all but wailed. "And that transplant surgery wasn't viable for my hair and skin type!" He bowed his head and ran fingertips through his thick head of hair. "Look, see? Look how well it's come in. But if I don't maintain it . . ."

"You used black magic. To grow hair."

"I . . ." He looked everywhere but at me. "I tried everything else first. I never meant to harm anyone. It never hurt anyone before."

"Irwin's a little more dependent on his essence than most," I told him. "You might have killed him."

Fabio's eyes widened in terror. "You mean he's . . . he's a . . ."

"Let's just say that his mother is his second-scariest parent and leave it at that," I said. I pointed at his chair and said, "Sit."

Fabio sat.

"Do you wish to live?"

"Yes. Yes, I don't want any trouble with the White Council."

Heavy footsteps came pounding up behind us. Steve and his un-bloodied buddy appeared in the doorway, carrying their batons. "Dr. Fabio!" Steve cried.

"Don't make me trash your guys," I told Fabio.

"Get out!" Fabio all but screamed at them.

They came to a confused stop. "But . . . sir?"

"Get out, get out!" Fabio screamed. "Tell the police there's no problem here when they arrive!"

"Sir?"

"Tell them!" Fabio screamed, his voice going up several octaves. "For God's sake, man! Go!"

Steve and his buddy went. They looked bewildered, but they went.

"Thank you," I said, when they left. No need to play bad cop at this point. If Fabio got any more scared, he might collapse into jelly. "Do you want to live, Doctor?"

He swallowed. He nodded once.

"Then I suggest you alter your hairstyle to complete baldness," I replied. "Or else learn to accept your receding hairline for what it is: the natural progression of your life. You will discontinue all use of magic from this point forward. And I do mean all. If I catch you with so much as a Ouija board or a deck of tarot cards, I'm going to make you disappear. Do you get me?"

It was a hollow threat. The guy hadn't broken any of the Laws, technically speaking, since Irwin hadn't died. And I had no intention of turning anyone over to the tender mercies of the Wardens if I could possibly avoid it. But this guy clearly had problems recognizing priorities. If he kept going the way he was, he might slide down into true practice of the black arts. Best to scare him away from that right now.

"I understand," he said in a very meek voice.

"Now," I said. "I'm going to go watch over Irwin. You aren't going to interfere. I'll be staying until his mother arrives."

"Are . . . are you going to tell her what I've done?"

"You bet your ass I am," I said. "And God have mercy on your soul."

IRWIN WAS AWAKE when I got back to the infirmary, and Nurse Jen had just finished stitching closed a cut on the wounded guard's scalp. She'd shaved a big, irregularly shaped section of his hair off to get it done, too, and he looked utterly ridiculous—even more so when she wrapped his entire cranium in bandages to keep the stitches covered.

I went into Irwin's room and said, "How you feeling?"

"Tired," he said. "But better than earlier today."

"Irwin," Nurse Jen said firmly.

"Yes, ma'am," Irwin said, and meekly placed the breathing mask over his nose and mouth.

"Your mom's coming to see you," I said.

The kid brightened. "She is? Oh, uh. That's fantastic!" He frowned. "It's not . . . because of my being sick? Her work is very important."

"Maybe a little," I said. "But mostly I figure it's because she loves you."

Irwin rolled his eyes but he smiled. "Yeah, well. I guess she's okay. Hey, is there anything else to eat?"

LATER, AFTER IRWIN had eaten (again), he slept.

"His temperature's back down, and his breathing is clear," Nurse

Jen said, shaking her head. "I could have sworn we were going to have to get him to an ICU a few hours ago."

"Kids," I said. "They bounce back fast."

She frowned at Irwin and then at me. Then she said, "It was Fabio, wasn't it? He was doing something."

"Something like what?" I asked.

She shook her head. "I don't know. I just know it . . . feels like something that's true. He's the one who didn't want you here. He's the one who sent security to run you out just as Irwin got worse."

"You might be right," I said. "And you don't have to worry about it happening again."

She studied me for a moment. Then she said simply, "Good."

I lifted my eyebrows. "That's one hell of a good sense of intuition you have, Nurse."

She snorted. "I'm still not going out with you."

"Story of my life," I said, smiling.

Then I stretched out my legs, settled into my chair, and joined Bigfoot Irwin in dreamland.

# CURSES

One of the most frequent requests I heard from fans who lived in Chicagoland and loved their Cubbies: What about the Billy Goat Curse in the world of the Dresden Files?

This is the story I wrote to answer that question—and because I honestly wanted to know myself, and sometimes writing the story is the only way for me to get it.

It is set between the events of *Small Favor* and *Turn Coat*.

**M**ost of my cases are pretty tame. Someone loses a piece of jewelry with a lot of sentimental value, or someone comes to me because they've just moved into a new house and it's a little more haunted than the seller's disclosure indicated. Nothing Chicago's only professional wizard can't handle, but the cases don't usually rake in much money, either.

So when a man in a two-thousand-dollar suit opened my office door and came inside, he had my complete attention.

I mean, I didn't take my feet down off my desk or anything. But I paid attention.

He looked my office up and down and frowned, as though he didn't much approve of what he saw. Then he looked at me and said, "Excuse me, is this the office of—"

"Dolce," I said.

He blinked. "Excuse me."

"Your suit," I said. "Dolce and Gabbana. Silk. Very nice. You might want to consider an overcoat, though, now that it's cooling off. Paper says we're in for some rain."

He studied me intently for a moment. He was a man in his late prime. His hair was dyed too dark, and the suit looked like it probably hid a few pounds. "You must be Harry Dresden."

I inclined my head toward him. "Agent or attorney?"

"A little of both," he said, looking around my office again. "I represent a professional entertainment corporation, which wishes to remain anonymous for the time being. My name is Donovan. My sources tell me that you're the man who might be able to help us."

My office isn't anything to write home about. It's on a corner, with windows on two walls, but it's furnished for function, not style—scuffed-up wooden desks, a couple of comfortable chairs, some old metal filing cabinets, a used wooden table, and a coffeepot that is old enough to have belonged to Neanderthals. I figured Donovan was worried that he'd exposed his suit to unsavory elements, and resisted an irrational impulse to spill my half cup of cooling coffee on it.

"That depends."

"On what?"

"What you need and whether you can afford me."

Donovan fixed me with a stern look. I bore up under it as best I could. "Do you intend to gouge me for a fee, Mr. Dresden?"

"For every penny I reasonably can," I told him.

He blinked at me. "You . . . You're quite up front about it, aren't you?"

"Saves time," I said.

"What makes you think I would tolerate such a thing?"

"People don't come to me until they're pretty desperate, Mr. Donovan," I said. "Especially rich people, and hardly ever corporations. Besides, you come in here all intriguey and coy, not wanting to reveal who your employer is. That means that in addition to whatever else you want from me, you want my discretion, too."

"So your increased fee is a polite form of blackmail?"

"Cost of doing business. If you want this done on the down low, you make my job more difficult. You should expect to pay a little more than a conventional customer when you're asking for more than they are."

He narrowed his eyes at me. "How much are you going to cost me?"

I shrugged a shoulder. "Let's find out. What do you want me to do?"

He stood up and turned to walk to the door. He stopped before he reached it, read the words HARRY DRESDEN, WIZARD backward in the frosted glass, and eyed me over his shoulder. "I assume that you have heard of any number of curses in local folklore."

"Sure," I said.

"I suppose you'll expect me to believe in their existence."

I shrugged. "They'll exist or not exist regardless of what you believe, Mr. Donovan." I paused. "Well. Apart from the ones that *don't* exist except in someone's mind. They're only real *because* somebody believes. But that edges from the paranormal over toward psychology. I'm not licensed for that."

He grimaced and nodded. "In that case . . ."

I felt a little slow off the mark as I realized what we were talking about. "A cursed local entertainment corporation," I said. "Like maybe a sports team."

He kept a poker face on, and it was a pretty good one.

"You're talking about the Billy Goat Curse," I said.

Donovan arched an eyebrow and then gave me an almost imperceptible nod as he turned around to face me again. "What do you know about it?"

I blew out my breath and ran my fingers back through my hair. "Uh, back in 1945 or so, a tavern owner named Sianis was asked to leave a World Series game at Wrigley. Seems his pet goat was getting rained on and it smelled bad. Some of the fans were complaining. Outraged at their lack of social élan, Sianis pronounced a curse on the stadium, stating that never again would a World Series game be played there. Well, actually he said something like, 'Them Cubs, they ain't gonna win no more,' but the World Series thing is the general interpretation."

"And?" Donovan asked.

"And I think if I'd gotten kicked out of a Series game I'd been looking forward to, I might do the same thing."

"You have a goat?"

"I have a moose," I said.

He blinked at that for a second, didn't understand it, and decided to ignore it. "If you know that, then you know that many people believe that the curse has held."

"Where the Series is concerned, the Cubbies have been filled with fail and dipped in suck sauce since 1945," I acknowledged. "No matter how hard they try, just when things are looking up, something seems to go bad at the worst possible time." I paused to consider. "I can relate."

"You're a fan, then?"

"More of a kindred spirit."

He looked around my office again and gave me a small smile. "But you follow the team."

"I go to games when I can."

"That being the case," Donovan said, "you know that the team has been playing well this year."

"And the Cubs want to hire yours truly to prevent the curse from screwing things up."

Donovan shook his head. "I never said that the Cubs organization was involved."

"Hell of a story, though, if they were."

Donovan frowned severely.

"The *Sun-Times* would run it on the front page. 'Cubs Hire Professional Wizard to Break Curse,' maybe. Rick Morrissey would have a ball with that story."

"My clients," Donovan said firmly, "have authorized me to commission your services on this matter, if it can be done quickly—and with the utmost discretion."

I swung my feet down from my desk. "Mr. Donovan," I said, "no one does discretion like me."

TWO HOURS AFTER I had begun my calculations, I dropped my pencil on the laboratory table and stretched my back. "Well. You're right."

"Of course I'm right," said Bob the Skull. "I'm always right."

I gave the dried, bleached human skull sitting on a shelf amid a stack of paperback romance novels a gimlet eye.

"For *some* values of right," he amended hastily. The words were conciliatory, but the flickering flames in the skull's eye sockets danced merrily.

My laboratory is in the subbasement under my basement apartment. It's dark, cool, and dank, essentially a concrete box that I have to enter by means of a folding staircase. It isn't a big room, but it's packed with the furnishings of one. Lots of shelves groan under the weight of books, scrolls, papers, alchemical tools, and containers filled with all manner of magical whatnot.

There's a silver summoning circle on the floor, and a tiny scale model of the city of Chicago on a long table running down the middle of the room. The only shelf not crammed full is Bob's, and even it gets a little crowded sometimes. Bob is my more-or-less-faithful, not-so-trusty assistant, a spirit of intellect that dwells within a specially enchanted skull. I might be a wizard, but Bob's knowledge of magic makes me look like an engineering professor.

"Are you sure there's nothing you missed?" I asked.

"Nothing's certain, boss," the skull said philosophically. "But you did the equations. You know the power requirements for a spell to continue running through all those sunrises."

I grunted sourly. The cycles of time in the world degrade ongoing magic, and your average enchantment doesn't last for more than a few days. For a curse to be up and running since 1945, it would have had to begin as a malevolent enchantment powerful enough to rip a hole through the crust of the planet. Given the lack of lava in the area, it would seem that whatever the Billy Goat Curse might be, I could be confident that it wasn't a simple magical working.

"Nothing's ever simple," I complained.

"What did you expect, boss?" Bob said.

I growled. "So the single-spell theory is out."

"Yep," Bob said.

"Which means that either the curse is being powered by something that renews its energy, or else someone is refreshing the thing all the time."

"What about this Sianis guy's family?" Bob said. "Maybe they're putting out a fresh whammy every few days or something."

I shook my head. "I called records in Edinburgh. The Wardens checked them out years ago when all of this first happened, and they aren't practitioners. Besides, they're Cub-friendly."

"The Wardens investigated the Greek guy but not the curse?" Bob asked curiously.

"In 1945 the White Council had enough to do trying to mitigate the bad mojo from all those artifacts the Nazis stockpiled," I said. "Once they established that no one's life was in danger, they didn't really care if a bunch of guys playing a game got cursed to lose it."

"So, what's your next move?"

I tapped my chin thoughtfully with one finger. "Let's go look at the stadium."

I PUT BOB in the mesh sack I sometimes tote him around in and, at his petulant insistence, hung it from the rearview mirror of my car, a battered old Volkswagen Beetle. He hung there, swinging back and forth and occasionally spinning one way or the other when something caught his eye.

"Look at the legs on that one!" Bob said. "And, whew, check *her* out! It must be chilly tonight!"

"There's a reason we don't get out more often, Bob," I sighed. I should have known better than to drive through the club district on my way to Wrigley.

"I love the girls' pants in this century," Bob said. "I mean, *look* at those jeans. One little tug and off they come."

I wasn't touching that one.

I parked the car a couple of blocks from the stadium, stuck Bob in a pocket of my black leather duster, and walked in. The Cubs were on the road, and Wrigley was closed. It was a good time to knock around inside. But since Donovan was evidently prepared to deny and disavow all knowledge, I wasn't going to be able to simply knock on the door and wander in.

So I picked a couple of locks at a delivery entrance and went inside. I didn't hit it at professional-burglar speed or anything—I knew a couple of guys who could open a lock with tools as fast as they could with a key—but I wasn't in any danger of getting a ticket for loitering, either. Once I was inside, I headed straight for the concourses. If I mucked around in the stadium's administrative areas, I would probably run afoul of a full-blown security system, and the only thing I could reliably do to that would be to shut it down completely—and most systems are smart enough to tip off their home-security company when that happens.

Besides. What I was looking for wouldn't be in any office.

I took Bob out of my pocket so that the flickering golden-orange lights of his eyes illuminated the area in front of me. "All right," I murmured. I kept my voice down, on the off chance that a night watchman might be on duty and nearby. "I'm angry at the Cubbies and I'm pitching my curse at them. Where's it going to stick?"

"There's really no question about that, is there?" Bob asked me.

"Home plate," we said together.

I started forward, walking silently. Being quiet when you sneak around isn't difficult, as long as you aren't in any rush. The serious professionals can all but sprint in perfect silence, but the main thing you need isn't agility—it's patience and calm. So I moved out slowly and calmly, and it must have worked, because nobody raised a hue or a cry.

The empty, unlit stadium was . . . just wrong. I was used to seeing Wrigley blazing with sunlight or its lights, filled with fans and music and the smell of overpriced, fattening, and inexplicably gratifying food. I was used to vendors shouting, the constant sea surge of crowd noise, and the buzz of planes passing overhead, trailing banners behind them.

Now Wrigley Field was vast and dark and empty. There was something silently sad about it—acres of seats with no one sitting, a green and beautiful field that no one was playing on, a scoreboard that didn't have anything on it to read or anyone to read it. If the gods and muses were to come down from Olympus and sculpt unfulfilled potential as a physical form, they wouldn't get any closer than that hollow house did.

I walked down the concrete steps and circled the infield until I could make my way to the seats behind home plate. Once there, I held Bob up and said, "What have we got?"

The skull's eyelights flared brighter for a second, and he snorted. "Oh yeah. Definitely tied the curse together right there."

"What's keeping it going?" I asked. "Is there a ley line passing underneath or something?"

"That's a negative, boss," Bob said.

"How fresh is it?"

"Maybe a couple of days," the skull replied. "Maybe more. It's an awfully tight weave."

"How so?"

"This spell resists deterioration better than most mortal magic. It's efficient and solid—way niftier than you could manage."

"Gee. Thanks."

"I call 'em like I see 'em," Bob said cheerfully. "So, either a more experienced member of the White Council is sponsoring this curse and refreshing it every so often, or else . . ."

I caught on. "Or else the curse was placed here by a nonmortal being."

"Yeah," Bob said. "But that could be almost anything."

I shook my head. "Not necessarily. Remember that the curse was laid upon the stadium during a game in the 1945 World Series."

"Ah yes," Bob said. "It would have been packed. Which means that whatever the being was, it could blend in. Either a really great veil or maybe a shapeshifter."

"Why?" I asked.

"What?"

"Why?" I repeated. "Why would this theoretical being have put out the curse on the Cubs?"

"Plenty of beings from the Nevernever really don't need a motivation."

"Sure they do," I said. "The logic behind what they do might be alien or twisted beyond belief, but it makes sense to them." I waved my hand at the stadium. "This being not only laid a curse on a nexus of human emotional power; it kept coming back week after week, year after year."

"I don't see what you're driving at, boss."

"Whoever's doing this is holding a grudge," I said thoughtfully. "This is vengeance for a genuine insult. It's personal."

"Maybe," Bob said. "But maybe the emotional state of the stadium supercharged Sianis's curse. Or maybe after the stadium evicted Sianis, who didn't have enough power to curse anybody anyhow, someone decided to make it stick."

"Or maybe . . ." My voice trailed off, and then I barked out a short bite of laughter. "Oh. Oh, that's *funny.*"

Bob spun in my hand to look up at me.

"It wasn't *Sianis* who put the whammy on the Cubs," I said, grinning. "It was the *goat.*"

THE LLYN Y FAN FACH Tavern and Inn was located down at the lakeside at the northern edge of the city. The place's exterior screamed PUB, as if it were trying to make itself heard over the roar of brawling football hooligans. It was all whitewashed walls and heavy timbers stained dark. The wooden sign hanging from a post above the door bore the tavern's name and a painted picture of a leek and a daffodil crossed like swords.

I sidled up to the tavern and went in. The inside matched the outside, continuing the dark-stained theme on its wooden floors, walls, and furnishings. It was just after midnight, which wasn't really all that late, as bar scenes went, but the Llyn y Fan Fach Tavern was all but empty.

A big red-haired guy sitting in a chair by the door scowled at me.

His biceps were thick enough to use steel-belted radials as armbands. He gave me the fish eye, which I ignored as I ambled on up to the bar.

I took a seat on a stool and nodded to the bartender. She was a pretty woman with jet-black hair and an obvious pride in her torso. Her white renaissance shirt had slipped entirely off both of her shapely shoulders and was being held up by only her dark leather bustier. She was busy wiping down the bar. The bustier was busy lifting and separating.

She glanced up at me and smiled. Her pale green eyes flicked over me, and the smile deepened. "Ah," she said, her accent thick and from somewhere closer to Cardiff than London. "You're a tall one, aren't you?"

"Only when I'm standing up."

Her eyes twinkled with merry wickedness. "Such a crime. What are you drinking, love?"

"Do you have any cold beer?" I asked.

"None of that Colonial piss here," she replied.

"Snob," I said, smiling. "Do you have any of McAnally's dark? McAnally's anything, really."

Her eyebrows went up. "Whew. For a moment there, I thought a heathen walked amongst us." She gave me a full smile, her teeth very square and straight and white, and walked over to me before bending over and drawing a dark bottle from beneath the bar.

I appreciated her in a polite and politically correct fashion. "Is the show included in the price of the drink?"

She opened the bottle with an expert twist of her wrist and set it down in front of me with a clean mug. "I'm a generous soul, love," she said, winking. "Why charge when I can engage in selfless charity?"

She poured the beer into the mug and set it on a napkin in front of me. She slid a bowl of bar nuts down my way. "Drinking alone?"

"That depends on whether you'll let me buy one for you."

She laughed. "A gentleman, is it? Sir, you must think me all manner of tart if you think I'd accept a drink from a stranger."

"I'm Harry," I said.

"And so we are strangers no longer," she replied, and got out another bottle of ale. She took her time about it, and she watched me as she did it. She straightened, also slowly, and opened her bottle before putting it gently to her lips and taking a slow pull. Then she arched an eyebrow at me and said, "See anything else you like? Something tasty, perhaps?"

"I suppose I am kind of an aural guy at the moment," I said. "Got a minute to talk to me, Jill?"

Her smile faded swiftly. "I've never seen you in here before. How is it you know my name?"

I reached into my shirt and tugged out my pentacle, letting it fall down against my T-shirt. Jill studied that for a few seconds, then took a second look at me. Her mouth opened in a silent *ah* of understanding. "The wizard. Dresden, isn't it?"

"Harry," I said.

She nodded and took another, warier sip of her beer.

"Relax," I said. "I'm not here on Council business. But a friend of mine among the Fair Folk told me that you were the person to talk to about the Tylwyth Teg."

She tilted her head to one side and smiled slightly. "I'm not sure how I could help you, Harry. I'm just a storyteller."

"But you know about the Tylwyth Teg."

"I know stories of them," she countered. "That's not the same as knowing them. Not in the way that your folk care about."

"I'm not doing politics between members of the Unseelie Accords right now," I said.

"But you're one of the magi," she said. "Surely you know what I do."

"I'm still pretty young for a wise guy. And nobody can know everything," I said. "My knowledge of the Fair Folk pretty much begins and ends with the Winter and Summer Courts. I know that the Tylwyth Teg are an independent kingdom of the Wyld. Stories might give me what I need."

The sparkle returned to her eyes for a moment. "This is the first time a man I've flirted with told me that *stories* were what he needed."

"I could gaze longingly at your décolletage while you talk, if you like."

"Given how much trouble I go to in order to show it off, it would seem polite."

I lowered my eyes demurely to her chest for a moment. "Well. If I must."

She let out a full-bodied laugh, which made attractive things happen to her upper body. "What stories are you interested in, specifically?"

I grinned at her. "Tell me about the Tylwyth Teg and goats."

Jill nodded thoughtfully and took another sip of beer. "Well," she said. "Goats were a favored creature among them. The Tylwyth Teg, if treated with respect by a household of mortals, would often perform tasks for them. One of the most common tasks was the grooming of goats—cleaning out their fur and brushing their beards for Sunday morning."

I took a notebook from my duster's pocket and started making notes. "Uh-huh."

"The Tylwyth Teg were shapeshifters," Jill continued. "They're a small folk, only a couple of feet tall, and though they could take what form they wished, they usually changed into fairly small animals—foxes, cats, dogs, owls, hares, and—"

"And goats?"

She lifted her eyebrows. "And goats, aye. Though the stories can become very odd at times. More than one Welsh farmer who managed to capture a bride of the Tylwyth Teg found himself waking up to a goat beside him in his bed, or took his wife's hand only to feel the shape of a cloven hoof beneath his fingertips."

"Weregoats," I muttered. "Jesus."

"They're masters of deceit and trickery," Jill continued. "And we mortals are well-advised to show them the proper respect, if we intrude upon them at all."

"What happens if we don't?"

Jill shook her head. "That would depend upon the offense, and which of the Tylwyth Teg were offended. They were capable of almost anything if their pride was wounded."

"The usual Fair Folk response?" I asked. "Bad fortune, children taken—that sort of thing?"

Jill shook her head. "Harry, love, the Queens of Winter and Summer do not kill mortals, and so frown upon their followers taking such action. But the high folk of the Tylwyth Teg have no such restrictions."

"They'd kill?" I asked.

"They can, have, and will take life in acts of vengeance," Jill said seriously. "They always respond in balance—but push them too far and they will."

"Damn," I said. "Those are some hard-core faeries."

Jill sucked in a sharp breath and her eyes glittered brightly. "What did you say?"

I became suddenly aware of the massive redhead by the door rising to his feet.

I swigged a bit of beer and put the notebook back in my pocket. "I called them faeries," I drawled.

The floorboards creaked under the weight of Big Red, walking toward me.

Jill stared at me with eyes that were hard and brittle like glass. "You of all, wizard, should know that word is an insult to . . . them."

"Oh, right," I said. "*They* get real upset when you call them that." A shadow fell across me. I sipped more beer without turning around and said, "Did someone just put up a building?"

A hand the size of a Christmas ham fell onto my shoulder, and Big Red growled, "You want me to leave some marks?"

"Come on, Jill," I said. "Don't be sore. It's not as though you're trying all that hard to hide. You left plenty of clues for the game."

Jill stared at me with unreadable eyes and said nothing.

I started ticking off points on my fingers. "Llyn y Fan Fach is a lake sacred to the Tylwyth Teg over in the Old World. You don't get a lot more Welsh than that leek-and-daffodil emblem. And as for calling yourself Jill, that's a pretty thin mask to cover the presence of one of the Jili Ffrwtan." I tilted my head back to indicate Big Red. "Changeling, right?"

Big Red's fingers tightened enough to hurt. I started to get a little bit concerned.

Jill held up a hand, and Big Red let go of me at once. I heard the floor creaking as he retreated. She stared at me for a moment more, then smiled faintly and said, "The mask is more than sufficient when no one is looking for the face behind it. What gave us away?"

I shrugged. "Someone has to be renewing the spell laid on Wrigley Field on a regular basis. It almost had to be someone local. Once I remembered that the Fair Folk of Wales had a rather singular affinity with goats, the rest was just a matter of legwork."

She finished off the beer in a long pull, her eyes sparkling again. "And my own reaction to the insult was the cherry on top."

I drained my mug and shrugged modestly. "I apologize for speaking so crudely, lady. It was the only way I could be sure."

"Powerful, clever, *and* polite," she murmured. She leaned forward onto the bar, and it got really hard not to notice her bosom. "You and I might get along."

I winked at her and said, "You're trying to distract me, and doing it well. But I'd like to speak to someone in authority over the enchantment laid on Wrigley."

"And who says our folk are behind such a thing?"

"Your cleavage," I replied. "Otherwise, why try to distract me?"

She let out another laugh, though this one was softer and more silvery, a tinkling and unearthly tone that made my ears feel like someone with fantastic lips was blowing gently into them. "Even if they are, what makes you think that we would alter that weaving now?"

I shrugged. "Perhaps you will. Perhaps you won't. I only request, please, to speak to one with authority over the curse, to discuss what might be done about it."

She studied me through narrowed eyes for another silent moment.

"I said please," I pointed out to her. "And I did buy you that beer."

"True," she murmured, and then gave me a smile that made my skin feel like I was standing close to a bonfire. She tossed her white cloth to one side and said, toward Big Red, "Mind the store for a bit?"

He nodded at her and settled back down into his chair.

The Jili Ffrwtan came out from behind the bar, hips swaying in deliciously feminine motion. I rose and offered her my arm in my best old-fashioned courtly style. It made her smile, and she laid her hand on my forearm lightly, barely touching. "This," she said, "should be interesting."

I smiled at her again and asked, "Where are we going?"

"Why, to Annwn, my love," the Jili Ffrwtan said, pronouncing it *ah-noon*. "We go to the land of the dead."

I FOLLOWED THE Jili Ffrwtan into the back room of the pub and down a narrow flight of stone stairs. The basement was all concrete walls and had a packed-earth floor. One wall of the place was stacked with an assortment of hooch. We walked past it while I admired the Jili Ffrwtan's shape and movement, and wondered if her hair felt as soft as it looked.

She gave me a sly look over one bare shoulder. "And tell me, young magus, what you know of my kind."

"That they are the high ladies of the Tylwyth Teg. And that they are surpassingly lovely, charming, and gracious, if you are any example, lady." *And that they could be psycho bitches from hell if you damaged their pride.*

She laughed again. "Base flattery," she said, clearly pleased. "But at least you do it well. You're quite articulate—for a mortal."

As we got farther from the light spilling from the staircase, the shadows grew thick, until she made a negligent gesture with one hand, and soft blue light with no apparent source filled the room around us. "Ah, here we are."

She stopped beside a ring of large brown mushrooms that grew up out of the floor. I extended my otherworldly senses toward the ring and could feel the quiver of energies moving through the air around the circle like a silent hum of high-tension electrical lines. The substance of mortal reality was thin here, easily torn. The ring of mushrooms was a doorway, a portal leading to the Nevernever, the spirit world.

I gave Jill a little bow and gestured with one hand. "After you, lady."

She smiled at me. "Oh, we must cross together, lest you get lost on the way." She slid her fingertips lightly down my forearm. Her warm fingers intertwined with mine, and the gesture felt almost obscenely intimate. My glands cut my brain out of every decision-making process they could, and it was an effort not to adjust my pants. The part of my head that was still on the job got real nervous right about then: There are way too many things in the universe that use sexual desire as a weapon, and I had to work not to jerk my hand away from the Jili Ffrwtan's.

It would be an awful idea to damage her pride with that kind of display.

*And besides*, my glands told me, *she looks great. And smells even better. And her skin feels amazing. And . . .*

"Quiet, you," I growled at my glands under my breath.

She arched an eyebrow at me.

I gave her a tight smile and said, "Not you. Talking with myself."

"Ah," she said. She flicked her eyes down to below my waist and back, smirking. Then she took a step forward, drawing me into the ring of mushrooms, and the basement blurred and went away, as if the shadow of an ancient mountain had fallen over us.

Then the shadow lifted, and we were elsewhere.

It's at this point that my senses pretty much broke down.

The darkness lifted away to light and motion and music like nothing I had ever seen before—and I've been to the wildest spots in Chicago and to a couple of parties that weren't even being held inside our reality.

We stood inside a ring of mushrooms and in a cave. But that doesn't

really describe it. Calling the hall of the Tylwyth Teg a cave is about
the same as calling the Taj Mahal a grave. It's technically accurate, but
it doesn't begin to cover it.

Walls soared up around me, walls in the shape of natural stone but
somehow surfaced in the polished beauty of marble, veined with
threads of silver and gold and even rarer metals, lit by the same source-
less radiance the Jili Ffrwtan had summoned back in Chicago. They
rose above me on every side, and since I'd just been to Wrigley, I had
a fresh perspective with which to compare them: If Wrigley was any
bigger, it wasn't by much.

The air was full of music. I call it music only because there aren't
any words adequate to describe it. By comparison to any music I'd ever
heard played, it was the difference between a foot-powder jingle and a
symphony by Mozart, throbbing with passion, merriment, pulsing
between an ancient sadness and a fierce joy. Every beat made me feel
like joining in—either to weep or to dance, or possibly both at the
same time.

And the dancers . . . I remember men and women and silks and
velvets and jewels and more gold and silver and a grace that made me
feel huge and awkward and slow.

There aren't any words.

The Jili Ffrwtan walked forward, taking me with her, and as she
went she changed, each step leaving her smaller, her clothing changing as well, until she was attired as the revelers were, in a jeweled gown
that left just as much of her just as attractively revealed as the previous
outfit. It didn't seem strange at the time that she should grow so much
smaller. I just felt like I was freakishly huge, the outsider, the intruder,
hopelessly oversized for that place. We moved forward through the
dancers, who spun and flitted out of our path. My escort kept on di-
minishing until I was walking half-hunched over, her entire hand covering about half of one of my fingers.

She led me to the far end of the hall, pausing several times to call
something aside, in a complex, musical tongue, to one of the other
Fair Folk. We walked past a miniature table laid out with a not-at-all-

miniature feast, and my stomach suddenly informed me that it had never once taken in an ounce of nutrition, and that it really was about time that I finally had something. I had actually taken a couple of steps toward the table before I forced myself to swerve away from it.

"Wise," said the Jili Ffrwtan. "Unless, of course, you wish to stay."

"It smells fine," I replied, my voice hoarse. "But it's no Burger King."

She laughed again, putting the fingers of one hand to her still proportionately impressive bosom, and we passed out of the great hall and into a smaller cavern—this one only the size of a train station. There were guards there—guards armored in bejeweled mail, faces masked behind mail veils, guards who barely came up over my knee, but guards nonetheless, bearing swords and spears and bows. They stood at attention and watched me with cold, hard eyes as we passed them. My escort seemed delightedly smug about the entire affair.

I cleared my throat and asked, "Who are we going to see?"

"Why, love, the only one who has authority over the curse upon Wrigley Field," she said. "His Majesty."

I swallowed. "The king of your folk? Gwynn ap Nudd, isn't it?"

"His Majesty will do," rang out a voice in a high tenor, and I looked up to see one of the Fair Folk sitting on a throne raised several feet above the floor of the chamber, so that my eyes were level with his. "Perhaps even His Majesty, sir."

Gwynn ap Nudd, ruler of the Tylwyth Teg, was tall—for his folk, anyway—broad shouldered, and ruggedly handsome. Though dressed in what looked like some kind of midnight blue fabric that had the texture of velvet but the supple sweep of silk, he had large-knuckled hands that looked rough and strong. Both his long hair and beard were streaked with fine, symmetrical lines of silver, and jewels shone on his fingers and upon his brow.

I stopped at once and bowed deeply, making sure my head went lower than the faerie king's, and I stayed there for a good long moment before rising again. "Your Majesty, sir," I said, in my politest voice. "You are both courteous and generous to grant me an audience.

It speaks well of the Tylwyth Teg as a people, that such a one should lead them."

King Gwynn stared at me for a long moment before letting out a grunt that mixed disbelief with wry satisfaction. "At least they sent one with half a sense of manners this time."

"I thought you'd like that, sire," said the Jili Ffrwtan, smiling. "May I present Harry Dresden, magus, a commander of the Order of the Grey Cloak, sometime mortal Champion of Queen Mab and Esquire of the Court of Queen Titania. He begs to speak to you regarding the curse upon the Field of Wrigley in the mortal citadel of Chicago."

"We know who he is," Gwynn said testily. "And we know why he is here. Return to your post. We will see to it that he is safely returned."

The Jili Ffrwtan curtsied deeply and revealingly. "Of course, sire." Then she simply vanished into a sparkling cloud of lights.

"Guards," King Gwynn called out. "You will leave us now."

The guards looked unhappy about it, but they lined up and filed out, every movement in sync with the others. Gwynn waited until the last of them had left the hall and the doors boomed shut before he turned back to me.

"So," he said. "Who do ye like for the Series this year?"

I blinked my eyes at him several times. It wasn't one of those questions I'd been expecting. "Um. American League, I'm kind of rooting for Tampa Bay. I'd like to see them beat out the Yankees."

"Aye," Gwynn said, nodding energetically. "Who wouldn't? Bloody Yankees."

"And in the National League," I said, "the Cubs are looking good at the moment, though I could see the Phillies pulling something out at the last minute." I shrugged. "I mean, since the Cubbies are cursed and all."

"Cursed?" Gwynn said. A fierce smile stretched his face. "Cursed, is it?"

"Or so it is widely believed," I said.

Gwynn snorted, then rose and descended from his throne. "Walk with me."

The diminutive monarch walked farther back into the cavern, past his throne and into what resembled some kind of bizarre museum. There were rows and rows of cabinets, each with shelves lined in black velvet and walls of crystalline glass. Each cabinet had a dozen or so artifacts in it; ticket stubs were some of the most common items, though there were also baseballs here and there among them, as well as baseball cards, fan booklets, team pennants, bats, batting gloves, and fielders' gloves.

As I walked beside him, careful to keep my pace slow enough to let him dictate how fast we were walking, it dawned on me that King Gwynn ap Nudd of the Tylwyth Teg was a baseball fan—as in *fanatic*—of the original vintage.

"It was you," I said suddenly. "You were the one they threw out of the game."

"Aye," King Gwynn said. "There was business to attend, and by the time I got there the tickets were sold out. I had to find another way into the game."

"As a goat?" I asked, bemused.

"It was a team-spirit thing," Gwynn said proudly. "Sianis had made up a sign and all, proclaiming that Chicago had already gotten Detroit's goat. Then he paraded me and the sign on the field before the game—it got plenty of cheers, let me tell you. And he did pay for an extra ticket for the goat, so it wasn't as though old Wrigley's successors were being cheated the price of admission. They just didn't like it that someone argued with the ushers and won!"

Gwynn's words had taken on the heat that you can only get from an argument that someone has rehearsed to himself about a million times. Given that he must have been practicing it since 1945, I knew better than to think that anything like reason was going to get in the way. So I just nodded and asked, "What happened?"

"Before the game was anywhere near over," Gwynn continued, his voice seething with outrage, "they came to Sianis and evicted him from the park. Because, they said, his goat smelled too awful!"

Gwynn stopped in his tracks and turned to me, scowling furiously as he gestured at himself with his hands. "Hello! I was a *goat*! Goats are *supposed* to smell awful when they are rained upon!"

"They are, Your Majesty, sir," I agreed soberly.

"And I was a *flawless* goat!"

"I have no doubts on that account, King Gwynn," I said.

"What kind of justice is it to be excluded from a Series game because one has flawlessly imitated a goat!?"

"No justice at all, Your Majesty, sir," I said.

"And to say that I, Gwynn ap Nudd, I the King of Annwn, I who defeated Gwythr ap Greidawl, I the counselor and ally to gods and heroes alike, *smelled*!" His mouth twisted up in rage. "How *dare* some jumped-up mortal ape say such a thing! As though mortals smell any *better* than wet goats!"

For a moment, I considered pointing out the conflicting logic of Gwynn both being a perfect (and therefore smelly) goat and being upset that he had been cast out of the game for *being* smelly. But only for a second. Otherwise, I might have been looking at coming back to Chicago about a hundred years too late to grab a late-night meal at BK.

"I can certainly see why you were upset and offended, Your Majesty, sir."

Some of the righteous indignation seemed to drain out of him, and he waved an irritated hand at me. "We're talking about something important here, mortal," he said. "We're talking about *baseball*. Call me Gwynn."

We had stopped at the last display cabinet, which was enormous by the standards of the furnishings of that hall, which is to say about the size of a human wardrobe. On one of its shelves was a single outfit of clothing; blue jeans, a T-shirt, a leather jacket, with socks and shoes. On all the rest were the elongated rectangles of tickets—season tickets, in fact, and hundreds of them.

But the single stack of tickets on the top shelf sat next to the only team cap I'd seen.

Both tickets and cap bore the emblem of the Cubs.

"It was certainly a serious insult," I said quietly. "And it's obvious that a balancing response was in order. But, Gwynn, the insult was given you unwittingly, by mortals whose very stupidity prevented them from knowing what they were doing. Few enough there that day are even alive now. Is it just that their children be burdened with their mistake? Surely that fact also carries some weight within the heart of a wise and generous king."

Gwynn let out a tired sigh and moved his right hand in a gesture that mimed pouring out water cupped in it. "Oh, aye, aye, Harry. The anger faded decades ago—mostly. It's the principle of the thing these days."

"That's something I can understand," I said. "Sometimes you have to give weight to a principle to keep it from being taken away in a storm."

He glanced up at me shrewdly. "Aye. I've heard as that's something you would understand."

I spread my hands and tried to sound diffident. "There must be some way of evening the scales between the Cubs and the Tylwyth Teg," I said. "Some way to set this insult to rights and lay the matter to rest."

"Oh, aye," King Gwynn said. "It's easy as dying. All we do is nothing. The spell would fade. Matters would resume their normal course."

"But clearly you don't wish to do such a thing," I said. "It's obviously an expenditure of resources for you to keep the curse alive."

The small king suddenly smiled. "Truth be told, I stopped thinking of it as a curse years ago, lad."

I arched my eyebrows.

"How do you regard it, then?" I asked him.

"As protection," he said. "From the *real* curse of baseball."

I looked from him to the tickets and thought about that for a moment. Then I said, "I understand."

It was Gwynn's turn to arch eyebrows at me. "Do ye, now?" He studied me for a time and then smiled, nodding slowly. "Aye. Aye, ye do. Wise, for one so young."

I shook my head ruefully. "Not wise enough."

"Everyone with a lick of wisdom thinks that," Gwynn replied. He regarded his tickets for a while, his hands clasped behind his back. "Now, ye've won the loyalty of some of the Wee Folk, and that is no quick or easy task. Ye've defied Sidhe queens. Ye've even stuck a thumb into the Erlking's eye, and that tickles me to no end. And ye've been clever enough to find us, which few mortals have managed, and gone out of your way to be polite, which means more from you than it would from some others."

I nodded quietly.

"So, Harry Dresden," King Gwynn said, "I'll be glad t' consider it, if ye say the Cubs wish me to cease my efforts."

I thought about it for a long time before I gave him my answer.

MR. DONOVAN SAT down in my office in a different ridiculously expensive suit and regarded me soberly. "Well?"

"The curse stays," I said. "Sorry."

Mr. Donovan frowned, as though trying to determine whether I was pulling his leg. "I would have expected you to declare it gone and collect your fee."

"I have this weird thing where I take professional ethics seriously," I said. I pushed a piece of paper at him and said, "My invoice."

He took it and turned it over. "It's blank," he said.

"Why type it up when it's just a bunch of zeroes?"

He stared at me even harder.

"Look at it this way," I said. "You haven't paused to consider the upside of the Billy Goat Curse."

"Upside?" he asked. "To losing?"

"Exactly," I said. "How many times have you heard people complaining that professional ball isn't about anything but money these days?"

"What does that have to do—"

"That's why everyone's so locked on the Series these days. Not necessarily because it means you're the best, because you've risen to a challenge and prevailed. The Series means millions of dollars for the club, for businesses, all kinds of money. Even the fans get obsessed with the Series, like it's the only significant thing in baseball. Don't even get me started on the stadiums all starting to be named after their corporate sponsors."

"Do you have a point?" Donovan asked.

"Yeah," I said. "Baseball is about more than money and victory. It's about facing challenges alone and on a team. It's about spending time with friends and family and neighbors in a beautiful park, watching the game unfold. It's . . ." I sighed. "It's about fun, Mr. Donovan."

"And you are contending that the curse is fun?"

"Think about it," I said. "The Cubs have the most loyal, diehard fan following in Major League ball. Those fans aren't in it to see the Cubs run rampant over other teams because they've spent more money hiring the best players. You know they aren't—because they all know about the curse. If you *know* your team isn't going to carry off the Series, then cheering them on becomes something more than yelling when they're beating someone. It's about tradition. It's about loyalty to the team and camaraderie with the other fans, and win or lose, just enjoying the damned game."

I spread my hands. "It's about *fun* again, Mr. Donovan. Wrigley Field might be the only stadium in professional ball where you can say that."

Donovan stared at me as though I'd started speaking in Welsh. "I don't understand."

I sighed again. "Yeah. I know."

My ticket was for general admission, but I thought I'd take a look around before the game got started. Carlos Zambrano was on the mound warming up when I sat down next to Gwynn ap Nudd.

Human sized, he was considerably over six feet tall, and he was dressed in the same clothes I'd seen back at his baseball shrine. Other than that, he looked exactly the way I remembered him. He was talking to a couple of folks in the row behind him, animatedly relating some kind of tale that revolved around the incredible arc of a single game-deciding breaking ball. I waited until he was finished with the story and turned back out to the field.

"Good day," Gwynn said to me.

I nodded just a little bit deeply. "And to you."

He watched Zambrano warming up and grinned. "They're going to fight through it eventually," he said. "There are so many mortals now. Too many players and fans want them to do it." His voice turned a little sad. "One day they will."

My equations and I had eventually come to the same conclusion. "I know."

"But you want me to do it now, I suppose," he said. "Or else why would you be here?"

I flagged down a beer vendor and bought one for myself and one for Gwynn.

He stared at me for a few seconds, his head tilted to one side.

"No business," I said, passing him one of the beers. "How about we just enjoy the game?"

Gwynn ap Nudd's handsome face broke into a wide smile, and we both settled back in our seats as the Cubs took the cursed field.

# EVEN HAND

In this tale, set between *Turn Coat* and *Changes*, I got to do one of the most enjoyable things a writer working on a really giant story possibly can do: write from the perspective of another pivotal character in a series.

John Marcone has been an underworld establishment in the Dresden Files since the first book of the series—longer than anyone except Bob, Murphy, and Harry himself. Keeping that position in the Dresden Files story world has required him to be a very smart, tough, resourceful, and dangerous human being. Marcone, much like Dresden, has been challenged by increasingly dangerous interlopers, and he has grown more cunning, dangerous, and ruthless by way of adapting to the challenges they've presented.

In this story, we get to see a little bit of Marcone operating in his own world—a place considerably more grey and nebulous than the relatively clear-cut moral environment Harry Dresden has created with his choices. It is probably worth remembering that Marcone, despite some of the more vile things he presides over, would probably have been considered a rather decent sort of leader for the majority of recorded human history—he is, in fact, rather strongly modeled on the ideals of medieval barons, who, it seems to me, would have made surpassingly excellent and dangerous crime lords. Here we see Marcone, operating from the bastion of his power, as the only mortal man considered competent and dangerous enough to join the Unseelie Accords of the varied supernatural nations.

**A** successful murder is like a successful restaurant: Ninety percent of it is about location, location, location.

Three men in black hoods knelt on the waterfront warehouse floor, their wrists and ankles trussed with heavy plastic zip ties. There were few lights. They knelt over a large, faded stain on the concrete floor, left behind by the hypocritically named White Council of Wizardry during their last execution.

I nodded to Hendricks, who took the hood off the first man, then stood clear. The man was young and good-looking. He wore an expensive yet ill-fitting suit and even more expensive yet tasteless jewelry.

"Where are you from?" I asked him.

He sneered at me. "What's it to y—"

I shot him in the head as soon as I heard the bravado in his voice. The body fell heavily to the floor.

The other two jumped and cursed, their voices angry and terrified.

I took the hood off the second man. His suit was a close cousin of the dead man's, and I thought I recognized its cut. "Boston?" I asked him.

"You can't do this to us," he said, more angry than frightened. "Do you know who we are?"

Once I heard the nasal quality of the word *are*, I shot him.

I took off the third man's hood. He screamed and fell away from me. "Boston," I said, nodding, and put the barrel of my .45 against the third man's forehead. He stared at me, showing the whites of his eyes. "You know who I am. I run drugs in Chicago. I run the numbers, the books. I run the whores. It's my town. Do you understand?"

His body jittered in what might have been a nod. His lips formed the word *yes*, though no sound came out.

"I'm glad you can answer a simple question," I told him, and lowered the gun. "I want you to tell Mr. Morelli that I won't be this lenient the next time his people try to clip the edges of my territory." I looked at Hendricks. "Put the three of them in a sealed trailer and rail-freight them back to Boston, care of Mr. Morelli."

Hendricks was a large, trustworthy man, his red hair cropped in a crew cut. He twitched his chin in the slight motion that he used for a nod when he disapproved of my actions but intended to obey me anyway.

Hendricks and the cleaners on my staff would handle the matter from here.

I passed him the gun and the gloves on my hands. Both would see the bottom of Lake Michigan before I was halfway home, along with the two slugs the cleaners would remove from the site. When they were done, there would be nothing left of the two dead men but a slight variation on the outline of the stain in the old warehouse floor, where no one would look twice in any case.

Location, location, location.

Obviously, I am not Harry Dresden. My name is something I rarely trouble to remember, but for most of my adult life, I have been called John Marcone.

I am a professional monster.

It sounds pretentious. After all, I'm not a flesh-devouring ghoul, hiding behind a human mask until it is time to gorge. I'm no vampire, draining the blood or soul from my victim—no ogre, no demon, no cursed beast from the spirit world dwelling amid the unsuspecting sheep of humanity. I'm not even possessed of the mystic abilities of a mortal wizard.

But they will never be what I am. One and all, those beings were born to be what they are.

I made a choice.

I walked outside of the warehouse and was met by my consultant, Gard—a tall blond woman without any makeup whose eyes continually swept her surroundings. She fell into step beside me as we walked to the car. "Two?"

"They couldn't be bothered to answer a question in a civil manner."

She opened the back door for me and I got in. I picked up my personal weapon and slipped it into the holster beneath my left arm while she settled down behind the wheel. She started driving and then said, "No. That wasn't it."

"It was business."

"And the fact that one of them was pushing heroin to thirteen-year-old girls and the other was pimping them out had nothing to do with it," Gard said.

"It was business," I said, enunciating. "Morelli can find pushers and pimps anywhere. A decent accountant is invaluable. I sent his bookkeeper back as a gesture of respect."

"You don't respect Morelli."

I almost smiled. "Perhaps not."

"Then why?"

I did not answer. She didn't push the issue, and we rode in silence back to the office. As she put the car in park, I said, "They were in my territory. They broke my rule."

"No children," she said.

"No children," I said. "I do not tolerate challenges, Ms. Gard. They're bad for business."

She looked at me in the mirror, her blue eyes oddly intent, and nodded.

There was a knock at my office door, and Gard thrust her head in, her phone's earpiece conspicuous. "There's a problem."

Hendricks frowned from his seat at a nearby desk. He was hunched over a laptop that looked too small for him, plugging away at his thesis. "What kind of problem?"

"An Accords matter," Gard said.

Hendricks sat up straight and looked at me.

I didn't look up from one of my lawyer's letters, which I receive too frequently to let slide. "Well," I said, "we knew it would happen eventually. Bring the car."

"I don't have to," Gard said. "The situation came to us."

I set aside the finished letter and looked up, resting my fingertips together. "Interesting."

Gard brought the problem in. The problem was young and attractive. In my experience, the latter two frequently lead to the former. In this particular case, it was a young woman holding a child. She was remarkable—thick, rich, silver-white hair, dark eyes, pale skin. She had on very little makeup, which was fortunate in her case, since she looked as if she had recently been drenched. She wore what was left of a grey business skirt suit, had a towel from one of my health clubs wrapped around her shoulders, and was shivering.

The child she held was too young to be in school and was also appealing, with rosy features, white blond hair, and blue eyes. Male or female, it hardly mattered at that age. They're all beautiful. The child clung to the girl as if it would not be separated, and was also wrapped in a towel.

The girl's body language was definitely protective. She had the kind of beauty that looked natural and . . . true. Her features and her bearing both spoke of gentleness and kindness.

I felt an immediate instinct to protect and comfort her.

I quashed it thoroughly.

I am not made of stone, but I have found it is generally best to behave as if I am.

I looked across the desk at her and said, "My people tell me you have asked for sanctuary under the terms of the Unseelie Accords, but that you have not identified yourself."

"I apologize, sir," she answered. "I was already being indiscreet enough just by coming here."

"Indeed," I said calmly. "I make it a point not to advertise the location of my business headquarters."

"I didn't want to add names to the issue," she said, casting her eyes down in a gesture of submission that did not entirely convince me. "I wasn't sure how many of your people were permitted access to this sort of information."

I glanced past the young woman to Gard, who gave me a slow, cautious nod. Had the girl or the child been other than they appeared, Gard would have indicated in the negative. Gard costs me a fortune and is worth every penny.

Even so, I didn't signal either her or Hendricks to stand down. Both of them watched the girl, ready to kill her if she made an aggressive move. Trust, but verify—that the person being trusted will be dead if she attempts betrayal.

"That was most considerate of you, Justine."

The girl blinked at me several times. "Y-you know me."

"You are a sometimes associate of Harry Dresden," I said. "Given his proclivities about those he considers to be held under his aegis, it is sensible to identify as many of them as possible. For the sake of my insurance rates, if nothing else. Gard."

"Justine, no last name you'll admit to," Gard said calmly. "Currently employed as Lara Raith's secretary and personal aide. You are the sometimes lover of Thomas Raith, a frequent ally of Dresden's."

I spread my hands slightly. "I assume the J notation at the bottom of Ms. Raith's typed correspondence refers to you."

"Yes," Justine said. She had regained her composure quickly—not something I would have expected of the servitor of a vampire of the White Court. Many of the . . . people, I suppose, I'd seen there had made lotus-eaters look self-motivated. "Yes, exactly."

I nodded. "Given your patron, one is curious as to why you have come to me, seeking protection."

"Time, sir," she replied quietly. "I lacked any other alternative."

Someone screamed at the front of the building.

My headquarters shifts position irregularly, as I acquire new buildings. Much of my considerable wealth is invested in real estate. I own more of the town than any other single investor. In Chicago, there is always money to be had by purchasing and renovating aging buildings. I do much of my day-to-day work out of one of my most recent renovation projects, once they have been modified to be suitable places to welcome guests. Then renovation of the building begins, and the place is generally crowded with contractors who have proven their ability to see and hear nothing.

Gard's head snapped up. She shook it as if to rid herself of a buzzing fly and said, "A presence. A strong one." Her blue eyes snapped to Justine. "Who?"

The young woman shuddered and wrapped the towel more tightly about herself. "Mag. A cantrev lord of the Fomor."

Gard spat something in a Scandinavian tongue that was probably a curse.

"Precis, please," I said.

"The Fomor are an ancient folk," she said. "Water dwellers, cousins of the jotuns. Extremely formidable. Sorcerers, shape changers, seers."

"And signatories," I noted.

"Yes," she said. She crossed to the other side of the room, opened a closet, and withdrew an athletic bag. She produced a simple, rather crude-looking broadsword from it and tossed it toward Hendricks. The big man caught it by the handle and took his gun into his left hand. Gard took a broad-bladed axe out of the bag and shouldered the weapon. "But rarely involved in mortal affairs."

"Ms. Raith sent me to the Fomor king with documents," Justine said, her voice coming out quietly and rapidly. Her shivering had increased. "Mag made me his prisoner. I escaped with the child. There wasn't time to reach one of my lady's strongholds. I came to you, sir. I beg your protection, as a favor to Ms. Raith."

"I don't grant favors," I said calmly.

Mag entered in the manner so many of these self-absorbed supernatural cretins seem to adore. He blasted the door into a cloud of flying splinters with what I presumed was magic.

*For God's sake.*

At least the vampires would call for an appointment.

The blast amounted to little debris. After a few visits from Dresden and his ilk, I had invested in cheap, light doors at dramatic (as opposed to tactical) entry points.

The Fomor was a pale, repellent humanoid. Seven feet tall, give or take, and distinctly froglike in appearance. He had a bloated belly, legs several inches too long to be proportionately human, and huge feet and hands. He wore a tunic of something that resembled seaweed beneath a long, flapping blue robe covered in the most intricate embroidery I had ever seen. A coronet of coral was bound about his head. His right hand was extended dramatically. He carried a twisted length of wood in his left.

His eyes bulged, jaundice yellow around septic green, and his teeth were rotted and filthy. "You cannot run from me," he said. His wide mouth made the words seem somehow slurred. "You are mine."

Justine looked up at me, evidently too frightened to turn her head, her eyes wide with fear. A sharper contrast would have been hard to manage. "Sir. Please."

I touched a button on the undersurface of my desk, a motion of less than two inches, and then made a steeple of my hands again as I eyed Mag and said, "Excuse me, sir. This is a private office."

Mag surged forward half a step, his eyes focused on the girl. "Hold your tongue, mortal, if you would keep it."

I narrowed my eyes.

Is it so much to ask for civility?

"Justine," I said calmly, "if you would stand aside, please."

Justine quickly, silently, moved out from between us.

I focused on Mag and said, "They are under my protection."

Mag gave me a contemptuous look and raised the staff. Darkness lashed at me, as if he had simply reached into the floorboards and cracks in the wall and drawn it into a sizzling sphere the size of a bowling ball.

It flickered away to nothingness about a foot in front of my steepled hands.

I lifted a finger and Hendricks shot Mag in the back. Repeatedly.

The Fomor went down with a sound like a bubbling teakettle, whipped onto his back as if the bullets had been a minor inconvenience, and raised the stick to point at Hendricks.

Gard's axe smashed it out of his grip, swooped back up to guard, and began to descend again.

"Stop," I said.

Gard's muscles froze just before she would have brought down the axe onto Mag's head. Mag had one hand uplifted, surrounded in a kind of negative haze, his long fingers crooked at odd angles—presumably some kind of mystic defense.

"As a freeholding lord of the Unseelie Accords," I said, "it would be considered an act of war if I killed you out of hand, despite your militant intrusion into my territory." I narrowed my eyes. "However, your behavior gives me ample latitude to invoke the defense-of-property-and-self clause. I will leave the decision to you. Continue this asinine behavior, and I will kill you and offer a weregild to your lord, King Corb, in accordance with the conflict resolution guidelines of section two, paragraph four."

As I told you, my lawyers send me endless letters. I speak their language.

Mag seemed to take that in for a moment. He looked at me, then Gard. His eyes narrowed. They tracked back to Hendricks, his head hardly moving, and he seemed to freeze when he saw the sword in Hendricks's hand.

His eyes flicked to Justine and the child and burned for a moment—not with adoration or even simple lust. There was a pure and possessive hunger there, coupled with a need to destroy that which he desired. I have spent my entire life around hard men. I know that form of madness when I see it.

"So," Mag said. His eyes traveled back to me and were suddenly heavy-lidded and calculating. "You are the new mortal lord. We half believed that you must be imaginary. That no one could be as foolish as that."

"You are incorrect," I said. "Moreover, you can't have them. Get out."

Mag stood up. The movement was slow, liquid. His limbs didn't seem to bend the proper way. "Lord Marcone," he said, "this affair is no concern of yours. I only wish to take the slaves."

"You can't have them. Get out."

"I warn you," Mag said. There was an ugly tone in his voice. "If you make me return for her—for them—you will not enjoy what follows."

"I do not require enjoyment to thrive. Leave my domain. I won't ask again."

Hendricks shuffled his feet a little, setting his balance.

Mag gathered himself up slowly. He extended his hand, and the twisted stick leapt from the floor and into his fingers. He gave Gard a slow and well-practiced sneer and said, "Anon, mortal lordling. It is time you learned the truth of the world. It will please me to be your instructor." Then he turned, slow and haughty, and walked out, his shoulders hunching in an odd, unsettling motion as he moved.

"Make sure he leaves," I said quietly.

Gard and Hendricks followed Mag from the room.

I turned my eyes to Justine and the child.

"Mag," I said, "is not the sort of man who is used to disappointment."

Justine looked after the vanished Fomor and then back at me, confusion in her eyes. "That was sorcery. How did you . . . ?"

I stood up from behind my desk and stepped out of the copper circle set into the floor around my chair. It was powered by the sorcerous equivalent of a nine-volt battery, connected to the control on the underside of my desk. Basic magical defense, Gard said. It had seemed like nonsense to me. It clearly was not.

I took my gun from its holster and set it on my desk.

Justine took note of my reply.

Of course, I wouldn't give the personal aide of the most dangerous woman in Chicago information about my magical defenses.

There was something hard and not at all submissive in her eyes. "Thank you, sir, for . . ."

"For what?" I said very calmly. "You understand, do you not, what you have done by asking for my help under the Accords?"

"Sir?"

"The Accords govern relations between supernatural powers," I said. "The signatories of the Accords and their named vassals are granted certain rights and obligations—such as offering a warning to a signatory who has trespassed upon another's territory unwittingly before killing him."

"I know, sir," Justine said.

"Then you should also know that you are most definitely not a signatory of the Accords. At best, you qualify in the category of servitors and chattel. At worst, you are considered to be a food animal."

She drew in a sharp breath, her eyes widening—not in any sense of outrage or offense, but in realization. Good. She grasped the realities of the situation.

"In either case," I continued, "you are property. You have no rights in the current situation, in the eyes of the Accords—and, more to the point, I have no right to withhold another's rightful property. Mag's behavior provided me with an excuse to kill him if he did not depart. He will not give me such an opening a second time."

Justine swallowed and stared at me for a moment. Then she glanced down at the child in her arms. The child clung harder to her and seemed to lean somewhat away from me.

One must admire such acute instincts.

"You have drawn me into a conflict that has nothing to do with me," I said quietly. "I suggest candor. Otherwise, I will have Mr. Hendricks and Ms. Gard show you to the door."

"You can't . . . ," she began, but her voice trailed off.

"I can," I said. "I am not a humanitarian. When I offer charity it is for tax purposes."

The room became silent. I was content with that. The child began to whimper quietly.

"I was delivering documents to the court of King Corb on behalf of my lady," Justine said. She stroked the child's hair absently. "It's in the sea. There's a gate there in Lake Michigan, not far from here."

I lifted an eyebrow. "You swam?"

"I was under the protection of their courier, going there," Justine said. "It's like walking in a bubble of air." She hitched the child up a little higher on her hip. "Mag saw me. He drove the courier away as I was leaving and took me to his home. There were many other prisoners there."

"Including the child," I guessed. Though it probably didn't sound that way.

Justine nodded. "I . . . arranged for several prisoners to flee Mag's home. I took the child when I left. I swam out."

"So you are, in effect, stolen property in possession of stolen property," I said. "Novel."

Gard and Hendricks came back into the office.

I looked at Hendricks. "My people?"

"Tulane's got a broken arm," he said. "Standing in that asshole's way. He's on his way to the doc."

"Thank you. Ms. Gard?"

"Mag is off the property," she said. "He didn't go far. He's summoning support now."

"How much of a threat is he?" I asked. The question was legitimate. Gard and Hendricks had blindsided the inhuman while he was focused on Justine and the child and while he wasted his leading magical strike against my protective circle. A head-on confrontation against a prepared foe could be a totally different proposition.

Gard tested the edge of her axe with her thumb and drew a smooth stone from her pocket. "Mag is a Fomor sorcerer lord of the first rank. He's deadly—and connected. The Fomor could crush you without a serious loss of resources. Confrontation would be unwise."

The stone made a steely, slithery sound as it glided over the axe's blade.

"There seems little profit to be had, then," I said. "It's nothing personal, Justine. Merely business. I am obliged to return stolen property to signatory members of the Accords."

Hendricks looked at me sharply. He didn't say anything. He didn't have to. I already knew the tone of whatever he would say. *Are there no prisons?* perhaps. Or, *No man is an island, entire of itself. It tolls for thee.* On and on.

Hendricks has no head for business.

Gard watched me, waiting.

"Sir," Justine said, her tone measured and oddly formal. "May I speak?"

I nodded.

"She isn't property," Justine said, and her voice was low and intense, her eyes direct. "She was trapped in a den of living nightmares, and there was no one to come save her. She would have died there. And I am *not* letting anyone take her back to that hellhole. I will die first." The young woman set her jaw. "She is not *property*, Mr. Marcone. She's a *child*."

I met Justine's eyes for a long moment.

I glanced aside at Hendricks. He waited for my decision.

Gard watched me. As ever, Gard watched me.

I looked down at my hands, my fingertips resting together with my elbows propped on the desk.

Business came first. Always.

But I have rules.

I looked up at Justine.

"She's a child," I said quietly.

The air in the room snapped tight with tension.

"Ms. Gard," I said, "please dismiss the contractors for the day, at pay. Then raise the defenses."

She pocketed the whetstone and strode quickly out, her teeth showing, a bounce in her step.

"Mr. Hendricks, please scramble our troubleshooters. They're to take positions across the street. Suppressed weapons only. I don't need patrolmen stumbling around in this. Then ready the panic room."

Hendricks nodded and got out his cell phone as he left. His huge, stubby fingers flew over its touchscreen as he sent the activation text message. Looking at him, one would not think him capable of such a thing. But that is Hendricks, generally.

I looked at Justine as I rose and walked to my closet. "You will go with the child into the panic room. It is, with the possible exception of Dresden's home, the most secure location in the city."

"Thank you," she said quietly.

I took off my coat and hung it up in the closet. I took off my tie and slipped it over the same hanger. I put my cuff links in my coat pocket, rolled up my sleeves, and skinned out of my gun's holster. Then I slipped on the armored vest made of heavy scales of composite materials joined to sleeves of quite old-fashioned mail. I pulled an old field jacket, olive drab, over the armor, belted it, holstered my sidearm at my side, opposite a combat knife, and took a military-grade assault shotgun—a weapon every bit as illegal as my pistol in the city of Chicago—from its rack.

"I am not doing it for you, young lady," I said. "Nor am I doing it for the child."

"Then why are you doing it?" she asked.

"Because I have rules," I said.

She shook her head gently. "But you're a criminal. Criminals don't have rules. They break them."

I stopped and looked at her.

Justine blanched and slid a step farther away from me, along the wall. The child made a soft, distressed sound. I beckoned curtly for her to follow me as I walked past her. It took her a moment to do so.

*Honestly.*

Someone in the service of a vampire ought to have a bit more fortitude.

This panic room looked like every other one I've had built: fluorescent lights, plain tile floor, plain drywall. Two double bunks occupied one end of the room. A business desk and several chairs took up the rest. A miniature kitchen nestled into one corner, opposite the miniature medical station in another. There was a door to a half bath and a bank of security monitors on the wall between them. I flicked one switch that activated the entire bank, displaying a dozen views from hidden security cameras.

I gestured for Justine to enter the room. She came in and immediately took a seat on the lower bunk of the nearest bed, still holding the child.

"Mag can find her," Gard told me when we all rendezvoused outside the panic room. "Once he's inside the building and gets past the forward area, he'll be able to track her. He'll head straight for her."

"Then we know which way he'll be moving," I said. "What did you find out about his support?"

"They're creatures," Gard said, "actual mortal beings, though like none you've seen before. The Fomor twist flesh to their liking and sell the results for favors and influence. It was probably the Fomor who created those cat things the Knights of the Blackened Denarius used."

I twisted my mouth in displeasure at the name. "If they're mortal, we can kill them."

"They'll die hard," Gard warned me.

"What doesn't?" I looked up and down the hallway outside the panic room. "I think the primary defense plan will do."

Gard nodded. She had attired herself in an armored vest, not unlike my own, over a long mail shirt. Medieval-looking, but then, modern armorers haven't aimed their craft at stopping claws of late. Hendricks, standing watch at the end of the hall, had on an armored vest but was otherwise covered in modified motorcyclist's armor. He carried an assault shotgun like mine, several hand grenades, and that same broadsword.

"Stay here," I said to Justine. "Watch the door. If anyone but one of us comes down the stairs, shut it."

She nodded.

I turned and started walking toward the stairway. I glanced at Gard. "What can we expect from Mag?"

"Pain."

Hendricks grunted. Skeptically.

"He's ancient, devious, and wicked," Gard clarified. "There is an effectively unlimited spectrum of ways in which he might do harm."

I nodded. "Can you offer any specific knowledge?"

"He won't be easy to get to," she said. "The Fomor practice entropy magic. They make the antitechnology effect Dresden puts off look like mild sunspot activity. Modern systems *are* going to experience problems near him."

We started up the stairs. "How long before he arrives?"

From upstairs, there was the crash of breaking plate glass. No alarm went off, but there was a buzzing, sizzling sound and a scream—Gard's outer defenses. Hendricks hit a button on his cell phone and then came with me as I rushed up the remaining stairs to the ground floor.

The lights went out as we went, and Hendricks's phone sputtered out a few sparks. Battery-powered emergency lights flicked on an instant later. Only about half of them functioned, and most of those were behind us.

Mag had waited for nightfall to begin his attack and then crippled our lights. Quite possibly he assumed that the darkness would give him an overwhelming advantage.

The hubris of some members of the supernatural community is astonishing.

The night-vision scopes mounted on my weapon and Hendricks's had been custom-made, based off of designs dating back to World War II, before night-vision devices had married themselves to the electronics revolution. They were heavy and far inferior to modern systems—but they would function in situations where electronic goggles would be rendered into useless junk.

We raised the weapons to our shoulders, lined an eye up with the scopes, and kept moving. We reached the first defensive position, folded out the reinforced composite barriers mounted there, and knelt behind them. The ambient light from the city outside and the emergency lights below us was enough for the scopes to do their jobs. I could make out the outline of the hallway and the room beyond. Sounds of quiet movement came closer.

My heart rate had gone up, but not alarmingly so. My hands were steady. My mouth felt dry, and my body's reaction to the prospect of mortal danger sent ripples of sensation up and down my spine. I embraced the fear and waited.

The Fomor's creatures exploded into the hallway on a storm of roars. I couldn't make out many details. They seemed to have been put together on the chassis of a gorilla. Their heads were squashed, ugly-looking things, with wide-gaping mouths full of sharklike teeth. The sounds they made were deep, with a frenzied edge of madness, and they piled into the corridor in a wave of massive muscle.

"Steady," I murmured.

The creatures lurched as they moved, like cheap toys that had not been assembled properly, but they were fast for all of that. More and more of them flooded into the hallway, and their charge was gaining momentum.

"Steady," I murmured.

Hendricks grunted. There were no words in it, but he meant *I know.*

The wave of Fomorian beings got close enough that I could see the patches of mold clumping their fur and tendrils and of mildew growing upon their exposed skin.

"Fire," I said.

Hendricks and I opened up.

The new military AA-12 automatic shotguns are not the hunting weapons I first handled in my patriotically delusional youth. They are fully automatic weapons with large circular drums that rather resembled the old tommy guns made iconic by my business predecessors in Chicago. One pulls the trigger and shell after shell slams through the weapon. A steel target hit by bursts from an AA-12 rapidly comes to resemble a screen door.

And we had two of them.

The slaughter was indescribable. It swept like a great broom down that hallway, tearing and shredding flesh, splattering blood on the walls, and painting them most of the way to the ceiling. Behind me, Gard stood ready with a heavy-caliber big-game rifle, calmly gunning down any creature that seemed to be reluctant to die before it could reach our defensive point. We piled the bodies so deep that the corpses formed a barrier to our weapons.

"Hendricks," I said.

The big man was already reaching for the grenades on his belt. He took one, pulled the pin, cooked it for a slow two count, and then flung it down the hall. We all crouched behind the barriers as the grenade went off with a deafening crunch of shock wave–driven air.

Hendricks threw another one. He might disapprove of killing, but he did it thoroughly.

When the ringing began to fade from my ears, I heard a sound like raindrops. It wasn't raining, of course; the gunmen in the building across the street had opened fire with silenced weaponry. Bullets whispered in through the windows and hit the floor and walls of the headquarters with innocuous-sounding thumps. Evidently Mag's servitors had been routed and were trying to flee.

An object the size of Hendricks's fist appeared from nowhere and arced cleanly through the air. It landed on the floor precisely between the two sheltering panels, a lump of pink-and-grey coral.

Gard hit me with a shoulder and drove me to the ground even as she shouted, "Down!"

The piece of coral didn't explode. There was a whispering sound, and hundreds of tiny holes appeared in the bloodstained walls and ceiling. Gard let out a pained grunt. My left calf jerked as something pierced it and burned as though the wound had been filled with salt.

I checked Hendricks. One side of his face was covered in a sheet of blood. Small tears were visible in his leathers, and he was beginning to bleed through the holes.

"Get him," I said to Gard, rising, as another coral spheroid rose into the air.

Before it could get close enough to be a threat, I blew it to powder with my shotgun. And the next and the next, while Gard dropped her rifle, got a shoulder under one of Hendricks's, and helped him to his feet as if he'd been her weight instead of two hundred and seventy pounds of muscle. She started down the stairs.

A fourth sphere came accompanied by mocking laughter, and when I pulled the trigger again, the weapon didn't function. Empty. I slapped the coral device out of the air with the shotgun's barrel and flung myself backward, hoping to clear the level of the floor on the stairwell before the pseudo-grenade detonated. I did not quite make it. Several objects struck my chest and arms, and a hot blade slipped across my unscarred ear, but the armor turned the truly dangerous projectiles.

I broke my arm tumbling backward down the stairs.

More laughter followed me down, but at least the Fomor wasn't spouting some kind of ridiculous monologue.

"I did my best," came Mag's voice. "I gave you a chance to return what was mine. But no. You couldn't keep yourself from interfering in my affairs, from stealing my property. And so now you will reap the consequences of your foolishness, little mortal. . . ."

There was more, but there is hardly a need to go into details. Given a choice between that egocentric drivel and a broken arm, I prefer the latter. It's considerably less excruciating.

Gard hauled me to my feet by my coat with her spare hand. I got under the stunned Hendricks's other arm and helped them both down the rest of the stairs. Justine stood in the doorway of the safe room, at the end of the hallway of flickering lights, her face white-lipped but calm.

Gard helped me get Hendricks to the door of the room and turned around. "Close the door. I may be able to discourage him out here."

"Your home office would be annoyed with me if I wasted your life on such a low-percentage proposition," I said. "We stick to the plan."

The Valkyrie eyed me. "Your arm is broken."

"I was aware, thank you," I said. "Is there any reason the counter-measure shouldn't work?"

Mag was going on about something, coming down the steps one at a time, making a production out of every footfall. I ignored the ass.

"None that I know of," Gard admitted. "Which is not the same answer as 'no.'"

"Sir," Justine said.

"We planned for this—or something very like it. We don't split up now. End of discussion. Help me with Hendricks."

"*Sir*," Justine said.

I looked up to see Mag standing on the landing, cloaked in random shadows, smiling. The emergency lights on the stairwell blew out with a melodramatic shower of dying sparks.

"Ah," I said. I reached inside the safe-room door, found the purely mechanical pull-cord wrapped unobtrusively around a nail head on the wall, and gave it a sharp jerk.

It set off the antipersonnel mines built into the wall of the landing.

There were four of them, which meant that a wash of fire and just under three-thousand-round shot acquainted themselves with the im-mediate vicinity of the landing and with Mag. A cloud of flame and flying steel enveloped the Fomor, but at the last minute the swirling blackness around him rose like a living thing, forming a shield be-tween Mag and the oncoming flood of destruction.

The sound of the explosions was so loud that it demolished my hearing for a moment. It began to return to me as the cloud of smoke and dust on the landing started to clear. I could hear a fire alarm going off.

Mag, smudged and blackened with residue but otherwise un-touched, made an irritated gesture, and the fire alarm sparked and fizzled—but not before setting off the automatic sprinklers. Water began pouring down from spigots in the ceiling.

Mag looked up at the water and then down at me, and his too-wide smile widened even more. "Really?" he asked. "Water? Did you actually think water would be a barrier to the magic of a Fomor lord?"

Running water was highly detrimental to mortal magic, or so Gard informed me, whether it was naturally occurring or not. The important element was quantity. Enough water would ground magic just as it could conduct electricity and short-circuit electronics. Evidently Mag played by different rules.

Mag made a point to continue down the stairs at exactly the same pace. He was somewhat hampered in that several of the stairs had been torn up rather badly in the explosion, but he made it to the hallway. Gard took up a position in the middle of the hallway, her axe held straight up beside her in both arms like a baseball player's bat.

I helped Hendricks into the safe room and dumped him on a bunk, out of any line of fire from the hallway. Justine took one look at his face and hurried over to the medical station, where she grabbed a first-aid kit. She rushed back to Hendricks's side. She broke open the kit and started laying out the proper gear for getting a clear look at a bloody wound and stopping the bleeding. Her hands flew with precise speed. She'd had some form of training.

From the opposite bunk, the child watched Justine with wide blue eyes. She was naked and had been crying. The tears were still on her little cheeks. Even now, her lower lip had begun to tremble.

But so far as anyone else knew, I was made of stone.

I turned and crossed the room. I sat down at the desk, a copy of the one in my main office. I put my handgun squarely in front of me. The desk was positioned directly in line with the door to the panic room. From behind the desk, I could see the entire hallway clearly.

Mag stepped forward and moved a hand as though throwing something. I saw nothing, but Gard raised her axe in a blocking movement, and there was a flash of light, and the image of a Norse rune, or something like it, was burned onto my retina. The outer edge of Gard's mail sleeve on her right arm abruptly turned black and fell to dust, so that the sleeve split and dangled open.

Gard took a grim step back as Mag narrowed his jaundiced eyes and lifted the crooked stick. Something that looked like the blend of a lightning bolt and an eel lashed through the air toward Gard, but she caught it on the broad blade of her axe, and there was another flash of light, another eye-searing rune. I heard her cry out, though, and saw that the edges of her fingernails had been burned black.

Step by step she fell back, while Mag hammered at her with things that made no sense, many of which I could not even see. Each time, the rune magic of that axe defeated the attack—and each time, it seemed to cost her something. A lightly singed face here. A long, shallow cut on her newly bared arm there. And the runes, I saw, were each in different places on the axe, being burned out one by one. Gard had a finite number of them.

As Gard's heels touched the threshold of the safe room, Mag let out a howl and threw both hands out ahead of him. An unseen force lifted Gard from her feet and flung her violently across the room, over my desk, and into the wall. She hit with bone-crushing force and slid down limply.

I faced the inhuman sorcerer alone.

Mag walked slowly and confidently into my safe room and stared at me across my desk. He was breathing heavily, from exertion or excitement or both. He smiled slowly and waved his hand again. An unpleasant shimmer went through the air, and I glanced down to see rust forming on the exposed metal of my gun, while cracking began to spread through the plastic grip.

"Go ahead, mortal," Mag said, drawing out the words. "Pick up the gun. Try it. The crafting of the weapon is fine, mortal, but you are not the masters of the world that you believe yourselves to be. Even today's cleverest smiths are no match for the magic of the Fomor."

I inclined my head in agreement. "Then I suppose," I said, "that we'll just have to do this old-school."

I drew the eighteenth-century German dragoon pistol from the open drawer beside my left hand, aimed, and fired. The ancient flint-lock snapped forward, ignited the powder in the pan, and roared, a wash of unnatural blue-white fire blazing forth from the antique weapon. I almost fancied that I could see the bullet, spinning and tumbling, blazing with its own tiny rune.

Though Mag's shadows leapt up to defend him, he had expended enormous energy moving through the building, hurling attack after attack at us. More energy had to be used to overcome the tremendous force of the claymores that had exploded virtually in his face. Perhaps, at his full strength, at the height of his endurance, his powers would have been enough to turn even the single, potent attack that had been designed to defeat them.

From the beginning, the plan had been to wear him down.

The blue bolt of lead and power from the heavy old flintlock pierced Mag's defenses and body in the same instant and with the same contemptuous energy.

Mag blinked at me, then lowered his head to goggle at the smoking hole in his chest as wide as my thumb. His mouth moved as he tried to gabble something, but no sound came out.

"Idiot," I said coldly. "It will be well worth the weregild to be rid of you."

Mag lurched toward me for a moment, intent on saying something, but the fates spared me from having to endure any more of him. He collapsed to the floor before he could finish speaking.

I eyed my modern pistol, crusted with rust and residue, and decided not to try it. I kept a spare .45 in the downstairs desk in any case. I took it from another drawer, awkwardly checked it one-handed, and then emptied the weapon into Mag's head and chest.

I am the one who taught Hendricks to be thorough.

I looked up from Mag's ruined form to find Justine staring at me, frozen in the middle of wrapping a bandage around my second's head.

"How is he?" I asked calmly.

Justine swallowed. She said, "He m-may need stitches for this scalp wound. I think he has a concussion. The other wounds aren't bad. His armor stopped most of the fragments from going in."

"Gard?" I asked without looking over my shoulder. The Valkyrie had an incredible ability to resist and recover from injury.

"Be sore for a while," she said, the words slurred. "Give me a few minutes."

"Justine, perhaps you will set my arm and splint it," I said. "We will need to abandon this renovation, I'm afraid, Gard. Where's the thermite?"

"In your upstairs office closet, right where you left it," she said in a *very* slightly aggrieved tone.

"Be a dear and burn down the building," I said.

She appeared beside my desk, looking bruised, exhausted, and functional. She lifted both eyebrows. "Was that a joke?"

"Apparently," I said. "Doubtless the result of triumph and adrenaline."

"My word," she said. She looked startled.

"Get moving," I told her. "Make the fire look accidental. I need to contact the young lady's patron so that she can be delivered safely back into her hands. Call Dr. Schulman as well. Tell him that Mr. Hendricks and I will be visiting him shortly." I pursed my lips. "And steak, I think. I could use a good steak. The Pump Room should do for the three of us, eh? Ask them to stay open an extra half an hour."

Gard showed me her teeth in a flash. "Well," she said, "it's no mead hall. But it will do."

I put my house in order. In the end, it took less than half an hour. The troubleshooters made sure the Fomorian creatures were dragged inside, then vanished. Mag's body had been bagged and transferred, to be returned to his watery kin, along with approximately a quarter of a million dollars in bullion, the price required in the Accords for the weregild of a person of Mag's stature.

Justine was ready to meet a car that was coming to pick her up, and Hendricks was already on the way to Schulman's attentions. He'd seemed fine by the time he left, growling at Gard as she fussed over him.

I looked around the office and nodded. "We know the defense plan has some merit," I said. I hefted the dragoon pistol. "I'll need more of those bullets."

"I was unconscious for three weeks after scribing the rune for that one," Gard replied. "To say nothing of the fact that the bullets themselves are rare. That one killed a man named Nelson at Trafalgar."

"How do you know?"

"I took it out of him," she said. "Men of his caliber are few and far between. I'll see what I can do." She glanced at Justine. "Sir?"

"Not just yet," I said. "I will speak with her alone for a moment, please."

She nodded, giving Justine a look that was equal parts curiosity and warning. Then she departed.

I got up and walked over to the girl. She was holding the child against her again. The little girl had dropped into an exhausted sleep.

"So," I said quietly. "Lara Raith sent you to Mag's people. He happened to abduct you. You happened to escape from him—despite the fact that he seemed to be holding other prisoners perfectly adequately—and you left carrying the child. And, upon emerging from Lake Michigan, you happened to be nearby, so you came straight here."

"Yes," Justine said quietly.

"Coincidences, coincidences," I said. "Put the child down."

Her eyes widened in alarm.

I stared at her until she obeyed.

My right arm was splinted and in a sling. With my left hand, I reached out and flipped open her suit jacket, over her left hip, where she'd been clutching the child all evening.

There was an envelope in a plastic bag protruding from the jacket's interior pocket. I took it.

She made a small sound of protest and aborted it partway.

I opened the bag and the envelope and scanned over the paper inside.

"These are account numbers," I said quietly. "Security passwords. Stolen from Mag's home, I suppose?"

She stared at me with very wide eyes.

"Dear child," I said, "I *am* a criminal. One very good way to cover up one crime is to commit another, more obvious one." I glanced down at the sleeping child again. "Using a child to cover your part of the scheme. Quite cold-blooded, Justine."

"I freed all of Mag's prisoners to cover up the theft of his records at my lady's bidding," she said quietly. "The child was . . . not part of the plan."

"Children frequently aren't," I said.

"I took her out on my own," she said. "She's free of that place. She will stay that way."

"To be raised among the vampires?" I asked. "Such a lovely child will surely go far."

Justine grimaced and looked away. "She was too small to swim out on her own. I couldn't leave her."

I stared at the young woman for a long moment. Then I said, "You might consider speaking to Father Forthill at St. Mary of the Angels. The Church appears to have some sort of program to place those endangered by the supernatural into hiding. I do not recommend you mention my name as a reference, but perhaps he could be convinced to help the child."

She blinked at me, several times. Then she said quietly, "You, sir, are not very much like I thought you were."

"Nor are you, Agent Justine." I took a deep breath and regarded the child again. "At least we accomplished something today." I smiled at Justine. "Your ride should be here by now. You may go."

She opened her mouth and reached for the envelope.

I slipped it into my pocket. "Do give Lara my regards. And tell her that the next time she sends you out to steal honey, she should find someone else to kill the bees." I gave her a faint smile. "That will be all."

Justine looked at me. Then her lips quivered up into a tiny, amused smile. She bowed her head to me, collected the child, and walked out, her steps light.

I debated putting a bullet in her head but decided against it. She had information about my defenses that could leave them vulnerable—and, more to the point, she knew that they were effective. If she should speak of today's events to Dresden . . .

Well. The wizard would immediately recognize that the claymores, the running water, and the magic-defense-piercing bullet had not been put into place to counter Mag or his odd folk at all.

They were there to kill Harry Dresden.

And they worked. Mag had proven that. An eventual confrontation with Dresden was inevitable—but murdering Justine would guarantee it happened immediately, and I wasn't ready for that, not until I had rebuilt the defenses in the new location.

Besides, the young woman had rules of her own. I could respect that.

I would test myself against Dresden in earnest one day—or he against me. Until then, I had to gather as many resources to myself as possible. And when the day of reckoning came, I had to make sure it happened in a place where, despite his powers, he would no longer have the upper hand.

Like everything else.

Location, location, location.

# BIGFOOT ON CAMPUS

This is the last of the trio of Bigfoot stories, and is set between *Turn Coat* and *Changes*. In this one, I got to play with the collision of a couple of different scions of supernatural beings, and to get a look at how that collision would play out against the background of the world of the Dresden Files.

This is also where Harry manages to insert himself into what he perceives as a parenting problem on behalf of River Shoulders, and in a quite arrogant, self-righteously wizardly fashion to boot. Naturally, his taking this position would come back to haunt him later, when he would have to face similar problems, and find out that the whole parenting gig is a lot harder than it looks from the outside.

It was also a chance for me to revisit, if mostly in memory, the campus of the University of Oklahoma and the town of Norman, where a number of excellent and nerdy friends I made in school live to this day.

The campus police officer folded his hands and stared at me from across the table. "Coffee?"

"What flavor is it?" I asked.

He was in his forties, a big, solid man with bags under his calm, wary eyes, and his name tag read DEAN. "It's coffee-flavored coffee."

"No mocha?"

"Fuck mocha."

"Thank God," I said. "Black."

Officer Dean gave me hot black coffee in a paper cup, and I sipped it gratefully. I was almost done shivering. It just came in intermittent bursts now. The old wool blanket Dean had given me was more gesture than cure.

"Am I under arrest?" I asked him.

Officer Dean moved his shoulders in what could have been a shrug. "That's what we're going to talk about."

"Uh-huh," I said.

"Maybe," he said in a slow, rural drawl, "you could explain to me why I found you in the middle of an orgy."

"Well," I said, "if you're going to be in an orgy, the middle is the best spot, isn't it?"

He made a thoughtful sound. "Maybe you could explain why there was a car on the fourth floor of the dorm."

"Classic college prank," I said.

He grunted. "Usually when that happens, it hasn't made big holes in the exterior wall."

"Someone was avoiding the cliché?" I asked.

He looked at me for a moment, and said, "What about all the blood?"

"There were no injuries, were there?"

"No," he said.

"Then who cares? Some film student probably watched *Carrie* too many times."

Officer Dean tapped his pencil's eraser on the tabletop. It was the most agitated thing I'd seen him do. "Six separate calls in the past three hours with a Bigfoot sighting on campus. Bigfoot. What do you know about that?"

"Well, kids these days, with their Internets and their video games and their iPods. Who knows what they thought they saw."

Officer Dean put down his pencil. He looked at me and said calmly, "My job is to protect a bunch of kids with access to every means of self-destruction known to man from not only the criminal element but also from themselves. I got chemistry students who can make their own meth, Ecstasy, and LSD. I got ROTC kids with access to automatic weapons and explosives. I got enough alcohol going through here on a weekly basis to float a battleship. I got a thriving trade in recreational drugs. I got lives to protect."

"Sounds tiring."

"About to get tired of you," he said. "Start giving it to me straight."

"Or you'll arrest me?" I asked.

"No," Dean said. "I bounce your face off my knuckles for a while. Then I ask again."

"Isn't that unprofessional conduct?"

"Fuck conduct," Dean said. "I got kids to look after."

I sipped the coffee some more. Now that the shivers had begun to subside, I finally felt the knotted muscles in my belly begin to relax. I slowly settled back into my chair. Dean hadn't blustered or tried to intimidate me in any way. He wasn't trying to scare me into talking. He was just telling me how it was going to be. And he drank his coffee old-school.

I kinda liked the guy.

"You aren't going to believe me," I said.

"I don't much," he said. "Try me."

"Okay," I said. "My name is Harry Dresden. I'm a professional wizard."

Officer Dean pursed his lips. Then he leaned forward slightly and listened.

The client wanted me to meet him at a site in the Ouachita Mountains in eastern Oklahoma. Looking at them, you might not realize they were mountains, they're so old. They've had millions of years of wear and tear on them, and they've been ground down to nubs. The site used to be on an Indian reservation, but they don't call them reservations anymore. They're Tribal Statistical Areas now.

I showed my letter and my ID to a guy in a pickup, who just happened to pull up next to me for a friendly chat at a lonely stop sign on a winding back road. I don't know what the tribe called his office, but I recognized a guardian when I saw one. He read the letter and waved me through in an even friendlier manner than he had used when he approached me. It's nice to be welcomed somewhere once in a while.

I parked at the spot indicated on the map and hiked a good mile and a half into the hills, taking a heavy backpack with me. I found a pleasant spot to set up camp. The mid-October weather was crisp, but I had a good sleeping bag and would be comfortable as long as it didn't start raining. I dug a fire pit and ringed it in stones, built a modest fire out of fallen limbs, and laid out my sleeping bag on a foam camp pad. By the time it got dark, I was well into preparing the dinner I'd brought with me. The scent of foil-wrapped potatoes baking in coals blended with that of the steaks I had spitted and roasting over the fire.

Can I cook a camp meal or what?

Bigfoot showed up half an hour after sunset.

One minute, I was alone. The next, he simply stepped out into view. He was huge. Not huge like a big person, but huge like a horse, with that same sense of raw animal power and mass. He was nine feet tall at least and probably tipped the scales at well over six hundred pounds. His powerful, wide-shouldered body was covered in long, dark brown hair. Even though he stood in plain sight in my firelight, I could barely see the buckskin bag he had slung over one shoulder and across his chest, the hair was so long.

"Strength of a River in His Shoulders," I said. "You're welcome at my fire."

"Wizard Dresden," River Shoulders rumbled. "It is good to see you." He took a couple of long steps and hunkered down opposite the fire from me. "Man. That smells good."

"Darn right, it does," I said. I proceeded with the preparations in companionable silence while River Shoulders stared thoughtfully at the fire. I'd set up my camp this way for a reason: It made me the host and River Shoulders my guest. It meant I was obliged to provide food and drink, and he was obliged to behave with decorum. Guest-and-host relationships are damned near laws of physics in the supernatural world: They almost never get violated, and when they do, it's a big deal. Both of us felt a lot more comfortable around each other this way.

Okay. Maybe it did a wee bit more to make me feel comfortable than it did River Shoulders, but he was a repeat customer, I liked him, and I figured he probably didn't get treated to a decent steak all that often.

We ate the meal in an almost ritualistic silence, too, other than River making some appreciative noises as he chewed. I popped open a couple of bottles of McAnally's Pale, my favorite brew by a veritable genius of hops back in Chicago. River liked it so much that he gave me an inquisitive glance when his bottle was empty. So I emptied mine and produced two more.

After that, I filled a pipe with expensive tobacco, lit it, took a few puffs, and passed it to him. He nodded and took it. We smoked and finished our beers. By then the fire had died down to glowing embers.

"Thank you for coming," River Shoulders rumbled. "Again, I come to seek your help on behalf of my son."

"Third time you've come to me," I said.

"Yes." He rummaged in his pouch and produced a small, heavy object. He flicked it to me. I caught it and squinted at it in the dim light. It was a gold nugget about as big as a Ping-Pong ball. I nodded and tossed it back to him. River Shoulders's brows lowered into a frown.

You have to understand. A frown on a mug like his looked indistinguishable from scowling fury. It turned his eyes into shadowed caves with nothing but a faint gleam showing from far back in them. It made his jaw muscles bunch and swell into knots the size of tennis balls on the sides of his face.

"You will not help him," the Bigfoot said.

I snorted. "You're the one who isn't helping him, big guy."

"I am," he said. "I am hiring you."

"You're his father," I said quietly. "And he doesn't even know your name. He's a good kid. He deserves more than that. He deserves the truth."

He shook his head slowly. "Look at me. Would he even accept my help?"

"You aren't going to know unless you try it," I said. "And I never said I wouldn't help him."

At that, River Shoulders frowned a little more.

I curbed an instinct to edge away from him.

"Then what do you want in exchange for your services?" he asked.

"I help the kid," I said. "You meet the kid. That's the payment. That's the deal."

"You do not know what you are asking," he said.

"With respect, River Shoulders, this is not a negotiation. If you want my help, I just told you how to get it."

He became very still at that. I got the impression that maybe people didn't often use tactics like that when they dealt with him.

When he spoke, his voice was a quiet, distant rumble. "You have no right to ask this."

"Yeah, um. I'm a wizard. I meddle. It's what we do."

"Manifestly true." He turned his head slightly away. "You do not know how much you ask."

"I know that kid deserves more than you've given him."

"I have seen to his protection. To his education. That is what fathers do."

"Sure," I said. "But you weren't ever there. And that matters."

Absolute silence fell for a couple of minutes.

"Look," I said gently. "Take it from a guy who knows. Growing up without a dad is terrifying. You're the only father he's ever going to have. You can go hire Superman to look out for Irwin if you want to, and he'd still be the wrong guy—because he isn't you."

River toyed with the empty bottle, rolling it across his enormous fingers like a regular guy might have done with a pencil.

"Do you want me on this?" I asked him. "No hard feelings if you don't."

River looked up at me again and nodded slowly. "I know that if you agree to help him, you will do so. I will pay your price."

"Okay," I said. "Tell me about Irwin's problem."


"WHAT'D HE SAY?" Officer Dean asked.

"He said the kid was at the University of Oklahoma for school," I said. "River'd had a bad dream and knew that the kid's life was in danger."

The cop grunted. "So . . . Bigfoot is a psychic?"

"Think about it. No one ever gets a good picture of one, much less a clean shot," I said. "Despite all the expeditions and TV shows and whatnot. River's people have got more going for them than being huge and strong. My guess is that they're smarter than humans. Maybe a lot smarter. My guess is they know magic of some kind, too."

"Jesus," Officer Dean said. "You really believe all this, don't you?"

"I want to believe," I said. "And I told you that you wouldn't."

Dean grunted. Then he said, "Usually they're too drunk to make sense when I get a story like this. Keep going."

I GOT TO Norman, Oklahoma, a bit before noon the next morning. It was a Wednesday, which was a blessing. In the Midwest, if you show up to a college town on a weekend, you risk running into a football game. In my experience, that resulted in universal problems with traffic, available hotel rooms, and drunken football hooligans.

Or wait: Soccer is the one with hooligans. Drunken American football fans are just . . . drunks, I guess.

River had provided me with a small dossier he'd had prepared, which included a copy of his kid's class schedule. I parked my car in an open spot on the street not too far from campus and ambled on over. I got some looks; I sort of stand out in a crowd. I'm a lot closer to seven feet tall than six, which might be one reason why River Shoulders liked to hire me—I look a lot less tiny than other humans to him. Add in the big black leather duster and the scar on my face, and I looked like the kind of guy you'd want to avoid in dark alleys.

The university campus was as confusing as all of them are, with buildings that had constantly evolved into and out of multiple roles over the years. They were all named after people I doubt any of the students had ever heard of or cared about, and there seemed to be no organizational logic at all at work there. It was a pretty enough campus, I supposed. Lots of redbrick and brownstone buildings. Lots of architectural doohickeys on many of the buildings, in a kind of quasiclassical Greek style. The ivy that was growing up many of the walls seemed a little too cultivated and obvious for my taste. Then again, I had exactly the same amount of regard for the Ivy League as I did for the Big 12. The grass was an odd color, like maybe someone had sprayed it with a blue-green dye or something, though I had no idea what kind of delusional creep would do something so pointless.

And, of course, there were students—a whole lot of kids, all of them with things to do and places to be. I could have wandered around all day, but I thought I'd save myself the headache of attempting to apply logic to a university campus and stopped a few times to ask for directions. Irwin Pounder, River Shoulders's son, had a physics course at noon, so I picked up a notebook and a couple of pens at the university bookstore and ambled on into the large classroom. It was a perfect disguise. The notebook was college ruled.

I sat near the back, where I could see both doors into the room, and waited. Bigfoot Irwin was going to stand out in the crowd almost as badly as I did. The kid was huge. River had shown me a photo he kept in his medicine bag, carefully laminated to protect it from the elements. Irwin's mom could have been a second-string linebacker for the Bears. Helena Pounder was a formidable woman, and over six feet tall. But her boy was a head taller than she already, and still had the awkward, too-lean look of someone who wasn't finished growing. His shoulders had come in, though, and it looked like he might have had to turn sideways to walk through doors.

I waited and waited, watching both doors, until the professor arrived and the class started. Irwin never arrived. I was going to leave, but it actually turned out to be kind of interesting. The professor was a lunatic but a really entertaining one. The guy drank liquid nitrogen, right there in front of everybody, and blew it out his nose in this huge jet of vapor. I applauded along with everyone else, and before I knew it, the lecture was over. I might even have learned something.

Okay.

Maybe there were some redeeming qualities to a college education.

I went to Irwin's next class, which was a freshman biology course, in another huge classroom.

No Irwin.

He wasn't at his four o'clock math class, either, and I emerged from it bored and cranky. None of Irwin's other teachers held a candle to Dr. Indestructo.

*Huh.*

Time for plan B.

River's dossier said that Irwin was playing football for OU. He'd made the team as a walk-on, and River had been as proud as any father would be about the athletic prowess of his son. So I ambled on over to the Sooners' practice field, where the team was warming up with a run.

Even among the football players, Irwin stood out. He was half a head taller than any of them, at least my own height. He looked gangly and thin beside the fellows around him, even with the shoulder pads on, but I recognized his face. I'd last seen him when he was about fourteen. Though his rather homely features had changed a bit, they seemed stronger and more defined. There was no mistaking his dark, intelligent eyes.

I stuck my hands in the pockets of my old leather duster and waited, watching the field. I'd found the kid, and, absent any particular danger, I was in no particular hurry. There was no sense in charging into the middle of Irwin's football practice and his life and disrupting everything. I'm just not that kind of guy.

Okay, well.

I try not to be.

"Seems to keep happening, though, doesn't it," I said to myself. "You show up on somebody's radar, and things go to DEFCON 1 a few minutes later."

"I'm sorry?" said a young woman's voice.

"AH," SAID OFFICER Dean. "This is where the girl comes in."

"Who said there was a girl?"

"There's always a girl."

"Well," I said, "yes and no."

SHE WAS BLOND, about five foot six, and my logical mind told me that every inch of her was a bad idea. The rest of me, especially my hindbrain, suggested that she would be an ideal mate. Preferably sooner rather than later.

There was nothing in particular about her that should have caused my hormones to rage. I mean, she was young and fit, and she had the body of the young and fit, and that's hardly ever unpleasant to look at. She had eyes the color of cornflowers and rosy cheeks, and she was a couple of notches above cute, when it came to her face. She was wearing running shorts, and her legs were smooth and generally excellent.

Some women just have it. And no, I can't tell you what *it* means because I don't get it myself. It was something mindless, something chemical, and even as my metaphorically burned fingers were telling me to walk away, the rest of me was going through that male physiological response the science guys in the Netherlands have documented recently.

Not that one.

Well, maybe a little.

I'm talking about the response where when a pretty girl is around, it hits the male brain like a drug and temporarily impairs his cognitive function, literally dropping the male IQ.

And, hey, how Freudian is it that the study was conducted in the Netherlands?

This girl dropped that IQ nuke on my brain, and I was standing there staring a second later while she smiled uncertainly at me.

"Um, sorry?" I asked. "My mind was in the Netherlands."

Her dimple deepened, and her eyes sparkled. She knew all about the brain nuke. "I just said that you sounded like a dangerous guy." She winked at me. It was adorable. "I like those."

"You're, uh. You're into bad boys, eh?"

"Maybe," she said, lowering her voice and drawing the word out a little, as if it was a confession. She spoke with a very faint drawl. "Plus, I like meeting new people from all kinds of places, and you don't exactly strike me as a local, darlin'."

"You dig dangerous guys who are just passing through," I said. "Do you ever watch those cop shows on TV?"

She tilted back her head and laughed. "Most boys don't give me lip like that in the first few minutes of conversation."

"I'm not a boy," I said.

She gave me a once-over with those pretty eyes, taking a heartbeat longer about it than she really needed. "No," she said. "No, you are not."

My inner nonmoron kept on stubbornly ringing alarm bells, and the rest of me slowly became aware of them. My glands thought that I'd better keep playing along. It was the only way to find out what the girl might have been interested in, right? Right. I was absolutely not continuing the conversation because I had gone soft in the head.

"I hope that's not a problem," I said.

"I just don't see how it could be. I'm Connie."

"Harry."

"So what brings you to Norman, Harry?"

"Taking a look at a player," I said.

Her eyes brightened. "Oooooh. You're a scout?"

"Maybe," I said, in the same tone she'd used earlier.

Connie laughed again. "I'll bet you talk to silly college girls like me all the time."

"Like you?" I replied. "No, not so much."

Her eyes sparkled again. "You may have found my weakness. I'm the kind of girl who likes a little flattery."

"And here I was thinking you liked something completely different."

She covered her mouth with one hand, and her cheeks got a little pinker. "Harry. That's not how one talks to young ladies in the South."

"Obviously. I mean, you look so outraged. Should I apologize?"

"Oh," she said, her smile widening. "I just have to collect you." Connie's eyes sparkled again, and I finally got it.

Her eyes weren't twinkling.

They were becoming increasingly flecked with motes of molten silver.

Cutie-pie was a frigging vampire.

I've worked for years on my poker face. Years. It still sucks pretty bad, but I've been working on it. So I'm sure my smile was only slightly wooden when I asked, "Collect me?"

I might not have been hiding my realization very well, but either Connie was better at poker than me or else she really was too absorbed in the conversation to notice. "Collect you," she said. "When I meet someone worthwhile, I like to have dinner with them. And we'll talk and tell stories and laugh, and I'll get a picture and put it in my memory book."

"Um," I said. "Maybe you're a little young for me."

She threw back her head and gave a full-throated laugh. "Oh, Harry. I'm talking about sharing a meal. That's all, honestly. I know I'm a terrible flirt, but I didn't think you were taking me seriously."

I watched her closely as she spoke, searching for the predatory calculation that I knew had to be in there. Vampires of the White Court—

"WAIT," DEAN SAID. "Vampires of the White Castle?"

I sighed. "White Court."

Dean grunted. "Why not just call her a vampire?"

"They come in a lot of flavors," I said.

"And this one was vanilla?"

"There's no such thing as . . ." I rubbed at the bridge of my nose. "Yes."

Dean nodded. "So why not just call 'em vanilla vampires?"

"I'll . . . bring it up at the next wizard meeting," I said.

"So the vampire is where all the blood came from?"

"No." I sighed. "This kind doesn't feed on blood."

"No? What do they eat, then?"

"Life energy."

"Huh?"

I sighed again. "Sex."

"Finally, the story gets good. So they eat sex?"

"Life energy," I repeated. "The sex is just how they get started."

"Like sticking fangs into your neck," Dean said. "Only instead of fangs, I guess they use—"

"Look, do you want the story or not?"

Dean leaned back in his chair and propped his feet up on his desk. "You kidding? This is the best one in years."

ANYWAY, I WATCHED Connie closely, but I saw no evidence of anything in her that I knew had to be there. Vampires are predators who hunt the most dangerous game on the planet. They generally aren't shy about it, either. They don't really need to be. If a White Court vampire wants to feed off a human, all she really has to do is crook her finger, and he comes running. There isn't any ominous music. Nobody sparkles. As far as anyone looking on is concerned, a girl winks at a boy and goes off somewhere to make out. Happens every day.

They don't get all coy asking you out to dinner, and they sure as hell don't have pictures in a memory book.

This was weird, and long experience has taught me that when the unexplained is bouncing around right in front of you, the smart thing is to back off and figure out what the hell is going on. In my line of work, what you don't know can kill you.

But I didn't get the chance. There was a sharp whistle from a coach somewhere on the field, and football players came rumbling off it. One of them came loping toward us, put a hand on top of the six-foot chain-link fence, and vaulted it in one easy motion. Bigfoot Irwin landed lightly, grinning, and continued directly toward Connie.

She let out a girlish squeal of delight and pounced on him. He caught her. She wrapped her legs around his hips, held his face in her hands, and kissed him thoroughly. They came up for air a moment later.

"Irwin," she said, "I met someone interesting. Can I collect him?"

The kid only had eyes for Connie. Not that I could blame him, really. His voice was a basso rumble, startlingly like River Shoulders's. "I'm always in favor of dinner at the Brewery."

She dismounted and beamed at him. "Good. Irwin, this is . . ."

The kid finally looked up at me and blinked. "Harry."

"Heya, Irwin," I said. "How're things?"

Connie looked back and forth between us. "You know each other?"

"He's a friend," Irwin said.

"Dinner," Connie declared. "Harry, say you'll share a meal with me."

Interesting choice of words, all things considered.

I think I had an idea what had caused River's bad dream. If a vampire had attached herself to Irwin, the kid was in trouble. Given the addictive nature of Connie's attentions, and the degree of control it could give her over Irwin . . . maybe he wasn't the only one who could be in trouble.

My, how little Irwin had grown. I wondered exactly how much of his father's supernatural strength he had inherited. He looked like he could break me in half without causing a blip in his heart rate. He and Connie looked at me with hopeful smiles, and I suddenly felt like maybe I was the crazy one. Expressions like that should not inspire worry, but every instinct I had told me that something wasn't right.

My smile probably got even more wooden. "Sure," I said. "Why not?"

THE BREWERY WAS a lot like every other sports bar you'd find in college towns, with the possible exception that it actually was a brewery. Small and medium-sized tanks stood here and there throughout the place, with signs on each describing the kind of beer that was under way. Apparently, the beer sampler was traditional. I made polite noises when I tried each, but they were unexceptional. Okay, granted, I was probably spoiled by having Mac's brew available back at home. It wasn't the Brewery's fault that their brews were merely excellent. Mac's stuff was epic, it was legend. Tough to measure up to that.

I kept one hand under the table, near a number of tools I thought

I might need, all the way through the meal, and waited for the other shoe to drop—only it never did. Connie and Irwin chattered away like any young couple, snuggled up to one another on adjacent chairs. The girl was charming, funny, and a playful flirt, but Irwin didn't seem discomfited by it. I kept my responses restrained, anyway. I didn't want to find out a couple of seconds too late that the seemingly innocent banter was how Connie got her psychic hooks into me.

But a couple of hours went by, and nothing.

"Irwin's never told me anything about his father," Connie said.

"I don't know much," Irwin said. "He's . . . kept his distance over the years. I've looked for him a couple of times, but I never wanted to push him."

"How mysterious," Connie said.

I nodded. "For someone like him, I think the word *eccentric* might apply better."

"He's rich?" Connie asked.

"I feel comfortable saying that money isn't one of his concerns," I said.

"I knew it!" Connie said, and looked slyly at Irwin. "There had to be a reason. I'm only into you for your money."

Instead of answering, Irwin calmly picked Connie up out of her chair, using just the muscles of his shoulders and arms, and deposited her on his lap. "Sure you are."

Connie made a little groaning sound and bit her lower lip. "God. I know it's not PC, but I've got to say, I am into it when you get all caveman on me, Pounder."

"I know." Irwin kissed the tip of her nose and turned to me. "So, Harry. What brings you to Norman?"

"I was passing through," I said easily. "Your dad asked me to look in on you."

"Just casually," Irwin said, his dark eyes probing. "Because he's such a casual guy."

"Something like that," I said.

"Not that I mind seeing you," Irwin said, "but in case you missed it, I'm all grown-up now. I don't need a babysitter. Even a cool, expensive one."

"If you did, my rates are very reasonable," Connie said.

"We'll talk," Irwin replied, sliding his arms around her waist. The girl wasn't exactly a junior petite, but she looked tiny on Irwin's scale. She hopped up and said, "I'm going to go make sure there isn't barbecue sauce on my nose, and then we can take the picture. Okay?"

"Sure," Irwin said, smiling. "Go."

Once she was gone from sight, Irwin looked at me and dropped his smile. "Okay," he said resignedly. "What does he want this time?"

There wasn't a load of time, so I didn't get all coy with the subject matter. "He's worried about you. He thinks you may be in danger."

Irwin arched his eyebrows. "From what?"

I just looked at him.

His expression suddenly turned into a scowl, and the air around us grew absolutely thick with energy that seethed for a point of discharge. "Wait. This is about Connie?"

I couldn't answer him for a second, the air felt so close. The last time I'd felt this much latent, waiting power, I'd been standing next to my old mentor, Ebenezar McCoy, when he was gathering his strength for a spell.

That pretty much answered my questions about River Shoulders's people having access to magical power. The kid was a freaking dynamo of it. I had to be careful. I didn't want to be the guy who was unlucky enough to ground out that storm cloud of waiting power. So I answered Irwin cautiously and calmly.

"I'm not sure yet. But I know for a fact that she's not exactly what she seems to be."

His nostrils flared, and I saw him make an effort to remain collected. His voice was fairly even. "Meaning what?"

"Meaning I'm not sure yet," I said.

"So, what? You're going to hang around here, butting into my life?"

I held up both hands. "It isn't like that."

"It's just like that," Irwin said. "My dad spends my whole life any-where else but here, and now he thinks he can just decide when to intrude on it?"

"Irwin," I said, "I'm not here to try to make you do anything. He asked me to look in on you. I promised I would. And that's all."

He scowled for a moment, then smoothed that expression away. "No sense in being mad at the messenger, I guess," he said. "What do you mean about Connie?"

"She's . . ." I faltered there. You don't just sit down with a guy and tell him, "Hey, your girlfriend is a vampire. Could you pass the ketchup?" I sighed. "Look, Irwin. Everybody sees the world a certain way. And we all kind of . . . Well, we all sort of decide together what's real and what isn't real, right?"

"Magic's real," Irwin said impatiently. "Monsters are real. Super-natural stuff actually exists. You're a professional wizard."

I blinked at him several times.

"What?" he asked, and smiled gently. "Don't let the brow ridge fool you. I'm not an idiot, man. You think you can walk into my life the way you have, twice, and not leave me with an itch to scratch? You made me ask questions. I went and got answers."

"Uh. How?" I asked.

"Wasn't hard. There's an Internet. And this organization called the Paranet, of all the cockamamie things, that got started a few years ago. Took me, like, ten minutes to find it online and start reading through their message boards. I can't believe everyone in the world doesn't see this stuff. It's not like anyone is trying very hard to keep it secret."

"People don't want to know the truth," I said. "That makes it sim-ple to hide. Wow, ten minutes? Really? I guess I'm not really an Inter-netty person."

"Internetty," Irwin said, seriously. "I guess you aren't."

I waved a hand. "Irwin, you need to know this. Connie isn't—"

The pretty vampire plopped herself back down into Irwin's lap and kissed his cheek. "Isn't what?"

"The kind to stray," I said, smoothly. "I was just telling Irwin how much I'd like to steal you away from him, but I figure you're the sort who doesn't play that kind of game."

"True enough," she agreed cheerfully. "I know where I want to sleep tonight." Maybe it was unconscious, the way she wriggled when she said it, but Irwin's eyes got a slightly glazed look to them.

I remembered being that age. A girl like Connie would have been a mind-numbing distraction to me back then even if she hadn't been a vampire. And Irwin was clearly in love, or as close to it as he could manage through the haze of hormones surrounding him. Reasoning with him wasn't going to accomplish anything—unless I made him angry. Passion is a huge force when you're Irwin's age, and I'd taken enough beatings for one lifetime. I'd never be able to explain the danger to him. He just didn't have a frame of reference. . . .

He just didn't know.

I stared at Connie for a second with my mouth open.

"What?" she asked.

"You don't know," I said.

"Know what?" she asked.

"You don't know that you're . . ." I shook my head and said to Irwin, "She doesn't know."

"HANG ON," DEAN said. "Why is that significant?"

"Vampires are just like people until the first time they feed," I said. "Connie didn't know that bad things would happen when she did."

"What kinda bad things?"

"The first time they feed, they don't really know it's coming. They have no control over it, no restraint—and whoever they feed on dies as a result."

"So she was the threat that Bigfoot dreamed about?"

"I'm getting to it."

IRWIN'S EXPRESSION HAD darkened again, into a glower almost exactly like River Shoulders's, and he stood up.

Connie was frowning at me as she was abruptly displaced. "Don't know wh— Oof, Pounder!"

"We're done," Irwin said to me. His voice wasn't exactly threatening, but it was absolutely certain, and his leashed anger all but made the air crackle. "Nice to see you again, Harry. Tell my dad to call. Or write. Or do anything but try to tell me how to live my life."

Connie blinked at him. "Wait . . . Wait, what's wrong?"

Irwin left a few twenties on the table and said, "We're going."

"What? What happened?"

"We're going," Irwin said. This time he did sound a little angry.

Connie's bewilderment suddenly shifted into some flavor of outrage. She narrowed her lovely eyes, and snapped, "I am not your pet, Pounder."

"I'm not trying to . . ." Irwin took a slow, deep breath, and said more calmly, "I'm upset. I need some space. I'll explain when I calm down. But we need to go."

She folded her arms and said, "Go calm down, then. But I'm not going to be rude to our guest."

Irwin looked at me, and said, "We going to have a problem?"

Wow. The kid had learned a lot about the world since the last time I'd seen him. He recognized that I wasn't a playful puppy dog. He realized that if I'd been sent to protect him, and I thought Connie was a threat, that I might do something about it. And he'd just told me that if I did, he was going to object. Strenuously. No protests, no threats, just letting me know that he knew the score and was willing to do something about it if I made him. The guys who are seriously capable handle themselves like that.

"No problem," I said, and made it a promise. "If I think something needs to be done, we'll talk first."

The set of his shoulders eased, and he nodded at me. Then he turned and stalked out. Warily, people watched him go.

Connie shook her head slowly and asked, "What did you say?"

"Um," I said. "I think he feels like his dad is intruding on his life."

"You don't say." She shook her head. "That's not your fault. He's usually so collected. Why is he acting like such a jerk?"

"Issues," I said, shrugging. "Everyone has a parental issue or two."

"Still. It's beneath him to behave that way." She shook her head. "Sometimes he makes me want to slap him. But I'd need to get a chair to stand on."

"I don't take it personally," I assured her. "Don't worry."

"It was about me," she said quietly. "Wasn't it? It's about something I don't know."

"Um," I said.

It was just possible that maybe I'd made a bad call when I decided to meddle between River and his kid. It wasn't my place to shake the pillars of Irwin's life. Or Connie's, for that matter. It was going to be hard enough on her to find out about her supernatural heritage. She didn't need to have the news broken to her by a stranger, on top of that. You'd think that, after years as a professional, I'd know enough to just take River's money, help out his kid, and call it a night.

"Maybe we should walk?" I suggested.

"Sure."

We left and started walking the streets of downtown Norman. The place was alive and growing, like a lot of college towns: plenty of old buildings, some railroad tracks, lots of cracks in the asphalt and the sidewalks. The shops and restaurants had that improvised look that a business district gets when it outlives its original intended purpose and subsequent generations of enterprise take over the space.

We walked in silence for several moments, until Connie finally said, "He's not an angry person. He's usually so calm. But when something finally gets to him . . ."

"It's hard for him," I said. "He's huge and he's very strong and he knows it. If he loses control of himself, someone could get hurt. He doesn't like the thought of that. So when he starts feeling angry, it makes him tense. Afraid. He's more upset about the fact that he feels so angry than about anything I said or did."

Connie looked up at me pensively for a long moment. Then she said, "Most people wouldn't realize that."

I shrugged.

"What don't I know?" she asked.

I shook my head. "I'm not sure it's my place to tell you."

"But it's about me."

"Yeah."

She smiled faintly. "Then shouldn't I be the one who gets to decide?"

I thought about that one for a moment. "Connie . . . you're mostly right. But some things, once said, can't be unsaid. Let me think about it."

She didn't answer.

The silence made me uncomfortable. I tried to chat my way clear of it. "How'd you meet Irwin?"

The question, or maybe the subject matter, seemed to relax her a little. "In a closet at a party. Someone spiked the punch. Neither of us had ever been drunk before, and . . ." She blushed. "And he's just so damned sexy."

"Lot of people wouldn't think so," I noted.

She waved a hand. "He's not pretty. I know that. It's not about that. There's . . . this energy in him. It's chemical. Assurance. Power. Not just muscles—it's who he is." Her cheeks turned a little pink. "It wasn't exactly love at first sight, I guess. But once the hangover cleared up, that happened, too."

"So you love him?" I asked.

Her smile widened, and her eyes shone the way a young woman's eyes ought to shine. She spoke with calm, simple certainty. "He's the one."

About twenty things to say leapt to my mind. I was going to say something about how she was too young to make that kind of decision.

I thought about how she hadn't been out on her own for very long, and how she had no idea where her relationship with Irwin was going to lead. I was going to tell her that only time could tell her if she and Irwin were good for one another and ready to be together, to make that kind of decision. I could have said something about how she needed to stop and think, not make blanket statements about her emotions and the future.

That was when I realized that everything I would have said was something I would have said to a young woman in love—not to a vampire. Not only that, but I heard something in her voice or saw something in her face that told me that my aged wisdom was, at least in this case, dead wrong. My instincts were telling me something that my rational brain had missed.

The kids had something real. I mean, maybe it hadn't gotten off on the most pure and virtuous foot, but that wasn't anything lethal in a relationship. The way they related to each other now? There was a connection there. You could imagine saying their names as a unit, and it fit: ConnieandIrwin. Maybe they had some growing to do, but what they had was real.

Not that it mattered. Being in love didn't change the facts. First, that Connie was a vampire. Second, that vampires had to feed. Third, they fed upon their lovers.

"HOLD ON," DEAN said. "You missed something."

"Eh?"

"Girl's a vampire, right?"

"Yeah."

"So," Dean said. "She met the kid in a closet at a party. They already got it on. She done had her first time."

I frowned. "Yeah."

"So how come Kid Bigfoot wasn't dead?"

I nodded. "Exactly. It bothered me, too."

———

THE GIRL WAS in love with Irwin, and it meant she was dangerous to him. Hell, she was dangerous to almost everyone. She wasn't even entirely human. How could I possibly spring something that big on her?

At the same time, how could I not?

"I should have taken the gold," I muttered to myself.

"What?" she asked.

That was when the town car pulled up to the curb a few feet ahead of us. Two men got out of the front seat. They wore expensive suits and had thick necks. One of them hadn't had his suit fitted properly—I could see the slight bulge of a sidearm in a shoulder holster. That one stood on the sidewalk and stared at me, his hands clasped in front of him. The driver went around to the rear passenger's door and opened it.

"Oh," Connie said. "Marvelous. This is all I need."

"Who is that?" I asked.

"My father."

The man who got out of the back of the limo wore a pearl grey suit that made his thugs' outfits look like secondhand clothing. He was slim, a bit over six feet tall, and his haircut probably cost him more than I made in a week. His hair was dark, with a single swath of silver at each temple, and his skin was weathered and deeply tanned. He wore rings on most of his manicured fingers, all of them sporting large stones.

"Hi, Daddy," Connie said, smiling. She sounded pleasant enough, but she'd turned herself very slightly away from the man as she spoke. A rule of thumb for reading body language is that almost no one can totally hide physical reflections of their state of mind. They can only minimize the signs of it in their posture and movements. If you mentally exaggerate and magnify their body language, it tells you something about what they're thinking.

Connie clearly didn't want to talk to this man. She was ready to flee from her own father should it become necessary. It told me something about the guy. I was almost sure I wasn't going to like him.

He approached the girl, smiling, and after a microhesitation, they exchanged a brief hug. It didn't look like something they'd practiced much.

"Connie," the man said, smiling. He had the same mild drawl his daughter did. He tilted his head to one side and regarded her thoughtfully. "You went blond. It's . . . charming."

"Thank you, Daddy," Connie said. She was smiling, too. Neither one of them looked sincere to me. "I didn't know you were in town. If you'd called, we could have made an evening of it."

"Spur-of-the-moment thing," he said easily. "I hope you don't mind."

"No, of course not."

Both of them were lying. *Parental issues, indeed.*

"How's that boy you've taken up with? Irving."

"Irwin," Connie said in a poisonously pleasant tone. "He's great. Maybe even better than that."

He frowned at that, and said, "I see. But he's not here?"

"He had homework tonight," Connie lied.

That drew a small, sly smile out of the man. "I see. Who's your friend?" he asked pleasantly, without actually looking at me.

"Oh," Connie said. "Harry, this is my father, Charles Barrowill. Daddy, this is Harry Dresden."

"Hi," I said brightly.

Barrowill's eyes narrowed to sudden slits, and he took a short, hard breath as he looked at me. He then flicked his eyes left and right around him, as if looking for a good place to dive or maybe a hostage to seize.

"What a pleasure, Mr. Dresden," he said, his voice suddenly tight. "What brings you out to Oklahoma?"

"I heard it was a nice place for perambulating," I said. Behind Barrowill, his guards had picked up on the tension. Both of them had become very still. Barrowill was quiet for a moment, as if trying to parse some kind of meaning from my words. Heavy seconds ticked by, like the quiet before a shootout in an old Western.

A tumbleweed went rolling by in the street. I'm not even kidding. An actual, literal tumbleweed. Man, Oklahoma.

Then Barrowill took a slow breath and said to Connie, "Darling, I'd like to speak to you for a few moments, if you have time."

"Actually . . ." Connie began.

"Now, please," Barrowill said. There was something ugly under the surface of his pleasant tone. "The car. I'll give you a ride back to the dorms."

Connie folded her arms and scowled. "I'm entertaining someone from out of town, Daddy. I can't just leave him here."

One of the guards' hands twitched.

"Don't be difficult, Connie," Barrowill said. "I don't want to make a scene."

His eyes never left me as he spoke, and I got his message loud and clear. He was taking the girl with him, and he was willing to make things get messy if I tried to stop him.

"It's okay, Connie," I said. "I've been to Norman before. I can find my way to a hotel easily enough."

"You're sure?" Connie asked.

"Definitely."

"Herman," Barrowill said.

The driver opened the passenger door again and stood next to it attentively. He kept his eyes on me, and one hand dangled, clearly ready to go for his gun.

Connie looked back and forth between me and her father for a moment, then sighed audibly and walked over to the car. She slid in, and Herman closed the door behind her.

"I recognize you," I said pleasantly to Barrowill. "You were at the Raith Deeps when Skavis and Malvora tried to pull off their coup. Front row, all the way on one end in the Raith cheering section."

"You have an excellent memory," Barrowill said.

"Got out in one piece, did you?"

The vampire smiled without humor. "What are you doing with my daughter?"

"Taking a walk," I said. "Talking."

"You have nothing to say to her. In the interests of peace between the Court and the Council, I'm willing to ignore this intrusion into my territory. Go in peace. Right now."

"You never told her, did you?" I asked. "Never told her what she was."

One of his jaw muscles twitched. "It is not our way."

"Nah," I said. "You wait until the first time they get twitterpated, experiment with sex, and kill whoever it is they're with. Little harsh on the kids, isn't it?"

"Connie is not some mortal cow. She is a vampire. The initiation builds character she will need to survive and prosper."

"If it was good enough for you, it's good enough for her?"

"Mortal," Barrowill said, "you simply cannot understand. I am her father. It is my obligation to prepare her for her life. The initiation is something she needs."

I lifted my eyebrows. "Holy . . . That's what happened, isn't it? You sent her off to school to boink some poor kid to death. Hell, I'd bet you had the punch spiked at that party. Except the kid didn't die—so now you're in town to figure out what the hell went wrong."

Barrowill's eyes darkened, and he shook his head. "This is no business of yours. Leave."

"See, that's the thing," I said. "It is my business. My client is worried about his kid."

Barrowill narrowed his eyes again. "Irving."

"Irwin," I corrected him.

"Go back to Chicago, wizard," he said. "You're in my territory now."

"This isn't a smart move for you," I said. "The kid's connected. If anything bad happens to him, you're in for trouble."

"Is that a threat?" he asked.

I shook my head. "Chuck, I've got no objection to working things out peaceably. And I've got no objection to doing it the other way. If you know my reputation, then you know what a sincere guy I am."

"Perhaps I should kill you now."

"Here, in public?" I asked. "All these witnesses? You aren't going to do that."

"No?"

"No. Even if you win, you lose. You're just hoping to scare me off." I nodded toward his goons. "Ghouls, right? It's going to take more than two, Chuck. Hell, I like fighting ghouls. No matter what I do to them, I never feel bad about it afterward."

Barrowill missed the reference, like the monsters usually do. He looked at me, then at his Rolex. "I'll give you until midnight to leave the state. After that, you're gone. One way or another."

"Hang on," I said, "I'm terrified. Let me catch my breath."

Barrowill's eyes shifted color slightly, from a deep green to a much paler, angrier shade of green-gold. "I react poorly to those who threaten my family's well-being, Dresden."

"Yeah. You're a regular Ozzie Nelson. John Walton. Ben Cartwright."

"Excuse me?"

"Mr. Drummond? Charles . . . in Charge? No?"

"What are you blabbering about?"

"Hell's bells, man. Don't any of you White Court bozos ever watch television? I'm giving you pop-reference gold here. Gold."

Barrowill stared at me with opaque, reptilian eyes. Then he said simply, "Midnight." He took two steps back before he turned his back on me and got into his car. His goons both gave me hard looks before they, too, got into the car and pulled away.

I watched the car roll out. Despite the attitude I'd given Barrowill, I knew better than to take him lightly. Any vampire is a dangerous foe—and one of them with holdings and resources and his own personal brute squad was more so. Not only that, but . . . from his point of view, I was messing around with his little girl's best interests. The vampires of the White Court were, to a degree, as dangerous as they were because they were partly human. They had human emotions, human motivations, human reactions. Barrowill could be as irrationally protective of his family as anyone else.

Except that they were also inhuman. All of those human drives were intertwined with a parasitic spirit they called a Hunger, where all the power and hunger of their vampire parts came from.

Take one part human faults and insecurities and add it to one part inhuman power and motivation. What do you get?

Trouble.

"BARROWILL?" OFFICER DEAN asked me. "The oil guy? He keeps a stable. Of congressmen."

"Yeah, probably the same guy," I said. "All vampires like having money and status. It makes their lives easier."

Dean snorted. "Every vampire. And every nonvampire."

"Heh," I said. "Point."

"You were in a fix," he said. "Tell the girl, you might wreck her. Don't tell her, and you might wreck her and Kid Bigfoot both. Either way, somebody's dad has a bone to pick with you."

"Pretty much."

"Seems to me a smart guy would have washed his hands of the whole mess and left town."

I shrugged. "Yeah. But I was the only guy there."

FOREST ISN'T EXACTLY the dominant terrain in Norman, but there are a few trees here and there. The point where I'd agreed to meet with River Shoulders was in the center of the Oliver Wildlife Preserve, which was a stand of woods that had been donated to the university for research purposes. As I hiked out into the little wood, it occurred to me that meeting River Shoulders there was like rendezvousing with

Jaws in a kiddie wading pool. But he'd picked the spot, so whatever floated the big guy's boat.

It was dark out, and I drew my silver pentacle amulet off my neck to use for light. A whisper of will and a muttered word, and the little symbol glowed with a dim blue light that would let me walk without bumping into a tree. It took me maybe five minutes to get to approximately the right area, and River Shoulders's soft murmur of greeting came to me out of the dark.

We sat down together on a fallen tree, and I told him what I'd learned.

He sat in silence for maybe two minutes after I finished. Then he said, "My son has joined himself to a parasite."

I felt a flash of mild outrage. "You could think of it that way," I said.

"What other way is there?"

"That he's joined himself to a girl. The parasite just came along for the ride."

River Shoulders exhaled a huge breath. It sounded like those pneumatic machines they use to elevate cars at the repair shop. "I see. In your view, the girl is not dangerous. She is innocent."

"She's both," I said. "She can't help being born what she is, any more than you or I."

River Shoulders grunted.

"Have your people encountered the White Court before?"

He grunted again.

"Because the last time I helped Irwin out, I remember being struck by the power of his aura when he was only fourteen. A long-term draining spell that should have killed him only left him sleepy." I eyed him. "But I don't feel anything around you. Stands to reason your aura would be an order of magnitude greater than your kid's. That's why you've been careful never to touch me. You're keeping your power hidden from me, aren't you?"

"Maybe."

I snorted. "Just the kind of answer I'd expect from a wizard."

"It is not something we care for outsiders to know," he said. "And we are not wizards. We see things differently than mortals. You people are dangerous."

"Heh," I said, and glanced up at his massive form beside mine. "Between the two of us, I'm the dangerous one."

"Like a child waving around his father's gun," River Shoulders said. Something in his voice became gentler. "Though some of you are better than others about it, I admit."

"My point is," I said, "the kid's got a life force like few I've seen. When Connie's Hunger awakened, she fed on him without any kind of restraint, and he wound up with nothing worse than a hangover. Could be that he could handle a life with her just fine."

River Shoulders nodded slowly. His expression might have been thoughtful. It was too dark, and his features too blunt and chiseled to be sure.

"The girl seems genuinely fond of him. And he of her. I mean, I'm not an expert in these things, but they seem to like each other, and even when they have a difference of opinions, they fight fair. That's a good sign." I squinted at him. "Do you really think he's in danger?"

"Yes," River Shoulders said. "They have to kill him now."

I blinked. "What?"

"This . . . creature. This Barrowill."

"Yeah?"

"It sent its child to this place with the intention that she meet a young man and feed upon him and unknowingly kill him."

"Yeah."

River Shoulders shook his huge head sadly. "What kind of monster does that to its children?"

"Vampires," I said. "It isn't uncommon, from what I hear."

"Because they hurt," River Shoulders said. "Barrowill remembers his own first lover. He remembers being with her. He remembers her death. And his wendigo has had its hand on his heart ever since. It shaped his life."

"Wendigo?"

River Shoulders waved a hand. "General term. Spirit of Hunger. Can't ever be sated."

"Ah, gotcha."

"Now, Barrowill. He had his father tell him that this was how it had to be. That it had to be that way to make him a good vampire. So this thing that turned him into a murdering monster is actually a good thing. He spends his whole life trying to convince himself of that." River nodded slowly. "What happens when his child does something differently?"

I felt like a moron. "It means that what his father told him was a lie. It means that maybe he didn't have to be like he is. It means that he's been lying to himself. About everything."

River Shoulders spread his hands, palms up, as if presenting the fact. "That kind of father has to make his children in his own image. He has to make the lie true."

"He has to make sure Connie kills Irwin," I said. "We've got to get him out of there. Maybe both of them."

"How?" River Shoulders said. "She doesn't know. He only knows a little. Neither knows enough to be wise enough to run."

"They shouldn't have to run," I growled.

"Avoiding a fight is always better than not avoiding one."

"Disagree," I said. "Some fights should be sought out. And fought. And won."

River Shoulders shook his head. "Your father's gun." I sensed a deep current of resistance in River Shoulders on this subject—one that I would never be able to bridge, I suspected. River just wasn't a fighter. "Would you agree it was wisest if they both fled?"

"In this case . . . it might, yeah. But I think it would only delay the confrontation. Guys like Barrowill have long arms. If he obsesses over it, he'll find them sooner or later."

"I have no right to take his child from him," River Shoulders said. "I am only interested in Irwin."

"Well, I'm not going to be able to separate them," I said. "Irwin nearly started swinging at me when I went anywhere close to that subject." I paused, then added, "But he might listen to you."

River Shoulders shook his head. "He's right. I got no right to walk in and smash his life to splinters after being so far away so long. He'd never listen to me. He's got a lot of anger in him. Maybe for good reasons."

"You're his father," I said. "That might carry more weight than you think."

"I should not have involved you in this," he said. "I apologize for that, wizard. You should go. Let me sort this out on my own."

I eyed River Shoulders.

The big guy was powerful, sure, but he was also slow. He took his time making decisions. He played things out with enormous patience. He was clearly ambivalent over what kind of involvement he should have with his son. It might take him months of observation and cogitation to make a choice.

Most of us don't live that way. I was sure Barrowill didn't. If the vampire was moving, he might be moving now. Like, right now.

"In this particular instance, River Shoulders, you are not thinking clearly," I said. "Action must be taken soon. Preferably tonight."

"I will be what I am," River said firmly.

I stood up from the log and nodded. "Okay," I said. "Me, too."

I PUT IN a call to my fellow Warden "Wild Bill" Meyers in Dallas, but got an answering service. I left a message that I was in Norman and needed his help, but I had little faith that he'd show up in time. The real downside to being a wizard is that we void the warrantees of anything technological every time we sneeze. Cell phones are worse than useless in our hands, and it makes communications a challenge at times, though that was far from the only possible obstacle. If Bill was in, he'd have picked up his phone. He had a big area for his beat and likely had problems of his own—but since Dallas was only three hours away (assuming his car didn't break down), I could hold out hope that he might roll in by morning.

So, I got in my busted-up old Volkswagen, picked up a prop, and drove up to the campus alone. I parked somewhere where I would probably get a ticket. I planned to ignore it. Anarchists have a much easier time finding parking spots.

I got out and walked toward one of the smaller dorm buildings on campus. I didn't have my wizard's staff with me, on account of how weird it looked to walk around with one, but my blasting rod was hanging from its tie inside my leather duster. I doubted I would need it, but better to have it and not need it than the other way around. I got my prop and trudged across a short bit of turquoise-tinted grass to the honors dorms, where Irwin lived. They were tiny, for that campus, maybe five stories, with the building laid out in four right-angled halls, like a plus sign. The door was locked. There's always that kind of security in a dorm building these days.

I rapped on the glass with my knuckles until a passing student noticed. I held up a cardboard box from the local Pizza 'Spress, and tried to look like I needed a break. I needn't have tried so hard. The kid's eyes were bloodshot and glassy. He was baked on something. He opened the door for me without blinking.

"Thanks."

"No problem," he said.

"He was supposed to meet me at the doors," I said. "You see a guy named, uh . . ." I checked the receipt that was taped to the box. "Irwin Pounder?"

"Pounder, hah," the kid said. "He'll be in his room. Fourth floor, south hall, third door on the left. Just listen for the noise."

"Music?"

He tittered. "Not exactly."

I thanked him and ambled up the stairs, which were getting to be a lot harder on my knees than they used to be. Maybe I needed orthopedic shoes or something.

I got to the second floor before I felt it. There was a tension in the air, something that made my heart speed up and my skin feel hot. A few steps farther, and I started breathing faster and louder. It wasn't until I got to the third floor that I remembered that the most dangerous aspect of a psychic assault is that the victim almost never realizes that it's actually happening.

I stopped and threw my mental defenses up in a sudden panic, and the surge of adrenaline and fear suddenly overcame the tremors of restless need that I'd been feeling. The air was thick with psychic power of a nature I'd experienced once before, back in the Raith Deeps. That was when Lara Raith had unleashed the full force of her come-hither against her own father, the White King, drowning his mind in imposed lust and desire to please her. He'd been her puppet ever since.

This was the same form of attack, though there were subtle differences. It had to be Barrowill. He'd moved even faster than I'd feared. I kept my mental shields up as I picked up my pace. By the time I reached the fourth floor, I heard the noise the amiable toker had mentioned.

It was sex. Loud sex. A lot of it.

I dropped the pizza and drew my blasting rod. It took me about five seconds to realize what was happening. Barrowill must have been pushing Connie psychically—forcing her to continue feeding and feeding after she would normally have stopped. He wanted her to kill Irwin like a good little vampire, and the overflow was spilling out onto the entire building.

Not that it takes much to make college kids interested in sex, but in this instance, they had literally gone wild. When I looked down the four hallways, doors were standing wide-open. Couples and . . . well, the only word that really applied was *clusters* of kids were in the act, some of them right out in the hall. Imagine an act of lust. It was going on in at least two of those four hallways.

I turned down Irwin's hall, channeling my will into my blasting rod—and yes, I'm aware of the Freudian irony here. The carved runes along its length began to burn with silver and scarlet light as the power built up in it. A White Court vampire is practically a pussycat compared to some of the other breeds on the planet, but I'd once seen one of them twist a pair of fifty-pound steel dumbbells around one another to make a point. I might not have much time to throw down on Barrowill in these narrow quarters, and my best chance was to put him down hard the instant I saw him.

I moved forward as silently as I knew how, stepping around a pair of couples who were breaking some sort of municipal statute, I was sure. Then I leaned back and kicked open the door to Irwin's room.

The place looked like a small tornado had gone through it. Books and clothing and bedclothes and typical dorm room décor had been scattered everywhere. The chair next to a small study desk had been knocked over. A laptop computer lay on its side, showing what I'd once been told was a blue screen of death. The bed had fallen onto its side, where two of the legs appeared to have snapped off.

Connie and Irwin were there, and the haze of lust rolling off the ingénue succubus was a second psychic cyclone. I barely managed to push away. Irwin had her pinned against the wall in a corner. His muscles strained against his skin, and his breath came in dry, labored gasps, but he never stopped moving.

He wasn't being gentle, and Connie apparently didn't mind. Her eyes were a shade of silver, metallic silver, as if they'd been made of chrome, reflecting the room around her like tiny, warped mirrors. She'd sunk her fingers into the drywall to the second knuckle on either side of her to hang on, and her body was rolling in a strained arch in time with his motion. They were gratuitously enthusiastic about the whole thing.

And I hadn't gotten laid in forever.

"Irwin!" I shouted.

Shockingly, I didn't capture his attention.

"Connie!"

I didn't capture hers, either.

I couldn't let the . . . the, uh, process continue. I had no idea how long it might take, or how resistant to harm Irwin might be, but it would be stupid to do nothing and hope for the best. While I was trying to figure out how to break it up before someone lost an eye, I heard the door of the room across the hall open behind me. The sights and sounds and the haze of psychic influence had my mental faculties running at less than peak performance. I didn't translate the sound into a threat until Barrowill slugged me on the back of the head with something that felt like a lump of solid ivory.

I don't even remember hitting the floor.

WHEN I WOKE up, I had a Sasquatch-sized headache and my wrists and ankles were killing me. Half a dozen of Barrowill's goons were all literally kneeling on me to hold me down. Every single one of them had a knife pressed close to one of my major arteries.

Also, my pants had shrunk by several sizes.

I was still in Irwin's dorm room, but things had changed. Irwin was on his back on the floor, Connie astride him. Her features had changed, shifted subtly. Her skin seemed to glow with pale light. Her eyes were empty white spheres. Her cheekbones stood out more harshly against her face, and her hair was a sweat-dampened, wild mane that clung to her cheeks and her parted lips. She was moving as if in slow motion, her fingernails digging into Irwin's chest.

Barrowill's psychic assault was still under way, and Connie's presence had become something so vibrant and penetrating that for a second I thought there might have been a minor earthquake going on. I had to get to that girl. I had to. If I didn't, I was going to lose my mind with need. My instant reaction upon opening my eyes was to struggle to get closer to her on pure reflex.

The goons held me down, and I screamed in protest—but at least being a captive had kept me from doing something stupid and gave me an instant's cold realization that my shields were down. I threw them up again as hard as I could, but the Barrowills had been in my head too long. I barely managed to grab hold of my reason.

The kid looked awful. His eyes were glazed. He wasn't moving with Connie so much as his body was randomly shaking in independent spasms. His head lolled from one side to the other, and his mouth was open. A strand of drool ran from his mouth to the floor.

Barrowill had righted the fallen chair. He sat on it with one ankle resting on his other knee, his arms folded. His expression was detached, clinical, as he watched his daughter killing the young man she loved.

"Barrowill," I said. My voice came out hoarse and rough. "Stop this."

The vampire directed his gaze to me and shook his head. "It's after midnight, Dresden. It's time for Cinderella to return to her real life."

"You son of a bitch," I snarled. "She's killing him."

A small smile touched one corner of his mouth. "Yes. Beautifully. Her Hunger is quite strong." He made a vague gesture with one hand. "Does he seem upset about it? He's a mortal. And mortals are all born to die. The only question is how and in how much pain."

"There's this life thing that happens in between," I snarled.

"And many more where his came from." Barrowill's eyes went chill. "His. And yours."

"What do you mean?"

"When she's finished, we leave. You're dessert."

A lump of ice settled in my stomach, and I swallowed. All things considered, I was becoming a little worried about the outcome of this situation. *Talk, Harry. Keep him talking. You've never met a vampire who didn't love the sound of his own voice. Something could change the situation if you play for time.*

"Why not do it before I woke up?" I asked.

"This way is more efficient," Barrowill said. "If a young athlete takes Ecstasy and his heart fails, there may be a candlelight vigil, but there won't be an investigation. Two dead men? One of them a private investigator? There will be questions." He shrugged a shoulder. "And I don't care for you to bequeath me your death curse, wizard. But once Connie has you, you won't have enough left of your mind to speak your own name, much less utter a curse."

"The Raiths are going to kill you if you drag the Court and the Council into direct opposition," I said.

"The Raiths will never know. I own twenty ghouls, Dresden, and they're always hungry. What they leave of your corpse won't fill a moist sponge."

Connie suddenly ceased moving altogether. Her skin had become pure ivory white. She shuddered, her breaths coming in ragged gasps. She tilted her head back and a low, throaty moan came out of her throat. I've had sex that wasn't as good as Connie sounded.

*Dammit, Dresden. Focus.*

I was out of time.

"The Council will find out, Chuck. They're wizards. Finding unfindable information is what they do."

He smirked. "I think we both know that their reputation is very well constructed."

We did both know that. *Dammit.* "You think nobody's going to miss me?" I asked. "I have friends, you know."

Barrowill suddenly leaned forward, focusing on Connie, his eyes becoming a few shades lighter. "Perhaps, Dresden. But your friends are not here."

Then there was a crash so loud that it shook the building. Barrowill's sleek, black Lincoln Town Car came crashing through the dorm room's door, taking a sizable portion of the wall with it. The ghouls holding me down were scattered by the debris, and fine dust filled the air.

I started coughing at once, but I could see what had happened. The car had come through from the far side of this wing of the dorm, smashing through the room where Barrowill had waited in ambush. The car had crossed the hall and wound up with its bumper and front tires resting inside Irwin's room. It had smashed a massive hole in the outer brick wall of the building, leaving it gaping open to the night.

That got everyone's attention. For an instant, the room was perfectly silent and perfectly still. The ghoul chauffeur still sat in the driver's seat—only his head wobbled loosely, leaning at a right angle to the rest of his neck.

"Hah," I cackled, wheezing. "Hah, hah. Heh, hah, hah, hah. Moron."

A large figure leapt up to the hole in the exterior wall and landed in the room across the hall, hitting with a crunch only slightly less massive than the car had made. I swear to you, if I'd heard that sound effect they used to use when Steve Austin jumped somewhere, I would not have been shocked. The other room was unlit, and the newcomer was a massive, threatening shadow.

He slapped a hand the size of a big cookie tray on the floor and let out a low, rumbling sound like nothing I'd ever heard this side of an amplified bass guitar. It was music. You couldn't have written it in musical notation any more than you could write the music of a thunderstorm, or write lyrics to the song of a running stream. But it was music nonetheless.

Power like nothing I had ever encountered surged out from that impact, a deep, shuddering wave that passed visibly through the dust in the air. The ceiling and the walls and the floor sang in resonance with the note and impact alike, and Barrowill's psychic assault was swept away like a sand castle before the tide. Connie's eyes flooded with color, changing from pure, empty whiteness back to a blue as deep and rich as a glacial lake, and the humanity came flooding back into her features. The sense of wild panic in the air suddenly vanished, and for another timeless instant, everything, everything in that night went utterly silent and still.

*Holy.*

*Crap.*

I've worked with magic for decades, and take it from me, it really isn't very different from anything else in life. When you work with magic, you rapidly realize that it is far easier to disrupt than to create, far more difficult to mend than to destroy. Throw a stone into a glass-smooth lake, and ripples will wash over the whole thing. Making waves with magic instead of a rock would have been easy.

But if you can make that lake smooth again—that's one hell of a trick.

That surge of energy didn't attack anything or anybody. It didn't destroy Barrowill's assault.

It made the water smooth again.

Strength of a River in His Shoulders opened his eyes, and his fury made them burn like coals in the shadows—but he simply crouched, doing nothing.

All of Barrowill's goons remained still, wide eyes flicking from River to Barrowill and back.

"Back off, Chuck," I said. "He's giving you a chance to walk away. Take him up on it."

The vampire's expression was completely blank as he stood among the debris. He stared at River Shoulders for maybe three seconds—and then I saw movement behind River Shoulders.

Clawed hands began to grip the edges of the hole behind River. Wicked, bulging red eyes appeared. Monstrous-looking things in the same general shape as a human appeared in complete silence.

Ghouls.

Barrowill didn't have six goons with him.

He'd brought them all.

Barrowill spat toward River, bared his teeth, and screamed, "Kill it!"

And it was on.

Everything went completely insane. The human-shaped ghouls in the room bounded forward, their faces and limbs contorting, tearing their way out of their cheap suits as they assumed their true forms. More ghouls poured in through the hole in the wall like a swarm of panicked roaches. I couldn't get an accurate count of the enemy—the action was too fast. But twenty sounded about right. Twenty flesh-rending, superhumanly strong and durable predators flung themselves onto River Shoulders in an overwhelming wave. He vanished beneath a couple of tons of hungry ghoul. It was not a fair fight.

Barrowill should have brought more goons.

There was an enormous bellow, a sound that could only have been made by a truly massive set of lungs, and ghouls exploded outward from River Shoulders like so much hideous shrapnel. Several were flung back out of the building. Others slammed into walls with so much force that they shattered the drywall. One of them went through the ceiling, then fell limply back down into the room—only to be caught by the neck in one of River Shoulders's massive hands. He squeezed, crushing the ghoul's neck like soft clay, and there was an audible pop. The ghoul spasmed once; then River flung the corpse into the nearest batch of monsters.

After that, it was clobbering time.

Barrowill moved fast, seizing Connie and darting out the door. I looked around frantically and spotted one of the knives the goons had been holding before they transformed. My hands and ankles had been bound in those plastic restraining strips, and I could barely feel my fingers, but I managed to pick up the knife and cut my legs free. Then I put it on the front bumper of the Lincoln, stepped on it with one foot to hold it in place, and after a few moments managed to cut my hands loose as well.

The dorm sounded like a medley of pay-per-view wrestling and *The Island of Dr. Moreau.* Ghouls shrieked. River Shoulders roared. Very, very disoriented students screamed. The walls and floor shook with impact again and again as River Shoulders flung ghouls around like so many softballs. Ghoulish blood spattered the walls and the ceiling, green-brown and putrid-smelling, and as strong as he was, River Shoulders wasn't pitching a shutout. The ghouls' claws and fangs had sunk into him, covering him in punctures and lacerations, and his scarlet blood mixed with theirs on the various surfaces.

I tried to think unobtrusive thoughts, stayed low, and went to Irwin. He still looked awful, but he was breathing hard and steady, and he'd already begun blinking and trying to focus his eyes.

"Irwin!" I shouted. "Irwin! Where's her purse?"

"Whuzza?" Irwin mumbled.

"Connie's purse! I've got to help Connie! Where is her purse?"

Irwin's eyes almost focused. "Connie?"

"Oh, never mind." I started ransacking the dorm room until I found Connie's handbag. She had a brush in it. The brush was liberally festooned with her blond hairs.

I swept a circle into the dust on the floor, tied the hair around my pentacle amulet, and invested the circle with a whisper of will. Then I quickly worked the tracking spell that was generally my bread and butter when I was doing investigator stuff. When I released the magic, it rushed down into Connie's borrowed hair, and my amulet lurched sharply out of plumb and held itself steady at a thirty- or forty-degree angle. Connie went thataway.

I ducked a flying ghoul, leapt over a dying ghoul, and staggered down the hall at my best speed while the blood went back into my feet.

I had gone down one whole flight of stairs without falling when the angle on the amulet changed again. Barrowill had gone down one floor, then taken off down one of the residential hallways toward the fire escape at the far end. He'd bypassed security by ripping the door off its hinges, then flinging it into the opposite wall. Kids were scattering out of the hallway, looking either horrified or disappointed. Some both. Barrowill had reached the far end, carrying his daughter over one shoulder, and was headed for the fire door.

Barrowill had been savvy enough to divest me of my accoutrements, but I was still a wizard, dammit, blasting rod or no. I drew up my will, aimed low, and snarled, *"Forzare!"*

Pure kinetic force lashed invisibly through the air and caught Barrowill at the ankles. It kicked both of his feet up into the air, and he took a pratfall onto the floor. Connie landed with a grunt and bounced to one side. She lay there dazed and blinking.

Barrowill slithered back up to his feet, spinning toward me and producing a pistol in one hand. I lurched back out of the line of fire as the gun barked twice, and bullets went by me with a double hiss. I went to my knees and bobbed my head out into the hall again for a quick peek, and jerked it back immediately. Barrowill was picking

Connie up. His bullet went through the air where my head would have been if I'd been standing.

"Don't be a moron, Harry," I said. "You came for the kid. He's safe. That's all you were obligated to do. Let it g— Oh, who am I kidding. There's a girl."

I didn't have to beat the vampire—I just had to slow him down long enough for River Shoulders to catch up to him . . . assuming River did pursue.

I took note of which wing Barrowill was fleeing through and rushed down the stairs to the ground floor. Then I left the building and sprinted to the far end of that wing.

Barrowill slammed the emergency exit open and emerged from the building. He was moving fast, but he also had his daughter to carry, and she'd begun to resist him, kicking and thrashing, slowing him down. She tugged him off-balance just as he shot at me again, and it went wide. I slashed at him with another surge of force, but this time I wasn't aiming for his feet—I went for the gun. The weapon leapt out of his hands and went spinning away, shattering against the bricks of the dorm's outer wall. Another blast knocked Connie off his shoulder, and she let out a little shriek. Barrowill staggered, then let out a snarl of frustration and charged me at a speed worthy of the Flash's understudy.

I flung more force at him, but Barrowill bobbed to one side, evading the blast. I threw myself away from the vampire and managed to roll with the punch he sent at my head. He caught me an inch or two over one eyebrow, the hardest and most impact-resistant portion of the human skull. That and the fact that I'd managed to rob it of a little of its power meant that he only sent me spinning wildly away, my vision completely obscured by pain and little silver stars. He was furious, his power rolling over me like a sudden deluge of ice water, to the point where crystals of frost formed on my clothing.

Barrowill followed up, his eyes murderous. And then Bigfoot Irwin bellowed, "Connie!" and slammed into Barrowill at the hip, using his body as a living spear. Barrowill was flung to one side, and Irwin pressed his advantage, still screaming, coming down atop the vampire and pounding him with both fists in elemental violence, his sunken eyes mad with rage. "Connie! Connie!"

I tried to rise but couldn't seem to make it past one knee. So all I could do was watch as the furious scion of River Shoulders unleashed everything he had on a ranking noble of the White Court. Barrowill could have been much stronger than a human being if he'd had the gas in the tank, but he'd spent his energy on his psychic assault, and it had drained him. He still thrashed powerfully, but he was no match for the enraged young man. Irwin slammed Barrowill's nose flat against his face. I saw one of the vampire's teeth go flying into the night air. Slightly too-pale blood began to splash against Irwin's fists.

Christ. If the kid killed Barrowill, the White Court would consider it an act of war. All kinds of horrible things could unfold. "Irwin!" I shouted. "Irwin, stop!"

Kid Bigfoot didn't listen to me.

I lurched closer to him but only made it about six inches before my head whirled so badly that I fell onto my side. "Irwin, stop!" I looked around and saw Connie staring dazedly at the struggle. "Connie!" I said. "Stop him! Stop him!"

Meanwhile, Irwin had beaten Barrowill to within an inch of his life—and now he raised his joined hands over his head, preparing for a sledgehammer blow to Barrowill's skull.

A small, pretty hand touched his wrist.

"Irwin," Connie said gently. "Irwin, no."

"He tried," Irwin panted. "Tried. Hurt you."

"This isn't the way," Connie said.

"Bad man," Irwin growled.

"But you aren't," Connie said, her voice very soft. "Irwin. He's still my daddy."

Connie couldn't have physically stopped Irwin—but she didn't need to. The kid blinked several times, then looked at her. He slowly lowered his hands, and Connie leaned down to kiss his forehead gently. "Shhhh," she said. "Shhhh. I'm still here. It's over, baby. It's over."

"Connie," Irwin said, and leaned against her.

I let out a huge sigh of relief and sank back onto the ground.

My head hurt.

OFFICER DEAN STARED at me for a while. He chewed on a toothpick and squinted at me. "Got some holes."

"Yeah?" I asked. "Like what?"

"Like all those kids saw a Bigfoot and them whatchamacalits. Ghouls. How come they didn't say anything?"

"You walked in on them while they were all still trying to put their clothes back on. After flinging themselves into random sex with whoever happened to be close to them. They're all denying that this ever happened right now."

"Hngh," Dean said. "What about the ghoul corpses?"

"After Irwin dragged their boss up to the fight, the ghouls quit when they saw him. River Shoulders told them all to get out of his sight and take their dead with them. They did."

Dean squinted and consulted a list. "Pounder is gone. So is Connie Barrowill. Not officially missing or nothing. Not yet. But where are they?"

I looked at Dean and shrugged.

I'D SEEN GHOULS in all kinds of situations before—but I'd never seen them whipped into submission. Ghouls fought to the grisly, messy end. That was what they did. But River Shoulders had been more than their match. He'd left several of them alive when he could have killed them to the last, and he'd found their breaking point when Irwin had dragged Barrowill in by his hair. Ghouls could take a huge beating, but River Shoulders had given them one like I'd never seen, and when he ordered them to take their master and their dead and never to return, they'd snapped to it.

"Thanks, Connie," I groaned, as she settled me onto a section of convenient rubble. I was freezing. The frost on my clothes was rapidly melting away, but the chill had settled inward.

The girl looked acutely embarrassed, but that wasn't in short supply in that dorm. That hallway was empty of other students for the moment, though. We had the place to ourselves, though I judged that the authorities would arrive in some form before long.

Irwin came over with a dust-covered blanket and wrapped it around her. He'd scrounged a ragged towel for himself, though it did more to emphasize his physique than to hide it. The kid was ripped.

"Thank you, Irwin," she said.

He grunted. Physically, he'd bounced back from the nearly lethal feeding like a rubber freaking ball. Maybe River Shoulders's water-smoothing spell had done something to help that. Mentally, he was slowly refocusing. You could see the gleam coming back into his eyes. Until that happened, he'd listened to Connie. A guy could do worse.

"I . . ." Connie shook her head. "I remember all of it. But I have no idea what just happened." She stared at River Shoulders for a moment, her expression more curious than fearful. "You . . . You stopped something bad from happening, I think."

"Yeah, he did," I confirmed.

Connie nodded toward him in a grateful little motion. "Thank you. Who are you?"

"Irwin's dad," I said.

Irwin blinked several times. He stared blankly at River Shoulders.

"Hello," River rumbled. How something that large and that powerful could sit there bleeding from dozens of wounds and somehow look sheepish was beyond me. "I am very sorry we had to meet like that. I had hoped for something quieter. Maybe with music. And good food."

"You can't stay," I said to River. "The authorities are on the way."

River made a rumbling sound of agreement. "This is a disaster. What I did . . ." He shook his head. "This was in such awful taste."

"Couldn't have happened to nicer guys, though," I said.

"Wait," Connie said. "Wait. What the hell just happened here?"

Irwin put a hand on her shoulder and said to me, "She's . . . she's a vampire. Isn't she?"

I blinked and nodded at him. "How did . . . ?"

"Paranet," he said. "There's a whole page."

"Wait," Connie said again. "A . . . what? Am I going to sparkle or something?"

"God, no," said Irwin and I together.

"Connie," I said, and she looked at me. "You're still exactly who you were this morning. And so is Irwin. And that's what counts. But right now, things are going to get really complicated if the cops walk in and start asking you questions. Better if they just never knew you were here."

"This is all so . . ." She shook her head. Then she stared at River Shoulders. Then at me. "Who are you?"

I pointed at me and said, "Wizard." I pointed at River. "Bigfoot." I pointed at Irwin. "Son of Bigfoot." I pointed at her. "Vampire. Seriously."

"Oh," she said faintly.

"I'll explain it," Irwin told her quietly. He was watching River Shoulders.

River held out his huge hands to either side and shrugged. "Hello, son."

Irwin shook his head slowly. "I . . . never really . . ." He sucked in a deep breath, squared off against his father, and said, "Why?"

And there it was. What had to be the Big Question of Irwin's life.

"My people," River said. "Tradition is very important to them. If I acknowledged you, they would have insisted that certain traditions be observed. It would have consumed your life. And I didn't want that for you. I didn't want that for your mother. I wanted your world to be wider than mine."

Bigfoot Irwin was silent for a long moment. Then he scratched at his head with one hand and shrugged. "Tonight . . . really explains a lot." He nodded slowly. "Okay. We aren't done talking. But okay."

"Let's get you out of here," River said. "Get you both taken care of. Answer all your questions."

"What about Harry?" Irwin said.

I couldn't get any more involved with the evident abduction of a scion of the White Court. River's mercy had probably kept the situation from going completely to hell, but I wasn't going to drag the White Council's baggage into the situation. "You guys go on," I told them. "I do this kind of thing all the time. I'll be fine."

"Wow, seriously?" Irwin asked.

"Yeah," I said. "I've been in messier situations than this. And it's probably better if Connie's dad has time to cool off before you guys talk again. River Shoulders can make sure you have that time."

Outside, a cart with flashing bulbs on it had pulled up.

"River," I said. "Time's up."

River Shoulders rose and nodded deeply to me. "I'm sorry that I interfered. It seemed necessary."

"I'm willing to overlook it," I said. "All things considered."

His face twisted into a very human-looking smile, and he extended his hand to Irwin. "Son."

Irwin took his father's hand, one arm still around Connie, and the three of them didn't vanish so much as . . . just become less and less relevant to the situation. It happened over the course of two or three seconds, as that same nebulous, somehow transparent power that River had used earlier enfolded them. And then they were all gone.

Boots crunched down the hall, and a uniformed officer with a name tag reading DEAN burst in, one hand on his gun.

DEAN EYED ME, then said, "That's all you know, huh?"

"That's the truth," I said. "I told you that you wouldn't believe it. You gonna let me go now?"

"Oh, hell, no," Dean said. "That's the craziest thing I've ever heard.

You're stoned out of your mind or insane. Either way, I'm going to put you in the drunk tank until you have a chance to sleep it off."

"You got any aspirin?" I asked.

"Sure," he said, and got up to get it.

My head ached horribly, and I was pretty sure I hadn't heard the end of this, but I was clear for now. "Next time, Dresden," I muttered to myself, "just take the gold."

Then Officer Dean put me in a nice, quiet cell with a nice, quiet cot, and there I stayed until Wild Bill Meyers showed up the next morning and bailed me out.

# BOMBSHELLS

This next story got written in that glorious time between the end of *Changes* and the beginning of *Ghost Story*, when fans were regularly screaming at me for answers and when I could regularly give answers that were somehow worse than the original questions. I realized, however, that I had agreed to several short stories in this same time period, when Dresden was or was not actually dead—which would make it something of a challenge to cast him as a protagonist of tales set during the same period.

The natural thing to do was to shift to the viewpoints of other characters—and to have a chance to show the impact of Dresden's absence on some of the characters who had been closest to him. In this case, I got the chance to write about life from the point of view of his apprentice, Molly, and how Dresden's apparent death had affected many of the people in his circle—but, more important, about how Dresden's *life* had affected those same people, and how it would show in their choices.

I miss my boss.

It's been most of a year since I helped him die, and ever since then I've been the only professional wizard in the city of Chicago.

Well, okay. I'm not, like, officially a wizard. I'm still sort of an apprentice. And no one really pays me, unless you count the wallets and valuables I lift from bodies sometimes, so I guess I'm more amateur than professional. And I don't have a PI license like my boss did, or an ad in the phone book.

But I'm all there is. I'm not as strong as he was, and I'm not as good as he was. I'm just going to have to be enough.

So, anyway, there I was, washing the blood off in Waldo Butters's shower.

I did a lot of living outdoors these days, which didn't seem nearly as horrible during the summer and early autumn as it did during the arctic chill of the previous superwinter. It was like sleeping on a tropical beach by comparison. Still, I missed things such as regular access to plumbing, and Waldo let me clean up whenever I needed to. I had the shower heat turned all the way up, and it was heaven. It was kind of a scourgey, scoury heaven, but heaven nonetheless.

The floor of the shower turned red for a few seconds, then faded to pink for a while as I sluiced the blood off. It wasn't mine. A gang of Fomor servitors had been carrying a fifteen-year-old boy down an alley toward Lake Michigan. If they'd gotten him there, he'd have been facing a fate worse than death. I intervened, but that bastard Listen cut his throat rather than give him up. I tried to save him while Listen and his buddies ran. I failed. And I'd been right there with him, feeling everything he did, feeling his confusion and pain and terror as he died.

Harry wouldn't have felt that. Harry would have saved the day. He would have smashed the Fomor goons around like bowling pins, picked the kid up like some kind of serial-movie action hero, and taken him to safety.

I missed my boss.

I used a lot of soap. I probably cried. I had begun ignoring tears months ago, and at times I honestly didn't know when they were falling. Once I was clean—physically, anyway—I just stood there soaking up the heat, letting the water course all over me. The scar on my leg where I'd been shot was still wrinkled, but the color had changed from purple and red to angry pink. Butters said it would be gone in a couple of years. I was walking normally again, unless I pushed myself too hard. But, yikes, my legs and various pieces needed to get reacquainted with a razor, even with medium-blond hair.

I was going to ignore them, but . . . grooming is important for keeping one's spirits up. A well-kept body for a well-kept mind and all that. I wasn't a fool. I knew I wasn't exactly flying level lately. My morale needed all the boost it could get. I leaned out of the shower and swiped Andi's pink plastic razor. I'd pay Waldo's werewolf girlfriend back for it later.

I wrapped up about the same time as the hot water ran out, got out of the shower, and toweled off. My things were in a pile by the door—some garage-sale Birkenstocks, an old nylon hiker's backpack, and my bloodied clothes. Another set gone. And the sandals had left partial tracks in blood at the scene, so I'd have to get rid of them, too. I was going to have to hit another thrift store at this rate. Normally, that would have cheered me up, but shopping just wasn't what it used to be.

I was carefully going over the tub and floor for fallen hairs and so on when someone knocked. I didn't stop scanning the floor. In my line of work, people can and will do awful things to you with discarded bits of your body. Not cleaning up after yourself is like asking for someone to boil your blood from twenty blocks away. No, thank you.

"Yes?" I called.

"Hey, Molly," Waldo said. "There's, uh . . . There's someone here to talk to you."

We'd prearranged a lot of things. If he'd used the word *feeling* at any point in his sentence, I would have known there was trouble outside the door. Not using it meant that there wasn't—or that he couldn't see it. I slipped on my bracelets and my ring and set both of my wands down where I could snatch them up instantly. Only then did I start putting clothes on.

"Who?" I called.

He was working hard not to sound nervous around me. I appreciated the effort. It was sweet. "Says her name is Justine. Says you know her."

I did know Justine. She was a thrall of the vampires of the White Court. Or at least a personal assistant to one and the girlfriend of another. Harry always thought well of her, though he was a big, goofy idiot when it came to women who might show the potential to become damsels in distress.

"But if he were here," I muttered to myself, "he'd help her."

I didn't wipe the steam off the mirror before I left the bathroom. I didn't want to look at anything in there.

Justine was a handful of years older than me, but her hair had turned pure white. She was a knockout, one of those girls all the boys assume are too pretty to approach. She had on jeans and a button-down shirt several sizes too large for her. The shirt was Thomas's, I was certain. Her body language was poised, very neutral. Justine was as good at hiding her emotions as anyone I'd ever seen, but I could sense leashed tension and quiet fear beneath the calm surface.

I'm a wizard, or damned close to it, and I work with the mind. People don't really get to hide things from me.

If Justine was afraid, it was because she feared for Thomas. If she'd come to me for help, it was because she couldn't get help from the White Court. We could have had a polite conversation that led up to that revelation, but I had less and less patience for the pleasantries lately, so I cut to the chase.

"Hello, Justine. Why should I help you with Thomas when his own family won't?"

Justine's eyes bugged out. So did Waldo's.

I was getting used to that reaction.

"How did you know?" Justine asked quietly.

When you're into magic, people always assume anything you do must be connected to it. Harry always thought that was funny. To him, magic was just one more set of tools that the mind could use to solve problems. The mind was the more important part of that pairing. "Does that matter?"

She frowned and looked away from me. She shook her head. "He's missing. I know he left on some kind of errand for Lara, but she says she doesn't know anything about it. She's lying."

"She's a vampire. And you didn't answer my first question." The words came out a little harsher and harder than they'd sounded in my head. I tried to relax a little. I folded my arms and leaned against a wall. "Why should I help you?"

It's not like I wasn't planning to help her. But I knew a secret about Harry and Thomas few others did. I had to know if Justine knew the secret, too, or if I'd have to keep it hidden around her.

Justine met my eyes with hers for a moment. The look was penetrating. "If you can't go to family for help," she said, "who can you turn to?"

I averted my eyes before it could turn into an actual soulgaze, but her words and the cumulative impression of her posture, her presence, her *self*, answered the question for me.

She knew.

Thomas and Harry were half brothers. She'd have gone to Harry for help if he were alive. I was the only thing vaguely like an heir to his power around these parts, and she hoped I would be willing to step into his shoes. His huge, stompy, terrifying shoes.

"You go to friends," I said quietly. "I'll need something of Thomas's. Hair or fingernail clippings would be . . ."

She produced a ziplock plastic bag from the breast pocket of the shirt and offered it to me without a word. I went over and picked it up. It had a number of dark hairs in it.

"You're sure they're his?"

Justine gestured toward her own snow-white mane. "It's not like they're easy to confuse."

I looked up to find Butters watching me silently from the other side of the room. He was a beaky little guy, wiry and quick. His hair had been electrocuted and then frozen that way. His eyes were steady and worried. He cut up corpses for the government, professionally, but he was one of the more savvy people in town when it came to the supernatural.

"What?" I asked him.

He considered his words before he spoke—less because he was afraid of me than because he cared about not hurting my feelings. That was the reverse of most people these days. "Is this something you should get involved in, Molly?"

What he really wanted to ask me was if I was sane. If I was going to help or just make things a lot worse.

"I don't know," I said honestly. I looked at Justine and said, "Wait here."

Then I got my stuff, took the hairs, and left.

The first thing Harry Dresden ever taught me about magic was a tracking spell.

"It's a simple principle, kid," he told me. "We're creating a link between two similar things out of energy. Then we make the energy give us an indicator of some kind, so that we can tell which way it's flowing."

"What are we going to find?" I asked.

He held up a rather thick grey hair and nodded back toward his dog, Mouse. He should have been named Moose. The giant, shaggy temple dog was pony-sized. "Mouse," Harry said, "go get lost and we'll see if we can find you."

The big dog yawned and padded agreeably toward the door. Harry let him out and then came over to sit down next to me. We were in his living room. A couple of nights before, I had thrown myself at him. Naked. And he'd dumped a pitcher of ice water over my head. I was still mortified, but he was probably right. It was the right thing for him to do. He always did the right thing, even if it meant he lost out. I still wanted to be with him so much, but maybe the time wasn't right yet.

That was okay. I could be patient. And I still got to be with him in a different way almost every day.

"All right," I said when he sat back down. "What do I do?"

In the years since that day, the spell had become routine. I'd used it to find lost people, secret places, missing socks, and generally to poke my nose where it probably didn't belong. Harry would have said that went with the territory of being a wizard. Harry was right.

I stopped in the alley outside Butters's apartment and sketched a circle on the concrete with a small piece of pink chalk. I closed the circle with a tiny effort of will, drew out one of the hairs from the plastic bag, and held it up. I focused the energy of the spell, bringing its different elements together in my head. When we'd started, Harry had let me use four different objects, teaching me how to attach ideas to them, to represent the different pieces of the spell, but that kind of thing wasn't necessary. Magic all happens inside the head of the wizard. You can use props to make things simpler, and in truly complex spells they make the difference between impossible and merely almost impossible. For this one, though, I didn't need the props anymore.

I gathered the different pieces of the spell in my head, linked them together, infused them with a moderate effort of will, and then with a murmured word released that energy down into the hair in my fingers. Then I popped the hair into my mouth, broke the chalk circle with a brush of my foot, and rose.

Harry always used an object as the indicator for his tracking spells—his amulet, a compass, or some kind of pendulum. I hadn't wanted to hurt his feelings, but that kind of thing really wasn't necessary. I could feel the magic coursing through the hair, making my lips tingle gently. I got out a cheap little plastic compass and a ten-foot length of chalk line. I set it up and snapped it to mark out magnetic north.

Then I took the free end of the line and turned slowly, until the tingling sensation was centered on my lips. Lips are extremely sensitive parts of the body, generally, and I've found that they give you the best tactile feedback for this sort of thing. Once I knew which direction Thomas was, I oriented the chalk line that way, made sure it was tight, and snapped it again, resulting in an extremely elongated V shape, like the tip of a giant needle. I measured the distance at the base of the V.

Then I turned ninety degrees, walked five hundred paces, and repeated the process.

Promise me you won't tell my high school math teacher about it, but after that I sat down and applied trigonometry to real life.

The math wasn't hard. I had the two angles measured against magnetic north. I had the distance between them in units of Molly-paces. Molly-paces aren't terribly scientific, but for purposes of this particular application, they were practical enough to calculate the distance to Thomas.

Using such simple tools, I couldn't get a measurement precise enough to know which door to kick down, but I now knew that he was relatively nearby—within four or five miles, as opposed to being at the North Pole or something. I move around the city a lot, because a moving target is a lot harder to hit. I probably covered three or four times that on an average day.

I'd have to get a lot closer before I could pinpoint his location any more precisely than that. So I turned my lips toward the tingle and started walking.

Thomas was in a small office building on a big lot.

The building was three stories, not huge, though it sat amid several much larger structures. The lot it stood upon was big enough to hold something a lot bigger. Instead, most of it was landscaped into a manicured lawn and garden, complete with water features and a very small, very modest wrought-iron fence. The building itself showed a lot of stone and marble in its design, and it had more class in its cornices than the towers nearby had in their whole structures. It was gorgeous and understated at the same time; on that block, it looked like a single, small, perfect diamond being displayed amid giant jars of rhinestones.

There were no signs outside it. There was no obvious way in, beyond a set of gates guarded by competent-looking men in dark suits. Expensive dark suits. If the guards could afford to wear those to work, it meant that whoever owned that building had money. Serious money.

I circled the building to be sure, and felt the tingling energy of the tracking spell confirming Thomas's location. But even though I'd been careful to stay on the far side of the street, someone inside noticed me. I could feel one guard's eyes tracking me, even behind his sunglasses. Maybe I should have done the initial approach under a veil, but Harry had always been against using magic except when it was truly necessary, and it was way too easy to start using it for every little thing if you let yourself.

In some ways, I'm better at the "how" of magic than Harry was. But I've come to learn that I might never be as smart as him when it came to the "why."

I went into a nearby Starbucks and got myself a cup of liquid life and started thinking about how to get in. My tongue was telling me all about what great judgment I had when I sensed the presence of supernatural power rapidly coming nearer.

I didn't panic. Panic gets you killed. Instead I turned smoothly on one heel and slipped into a short hallway leading to a small restroom. I went inside, shut the door behind me, and drew my wands from my hip pocket. I checked the energy level on my bracelets. Both of them were ready to go. My rings were all full up, too, which was about as ideal as things could get.

So I ordered my thoughts, made a small effort of will, whispered a word, and vanished.

Veils were complex magic, but I had a knack for them. Becoming truly and completely invisible was a real pain in the neck: Passing light completely through you was a literal stone-cold bitch, because it left you freezing cold and blind as a bat to boot. Becoming unseen, though, was a different proposition entirely. A good veil would reduce your visibility to little more than a few flickers in the air, to a few vague shadows where they shouldn't be, but it did more than that. It created a sense of ordinariness in the air around you, an aura of boring unremarkability that you usually only felt in a job you didn't like, around three thirty in the afternoon. Once you combined that suggestion with a greatly reduced visible profile, remaining unnoticed was at least as easy as breathing.

As I vanished into that veil, I also called up an image, another combination of illusion and suggestion. This one was simple: me, as I'd appeared in the mirror a moment before, clean and seemingly perky and toting a fresh cup of creamy goodness. The sensation that went with it was just a kind of heavy dose of me: the sound of my steps and movement, the scent of Butters's shampoo, the aroma of my cup of coffee. I tied the image to one of the rings on my fingers and left it there, drawing from the energy I'd stored in a moonstone. Then I turned around, with my image layered over my actual body like a suit made of light, and walked out of the coffee shop.

Once outside, the evasion was a simple maneuver, the way all the good ones are. My image turned left and I turned right.

To anyone watching, a young woman had just come out of the store and gone sauntering down the street with her coffee. She was obviously enjoying her day. I'd put a little extra bounce and sway into the image's movements, to make her that much more noticeable (and therefore a better distraction). She'd go on walking down that street for a mile or more before she simply vanished.

Meanwhile, the real me moved silently into an alleyway and watched.

My image hadn't gone a hundred yards before a man in a black turtleneck sweater—a servitor of the Fomor—stepped out of an alley and began following it. Those jerks were everywhere these days, like roaches, only more disgusting and harder to kill.

Only . . . that was just too easy. One servitor wouldn't have set my instinct alarms to jingling. They were strong, fast, and tough, sure, but no more so than any number of creatures. They didn't possess mounds of magical power; if they had, the Fomor would never have let them leave in the first place.

Something else was out there. Something that had wanted me to be distracted, watching the apparent servitor follow the apparent Molly. And if something knew me well enough to set up this sort of diversion to ensnare my attention, then it knew me well enough to find me, even beneath my veil. There were a really limited number of people who could do that.

I slipped a hand into my nylon backpack and drew out my knife, the M9 Bayonet my brother had brought home from Afghanistan. I drew the heavy blade out, closed my eyes, and turned quickly with the knife in one hand and my coffee in the other. I flicked the lid off the coffee with my thumb and slewed the liquid into a wide arc at about chest level.

I heard a gasp and oriented on it, opened my eyes, and stepped toward the source of the sound, driving the knife into the air before me at slightly higher than the level of my own heart.

The steel of the blade suddenly erupted with a coruscation of light as it pierced a veil that hung in the air only inches away from me. I stepped forward rapidly through the veil, pushing the point of the knife before me toward the suddenly revealed form behind the veil. She was a woman, taller than me, dressed in ragged, coffee-stained clothes, but with her long, fiery autumn hair unbound and wind tossed. She twisted to one side, off-balance, until her shoulders touched the brick wall of the alley.

I did not relent, driving the blade toward her throat—until at the last second, one pale, slender hand snapped up and grasped my wrist, quick as a serpent but stronger and colder. My face wound up only a few inches from hers as I put the heel of one hand against the knife and leaned against it slightly—enough to push against her strength, but not enough to throw me off-balance if she made a quick move. She was lean and lovely, even in the rags, with wide, oblique green eyes and perfect bone structure that could be found only in a half dozen supermodels—and in every single one of the Sidhe.

"Hello, Auntie," I said in a level voice. "It isn't nice to sneak up behind me. Especially lately."

She held my weight off of her with one arm, though it wasn't easy for her. There was a quality of strain to her melodic voice. "Child," she breathed. "You anticipated my approach. Had I not stopped thee, thou wouldst have driven cold iron into my flesh, causing me agonies un-told. Thou wouldst have spilled my life's blood upon the ground." Her eyes widened. "Thou wouldst have killed me."

"I wouldst," I agreed pleasantly.

Her mouth spread into a wide smile, and her teeth were daintily pointed. "I have taught thee well."

Then she twisted with a lithe and fluid grace, away from the blade and to her feet a good long step away from me. I watched her and lowered the knife—but I didn't put it away. "I don't have time for les-sons right now, Auntie Lea."

"I am not here to teach thee, child."

"I don't have time for games, either."

"Nor did I come to play with thee," the Leanansidhe said, "but to give thee warning: Thou art not safe here."

I quirked an eyebrow at her. "Wow. Gosh."

She tilted her head at me in reproof, and her mouth thinned. Her eyes moved past me to look down the alley, and she shot a quick glance behind her. Her expression changed. She didn't quite lose the smug superiority that always colored her features, but she toned it down a good deal, and she lowered her voice. "Thou makest jests, child, but thou art in grave peril—as am I. We should not linger here." She shifted her eyes to mine. "If thou dost wish to brace this foe, if thou wouldst recover my Godson's brother, there are things I must tell thee."

I narrowed my eyes. Harry's Faerie Godmother had taken over as my mentor when Harry died, but she wasn't exactly one of the good faeries. In fact, she was the second in command to Mab, the Queen of Air and Darkness, and she was a bloodthirsty, dangerous being who divided her enemies into two categories: those who were dead, and those in which she had not yet taken pleasure. I hadn't known that she knew about Harry and Thomas—but it didn't shock me.

Lea was a murderous, cruel creature—but as far as I knew, she had never lied to me. Technically.

"Come," said the Leanansidhe. She turned and walked briskly toward the far end of the alley, gathering a seeming and a veil around her as she went, to hide herself from notice.

I glanced back toward the building where Thomas was being held, ground my teeth, and followed her, merging my veil with hers as we left.

We walked Chicago's streets unseen by thousands of eyes. The people we passed all took a few extra steps to avoid us without really thinking about it. It's important to lay out an avoidance suggestion like that when you're in a crowd. Being unseen is kind of pointless if dozens of people keep bumping into you.

"Tell me, child," Lea said, shifting abruptly out of her archaic dialect. She did that sometimes, when we were alone. "What do you know of svartalves?"

"A little," I said. "They're from Northern Europe originally. They're small and they live underground. They're the best magical craftsmen on earth; Harry bought things from them whenever he could afford it, but they weren't cheap."

"How dry," the faerie sorceress said. "You sound like a book, child. Books frequently bear little resemblance to life." Her intense green eyes glittered as she turned to watch a young woman with an infant walk by us. "What do you *know* of them?"

"They're dangerous," I said quietly. "Very dangerous. The old

Norse gods used to go to them for weapons and armor and they didn't try to fight them. Harry said he was glad he never had to fight a svartalf. They're also honorable. They signed the Unseelie Accords and they uphold them. They have a reputation for being savage about protecting their own. They aren't human, they aren't kind, and only a fool crosses them."

"Better," the Leanansidhe said. Then she added, in an offhand tone, "Fool."

I glanced back toward the building I'd found. "That's their property?"

"Their fortress," Lea replied, "the center of their mortal affairs, here at the great crossroads. What else do you recall of them?"

I shook my head. "Um. One of the Norse goddesses got jacked for her jewelry—"

"Freya," Lea said.

"And the thief—"

"Loki."

"Yeah, him. He pawned it with the svartalves or something, and there was a big to-do about getting it back."

"One wonders how it is possible to be so vague and so accurate at the same time," Lea said.

I smirked.

Lea frowned at me. "You knew the story perfectly well. You were . . . tweaking my nose, I believe is the saying."

"I had a good teacher in snark class," I said. "Freya went to get her necklace back, and the svartalves were willing to do it—but only if she agreed to kiss each and every one of them."

Lea threw her head back and laughed. "Child," she said, a wicked edge to her voice, "remember that many of the old tales were translated and transcribed by rather prudish scholars."

"What do you mean?" I asked.

"That the svartalves most certainly did not agree to give up one of the most valuable jewels in the universe for a society-wide trip to first base."

I blinked a couple of times and felt my cheeks heat up. "You mean she had to . . ."

"Precisely."

"*All* of them?"

"Indeed."

"Wow," I said. "I like to accessorize as much as the next girl, but that's over the line. Way over. I mean, you can't even *see* the line from there."

"Perhaps," Lea said. "I suppose it depends upon how badly one needs to recover something from the svartalves."

"Uh. You're saying I need to pull a train to get Thomas out of there? 'Cause that just isn't going to happen."

Lea showed her teeth in another smile. "Morality is amusing."

"Would you do it?"

Lea looked offended. "For the sake of another? Certainly not. Have you any idea of the obligation that would incur?"

"Um. Not exactly."

"This is not my choice to make. You must ask yourself this question: Is your untroubled conscience more valuable to you than the vampire's life?"

"No. But there's got to be another way."

Lea seemed to consider that for a moment. "Svartalves love beauty. They covet it the way a dragon lusts for gold. You are young, lovely, and . . . I believe the phrase is *smoking hot*. The exchange of your favors for the vampire, a straightforward transaction, is almost certain to succeed, assuming he still lives."

"We'll call that one plan B," I said. "Or maybe plan X. Or plan XXX. Why not just break in and burgle him out?"

"Child," the Leanansidhe chided me. "The svartalves are quite skilled in the Art, and this is one of their strongholds. *I* could not attempt such a thing and leave with my life." Lea tilted her head to one side and gave me one of those alien looks that made my skin crawl. "Do you wish to recover Thomas or not?"

"I wish to explore my options," I said.

The faerie sorceress shrugged. "Then I advise you to do so as rapidly as possible. If he yet lives, Thomas Raith might count the remainder of his life in hours."

I opened the door to Waldo's apartment, shut and locked it behind me, and said, "Found him."

As I turned toward the room, someone slapped me hard across the face.

This wasn't a "Hey, wake up" kind of slap. It was an openhanded blow, one that would have really hurt if it was delivered with a closed fist. I staggered to one side, stunned.

Waldo's girlfriend, Andi, folded her arms and stared at me through narrowed eyes for a moment. She was a girl of medium height, but she was a werewolf and she was built like a pinup model who was thinking about going into professional wrestling. "Hi, Molly," she said.

"Hi," I said. "And— Ow."

She held up a pink plastic razor. "Let's have a talk about boundaries."

Something ugly way down deep inside me somewhere unsheathed its claws and tensed up. That was the part of me that wanted to catch up to Listen and do things involving railroad spikes and drains in the floor. Everyone has that inside them somewhere. It takes fairly horrible things to awaken that kind of savagery, but it's in all of us. It's the part of us that causes senseless atrocities, that makes war hell.

No one wants to talk about it or think about it, but I couldn't afford that kind of willing ignorance. I hadn't always been this way, but after a year fighting the Fomor and the dark underside of Chicago's supernatural scene, I was somebody else. That part of me was awake and active and constantly pushing my emotions into conflict with my rationality.

I told that part of me to shut up and sit its ass down.

"Okay," I said. "But later. I'm kind of busy."

I started to brush past her into the room, but she stopped me short by placing a hand against my sternum and shoving me back against the door. It didn't look like she was trying, but I hit the wood firmly.

"Now's good," she said.

In my imagination, I clenched my fists and counted to five in an enraged scream. I was sure Harry had never had to deal with this kind of nonsense. I didn't have time to lose, but I didn't want to start something violent with Andi, either. I'd catch all kinds of hell if I threw down. I allowed myself the pleasure of gritting my teeth, took a deep breath, and nodded. "Okay. What's on your mind, Andi?"

I didn't add the words *you bitch*, but I thought them really loud. I should probably be a nicer person.

"This is not your apartment," Andi said. "You don't get to roll in and out of here whenever you damned well please, no matter the hour, no matter what's going on. Have you even stopped to think about what you're doing to Butters?"

"I'm not doing anything to Butters," I said. "I'm just borrowing the shower."

Andi's voice sharpened. "You came here today covered in blood. I don't know what happened, but you know what? I don't care. All I care about is what kind of trouble you might draw down onto other people."

"There was no trouble," I said. "Look, I'll buy you a new razor."

"This isn't about property or money—Christ," Andi said. "This is about respect. Butters is there for you whenever you need help, and you barely do so much as thank him for it. What if you'd been followed here? Do you have any idea how much trouble he could get into for helping you out?"

"I wasn't followed," I said.

"Today," Andi said. "But what about next time? You have power. You can fight. I don't have what you do, but even I can fight. Butters can't. Whose shower are you going to use if it's his blood all over you?"

I folded my arms and looked carefully away from Andi. In some part of my brain I knew that she had a point, but that reasoning was coming in a distant second to my sudden urge to slap her.

"Look, Molly," she said, her voice becoming gentler. "I know things haven't been easy for you lately. Ever since Harry died. When his ghost showed up. I know it wasn't fun."

I just looked at her without speaking. *Not easy or fun.* That was one way to describe it.

"There's something I think you need to hear."

"What's that?"

Andi leaned forward slightly and sharpened her words. "Get over it."

The apartment was very quiet for a moment, and the inside of me wasn't. That ugly part of me started getting louder and louder. I closed my eyes.

"People die, Molly," Andi continued. "They leave. And life goes on. Harry may have been the first friend you lost, but he won't be the last. I get that you're hurting. I get that you're trying to step into some really big shoes. But that doesn't give you the right to abuse people's better natures. A *lot* of people are hurting lately, if you didn't notice."

If I didn't notice. God, I would absolutely *kill* to be able not to notice people's pain. Not to live it beside them. Not to sense its echoes hours or days later. The ugly part of me, the black part of my heart, wanted to open a psychic channel to Andi and *show* her the kind of thing I went through on a regular basis. Let *her* see how she would like my life. And we'd see if she was so righteous afterward. It would be wrong, but . . .

I took a slow breath. *No.* Harry told me once that you can always tell when you're about to rationalize your way to a bad decision. It's when you start using phrases such as *It would be wrong, but* . . . His advice was to leave the conjunction out of the sentence: *It would be wrong.* Period.

So I didn't do anything rash. I didn't let the rising tumult inside me come out. I spoke softly. "What is it you'd like me to do, exactly?"

Andi huffed out a little breath and waved a vague hand. "Just . . . get your head out of your ass, girl. I am not being unreasonable here, given that my boyfriend gave you a key to his freaking apartment."

I blinked once at that. Wow. I hadn't even really considered that aspect of what Butters had done. Romance and romantic conflict hadn't exactly been high on my list lately. Andi had nothing to worry about on that front, but I guess she didn't have way too much awareness of people's emotions to tip her off to that fact. Now I could put a name to some of the worry in her. She wasn't jealous, exactly, but she was certainly aware of the fact that I was a young woman a lot of men found attractive, and that Waldo was a man.

And she loved him. I could feel that, too.

"Think about him," Andi said quietly. "Please. Just try to take care of him the way he takes care of you. Call ahead. If you'd just walked in covered with blood next Saturday night, he would have had something very awkward to explain to his parents."

I most likely would have sensed the unfamiliar presences inside the apartment before I got close enough to touch the door. But there was no point in telling Andi that. It wasn't her fault that she didn't really understand the kind of life I lived. Certainly, she didn't deserve to die for it, no matter what the opinion of my inner Sith.

I had to make my choices with my head. My heart was too broken to be trusted.

"I'll try," I said.

"Okay," Andi said.

For a second, the fingers of my right hand quivered, and I found the ugly part of me about to hurl power at the other woman, blind her, deafen her, drown her in vertigo. Lea had shown me how. But I reeled the urge to attack back under control. "Andi," I said instead.

"Yes?"

"Don't hit me again unless you intend to kill me."

I didn't mean it as a threat, exactly. It was just that I tended to react with my instincts when things started getting violent. The psychic turbulence of that kind of conflict didn't make me fall over screaming in pain anymore, but it did make it really hard to think clearly over the furious roaring of ugly me. If Andi hit me like that again . . . well. I wasn't completely sure how I would react.

I'm not Mad Hatter insane. I'm pretty sure. But studying survival under someone like Auntie Lea leaves you ready to protect yourself, not to play well with others.

Threat or not, Andi had seen her share of conflict, and she didn't back down. "If I don't think you need a good smack in the face, I won't give you one."

Waldo and Justine had gone out to pick up some dinner, and got back about ten minutes later. We all sat down to eat while I reported on the situation.

"Svartalfheim," Justine breathed. "That's . . . that's not good."

"Those are the Norse guys, right?" Butters asked.

I filled them in between bites of orange chicken, relaying what I had learned from the Leanansidhe. There was a little silence after I did.

"So," Andi said after a moment. "The plan is to . . . boink him free?"

I gave her a look.

"I'm just asking," Andi said in a mild voice.

"They'd never sell," Justine said, her voice low, tight. "Not tonight."

I eyed her. "Why not?"

"They concluded an alliance today," she said. "There's a celebration tonight. Lara was invited."

"What alliance?" I asked.

"A nonaggression pact," Justine said, "with the Fomor."

I felt my eyes widen.

The Fomor situation just kept getting worse and worse. Chicago was far from the most preyed-upon city in the world, and they had still made the streets a nightmare for those of even modest magical talent. I didn't have access to the kind of information I had when I was working with Harry and the White Council, but I'd heard things through the Paranet and other sources. The Fomor were kind of an all-star team of bad guys, the survivors and outcasts and villains of a dozen different pantheons that had gone down a long time ago. They'd banded together under the banner of a group of beings known as the Fomor, and had been laying quiet for a long time—for thousands of years, in fact.

Now they were on the move—and even powerful interests like Svartalfheim, the nation of the svartalves, were getting out of the way.

Wow, I was so not wizard enough to deal with this.

"Lara must have sent Thomas in for something," Justine said. "To steal information, to disrupt the alliance somehow. Something. Trespassing would be bad enough. If he was captured spying on them . . ."

"They'll have a demonstration," I said quietly. "They'll make an example."

"Couldn't the White Court get him out?" Waldo asked.

"If the White Court seeks the return of one of their own, it would be like admitting they sent an agent in to screw around with Svartalfheim," I said. "Lara can't do that without serious repercussions. She'll deny that Thomas's intrusion had anything to do with her."

Justine rose and paced the room, her body tight. "We have to go. We have to do something. I'll pay the price; I'll pay it ten times. We have to *do* something!"

I took a few more bites of orange chicken, frowning and thinking.

"Molly!" Justine said.

I looked at the chicken. I liked the way the orange sauce contrasted with the deep green of the broccoli and the soft white contours of the rice. The three colors made a pleasant complement. It was . . . beautiful, really.

"They covet beauty like a dragon covets gold," I murmured.

Butters seemed to clue in to the fact that I was onto something. He leaned back in his chair and ate steadily from a box of noodles, his chopsticks precise. He didn't need to look to use them.

Andi picked up on it a second later and tilted her head to one side. "Molly?" she asked.

"They're having a party tonight," I said. "Right, Justine?"

"Yes."

Andi nodded impatiently. "What are we going to do?"

"We," I said, "are going shopping."

I'm kind of a tomboy. Not because I don't like being a girl or anything, because for the most part I think it's pretty sweet. But I like the outdoors and physical activities, and learning stuff and reading things and building things. I've never really gotten very deep into the girly parts of being a girl. Andi was a little bit better at it than me. The fact that her mother hadn't brought her up the way mine had probably accounted for it. In my house, makeup was for going to church and for women with easy morals.

I know, I know. The mind boggles at the contradiction. I had issues way before I got involved with magic, believe me.

I wasn't sure how to accomplish what we needed in time to get to the party, but once I explained what we needed, I found out that when it came to being a girly girl, Justine had her shit wired tight.

Within minutes a town car picked us up and whisked us away to a private salon in the Loop, where Justine produced a completely unmarked, plain white credit card. About twenty staff members—wardrobe advisors, hairdressers, makeup artists, tailors, and accessory technicians—leapt into action and got us kitted out for the mission in a little more than an hour.

I couldn't really get away from the mirror this time. I tried to look at the young woman in it objectively, as if she were someone else, and not the one who had helped kill the man she loved and who had then failed him again by being unable to prevent even his ghost from being destroyed in its determination to protect others. That bitch deserved to be run over by a train or something.

The girl in the mirror was tall and had naturally blond hair that had been rapidly swirled up off of her neck and suspended with gleaming black chopsticks. She looked lean, probably too much so, but had a little too much muscle tone to be a meth addict. The little black dress she wore would turn heads. She looked a little tired, even with the expertly applied makeup. She was pretty—if you didn't know her, and if you didn't look too hard at what was going on in her blue eyes.

A white stretch limo pulled up to get us, and I managed to dodder out to it without falling all over myself.

"Oh, my God," Andi said when we got in. The redhead stuck her feet out and wiggled them. "I love these shoes! If I have to wolf out and eat somebody's face, I am going to cry to leave these behind."

Justine smiled at her but then looked out the window, her lovely face distant, worried. "They're just shoes."

"Shoes that make my legs and my butt look awesome!" Andi said.

"Shoes that hurt," I said. My wounded leg might have healed up, but moving around in these spiky torture devices was a new motion, and a steady ache was spreading up through my leg toward my hip. The last thing I needed was for my leg to cramp up and drop me to the ground, the way it had kept doing when I first started walking on it again. Any shoes with heels that high should come with their own safety net. Or a parachute.

We'd gone with similar outfits: stylish little black dresses, black chokers, and black pumps that proclaimed us hopeful that we wouldn't spend much time on our feet. Each of us had a little Italian leather clutch, too. I'd put most of my magical gear in mine. All of us had our hair up in styles that varied only slightly. There were forged Renaissance paintings that had not had as much artist's attention as our faces.

"It just takes practice wearing them," Justine said. "Are you sure this is going to work?"

"Of course it is," I said calmly. "You've been to clubs, Justine. The three of us together would skip the line to any place in town. We're a matched set of hotness."

"Like the Robert Palmer girls," Andi said drily.

"I was going to go with Charlie's Angels," I said. "Oh, speaking of"—I opened the clutch and drew out a quartz crystal the size of my thumb—"Bosley, can you hear me?"

A second later, the crystal vibrated in my fingers and we heard Waldo's faint voice coming from it. "Loud and clear, Angels. You think these will work once you get inside?"

"Depends on how paranoid they are," I said. "If they're paranoid, they'll have defenses in place to cut off any magical communications. If they're murderously paranoid, they'll have defenses in place that let us talk so that they can listen in, and then they'll kill us."

"Fun," Butters said. "Okay, I've got the Paranet chat room up. For what it's worth, the hivemind is online."

"What have you found out?" Andi asked.

"They'll look human," Waldo replied. "Their real forms are . . . Well, there's some discussion, but the basic consensus is that they look like aliens."

"Ripley or Roswell?" I asked.

"Roswell. More or less. They can wear flesh forms, though, kind of like the Red Court vampires did. So be aware that they'll be disguised."

"Got it," I said. "Anything else?"

"Not much," he said. "There's just too much lore floating around to pick out anything for sure. They might be allergic to salt. They might be supernaturally OCD and flip out if you wear your clothes inside out. They might turn to stone in sunlight."

I growled. "It was worth a shot. Okay. Keep the discussion going, and I'll get back to you if I can."

"Got it," he said. "Marci just got here. I'll bring the laptop with me and we'll be waiting for you on the east side of the building when you're ready to go. How do you look, Andi-licious?"

"Fabulous," Andi said confidently. "The hemlines on these dresses stop about an inch short of Slutty Nymphomaniac."

"Someone take a picture," he said cheerfully, but I could hear the worry in his voice. "I'll see you soon."

"Don't take any chances," I said. "See you soon."

I put the crystal away and tried to ignore the butterflies in my stomach.

"This isn't going to work," Justine murmured.

"It is going to work," I told her, keeping my tone confident. "We'll breeze right in. The Rack will be with us."

Justine glanced at me with an arched eyebrow. "The Rack?"

"The Rack is more than just boobs, Justine," I told her soberly. "It's an energy field created by all living boobs. It surrounds us, penetrates us, and binds the galaxy together."

Andi started giggling. "You're insane."

"But functionally so," I said, and adjusted myself to round out a little better. "Just let go your conscious self and act on instinct."

Justine stared blankly at me for a second. Then her face lightened and she let out a little laugh. "The Rack will be with us?"

I couldn't stop myself from cracking a smile. "Always."

The limo joined a line of similar vehicles dropping people off at the entrance to the svartalf stronghold. A valet opened our door, and I swung my legs out and tried to leave the car without flashing everyone in sight. Andi and Justine followed me out, and I started walking confidently toward the entrance with the other two flanking me. Our heels clicked in near unison, and I suddenly felt every eye in sight swivel toward us. A cloud of thought and emotion rolled out in response to our presence—pleasure, mostly, along with a mixed slurry of desire, outright lust, jealousy, anxiety, and surprise. It hurt to feel all of that scraping against the inside of my head, but it was necessary. I didn't sense any outright hostility or imminent violence, and the instant of warning I might get between sensing an attacker's intention and the moment of attack might save our lives.

A security guard at the door watched us intently as we approached, and I could feel the uncomplicated sexual attraction churning through him. He kept it off his face and out of his voice and body, though. "Good evening, ladies," he said. "May I see your invitations?"

I arched an eyebrow at him, gave him what I hoped was a seductive smile, and tried to arch my back a little more. Deploying the Rack had worked before. "You don't need to see our invitation."

"Um," he said. "Miss, I kind of do."

Andi stepped up beside me and gave him a sex-kitten smile that made me hate her a little, just for a second. "No, you don't."

"Uh," he said, "yeah. Still do."

Justine stepped up on my other side. She looked more sweet than sexy, but only barely. "I'm sure it was just an oversight, sir. Couldn't you ask your supervisor if we might come to the reception?"

He stared at us for a long moment, clearly hesitant. Then one hand slowly went to the radio at his side and he lifted it to his mouth. A moment later a slight, small man in a silk suit appeared from inside the building. He took a long look at us.

The interest I'd felt from the guard was fairly normal. It had just been a spark, the instinct-level response of any male to a desirable female.

What came off of the new guy was . . . It was more like a road flare. It burned a thousand times hotter and brighter, and it kept *on* burning. I'd sensed lust and desire in others before. This went so much deeper and wider than mere lust that I didn't think there was a word for it. It was a vast and inhuman yearning, blended with a fierce and jealous love, and seasoned with sexual attraction and desire. It was like standing near a tiny sun, and I suddenly understood exactly what Auntie Lea had been trying to tell me.

Fire is hot. Water is wet. And svartalves are suckers for pretty girls. They could no more change their nature than they could the course of the stars.

"Ladies," the new guy said, smiling at us. It was a charming smile, but there was something distant and disquieting in his face all the same. "Please, wait just a moment for me to alert my other staff. We would be honored if you would join us."

He turned and went inside.

Justine gave me a sidelong look.

"The Rack can have a powerful influence over the weak-minded," I said.

"I'd feel better if he hadn't left on a Darth Vader line," Andi breathed. "He smelled odd. Was he . . . ?"

"Yeah," I whispered back. "One of them."

The man in the silk suit reappeared, still smiling, and opened the door for us. "Ladies," he said, "I am Mr. Etri. Please, come inside."

I had never in my life seen a place more opulent than the inside of the svartalves' stronghold. Not in magazines, not in the movies. Not even on *Cribs*.

There were tons of granite and marble. There were sections of wall that had been inlaid with precious and semiprecious stones. Lighting fixtures were crafted of what looked like solid gold, and the light switches looked like they'd been carved from fine ivory. Security guards were stationed every twenty or thirty feet, standing at rigid attention like those guys outside Buckingham Palace, only without the big hats. Light came from everywhere and from nowhere, making all shadows thin and wispy things without becoming too bright for the eyes. Music drifted on the air, some old classical thing that was all strings and no drumbeat.

Etri led us down a couple of hallways to a vast cathedral of a ballroom. It was absolutely palatial in there—in fact, I was pretty sure that the room shouldn't have *fit* in the building we'd just entered—and it was filled with expensive-looking people in expensive-looking clothing.

We paused in the entry while Etri stopped to speak to yet another security guy. I took the moment it offered to sweep my gaze over the room. The place wasn't close to full, but there were a lot of people there. I recognized a couple of celebrities, people you'd know if I told you their names. There were a number of the Sidhe in attendance, their usual awe-inspiring physical perfection muted to mere exotic beauty. I spotted Gentleman Johnnie Marcone, the head of Chicago's outfit, in attendance, with his gorilla, Hendricks, and his personal attack witch, Gard, floating around near him. There were any number of people who I was sure weren't people; I could sense the blurring of perception in the air around them as if they were cut off from me by a thin curtain of falling water.

But I didn't see Thomas.

"Molly," Justine whispered, barely audible. "Is he . . . ?"

The tracking spell I'd focused on my lips was still functioning, a faint tingle telling me that Thomas was nearby, deeper into the interior of the building. "He's alive," I said. "He's here."

Justine shuddered and took a deep breath. She blinked slowly once, her face showing nothing as she did. I felt the surge of simultaneous relief and terror in her presence, though, a sudden blast of emotion that cried out for her to scream or fight or burst into tears. She did none of that, and I turned my eyes away from her in order to give her the illusion that I hadn't noticed her near meltdown.

In the center of the ballroom, there was a small, raised platform of stone with a few stairs leading up onto it. Upon the platform was a podium of the same material. Resting on the podium was a thick folio of papers and a neat row of fountain pens. There was something solemn and ceremonial about the way it was set up.

Justine was looking at it, too. "That must be it."

"The treaty?"

She nodded. "The svartalves are very methodical about business. They'll conclude the treaty precisely at midnight. They always do."

Andi tapped a finger thoughtfully on her hip. "What if something happened to their treaty first? I mean, if someone spilled a bunch of wine on it or something. That would be attention getting, I bet— maybe give a couple of us a chance to sneak farther in."

I shook my head. "No. We're guests here. Do you understand?"

"Uh. Not really."

"The svartalves are old-school," I said. "*Really* old-school. If we break the peace when they've invited us into their territory, we're violating our guest right and offering them disrespect as our hosts—right out in the open, in front of the entire supernatural community. They'll react . . . badly."

Andi frowned and said, "Then what's our next move?"

Why do people keep asking me that? Is this what all wizard types go through? I'd probably asked Harry that question a hundred times, but I never realized how hard it was to hear it coming toward you. But Harry always knew what to do next. All I could do was improvise desperately and hope for the best.

"Justine," I said, "do you know any of the players here?"

As Lara Raith's personal assistant, Justine came in contact with a lot of people and not-quite-people. Lara had so many fingers in so many pies that I could barely make a joke about it, and Justine saw, heard, and thought a lot more than anyone gave her credit for. The white-haired girl scanned the room, her dark eyes flicking from face to face. "Several."

"All right. I want you to circulate and see what you can find out," I said. "Keep an eye out. If you see them sending the brute squad after us, get on the crystal and warn us."

"Okay," Justine whispered. "Careful."

Etri returned and smiled again, though his eyes remained oddly, unsettlingly without expression. He flicked one hand, and a man in a tux floated over to us with a tray of drinks. We helped ourselves, and Etri did, too. He lifted his glass to us and said, "Ladies, be welcome. To beauty."

We echoed him and we all sipped. I barely let my lips touch the liquid. It was champagne, really good stuff. It fizzed and I could barely taste the alcohol. I wasn't worried about poison. Etri had quite diffidently allowed us to choose our glasses before taking one of his own.

I was actually more worried about the fact that I'd stopped to consider potential poisoning, and to watch Etri's actions carefully as he served us. Is it paranoid to worry about things like that? It seemed reasonable to me at the time.

Man, maybe I'm more messed up than I thought I was.

"Please enjoy the reception," Etri said. "I'm afraid I must insist on a dance with each of you lovely young ladies when time and duty allow. Who shall be first?"

Justine gave him a Rack-infused smile and lifted her hand. If you twisted my arm, I'd tell you that Justine was definitely the prettiest girl in our little trio, and Etri evidently agreed. His eyes turned warm for an instant before he took Justine's hand and led her out onto the dance floor. They vanished into the moving crowd.

"I couldn't do this ballroom stuff, anyway," Andi said. "Not nearly enough booty bouncing. Next-move time?"

"Next-move time," I said. "Come on."

I turned to follow the tingle in my lips and the two of us made our way to the back side of the ballroom, where doors led deeper into the facility. There were no guards on the doors, but as we got closer, Andi's steps started to slow. She glanced over to one side, where there was a refreshments table, and I saw her begin to turn toward it.

I caught her arm and said, "Hold it. Where are you going?"

"Um," she said, frowning. "Over there?"

I extended my senses and felt the subtle weaving of magic in the air around the doorway, cobweb fine. It was a kind of veil, designed to direct the attention of anyone approaching it away from the doorway and toward anything else in the room. It made the refreshment table look yummier. If Andi had spotted a guy, he would have looked a lot cuter than he actually was.

I'd been having a powerful faerie sorceress throwing veils and glamours at me for almost a year, building up my mental defenses, and a few months ago I'd gone twelve rounds in the psychic boxing ring with a heavyweight-champion necromancer. I hadn't even noticed the gentle magical weaving hitting my mental shields.

"It's an enchantment," I told her. "Don't let it sway you."

"What?" she asked. "I don't feel anything. I'm just hungry."

"You wouldn't feel it," I said. "That's how it works. Take my hand and close your eyes. Trust me."

"If I had a nickel for every time a bad evening started with a line like that," she muttered. But she put her hand in mine and closed her eyes.

I walked her toward the doorway and felt her growing tenser as we went, but then we passed through it and she let out her breath explosively, blinking her eyes open. "Wow. That felt . . . like nothing at all."

"It's how you recognize quality enchantment," I said. "If you don't know it's got you, you can't fight it off." The hallway we stood in looked much like any in any office building. I tried the nearest door and found it locked. So were the next couple, but the last was an empty conference room, and I slipped inside.

I fumbled the crystal out of my little clutch and said, "Bosley, can you hear me?"

"Loud and clear, Angels," came Waldo's voice. Neither of us used real names. The crystals were probably secure, but a year with Lea's nasty trickery as a daily feature of life had taught me not to make many assumptions.

"Were you able to come up with those floor plans?"

"About ninety seconds ago. The building's owners filed everything with the city in triplicate, including electronic copies, which I am now looking at, courtesy of the hivemind."

"Advantage, nerds," I said. "Tell them they did good, Boz."

"Will do," Waldo said. "These people you're visiting are thorough, Angels. Be careful."

"When am I not careful?" I said.

Andi had taken up a guard position against the wall next to the door, where she could grab anyone who opened it. "Seriously?"

I couldn't help but smile a little. "I think our lost lamb is in the wing of the building to the west of the reception hall. What's there?"

"Um . . . offices, it looks like. Second floor, more offices. Third floor, more offi— Hello there."

"What'd you find?"

"A vault," Waldo said. "Reinforced steel. Huge."

"Ha," I said. "A reinforced-steel vault? Twenty bucks says it's a dungeon. We start there."

"Whatever it is, it's in the basement. There should be a stairway leading down to it at the end of the hallway leading out of the reception hall."

"Bingo," I said. "Stay tuned, Bosley."

"Will do. Your chariot awaits."

I put the crystal away and began putting on my rings. I got them all together, then began to pick up my wands, and realized that I couldn't carry them in each hand while also carrying the little clutch. "I knew I should have gone for a messenger bag," I muttered.

"With that dress?" Andi asked. "Are you kidding?"

"True." I took the crystal out and tucked it into my décolletage, palmed one of the little wands in each hand, and nodded to Andi. "If it's a vault or a dungeon, there will be guards. I'm going to make it hard for them to see us, but we might have to move fast."

Andi looked down at her shoes and sighed mournfully. Then she stepped out of them and peeled the little black dress off. She hadn't been wearing anything underneath. She closed her eyes for a second and then her form just seemed to blur and melt. Werewolves don't do dramatic, painful transformations except right at first, I've been told. This looked as natural as a living being turning in a circle and sitting down. One moment Andi was there, and the next there was a great, russet-furred wolf sitting where she'd been.

It was highly cool magic. I was going to have to figure out how that was done one of these days.

"Don't draw blood unless it's absolutely necessary," I said, stepping out of my own torturous shoes. "I'm going to try to make this quick and painless. If there's any rough stuff, not killing anyone will go a long way with the svartalves."

Andi yawned at me.

"Ready?" I asked.

Andi bobbed her lupine head in a sharp, decisive nod. I drew the concealing magic of my top-of-the-line veil around us, and the light suddenly went dim, the colors leaching out of the world. We would be almost impossible to see. And anyone who came within fifty or sixty feet of us would develop a sudden desire for a bit of introspection, questioning their path in life so deeply that there was practically no chance we'd be detected as long as we were quiet.

With Andi walking right beside me, we stole out into the hallway. We found the stairwell Waldo had told us about, and I opened the door to it slowly. I didn't go first. You can't do much better than having a werewolf as your guide, and I'd worked with Andi and her friends often enough in the past year to make our movements routine.

Andi went through first, moving in total silence, her ears perked, her nose twitching. Wolves have incredible senses of smell. Hearing, too. If anyone was around, Andi would sense them. After a tense quarter of a minute, she gave me the signal that it was all clear by sitting down. I eased up next to her and extended my senses, feeling for any more magical defenses or enchantments. There were half a dozen on the first section of the stairwell—simple things, the sorcerous equivalent of trip wires.

Fortunately, Auntie Lea had shown me how to circumvent enchantments such as these. I made an effort of will and modified our veil, and then I nodded to Andi and we started slowly down the stairs. We slipped through the invisible fields of magic without disturbing them and crept down to the basement.

I checked the door at the bottom of the stairs and found it unlocked.

"This seems way too easy," I muttered. "If it's a prison, shouldn't this be locked?"

Andi let out a low growl, and I could sense her agreement and suspicion.

My mouth still tingled, much more strongly now. Thomas was close. "Guess there's not a lot of choice here." I opened the door, slowly and quietly.

The door didn't open onto some kind of dungeon. It didn't open up to show us a vault, either. Instead, Andi and I found ourselves staring at a long hallway every bit as opulent as those above, with large and ornate doors spaced generously along it. Each door had a simple number on it, wrought in what looked like pure silver. Very subdued lighting was spaced strategically along its length, leaving it comfortably dim without being dark.

Andi's low growl turned into a confused little sound and she tilted her head to one side.

"Yeah," I said, perplexed. "It looks like . . . a hotel. There's even a sign showing fire-escape routes on the wall."

Andi gave her head a little shake, and I sensed enough of her emotions to understand her meaning. *What the hell?*

"I know," I said. "Is this . . . living quarters for the svartalves? Guest accommodations?"

Andi glanced up at me and flicked her ears. *Why are you asking me? I can't even talk.*

"I know you can't. Just thinking out loud."

Andi blinked, her ears snapping toward me, and she gave me a sidelong glance. *You heard me?*

"I didn't so much hear you as just . . . understand you."

She leaned very slightly away from me. *Just when I thought you couldn't get any more weird and disturbing.*

I gave her a maliciously wide smile and the crazy eyes I used to use to scare my kid brothers and sisters.

Andi snorted and then began testing the air with her nose. I watched her closely. Her hackles rose and I saw her crouch down. *There are things here. Too many scents to sort out. Something familiar, and not in a good way.*

"Thomas is close. Come on." We started forward, and I kept my face turned directly toward the tingling signature of my tracking spell. It began to bear to the right, and as we got to the door to room 6, the tingle suddenly swung to the very corner of my mouth, until I turned to face the doorway directly. "Here, in six."

Andi looked up and down the hall, her eyes restless, her ears trying to swivel in every direction. *I don't like this.*

"Too easy," I whispered. "This is way too easy." I reached out toward the doorknob and stopped. My head told me this situation was all wrong. So did my instincts. If Thomas was a prisoner being held by Svartalfheim, then where were the cages, the chains, the locks, the bars, the guards? And if he wasn't being held against his will, what *was* he doing here?

When you find yourself in a situation that doesn't make any sense, it's usually for one reason: You have bad information. You can get bad information in several ways. Sometimes you're just plain wrong about what you learn. More often, and more dangerously, your information is bad because you made a faulty assumption.

Worst of all is when someone deliberately feeds it to you—and, like a sucker, you trust her and take it without hesitation.

"Auntie," I breathed. "She *tricked* me." Lea hadn't sent me into the building to rescue Thomas—or at least not only for that. It was no freaking coincidence that she'd taught me how to specifically circumvent the magical security the svartalves were using, either. She'd had another purpose in bringing me here on this night.

I replayed our conversation in my mind and snarled. Nothing she told me was a lie, and all of it had been tailored to make me reach the wrong conclusion—that Thomas had to be rescued and that I was the only one who would do it. I didn't know why the Leanansidhe thought I needed to be where I was, but she sure as hell had made sure I would get there.

"That conniving, double-speaking, treacherous *bitch*. When I catch up with her, I'm going to—"

Andi let out a sudden, very low growl, and I shut up in the nick of time.

The door from the upstairs opened, and that bastard Listen and several turtlenecks started walking down the hall toward us.

Listen was a lean and fit-looking man of middling height. His hair was cropped military short, his skin was pale, and his dark eyes looked hard and intelligent. The werewolves and I had tried to bring him down half a dozen different times, but he always managed to either escape or turn the tables and make us run for our lives.

Vicious bad guys are bad enough. Vicious, resourceful, ruthless, professional, *smart* bad guys are way worse. Listen was one of the latter, and I hated his fishy guts.

He and his lackeys were dressed in the standard uniform of the Fomor servitors: black slacks, black shoes, and a black turtleneck sweater. The high neck of the sweater covered up the gills on both sides of their necks, so that they could pass as mortals. They weren't, or at least they weren't anymore. The Fomor had changed them, making them stronger, faster, and all but immune to pain. I'd never managed to set up a successful ambush before, and now one had fallen right into my lap. I absolutely *ached* to avenge the blood I'd washed from my body early that very day.

But the servitors had weird minds, and they kept getting weirder. It was damned difficult to get into their heads the way I would need to do, and if that first attack failed in close quarters like these, that crew would tear Andi and me apart.

So I ground my teeth. I put my hand on Andi's neck and squeezed slightly as I crouched down beside her, focusing on the veil. I had to tamp down on the introspection suggestion: Listen had nearly killed me a few months before, when he noticed a similar enchantment altering the course of his thoughts. That had been damned scary, but I'd worked on it since then. I closed my eyes and spun the lightest, finest cobwebs of suggestion that my gifts could manage while simultaneously drawing the veil even tighter around us. The light in the hallway shrunk to almost nothing, and the air just over my skin became noticeably cooler.

They came closer, Listen clearly in the lead, walking with swift and silent purpose. The son of a bitch passed within two feet of me. I could have reached out and touched him with my hand.

None of them stopped.

They went down the hall to room 8, and Listen pushed a key into a door. He opened it, and he and his buddies began to enter the room.

This was an opportunity I couldn't pass up. For all the horror the Fomor had brought to the world since the extinction of the Red Court, we still didn't know why they did what they did. We didn't know what they wanted, or how they thought their current actions would get it for them.

So I moved in all the silence the past year had taught me the hard way, and stalked up to the line of servitors passing into the chamber. After a startled second, Andi joined me just as quietly. We barely slipped through the door before it shut.

No one looked back at us as we passed into a palatial suite, furnished as lavishly as the rest of the building. In addition to the half dozen turtlenecks in Listen's party, another five were standing around the room in a guard position, backs straight, their arms clasped behind them.

"Where is he?" Listen asked a guard standing beside a door. The guard was the biggest turtleneck there, with a neck like a fireplug.

"Inside," the guard said.

"It is nearly time," Listen said. "Inform him."

"He left orders that he was not to be disturbed."

Listen seemed to consider that for a moment. Then he said, "A lack of punctuality will invalidate the treaty and make our mission impossible. Inform him."

The guard scowled. "The lord left orders that—"

Listen's upper body surged in a sudden motion, so fast that I could only see it *as* motion. The big guard let out a sudden hiss and a grunt, and blood abruptly fountained from his throat. He staggered a step, turned to Listen, and raised a hand.

Then he shuddered and collapsed on the floor, blood pumping rapidly from a huge and jagged wound in his neck.

Listen dropped a chunk of meat the size of a baseball from his bare, bloody fingers, and bent over to wipe them clean on the dead turtleneck's sweater. The blood didn't show against the black. He straightened up again and then knocked on the door.

"My lord. It is nearly midnight."

He did it again exactly sixty seconds later.

And he repeated it three more times before a slurred voice answered, "I left orders that I was not to be disturbed."

"Forgive me, my lord, but the time is upon us. If we do not act, our efforts are for nothing."

"It is not for you to presume what orders may or may not be ignored," said the voice. "Execute the fool who allowed my sleep to be disturbed."

"It is already done, my lord."

There was a somewhat mollified grunt from the far side of the door, and a moment later it opened, and for the first time I saw one of the lords of the Fomor.

He was a tall, extremely gaunt being, yet somehow not thin. His hands and feet were too large, and his stomach bulged as if it contained a basketball. His jowls were oversized as well, his jaws swollen as if he had the mumps. His lips were too wide, too thick, and too rubbery-looking. His hair was too flattened, too limp, like strands of seaweed just washed up onto shore, and on the whole he looked like some kind of gangling, poisonous frog. He was dressed only in a blanket draped across his shoulders. *Ew.*

There were three women in the room behind him, naked and scattered and dead. Each had livid purple bruises around her throat and glassy, staring eyes.

The turtlenecks all dropped to the floor in supplication as the Fomor entered, though Listen only genuflected upon one knee.

"He is here?" asked the Fomor.

"Yes, my lord," Listen said, "along with both of his bodyguards."

The Fomor croaked out a little laugh and rubbed his splay-fingered hands together. "Mortal upstart. Calling himself a baron. He will pay for what he did to my brother."

"Yes, my lord."

"No one is allowed to murder my family but me."

"Of course, my lord."

"Bring me the shell."

Listen bowed and nodded to three of the other turtlenecks. They hurried to another door and then emerged, carrying between them an oyster shell that must have weighed half a ton. The thing was monstrous and covered in a crust of coral or barnacles or whatever those things are that grow on the hulls of ships. It was probably seven feet across. The turtlenecks put it down on the floor in the middle of the room.

The Fomor crossed to the shell, touched it with one hand, and murmured a word. Instantly, light blossomed all across its surface, curling and twisting in patterns or maybe letters I had never seen before. The Fomor stood over it for a time, one hand outstretched, bulbous eyes narrowed, saying something in a hissing, bubbling tongue.

I didn't know what he was doing, but he was moving a lot of energy around, whatever it was. I could feel it filling the air of the chamber, making it seem tighter and somehow harder to breathe.

"My lord?" asked Listen abruptly. "What are you doing?"

"Making a present for our new allies, of course," the Fomor said. "I can hardly annihilate the svartalves along with everyone else. Not yet."

"This is not according to the plans of the Empress."

"The Empress," spat the Fomor, "told me that I ought not harm our new allies. She said nothing of the puling scum attending their festivities."

"The svartalves value their honor dearly," Listen said. "You will shame them if their guests come to harm whilst under their hospitality, my lord. It could defeat the point of the alliance."

The Fomor spat. A glob of yellowy, mucuslike substance splattered the floor near Listen's feet. It hissed and crackled against the marble floor. "Once the treaty is signed, it is done. My gift will be given to them in the moments after: I will spare their miserable lives. And if the rest of the scum turn against the svartalves, they will have no choice but to turn to *us* for our strength." He smirked. "Fear not, Listen. I am not so foolish as to destroy one of the Empress's special pets, even in an accident. You and your fellows will survive."

I suddenly recognized the tenor of energy building up in the giant shell on the floor and my heart just about stopped.

*Holy crap.*

Lord Froggy had himself a *bomb*.

Like, right *there*.

"My life belongs to my masters, to spend as they will, my lord," Listen said. "Have you any other instruction?"

"Seize whatever treasure you might from the dead before we depart."

Listen bowed his head. "How efficacious do you anticipate your gift to be?"

"The one I made for the Red Court in the Congo was deadly enough," Lord Froggy said, a smug tone in his voice.

My heart pounded even harder. During its war with the White Council, the Red Court had used some kind of nerve gas on a hospital tending wounded wizards. The weapon had killed tens of thousands of people in a city far smaller and less crowded than Chicago.

My bare feet felt tiny and cold.

Lord Froggy grunted and fluttered his fingers, and the bombshell vanished, hidden by a veil as good as anything I could do. The Fomor lord abruptly lowered his hand, smiling. "Bring my robes."

The turtlenecks hurriedly dressed Lord Froggy in what might have been the tackiest robe in the history of robekind. Multiple colors wavered over it in patterns like the ripples on water, but seemed random, clashing with one another. It was beaded with pearls, some of them the size of big supermarket gumballs. They put a crownlike circlet on his head after that, and then Lord Froggy and company headed out the door.

I crouched as far to the side as I could, almost under the minibar, with Andi huddling right beside me, holding my veil in tight. Lord Froggy blew right by me, with the turtlenecks walking in two columns behind him, their movements precise and uniform—until one of the last pair stopped, his hand holding the door open.

It was Listen.

His eyes swept the room slowly, and he frowned.

"What is it?" asked the other turtleneck.

"Do you smell something?" Listen asked.

"Like what?"

"Perfume."

*Oh, crap.*

I closed my eyes and focused on my suggestion frantically, adding threads of anxiety to it, trying to keep it too fine for Listen to pick up on.

After a moment, the other turtleneck said, "I've never really liked perfume. We should not be so far from the lord."

Listen hesitated a moment more before he nodded and began to leave.

"Molly!" said Justine's voice quite clearly from the crystal tucked into my dress. "Miss Gard freaked out about two minutes ago and all but carried Marcone out of here. Security is mobilizing."

Sometimes I think my life is all about bad timing.

Listen whirled around toward us at once, but Andi was faster. She bounded from the floor into a ten-foot leap and slammed against the doorway, hammering it closed with the full weight of her body. In a flickering instant, she was a naked human girl again, straining against the door as she reached up and manually snapped its locks closed.

I fished the crystal out of my dress and said, "There's a bomb on the premises, down in the guest wing. I repeat, a *bomb* in the guest wing, in the Fomor ambassador's quarters. Find Etri or one of the other svartalves and tell them that the Fomor are planning to murder the svartalves' guests."

"Oh, my God," Justine said.

"Holy crap!" chimed in Butters.

Something heavy and moving fast slammed into the door from the other side, and it jumped in its frame. Andi was actually knocked back off of it a few inches, and she reset herself, pressing her shoulder against it to reinforce it. "Molly!"

This was another one of those situations in which panic can get you killed. So while I wanted to scream and run around in circles, what I did was close my eyes for a moment as I released the veil and took a slow, deep breath, ordering my thoughts.

First: If Froggy and the turtlenecks managed to get back into the room, they'd kill us. There were already at least four dead bodies in the suite. Why not add two more? And, all things considered, they'd probably be able to do it. So priority one was to keep them out of the room, at least until the svartalves sorted things out.

Second: the bomb. If that thing went off, and it was some kind of nerve agent like the Red Court used in Africa, the casualties could be in the hundreds of thousands, and would include Andi and Thomas and Justine—plus Butters and Marci, waiting outside in the car. The bomb had to be disarmed or moved to somewhere safe. Oh, and it would probably need to not be invisible for either of those things to happen.

And three: Rescue Thomas. Can't forget the mission, regardless of how complicated things got.

The door boomed again.

"Molly!" Andi screamed, her fear making her voice vibrant, piercing.

"Dammit," I growled. "What would Harry do?"

If Harry were here, he would just hold the stupid door shut. His magic talents had been, like, superhero strong when it came to being able to deliver massive amounts of energy. I'm fairly sure he could have stopped a speeding locomotive. Or at least a speeding semitrailer. But my talents just didn't run to the physical.

Harry had once told me that when you had one problem, you had a problem. But when you had several problems, you might also have several solutions.

I stood up and dropped my wands into my hands, gripping them hard. I faced the doorway and said, "Get ready."

Andi flashed me a glance. "For what?"

"To open the door," I said. "Then shut it behind me."

"*What?*"

"Close your eyes. Go on three," I said, and bent my knees slightly. "One!"

The door rattled again.

"Two!"

"Are you insane?" Andi demanded.

"Three!" I screamed, and sprinted for the door, lifting both wands.

Andi squeezed her eyes shut and swung the door open, and I deployed the One-Woman Rave.

Channeling the strength of my will, light and sound burst from the ends of the two wands. Not light like from a flashlight; more like the light of a small nuclear explosion. The sound wasn't loud like a scream or a small explosion, or even the howl of a passing train. It was like standing on the deck of one of those old World War II battleships when they fired their big guns—a force that could stun a full-grown man and knock him on his ass.

I charged ahead with a wall of sound and furious light leading the way, and burst into the hall among the scattered forms of the startled, dazed turtlenecks.

And then I started playing nasty.

A few seconds later, the scattered turtlenecks were all on their feet again, though they looked a little disoriented and were blinking. Down the hallway, one of the turtlenecks was helping Lord Froggy to his feet, his lank hair disheveled, his robes in disarray. His ugly face was contorted in fury. "What is happening here, Listen?" he demanded. He was screaming at the top of his lungs. I doubt his ears were working very well.

"My lord," Listen said, "I believe this is more of the work of the Ragged Lady."

"What!? Speak up, fool!"

Listen's cheek twitched once. Then he repeated himself in a shout.

Froggy made a hissing sound. "Meddling bitch," he snarled. "Break down that door and bring me her *heart*."

"Yes, my lord," Listen said, and the turtlenecks grouped up around the door to room 8 again.

They didn't use any tools. They didn't need any. They just started kicking the door, three of them at a time, working in unison, driving the heels of their shoes at the wood. In three kicks, cracks began to form and the door groaned. In five, it broke and swung in loosely on its hinges.

"Kill her!" snarled Lord Froggy, pacing closer to the broken door. "*Kill* her!"

All but two of the turtlenecks poured into the room.

From behind my renewed veil, I figured the timing was about right to discontinue my illusion just as the door bounced back after they'd rushed through it. The silver numeral 8 hanging on the door blurred and melted back into a silver numeral 6.

Lord Froggy's eyes widened in sudden, startled realization.

One of the turtlenecks flew back out the door to room 6 and smashed into the wall on the far side. He hit like a rag doll and flopped to the ground. There was a body-shaped outline in cracked marble and flecks of fresh blood left on the wall behind him.

And from the other side of the broken door, Thomas Raith, vampire, said, "It's Listen, right? Wow. Did you clowns ever pick the wrong room."

"We made a mistake," Listen said.

"Yes. Yes, you did."

And things started going crunch and thump in the room beyond.

Lord Froggy hissed and swiveled his bulgy head around on his gangly neck. "Ragged bitch," he hissed. "I know you are here."

This time, I knew exactly what Harry would do. I lifted my sonic wand and sent my voice down to the far end of the hall, behind him. "Hi there, Froggy. Is it as hard as it looks, holding up villain clichés, or does it come naturally to you?"

"You *dare* mock *me*?" the Fomor snarled. He threw a spiraling corkscrew of deep green energy down the hall, and it hissed and left burn marks on everything it touched, ending at the doors. When it hit *them*, there was a snarling, crackling sound, and the green light spread across their surface in the pattern of a fisherman's net.

"Hard to do anything else to a guy with a face like yours," I said, this time from directly beside him. "Did you kill those girls, or did they volunteer once they saw you with your shirt off?"

The Fomor snarled and swatted at the air beside him. Then his eyes narrowed, and he started muttering and weaving his spatulate fingers in complicated patterns. I could feel the energy coming off of him at once, and knew exactly what he was trying to do: Unravel my veil. But I'd been playing that game with Auntie Lea for months.

Lord Froggy hadn't.

As his questing threads of magic spread out, I sent out whispers of my own power to barely brush them, guiding them one by one out and around the area covered by my veil. I couldn't afford to let him find me. Not like that, anyway. He wasn't thinking, and if I didn't get him to, it was entirely possible that he'd be too stupid to fool.

I couldn't have him giving up and leaving, either, so when I was sure I'd compromised his seeking spell I used the sonic wand again, this time directly above his head. "This kind of thing really isn't for amateurs. Are you sure you shouldn't sit this one out and let Listen give it a shot?"

Lord Froggy tilted his head up and then narrowed his eyes. He lifted a hand and spat a hissing word, and fire leapt up from his fingers to engulf the ceiling above him.

It took about two seconds for the fire alarm to go off, and another two before the sprinkler system kicked in. But I was back at the door to room 8 when the falling water began to dissolve my veil. Magic is a kind of energy, and follows its own laws. One of those laws is that water tends to ground out active magical constructs, and my veil started melting away like it was made of cotton candy.

"Hah!" spat the Fomor, spotting me. I saw him send a bolt of viridian light at me. I threw myself facedown on the floor and it passed over me, splashing against the door. I whipped over onto my back, just in time to raise a shield against a second bolt and a third. My physical shields aren't great, but the Fomor's spell was pure energy, and that made it easier for me to handle. I deflected the bolts left and right, and they blasted chunks of marble the size of bricks out of the walls when they struck.

Lord Froggy's eyes flared even larger and more furious that he'd missed. "Mortal cow!"

Okay, now. That stung. I mean, maybe it's a little shallow, and maybe it's a little petty, and maybe it shows a lack of character of some kind that Froggy's insult to my appearance got under my skin more effectively than attempted murder.

"*Cow?*" I snarled as water from the sprinkler system started soaking me. "I *rock* this dress!"

I dropped one of my wands and thrust my palm out at him, sending out an invisible bolt of pure memory, narrowed and focused with magic, like light passing through a magnifying glass. Sometimes you don't really remember traumatic injuries, and my memory of getting shot in the leg was pretty blurry. It hadn't hurt so much when I actually got shot, and I'd had a few things occupying my attention. Mostly, I'd just felt surprised and then numb—but when they were tending the wound in the helicopter later, now, *that* was pain. They'd dug the bullet out with forceps, cleaned the site with something that burned like Hell itself, and when they'd put the pressure bandage on it and tightened the straps, it hurt so bad that I'd thought I was going to die.

*That's* what I gave to Lord Froggy, with every bit of strength I could muster.

He wove a shield against the attack, but I guess he wasn't used to handling something so intangible as a memory. Even with the falling water weakening it, I felt the strike smash through his defense and sink home, and Froggy let out a sudden, high-pitched shriek. He staggered and fell heavily against the wall, clutching at his leg.

"Kill her!" he said, his voice two octaves higher than it had been a moment before. "Kill her, kill her, kill her!"

The remaining pair of turtlenecks in the hallway plunged toward me. A wave of fatigue from my recent efforts, especially that last one, almost held me pinned to the floor—but I scrambled to my feet, lurched to the door to room 8, and pounded against it with one fist. "Andi! Andi, it's Molly! Andi, let me—"

The door jerked open and I fell into the room. I snapped my legs up into a fetal curl, and Andi slammed the door shut behind me and hit the locks.

"What the *hell*, Molly?" she demanded. Andi was soaking wet, along with everything else in the room—including the Fomor's bomb.

I got up and scrambled toward it. "I couldn't take apart the veil over the bomb from the outside," I panted. "We didn't have time to build up a fire, and I can't call up enough of my own to set off the alarms. I had to get Froggy to do it for me."

The door shuddered under more blows from the turtlenecks.

"Hold them off," I told her. "I'll disarm the bomb."

"Can you *do* that?" Andi asked.

"Piece of cake," I lied.

"Okay," Andi said. She grimaced. "I'm going to smell like wet dog all night."

She turned to face the door in a ready position as I reached the giant shell. I forced the battering enemies at the door out of my thoughts and focused my complete attention on the shell before me. Then I extended my senses toward it and began feeling out the energy moving through it.

There was a *lot* of energy involved in this thing, power stored up inside and ready to explode. A thin coating of enchantment lined the shell's exterior, kind of the magical equivalent of a control panel. The water was eroding it slowly, but not fast enough to start melting the core enchantment and dispersing the stored energy. But if I didn't move fast, the water *would* destroy the surface enchantment and make it impossible for *anyone* to disarm the bomb.

I closed my eyes and put one hand out over the shell like Froggy had done. I could feel the energy of the shell reaching up to my fingers, ready to respond, and I began pouring my own energy down into it, trying to feel it out. It was a straightforward spell, nothing complicated, but I didn't know what anything did—it was like having a remote control for the TV, if someone had forgotten to label any of the buttons. I couldn't just start pushing them randomly.

On the other hand, I couldn't *not* do it, either.

It would have to be an educated guess.

On a TV remote, the power button is almost always a little apart from the others, or else somehow centered. That's what I was looking for—to turn the bomb off. I started eliminating all the portions of the spell that seemed too complex or too small, narrowing my choices bit by bit. It came down to two. If I guessed wrong . . .

I burst out into a nervous giggle. "Hey, Andi. Blue wire or red wire?"

A turtleneck's foot smashed a hole in the door, and Andi whipped her head around to give me an incredulous look. "Are you fucking *kidding* me?" she shouted. "Blue, you *always* cut the blue!"

Half of the door broke down and crashed to the floor. Andi blurred into her wolf form and surged forward, ripping at the first turtleneck as he tried to come in.

I turned my attention back to the bomb and picked the second option. I focused my will on it. It took me a couple of tries, because I was freaking terrified, and pants-wetting fear is generally not conducive to lucidity.

"Hey, God," I whispered. "I know I haven't been around much lately, but if you could do me a solid here, it would be really awesome for a lot of people. Please let me be right."

I cut the blue wire.

Nothing happened.

I felt a heavy, almost paralytic surge of relief—and then Lord Froggy hopped over the two turtlenecks struggling with Andi and smashed into me.

I went down hard on the marble floor, and Froggy rode me down, pinning me beneath his too-gaunt body. He wrapped the fingers of one hand all the way around my neck with room enough for them to overlap his thumb and squeezed. He was hideously strong. My breath stopped instantly, and my head began to pound and my vision to darken.

"Little *bitch*," he hissed. He started punching me with his other hand. The blows landed on my left cheekbone. They should have hurt, but I think something was wrong with my brain. I registered the impact but everything else was swallowed by the growing darkness. I could feel myself struggling, but I didn't get anywhere. Froggy was way, way stronger than he looked. My eyes weren't focusing very well, but I found myself staring down a dark tunnel toward one of the dead girls on the bedroom floor, and the dark purple band of bruising around her throat.

Then the floor a few feet away rippled, and an odd-looking grey creature popped up out of it.

The svartalf was maybe four-six and entirely naked. His skin was a mottled shade of grey, and his eyes were huge and entirely black. His head was a little larger than most people's and he was bald, though his eyebrows were silvery white. He did look kind of Roswellian, only instead of being superskinny he was built like a professional boxer, lean and strong—and he carried a short, simple sword in his hand.

"Fomor," said the svartalf calmly. I recognized Mr. Etri's voice. "One should not strike ladies."

Froggy started to say something, but then Etri's sword went *snicker-snack*, and the hand that was choking the life out of me was severed cleanly from the Fomor's wrist. Froggy screamed and fell away from me, spitting words and trying to summon power as he scrambled away on three limbs.

"You have violated guest right," Etri continued calmly. He made a gesture, and the marble beneath Lord Froggy turned suddenly liquid. Froggy sank about three inches, and then the floor hardened around him again. The Fomor screamed.

"You have attacked a guest under the hospitality and protection of Svartalfheim," he said, his tone of voice never changing. The sword swept out again and struck the nose from Froggy's face, spewing ichor everywhere and drawing even more howling. Etri stood over the fallen Fomor and looked down at him with absolutely no expression on his face. "Have you anything to say on your own behalf?"

"No!" Froggy screamed. "You cannot do this! I have harmed none of your people!"

There was a pulse of rage from Etri so hot that I thought the falling water would burst into steam when it struck him. "Harmed us?" he said quietly. He glanced at the shell and then back at Froggy with pure contempt. "You would have used our alliance as a pretext to murder innocent thousands, making us your accomplices." He crouched down to put his face inches from Froggy's, and said in a calm, quiet, pitiless voice, "You have stained the honor of Svartalfheim."

"I will make payment!" Froggy gabbled. "You will be compensated for your pains!"

"There is but one price for your actions, Fomor. And there are no negotiations."

"No," Froggy protested. "No. NO!"

Etri turned away from him and surveyed the room. Andi was still in wolf form. One of the turtlenecks was bleeding out onto the marble floor, the sprinklers spreading the blood into a huge pool. The other was crouched in a corner with his arms curled around his head, covered in bleeding wounds. Andi faced him, panting, blood dripping from her reddened fangs, a steady growl bubbling in her chest.

Etri turned to me and offered me his hand. I thanked him and let him pull me up to a sitting position. My throat hurt. My head hurt. My face hurt. *It's killing me, nyuk, nyuk, nyuk. C'mere, you.*

You know you've been punched loopy when you're doing a one-person Three Stooges routine in your internal monologue.

"I apologize," Etri said, "for interfering in your struggle. Please do not presume that I did so because I thought you unable to protect yourself."

My voice came out in a croak. "It's your house, and your honor that was at stake. You had the right."

The answer seemed to please him and he inclined his head slightly. "I further apologize for not handling this matter myself. It was not your responsibility to discover or take action against this scum's behavior."

"It was presumptuous of me," I said. "But there was little time to act."

"Your ally alerted us to the danger. You did nothing improper. Svartalfheim thanks you for your assistance in this matter. You are owed a favor."

I was about to tell him that no such thing was necessary, but I stopped myself. Etri wasn't uttering social pleasantries. This wasn't a friendly exchange. It was an audit, an accounting. I just inclined my head to him. "Thank you, Mr. Etri."

"Of course, Miss Carpenter."

Svartalves in security uniforms, mixed with mortal security guards, came into the room. Etri went to them and quietly gave instructions.

The Fomor and his servitors were trussed up and taken from the room.

"What will happen to them?" I asked Etri.

"We will make an example of the Fomor," Etri said.

"What of your treaty?" I asked.

"It was never signed," he said. "Mostly because of you, Miss Carpenter. While Svartalfheim does not pay debts which were never incurred, we appreciate your role in this matter. It will be considered in the future."

"The Fomor don't deserve an honorable ally."

"It would seem not," he said.

"What about the turtlenecks?" I asked.

"What of them?"

"Will you . . . deal with them?"

Etri just looked at me. "Why would we?"

"They were sort of in on it," I said.

"They were property," said the svartalf. "If a man strikes you with a hammer, it is the man who is punished. There is no reason to destroy the hammer. We care nothing for them."

"What about them?" I asked, and nodded toward the dead girls in the Fomor's chamber. "Do you care what happened to them?"

Etri looked at them and sighed. "Beautiful things ought not be destroyed," he said. "But they were not our guests. We owe no one for their end and will not answer for it."

"There is a vampire in your custody," I said, "is there not?"

Etri regarded me for a moment and then said, "Yes."

"You owe me a favor. I wish to secure his release."

He arched an eyebrow. Then he bowed slightly and said, "Come with me."

I followed Etri out of the suite and across the hall to room 6. Though the door was shattered, Etri stopped outside of it respectfully and knocked. A moment later, a female voice said, "You may enter."

We went in. It was a suite much like the Fomor's, only with way more throw pillows and plush furniture. It was a wreck. The floor was literally covered with shattered furniture, broken décor, and broken turtlenecks. Svartalf security was already binding them and carrying them from the room.

Listen walked out on his own power, his hands behind his back, one of his eyes swollen halfway shut. He gave me a steady look as he went by and said nothing.

Bastard.

Etri turned toward the curtained door to the suite's bedroom and spoke. "The mortal apprentice who warned us has earned a favor. She asks for the release of the vampire."

"Impossible," answered the female voice. "That account has been settled."

Etri turned to me and shrugged. "I am sorry."

"Wait," I said. "May I speak to him?"

"In a moment."

We waited. Thomas appeared from the doorway to the bedroom dressed in a black terry-cloth bathrobe. He'd just gotten out of the shower. Thomas was maybe a finger's width under six feet tall, and there wasn't an inch of his body that didn't scream *sex symbol*. His eyes were a shade of deep crystalline blue, and his dark hair hung to his wide shoulders. My body did what it always did around him and started screaming at me to make babies. I ignored it. Mostly.

"Molly," he said. "Are you all right?"

"Nothing a bucket of aspirin won't help," I said. "Um. Are you okay?"

He blinked. "Why wouldn't I be?"

"I thought . . . you know. You'd been captured as a spy."

"Well, sure," he said.

"I thought they would, uh. Make an example of you?"

He blinked again. "Why would they do that?"

The door to the bedroom opened again, and a female svartalf appeared. She looked a lot like Etri—tiny and beautiful, though she had long silver hair instead of a cue ball. She was wearing what might have been Thomas's shirt, and it hung down almost to her ankles. She had a decidedly . . . smug look about her. Behind her, I saw several other sets of wide, dark eyes peer out of the shadowy bedchamber.

"Oh," I said. "*Oh*. You, uh. You made a deal."

Thomas smirked. "It's a tough, dirty job . . ."

"And one that is not yet finished," said the female svartalf. "You are ours until dawn."

Thomas looked from me to the bedroom and back and spread his hands. "You know how it is, Molly. Duty calls."

"Um," I said. "What do you want me to tell Justine?"

Again he gave me a look of near incomprehension. "The truth. What else?"

"Oh, thank goodness," Justine said as we were walking out. "I was afraid they'd have starved him."

I blinked. "Your boyfriend is banging a roomful of elf girls and you're *happy* about it?"

Justine tilted her head back and laughed. "When you're in love with an incubus, it changes your viewpoint a little, I think. It isn't as though this is something new. I know how he feels about me, and he needs to feed to be healthy. So what's the harm?" She smirked. "And besides. He's *always* ready for more."

"You're a very weird person, Justine."

Andi snorted, and nudged me with her shoulder in a friendly way. She'd recovered her dress and the shoes she liked. "Look who's talking."

After everyone was safe home, I walked from Waldo's apartment to the nearest parking garage. I found a dark corner, sat down, and waited. Lea shimmered into being about two hours later and sat down beside me.

"You tricked me," I said. "You sent me in there blind."

"Indeed. Just as Lara did her brother—except that my agent succeeded where hers failed."

"But why? Why send us in there?"

"The treaty with the Fomor could not be allowed to conclude," she said. "If one nation agreed to neutrality with them, a dozen more would follow. The Fomor would be able to divide the others and contend with them one by one. The situation was delicate. The presence of active agents was intended to disrupt its equilibrium—to show the Fomor's true nature in a test of fire."

"Why didn't you just tell me that?" I asked.

"Because you would neither have trusted nor believed me, obviously," she said.

I frowned at her. "You should have told me anyway."

"Do not be ridiculous, child." Lea sniffed. "There was no time to humor your doubts and suspicions and theories and endless questions. Better to give you a simple prize upon which to focus: Thomas."

"How did you know I would find the bomb?"

She arched an eyebrow. "Bomb?" She shook her head. "I did not know what was happening in any specific sense. But the Fomor are betrayers. Ever have they been; ever will they be. The only question is what form their treachery will take. The svartalves had to be shown."

"How did you know I would discover it?"

"I did not," she said. "But I know your mentor. When it comes to meddling, to unearthing awkward truths, he has taught you exceedingly well." She smiled. "You have also learned his aptitude for taking orderly situations and reducing them to elemental chaos."

"Meaning what?" I demanded.

Her smile was maddeningly smug. "Meaning that I was confident that whatever happened, it would not include the smooth completion of the treaty."

"But you could have done everything I did."

"No, child," Lea said. "The svartalves would never have asked me to be their guest at the reception. They love neatness and order. They would have known my purposes were not orderly ones."

"And they didn't know that about me?"

"They cannot judge others except by their actions," Lea said. "Hence their treaty with the Fomor, who had not yet crossed their paths. My actions have shown me to be someone who must be treated with caution. You had . . . a clean record with them. And you are smoking hot. All is well, your city saved, and now a group of wealthy, skilled, and influential beings owes you a favor." She paused for a moment and then leaned toward me slightly. "Perhaps some expression of gratitude is in order."

"From me to you?" I asked. "For that?"

"I think your evening turned out quite well," Lea said, her eyebrows raised. "Goodness, but you are a difficult child. How he manages to endure your insolence I will never know. You probably think you have earned some sort of reward from me." She rose and turned to go.

"Wait!" I said suddenly.

She paused.

I think my heart had stopped beating. I started shaking, everywhere. "You said that you know Harry. Not knew him. *Know*. Present tense."

"Did I?"

"You said you don't know how he manages to put up with me. *Manages*. Present tense."

"Did I?"

"Auntie," I asked her, and I could barely whisper. "Auntie, is Harry . . . Is he alive?"

Lea turned to me very slowly, and her green eyes glinted with wicked knowledge. "I did not say that he was alive, child. And neither should you. Not yet."

I bowed my head and started crying. Or laughing. Or both. I couldn't tell. Lea didn't wait around for it. Emotional displays made her uncomfortable.

Harry. Alive.

I *hadn't* killed him.

Best reward ever.

"Thank you, Auntie," I whispered. "Thank you."

# COLD CASE

I really enjoyed writing, in the previous tale, from Molly's viewpoint at one of the lowest points of her life. I wanted to keep following her personal story after the events of *Ghost Story*, where she faces an uncertain future but is beginning to rebuild who she is and what she wants out of her life. Molly has always had issues with her mother—and now, as the new Winter Lady of the Unseelie Court, she has found herself faced with one of the more terrifying mother figures imaginable in Mab, the Queen of Air and Darkness. I wanted to get a look at that interplay, but I had to write the story to do it.

I also wanted to get a little bit more into the actual role of the Winter Lady in the circles of power that are the Faerie Courts, and why her role is so important, and why it was so distressing that Maeve had been shirking her duties for such a long time.

And finally, I wanted to show more of Molly, who has been through so much and learned such bitter lessons—and to demonstrate why it might just be possible that Mab may have bitten off more than she could chew in the inestimable Miss Carpenter.

"**Y**ou understand what you must do," said Mab, the Queen of Air and Darkness.

It wasn't phrased as a question.

I gripped the handrail on the side of the yacht and held on as it *whump*ed and *thump*ed through choppy water on the way toward a bleak shore. "I get it," I told her. "Collect the tribute from the Miksani."

Mab stared at me for a long moment, and that made me uncomfortable. It takes a lot to make that happen. I mean, you should see the stares my mother can give—Charity Carpenter is terrifying. And I got to where I could shake those off like nothing.

"Lady Molly," Mab said. "Regard me."

Not *Look at me*. Oh no. Not nearly dramatic enough.

I looked up at her.

We weren't around any mortals at the moment, but we were technically moving through the mortal world, among the Aleutians, and Mab was dressed in mortal clothing. The Queen of the Winter Court of the Fae wore white furs and a big, poufy white hat like you might see on a Northern European socialite in an old Bond movie. No mortal alive would have been wearing white heels on the frozen, dripping, bucking deck of the yacht in those seas, in the beginnings of a howling winter storm, but she was Mab. She would take the path of least resistance when practical, but her willingness to tolerate the possible alarm and outrage of the human race extended only so far. She would wear what she felt like wearing. And at the moment, it would seem that she mostly felt like wearing an expression of stern disapproval.

My own clothing, I knew, disappointed her gravely, but I was used to doing that to mother figures. I was dressed in flannel-lined winter jeans and large, warm boots, with several layers of sweaters, a heavy bomber jacket, and an old hunter's cap with ear flaps that folded down. Practical, sturdy, and serviceable.

I didn't need them any more than Mab needed the furs, but it seemed like it would be simpler to blend in—to a point, anyway.

"Appearances matter, young lady," Mab said, her voice hard-edged. "First impressions *matter.*"

"You never get a second chance to make a first impression," I said, rolling my eyes.

I might have sounded a bit like this guy I know. Maybe a little.

Mab stared at me for a long second before she gave me a wintry smile. "Wisdom wrapped in witless defiance."

"*Witless,*" I sputtered.

"I am offering you advice," Queen Mab said. "You have been a Queen of Faerie for less than a week. You would be wise to listen."

The yacht began to slow and then slewed to one side, throwing a wave of icy spray toward the rocky shore. It handled too well to be a mortal craft, but out here, where few eyes could see, the Sidhe who piloted her were only so willing to be inconvenienced by seas that would have daunted experienced mortal captains and advanced mortal vessels.

*Not mortal,* I told myself sternly, in my inner, reasonable voice. *Human. Human. Just like me.*

"Thanks for that," I said to Mab. "Look, I get it. My predecessor hasn't performed her duties properly for, like, two hundred years. I've got a huge backlog. I've got a lot of work facing me. I understand already."

Mab gave me another long stare before saying, "You do not understand." Then she turned and walked back toward her cabin, the one that was bigger on the inside than it was on the outside. "But you will."

I frowned after her for a second, then glanced at the thrashing twenty yards of sea between myself and the land and asked, "How am I supposed to go ashore?"

Mab moved her eyes in what might have been an impatient glance, if she'd actually moved them all the way to me, and went into her cabin and shut the door behind her without a word.

I was left standing on the pitching deck. I glanced up at the Sidhe piloting the yacht. They were both male, both tall, both dark of hair and eye. Which was not my type. Even a little, dammit. One noticed me and met my gaze boldly, his mouth curling up into a little smirk, and my heart went pitty-pat. Or something did. I mean, he was a damned attractive man.

*Except he's not a man. He's one of the Sidhe. He's picked a look he knows you like for his glamour, and he'd cheerfully do things with you no human could possibly be flexible enough to manage, but he wouldn't* care.

My reasonable voice sounded a lot like my mom's, which was more than a bit spooky.

Besides, I didn't need him to care. I just needed him to look pretty while I tore his clothes off and . . .

I shook my head and looked away, out at the ocean. Being the Winter Lady brought a host of challenges with it. One of the most annoying was what had happened to my libido, which had never exactly lacked for health. These days, I was like an adolescent boy bunny rabbit. Everything had sex in it, no matter how much it didn't or how hard I tried not to notice it. It was annoying, because I had a job to do.

The two extremely sexy Sidhe stared at me, being all smoldery and distracting, but not doing a damned thing to help me get ashore or prove myself on my first mission for the Queen of Air and Darkness. And since the last Winter Lady who had failed Mab wound up with a bullet in her skull, I figured I'd better not screw it up.

Which is what she'd meant about first impressions. It had been a polite threat, and, as I realized that, my legs felt a little wobbly.

*Fine, then.*

I called upon Winter. Big-time. I let the endlessly empty cold fill me, subsume me, and winds rose around me as the power of Winter flowed in. I let it freeze everything—my concerns of what would happen if I failed Mab, my curiosity about what was coming next, the lust inspired by the pilots (whom I suddenly realized had probably been placed where they had precisely to test my focus and resolve).

And then I let it out.

All my life, magically speaking, I had been used to being a spinner of cobwebs of illusion and mental magic. I'd always had enormous finesse, and always lacked the kind of power I had seen my mentor wield. I'd forced myself to adjust to the idea that I would always have to be subtle, indirect, manipulative—that only indirect power was mine to command.

That was no longer true.

There was a thunder crack that thrummed from the surface of the sea as Winter's ice froze the ocean ten feet down for half a mile in every direction. The yacht suddenly locked into place, no longer pitching and rolling.

I'd have to do the math to be sure, but I thought that little trick had taken as much energy to accomplish as fairly large military-grade munitions. The two pilots just stared at me, suddenly uncertain about what they were attempting to play with.

*That's right, pretty boys. Mess with me, I'll hit you so hard, your children will be born bruised.*

I gave them a sunny little smile, vaulted the side rail, and walked to shore through howling winds before the ice started breaking up again.

THEY ACTUALLY NAMED the town Unalaska, Alaska. Despite the appeal of an innately oxymoronic name, Unalaska struck me as something closer to a colony on an alien world than as a mortal village. It's a collection of homes and businesses around Dutch Harbor, famous for being the central port for the fishing boats on that show about how dangerous it is to catch crabs.

(Actual crabs. Literal ones, like, in the water. Sheesh, this Winter mantle thing is so childish sometimes, because it's definitely not me.)

The buildings are all squat, sturdy, and on the small side—the better to resist massive winds and snows and rains and frozen ocean spray that turns to coatings of ice when whipped up by a storm. The town was surrounded by looming, steep, formidable mountains devoid of human markings, and clung to the limited flat spaces at their feet like some kind of lichen stubbornly hanging on in the shade of a large stone. The icy sea filled whatever vision was not occupied by the sky or the mountains, cold and uncaring and implacable. The sky overhead was a neutral grey, promising neither sunlight nor storms yet ready to deliver both with an impartial hand and little warning.

It wasn't a place that was inviting, kind, or merciful to mere humanity, and yet there they were.

*We were. There we were.*

I trudged through freezing winds and half an inch of sleet that had hardened into something between ice and snow and didn't shiver.

Harry Dresden once warned me about lying to myself.

I tried not to think about that too hard as I walked through the endless twilight of an Aleutian autumn and into town. I threw a glamour, nothing fancy, over myself as I went. I muddled my features from stark-boned beauty down to something much plainer. I darkened my hair, my skin, both of which were paler than usual these days. I added on a few pounds, because I'd never really recovered the weight I'd lost when I was playing grim-dark superhero on the streets of Chicago, when Harry had been mostly dead. Everything about the look said *unremarkable*, and I added on the barest hint of an aura that I was an awfully boring person. It would be easier to move around that way.

Then I opened my senses to try to track down the elusive Fae who lived among the human population in Unalaska.

THE WIND WAS kicking up, with more rain and sleet on the way, and apparently the inhabitants of Unalaska knew it. No one was on the streets, and a few cars moved about furtively, like mice getting out of the way of a predator. I sensed a trickle of quivery energy coming from one low building, a place called the Elbow Room, and I went on in.

I was immediately subsumed in the energy of a crowded, raucous little dive. Music and the scent of beer, seared meat, and smoke flooded into my face, but worse were the sudden emotions that filled my head. There was drunken elation and drunken dread and drunken sullen anger and drunken lust; mainly, though, there were sober versions of all of those emotions as well. Threads of frustration and tension wove through the other emotions—servers, I imagined, overworked and cautious. Wariness rode steadily through the room from one corner, doubtless the bouncer, and cheerful greed hummed tunelessly under the rest, doubtless from the dive's owner.

I'm a wizard and I specialize in delicate magicks. I'm awfully sensitive to people's emotions, and running into this batch was like walking into a wall of none-too-clean water. It took me a moment to get my balance back, adjust, and walk inside.

"Close the door!" someone shouted. I took note of a young man, his face reddened and chapped by frigid wind. "Christ, I been cold enough to freeze my balls off for days!"

"That explains a whole hell of a lot, Clint!" shouted another man from the far side of the bar, to a round of general, rough laughter.

I closed the door behind me and tried to ignore the sullen, swelling anger radiating off Clint. There was something very off about his vibe. When it comes to emotions, people and monsters have a lot in common. It takes a very, very alien mind to feel emotions that are significantly different from those you'd find in human beings—and there's a vast range of them, too. Throw in mind-altering substances, like hormones and drugs, and it's absolutely unreal the variety available.

But I recognized an angry sexual predator when I sensed one.

I faked a few shivers against the cold as I wedged myself in at the bar and nodded to the bartender, a woman who looked as if she might wrestle Kodiaks for fun on her days off, if she ever took a day off. I put down some cash, secured a beer, and felt an ugly presence crawling up my spine.

I took a sip of the beer, some kind of Russian monstrosity that tasted as if it had been brewed from Stalin's sweat and escaped a Soviet gulag, and turned casually to find Clint standing behind me, about three inches too close, and breathing a little too hard.

"I don't know you," he said.

"Wow," I said.

"What?"

"That's got to be the best opening line in history," I said, and swigged some more beer. Hairs probably didn't start popping out on my chest, making little *bing* noises as they did, but I can't swear to it. "Did you want something?"

"I don't know you," he repeated. His breath was coming faster, and there was a kind of glossy film on his eyes I didn't like much. "Everyone knows everyone here. You're new."

"But not interested," I said, and turned away.

He clamped a hand down on my shoulder, painfully hard, and spun me back around. "I'm talking to you."

Once upon a time, that sudden physicality would have made my adrenaline spike and my heart pound with apprehension. Now my whole head suddenly went icy-hot with anger instead. I felt my lips pull back from my teeth. "Oh, pumpkin," I said. "You should walk away. You aren't going to like how this one plays out."

"You need to come with me," Clint said. He started to pull at me. He was strong. Wobbly on his feet, but strong.

"Take your hand off me before I lose my temper," I said, my voice very sharp, and pitched to carry to everyone in the room, even over the noise and music.

And I got almost no reaction from the room at all.

Now, *that* was interesting enough to notice. Places like this were full of your usual blue-collar crowd. You wouldn't find many philosophers or intellectuals here, but there would be plenty of basically decent people who wouldn't think twice about taking a swing at an aggressor.

Except no one was even looking at me. Not one eye in the entire room. Everyone was staring at a tiny TV screen on a wall, playing a sports broadcast so grainy and blurred that I couldn't even tell which game it was. Or they were focused on their drinks. Or at random spots on the wall. And the whole place filled with the sudden, sour psychic stench of fear. I turned my eyes to the two men at the bar next to me, and they only traded a look with the bartender, one that practically screamed out the words, *Oh no, not this again.*

What? Was Clint really *that* scary?

Apparently.

Certainly no help was coming. Which meant it was up to me.

"Let's do this the fun way," I said. "I'm going to count down from three to one, and when I get to one, if you are still touching me, I'm going to put you on a therapist's couch for the rest of your natural life."

"With me," Clint insisted, breathing harder. I'm not even sure he realized I had said anything.

"Three," I said.

"Show you something," Clint growled.

"Two," I replied, drawing out the number, the way Mary Poppins might have to unruly children.

"Yeah," Clint said. "Yeah. Show you something."

"O—" I began to say.

I didn't get to finish the word. A man seized the middle finger of Clint's hand, the one on my shoulder, snagged the other fingers with his other hand, and bent the single finger back. There was a snapping sound like a small tree branch breaking, and Clint let out a scream.

The newcomer moved with calm efficiency. Before Clint could so much as turn to face him, the new guy lifted a foot and drove his heel down hard at a downward angle into the side of Clint's knee. There was a second crack, louder, and Clint dropped to the floor in a heap.

"I don't think the lady likes you doing that," the newcomer said, his voice polite. He was a little over medium height, maybe an inch or two shorter than me, and built like a gymnast, all compact muscle and whipcord. He wore nondescript clothes much like my own, his features were darkly handsome, and his black eyes glittered with a feverish, intelligent heat.

I also knew him. Carlos Ramirez was a wizard, and a Warden of the White Council. He was only a couple of years older than me, and hotter than a boy-band bad boy's mug shot, and I instantly wanted to jump him.

*Whoa. Down, girl. Just because you're the Winter Lady doesn't mean you have to behave like your predecessor did. Look where it got her.*

"Miss?" he asked me. "Are you all right?"

"Yes, fine," I said.

"I apologize for that," he said. "Some things just shouldn't happen. Excuse me for a moment."

And with that, Carlos reached down, snagged Clint by the back of his coat, and dragged him to the door. Clint started feebly thrashing and swatting at Carlos, but the young wizard didn't seem to notice. He dragged Clint to the door and tossed him out into the sleet. Then he shut the door again and turned back to face the room.

Everyone was staring at him. The jukebox was wailing a song about broken hearts, but the talk in the room had died completely. The fear I'd sensed earlier had ratcheted up a notch. For a frozen moment, no one moved. Then one of the customers reached for his wallet and started counting bills onto his table. Everyone else started following suit.

Within five minutes the place was empty except for us and the bartender.

"What the hell is this about?" Carlos murmured, watching the last patrons depart. He looked over his shoulder at the bartender. "Was that guy the sheriff's kid or something?"

The bartender shook her head and said, "I'm closing. You two need to leave."

Carlos held up a twenty between two fingers. "Beer first?"

The bartender gave him an exasperated look, took a step to her left, and then said, "Do you understand me, mister? *You need to leave. Both of you.*"

"That a pistol or shotgun you got back there?" Carlos asked.

"Stick around. You'll find out," the bartender said.

The fear coming off her was nauseating, a mortal dread. I shook my head and said to Carlos, "Maybe we should."

"Mostly frozen water is falling from the sky, I'm starving, and I haven't had a drink yet," Carlos said. He asked the bartender, "There another place for one?"

"Charlie's," she replied instantly. "Other side of the bay. Green neon sign. Good burgers."

Carlos squinted his eyes and studied the bartender, as if weighing the value of heeding her words versus the personal pleasure he would take in being contrary.

Harry Dresden has had a horrible influence on far too many people, and has much to answer for.

"Okay," he said mildly. "Miss, would you care to join me for a meal?"

"That would be lovely," I said.

So WE LEFT and started trudging through the sleet.

The sound of it hitting the ground and the sidewalks and roads was a wet rattle. I didn't need to, but I hunched my shoulders as if against the cold and dropped my chin down to my neck as much as I could. "Goodness, this is brisk," I said.

"Is it?" Carlos asked.

"Aren't you cold?"

"Of course I am," Carlos said. "But I figured the Winter Lady would think this was a balmy day."

I stopped in my tracks and stared at him for a moment.

He offered me a sudden, mischievous smile. "Hi, Molly."

I tilted my head to one side. "Mmm. What gave it away?"

He gestured toward his eyelids with two fingertips. "Seeing ointment," he said. "Cuts right through glamour. I've got eyes all over this town. When they spotted a lone young woman walking in from the far side of the island, I figured it was worth taking a peek."

"I see," I said. "Carlos, tell me something."

"What's that?"

"Do you mean to arrest me and take me before the White Council? Because that isn't going to fit into my schedule."

I'd had some issues with the White Council's Laws of Magic in the past. The kind of issues that would have gotten my head hacked off if Harry hadn't interceded on my behalf. But then he mostly died, and I'd been on my own, outside of his aegis. The Wardens, including Carlos Ramirez, had hunted me. I'd evaded them—always moving, always watching, always afraid that one of the grim men and women in grey cloaks would step out of a tear in the fabric of reality right in front of me and smite me. I'd had a recurring nightmare about it, in fact.

But they'd never caught up with me.

"Molly, please," Ramirez said. "If I'd wanted to find you and take you to the Council, I would have found you. Give me that much credit. I even sandbagged a couple of the ops sent to bring you in."

I frowned at him. "Why would you do that?"

"Because Harry liked you," he said simply. "Because he thought it was worth sticking his neck out to help you. Besides, I had my own area to cover, and in the absence of a Warden, you were giving the Fomor hell."

They hadn't been the only ones with a surplus of hell. I hadn't been having much fun, either. "Why didn't the Council appoint a replacement, then?"

"They tried. They couldn't get anyone to volunteer to take Dresden's place as the Warden of the Midwest."

"Why not, I wonder."

"Lots and lots of problems and not enough Wardens," Carlos replied. "With the Fomor going nutballs, we're up to our necks and sinking already. Plus, everyone they asked had a good opinion of Harry, and nobody wanted to inherit the enemies he'd made."

"So, to clarify," I said, "you're not here to bring me in."

"Correct, Miss Carpenter. It would be a little awkward now that you're royalty. And, frankly, I have no intention of crossing Mab if I can possibly help it. Ever."

"Then why *are* you here?" I asked.

A boyish smile flickered over his face, and something inside me did a little quivering barrel roll. "Maybe I just wanted to meet the famous new Queen of the Winter Court," he said.

I fluttered my eyelashes at him and said, "Don't you trust me, Carlos?"

The smile faded a little and then turned wry. "It isn't personal, Molly. But from what I hear, you're a sovereign executive entity of a foreign supernatural nation, one that is on formal and unsteady ground with the White Council."

I felt myself grinning more widely at his mistake. "So it's Council business, then," I said.

His lips pressed into a grimace and he said, "No comment."

"So formal," I said. "What did you think of that scene in the bar?"

"Weird, right?" he said.

"Do you know what I think I'd like to do?"

"Circle back and watch the place to see why everyone was leaving?"

I winked at him. "I was going to say, 'Find a warm spot to make out,' but, sure, we can do that if you'd rather."

Carlos blinked several times.

Actually, I kind of blinked, too.

The past few years had been hard ones. I'd gotten used to walling people away. My libido had shriveled up from lack of use. I'd barely been able to allow Harry to come near me. And now here I was, flirting with the really, exceptionally cute Carlos Ramirez, as if I were a girl who enjoyed flirting.

I remembered that girl. I used to be that girl. Was that also a part of what Mab had done for me when she arranged to have me ascend to be the Winter Lady? Because if it was . . .

I liked it.

Should that be scaring me? I decided that I didn't want to worry about that. It was just such a relief to *feel* that kind of feeling again.

I pursed my lips, blew Carlos a little kiss, and turned to circle back toward the Elbow Room. It took him about five seconds to begin to follow me.

WE FOUND A shadowy spot next to a building within sight of the Elbow Room. I flicked up a veil to make sure we wouldn't be observed, and we settled down to wait.

It didn't take long. Within five or ten minutes, a silent column of men, twenty strong, came down the road, their feet crunching through the half-frozen sleet. Clint was at the head of the column with another man, a very tall, very lean character with a captain's peaked cap, leathery skin, and the dull, flat eyes of a dead fish. They marched up to the Elbow Room and filed inside, neat as a military unit on parade. No one said a word the entire time.

"Huh," Carlos noted. "That's not odd at all."

"No kidding. Dive Bar of the Damned." I frowned. "They look like locals to you?"

"Waterproof boots and coats," he said. "Fishermen, likely."

"Like, Clint's shipmates? Do shipmates come get involved in bar fights for their fellow shipmates?"

"Do I look like somebody who knows something like that? I'm from LA." He scratched his nose. "The question I'm having trouble with is, are there people who are willing to get into a fight for the sake of a jackhole like Clint?" He squinted. "Can I ask you something, Molly?"

I grinned at him. "It's pretty early in the season to entertain any more proposals, Carlos."

In the dark it was hard to tell, but I think his cheeks turned a few shades of color. It was actually kind of adorable. "What are *you* doing here?" he asked.

"Talking to the Miksani," I said, or tried to say. To my intense surprise, what came out was, "Talking to prospective make-out partners."

Carlos grimaced. "I'm serious."

I tried to say, *Miksani*, but what came out was, "So am I."

"Fine," he said, "be that way."

Why the hell would that be happening to me? Unless . . . it was a part of Winter Law.

The Winter Court of Faerie had an ironclad code of law laid out by Mab herself. It didn't work like mortal law did. If you broke it, you didn't get punished. You didn't break it. Period. You were physically incapable of doing so. When Mab laid down the law, the beings of her Court followed it, whether they wanted to or not. They actually knew the law, on a subconscious level, but it took a real effort to summon it to your conscious mind. I took a slow breath and realized that any of the Hidden Peoples of the Winter Court were entitled to their privacy and could not be outed to the mortals or anyone else without their prior consent.

I let out a breath through my teeth and said, "It's not personal. I can't talk about it."

He frowned at me for a moment and then said, "What about a trade?"

"I'll show you mine if you show me yours?" I asked. "I like the way you think."

"Wow," he said, and now I was certain his cheeks were flaming. "Wow, Molly. That's not . . . It isn't . . . Could you please take this seriously for a minute?"

I smiled at him, and as I did, I realized that a trade changed everything with regard to the law. Bargains had to be balanced in the proper proportions and in similar coin. That, too, was Winter Law. If Carlos told me why he was present, I'd be free to say more about my purpose in kind.

"Deal," I said.

"We got a report from Elaine Mallory through the Paranet," Carlos said, watching the door to the Elbow Room. "Vague descriptions of a strange vibe and unusually odd activity here in Unalaska. People going missing, weird behavior, energy out of whack—that kind of thing. Someone had to check it out."

"Huh," I said.

"Your turn."

"Mab sent me," I said. "I'm here to collect on a debt."

I felt his eyes on me for a moment, and then he said, "You're . . . Mab's bagman?"

"Bagperson," I said. "Though I think it's more like a tax collector."

"They're just bagmen for the government," he replied. "What happened? One of the Miksani piss Mab off?"

I lifted my eyebrows at him. "You know of them?"

"Duh. Wizard," he said. "Jeez, Molly, give me a little credit."

I found myself smiling at him. "It's internal Winter Court business."

He nodded. "It occurs to me that if there is a tribe of Fae here, they probably know a whole lot about strange things happening in their town."

"That does seem reasonable," I said.

"It seems like we both might benefit from mutual cooperation," he said. "If I help you with your job, maybe you could help me with mine."

Help from a mortal, on my first job? Mab wouldn't like that.

On the other hand, I was pretty sure that when it came to me filling the role of the Winter Lady, Mab wasn't going to like a lot of things I did. She might as well get used to it now.

"I think that could work out," I said. "Provided you help me with my job first."

"Molly," he said, and put his hand on his chest. "You wound me. Do you think I'd welch on you?"

"Not if we do my job first," I said sweetly. "You know Winter well enough by now to know that I'll do what I say I will."

"Yes," he said simply. He offered me his hand and said, "Do we have a deal?"

I reached for his hand, but apparently bargains weren't closed with handshakes under Winter Law. So I drew him toward me by his hand, leaned over, and placed a soft kiss on his mouth.

Suddenly there was nothing else in the world that mattered. Nothing at all. Just the soft heat of his lips on mine, the way he drew in a sudden, shocked breath, and then an abrupt ardor in returning the kiss. Something shuddered through me, a frisson of pleasure like the deep-toned toll of an enormous bell. The kiss was a symbol. Both parties had to agree to a kiss to make it happen like this one.

After a time, the kiss ended and my lips parted from his, just a little. I sat there panting, my eyes only half-open, focused on nothing. My heart was racing and sending bursts of lust running through my body that began to pool in my hips.

I wasn't sure what the hell was happening to me exactly, but it felt incredibly . . . *right*.

That probably should have scared me a little.

Carlos opened his eyes, and they were absolutely aflame with intensity.

"We have a deal, wizard," I whispered. Then I shivered and rose, stepping away from him before my mouth decided it needed to taste his again. "Let us begin."

I focused my will, quietly murmured, "Kakusu," and brought up the best veil I could manage—which is to say, world-class. It was one of the first things I learned to do, and I was good at it. The light around us dimmed very slightly, and we vanished from the view of anyone who wasn't going to extreme supernatural measures to spot us. The mix of sleet and rain could be problematic, since anyone who looked closely enough would see it bouncing off an empty hole in the air. But nothing is perfect, is it?

I nodded to Carlos, and we padded quietly across the street to circle the Elbow Room. A building that spends half the year mostly buried in snow doesn't go in for a lot of windows. The only two in the place were side by side, deeply recessed, and high up on the wall, to let in light.

We both reached up and got a grip on the slippery sills, and then quietly pulled ourselves up to peer into the bar.

The fishermen were standing facing the bar in two neat lines. Their scrawny leader in the captain's hat was staring at the bartender, who stood behind the bar, gripping a cloth like some kind of useless talisman. Her face had gone pale and was covered in beads of sweat. She trembled so violently that it threatened her balance, and she just kept repeating the same phrase, loudly enough to be heard through the window, over the sleet: "I don't know, I don't know, I don't know, I don't know, I don't know."

Captain Fisherman took a step forward, toward her, and the strain on her face immediately increased, along with the volume and desperation of her voice. "I don't know, I don't know, I don't know!"

"Psychic interrogation," I noted. Invading a human being's mind was a monstrous act. It inflicted untold amounts of horrible damage, not to their brain but to their *mind*. The sensations it could cause were technically known as pain, but the word really doesn't do them justice. If someone went digging in your head long enough, they'd leave you a mindless vegetable, or hopelessly insane.

I knew, because I'd done it. I'd had the noblest intentions in the world, but I'd been younger, dumber, and a lot surer of myself, and people had been hurt.

Carlos let out a growl beneath his breath. "And we have a Third Law violation. And there's no way that's an accident or even badly misguided benevolence."

"Assuming he's mortal," I whispered. "If he isn't, then the laws don't apply to him."

"Either way, his head is coming off."

"Cool," I said. "Who is he?"

"Who cares?"

"What's he doing here?"

"Breaking the Laws."

"Uh-huh," I said. "I wonder how many friends he has."

In my peripheral vision, I could see the muscles along Carlos's jaw contract and then relax again. I glanced aside and saw him visibly force down his anger and shake his head a little. "I'm taking him down. Just as soon as I find out exactly who he is, how many buddies he has, and what designs he has on this town."

"Oh," I said innocently. "Is that not what you meant the first time?"

He started to mutter an answer when his fingers slipped on the slickened windowsill and he fell.

He didn't make much noise—a little scrape on the wall and a *thump* as he hit the ground—but the captain's head whipped around in a turn at least forty-five degrees too great to take place on a human neck, his eyes narrowed. He paused for about two seconds, and then spun on a heel and started walking for the door.

"Company," I hissed to Carlos. I dropped down quietly from the window. My feet did not slip on the ice, because, hey, Queen of Winter over here. I moved quickly and crouched over him, putting my hands lightly on his chest. "Stay flat and stay still. I'll keep you covered."

He looked down at my hands and gave me a quick glance; then his expression went focused and stoic and he lay back on the sleet-covered ground.

I did everything I could to shore up the veil covering us both. The captain stepped out of the Elbow Room and looked around, and I got a close look at the man for the first time.

There was visibly something wrong with him. At a casual glance, it might have looked like he'd simply been exposed to a little too much cold and ultraviolet radiation and freezing salt water. But the cracks in his skin were a little too sharp edged, the reddened portions a little too brightly colored for that. I got the slow and horrible impression that his skin was trying to contain too much mass, like an overstuffed sausage. There were what looked like the beginnings of cataracts in his eyes—only their edges quivered and wobbled, like living things.

That was pretty weird, even by my standards.

It got absolutely hentai-level weird when the man opened his mouth and then opened it a little wider, and then opened it until his jaw visibly unhinged and a writhing tangle of purplish red tentacles emerged and thrashed wildly at the air, as if grasping for scents.

I felt my mouth stretch into a widening grin. A sleet storm was a terrible place for scent hunting. I couldn't tell you how I knew that, but I knew it as certainly as I knew that he hadn't noticed the flaws in my veil. This was not the territory of this creature, whatever it was. It was mine.

The tentacles withdrew with a whipping motion, like a frog recovering its tongue. The captain swayed from foot to foot, looking around the night for a moment, and then turned and paced back into the bar. A moment later, the whole weirdly silent column of fisherman freaks, including Clint, marched out of the bar and back down the hill toward the harbor. Clint was walking on his broken knee as if it didn't particularly bother him that it was bent inward like that.

"What the hell?" Carlos breathed as they walked away. "What was *that*?"

"Right?" I asked him. An absolutely mad giggle came wriggling up out of my belly. "That was the most messed-up thing I have ever seen from that close." I looked down at him, put my hand up to my mouth, and made gargling sounds while wiggling my fingers like tentacles.

And suddenly I realized that I was straddling Carlos Ramirez. And that he was staring at me with dark eyes that I felt like I could look at for a good, long while.

"Do you know what I want to do?" I asked him.

He licked his lips and then glanced at the retreating group. "Follow them?"

"Yes, all right," I said, and swallowed. "Follow them. We can also do that." I rose and helped him up.

"Wait. What?"

"I'm flirting with you, dummy," I said, and smiled at him. "What, you can't work and banter at the same time? After all your big talk?"

He lifted a hand, closed his eyes, and pinched the bridge of his nose for a moment. "*Dios*. This . . . is very much not what I was expecting for this evening. And hang on." He ducked back around the corner of the Elbow Room, and a moment later emerged with a small bundle of gear. In a few seconds, he was donning the grey cloak of the Wardens of the White Council and buckling on a weapons belt that bore a sword on one side and a large pistol on the other.

"Swords and guns," I said. "Hot." I picked up a corner of the cloak and wrinkled my nose. "This, though . . . Not."

"Wardens do a lot of good," he said quietly. "It isn't always pretty, what we do, but it needs to be done." He nodded toward the retreating backs of the captain and his crew. "Like those . . . things. Someone has to do something." He smiled faintly as he started walking in their wake. "You and Dresden can't be everywhere."

I watched him for a moment, taking in details. "You're limping," I noted. It was a weakness, and it stood out to me. It might not have before.

"Should have seen me a month ago," he said. "Could barely get out of my chair. Chupacabra kicked me in the back. Come on."

I could see the pain in his movements now, and cataloged them on pure reflex. His back was too rigid, much more so than it had been before. The fall from the window had aggravated injuries that hadn't healed properly. That could be used against him.

I wish thoughts like that didn't come to me so naturally, but after months fighting the Fomor on Chicago's streets, months under the instruction of the Leanansidhe, they were second nature.

I folded my arms against a little chill that had nothing to do with the weather and hurried after the handsome young Warden.

———

THE WEATHER CONTINUED worsening as we reached the waterfront. It wasn't far from the Elbow Room, but *far* was a relative term when a viciously cold wind was driving sleet and icy spray up the slope and into our faces. To me, it was brisk but actually a little bit pleasant. But for the sake of camaraderie, and definitely not because I wanted to conceal my increasing levels of weirdness from Carlos, I emulated him. I bowed my head against the wind and hunched my shoulders while hugging my own stomach.

"Who would live in this?" Carlos growled, shuddering.

"People smart enough to stay indoors during this kind of weather?" I suggested. "Tentacular parasites? Obstinate wizards? You come to Alaska but you don't plan for the cold?"

He couldn't really roll his eyes very well when his lashes were becoming steadily encased in ice, but he came close. "Maybe you'd like it back in your cell, Your Highness."

I flashed him a quick grin, and then we kept on following the captain and his crew. They wasted no time in marching back to a waterfront pier and boarding a ship with the name *Betsy Lee* painted across her stern. They filed up the gangplank, neat as you please, and went belowdecks, all without hesitating or looking back—and all in total silence.

We watched for a moment more, and then Carlos nodded and said, "I'm thinking freak fuel explosion. Boat burns to the water in moments, takes them with it."

"Wow," I said.

"Not yet," he said. "Not until I'm sure it's only them. Just thinking of the shape of things to come."

I looked up and down the waterfront, what I could see of it through the weather, and said, "Well, we're not sitting out here all night and babysitting the boat." And we weren't going to be moving quietly around the *Betsy Lee*, either, not with all that ice on the deck.

But I could.

"I'm going to take a peek around," I said. "Right back."

"Whoa," Carlos said. "What? Molly . . ."

I ignored him and ran lightly over the short distance to the dock and down it, and then leapt lightly out onto the deck of the ship. My feet didn't slip, and a continuous series of rippling shivers ran up and down my spine. I was putting myself in danger, treading into the territory of what was clearly a dangerous predator, and it felt really, really good.

Is that what happened to Maeve? Had she gotten a little too fond of the feeling of danger? I mean, she'd spent years defying freaking *Mab*. Could it get more dangerous than that?

I shook my head and started scouting the ship, relying on my instincts. Harry'd always been a good source of advice about problems. He dealt with them on a continuous basis, after all, and in his studied opinion, if you had one problem, you had a problem. But if you had *multiple* problems, you might also have an opportunity. One problem, he swore, could often be used to solve another, and he had stories about a zombie tyrannosaurus to prove it.

The Miksani had several centuries' worth of a spotless record in paying tribute to Mab. They'd stopped only a few years ago. As diverse and fickle as the beings of Faerie could be, they rarely did things for no reason. And, lo and behold, in this same little town in the middle of more nowhere than any other little town I had ever seen, tentacular weirdo critters were conducting a quiet reign of terror.

Chances that these two facts were unrelated? Probably close to zero.

I didn't want to take foolish risks in the confined spaces belowdecks—that was a losing proposition for me, if it came to a confrontation. So I conducted a quick survey of the deck, the bridge, and the fishing paraphernalia stored on it, keeping my steps as light and silent as I could. I spotted it just before deciding to leave again: a single, dark feather gleaming with opalescence, pinned between two metal frames of what I presumed to be crab cages, stored and ready to drop into the sea.

I felt a little surge of triumph, took it, and leapt lightly back to the deck. I rejoined Carlos a moment later. He was sliding his gun into its holster. He'd been ready to start shooting if I got into trouble. And they say there are no gentlemen anymore.

"What'd you find?"

I held it up, grinning.

"Feather?"

"Not just a feather," I said. "A cormorant feather."

He peered at me. "How do you know that?"

I didn't want to say something like *I Googled it under Winter Law*, but the mantle of power I'd inherited from Maeve knew all about Mab's subjects, and the knowledge it contained flowed through me as certainly as lessons learned in childhood. "How do you think?" I asked instead.

He struck his head lightly with the heel of his hand and said, "Durr. The Miksani."

"Elementary, Watson," I said, and winked at him before I started walking. "I suggest you bring your pistol, just in case."

"Just in case of what?" he asked, turning to follow.

"In case the Miksani decide they aren't in the mood for company."

ILIULIUK BAY IS the next-best thing to four miles long, and that makes for a lot of shoreline. We had to walk around the bay to get to the portion of Unalaska that was physically farthest from the dock where the *Betsy Lee* was moored. The weather stopped worsening and held steady at torturously miserable levels. Carlos drew up his cloak's hood and trudged along stoically.

It took time, but we reached a log building on the edge of town that bore a sign that read UNALASKA FISH MARKET. A pair of cormorants—large, dark seabirds—huddled on a protruding log at the building's corner, taking partial shelter from the night beneath the eaves of the building's roof. I could feel their dark, bright eyes on me as I approached the darkened building, but I didn't head for the door. Instead I went straight to the birds.

"Greetings to the Miksani from the mistress of Arctis Tor," I said in formal tones. "I, her appointed representative, have come for the tribute rightfully due the Winter Court. I believe that a meeting with your elders could produce positive results for all parties."

The birds stared at me hard. Then, as one, their eyes swiveled to Carlos.

He lifted a hand and said, "Warden Ramirez of the White Council of Wizardry. I apologize for showing up at the last minute, but I come in peace, and would appreciate a meeting with your elders as well."

The two birds stared at him for a moment and then looked at each other. One winged away into the night.

The other flapped its wings, soared down to the ground not far from us, and shimmered. A second later, the cormorant was gone, and an entirely naked young woman crouched where it had been a moment before. She had the bronze skin and almond eyes of someone with a generous helping of Native American blood in her veins, and her hair was nearly longer than she was, dark and glossy, with faint flickers of opalescence in it. She couldn't have been older than me, and she was built like a swimmer, all supple muscle and muted curves.

Her eyes were agate hard. The anger boiled off her in waves.

"Now?" she demanded of me. "Now you come?"

"I'm kind of new at this," I said. "This was actually my first stop. I'm Molly, the new Winter Lady."

The girl narrowed her eyes, staring a hole in me as she did. She was silent for a full minute before she spat, "Nauja."

"It's nice to meet you, Nauja," I said.

The simple pleasantry got a suspicious look and narrowed eyes in response. Apparently, Maeve had left quite an impression on the locals. That girl had been a real piece of work.

"I have nothing to say to you," Nauja said, her tone carefully neutral. She turned to Carlos and inclined her head in something resembling politeness, only a lot stiffer. "Wizard Ramirez. We have heard of you, even here. You have done much for one so young."

Carlos gave her his easy, confident grin. "Just wait until I'm old enough to get my driver's license."

Nauja stared at him for a second and then looked down sharply, her cheeks turning a few shades pinker. Not that I could really blame her. Carlos was pretty darned cute, and he could *kiss*. My lips tingled faintly in memory, and I folded my arms so that I could rub at my mouth unobtrusively.

Maybe three minutes later, the door to the fish market opened and candlelight shone weakly out into the foul weather of the night. Nauja rose immediately and walked inside. There was a young man about her age waiting inside, wearing a heavy flannel robe. He had another one waiting, and wrapped it around her shoulders carefully before nodding to us and standing aside so that we could enter.

We went in, and the young man shut the door behind us. It took a couple of seconds for our eyes to adjust to the low candlelight, and then I saw why the Miksani were so upset.

They were in the middle of a funeral.

A dead man of middle years, resembling Nauja enough to be her father or uncle, lay on a table in the middle of the room. He was dressed in a mix of practical modern clothing and native garb, maybe sealskin, richly decorated in beads and ivory. His hands were folded on his chest, and a bone knife or spearhead of some kind lay beneath them. Nauja and her male counterpart took up positions on either side of a woman of middle age who stood beside the body, her expression drawn with grief. The three of them stared at me expectantly.

Carlos stepped close enough to me that he was almost touching. His hip bumped mine deliberately, and he looked up at the rafters of the little market building.

Dozens of bright eyes were staring down at us. I couldn't tell how many cormorants lurked in the rafters, but they were everywhere, and waiting with the silent patience of predators.

I dragged my eyes from them back to the elder woman facing me.

"I am Molly, the new Winter Lady," I said in what I hoped was a respectful, quiet tone. "I've come for the tribute."

"I am Aluki," said the woman in a quiet voice. She gestured toward the bier. "This is my husband, Tupiak. We sent to you for help years ago."

"I take it no help came," I said.

Aluki stared at me. Nauja looked like she wanted to fling herself on me and rip my eyes out.

"Well, the problem has been addressed, and now I'm here," I said. "Let's set things straight."

"What do you know of our troubles?" Aluki said.

"I know they're on the *Betsy Lee*," I said.

Nauja's eyes suddenly became huge and black, and she all but quivered in place.

Carlos stepped between us and nodded respectfully. "Elder Aluki, I am Warden Ramirez of the White Council of Wizardry. We've been made aware of difficulties in this place. I'm here to help. If I can be of service in restoring balance to the Miksani, I will be glad to do so."

Aluki inclined her head to Carlos. "We are not a wealthy people, Warden. I cannot ask for your help."

Of course not. The Miksani were of Winter, and the Fae never gave or accepted gifts or services without equal recompense. The scales of obligation had to remain balanced at all times.

"You need not," Carlos responded. "I've come to a bargain with Lady Molly, who has already offered payment on your behalf."

Oh, that was an excellent gesture on Carlos's part. And it worked. Aluki gave me another glance, one more thoughtful, before she nodded.

"My predecessor," I said, "failed to make me aware of her obligations before she passed. Please tell me how Winter may assist you."

"No," Nauja hissed, surging toward me.

Aluki stopped the younger Miksani with a lifted hand, her eyes on me. Then she said, "Our enemy has arisen from the deeps and taken mortal shells. Each season, they take some of our number."

"Take?" Carlos asked. He nodded toward the dead Miksani. "Like that?"

Aluki shook her head and spoke in a level, weary tone. "The enemy has power. Our people survive by hiding among the mortals. Few of us are warriors. Only Tupiak, Nauja, and Kunik had the power to challenge the enemy. They tried to rescue those who had been taken. They failed. My husband was wounded and did not survive."

"Your enemy has captives?" I asked. "Right now?"

She nodded and said, "On the ship, belowdecks. While they are captive, there will be no tribute."

"Well, then," I said. I exchanged a glance with Carlos. He gave me a wolfish grin and nodded. I nodded back and said to Aluki, "The Warden and I are going to go get them out of there."

She lifted her chin. "You can do this?"

"I can," I said. "I will."

There was a low thrum in the air as I spoke the words, and I felt something go *click* somewhere in my head. I had just made a promise.

And Winter *kept* its promises.

Aluki stared at me for a moment, then sagged, bowed her head, and nodded. "Very well."

"Your people who were taken," I said, "how will I know them?"

Nauja bared her teeth and spoke with her jaw clenched. "They took our children."

"God, I love hero work," Carlos said as we stepped back out into the storm. "No murky grey area, no anguished questions, no conflicting morality. Bad guys took some kids, and we're gonna go get 'em out."

"Right?" I asked him, and nodded. "This must be what my dad felt, all the time."

"Knights of the Cross never have any missions they question?" Carlos asked.

"I think they get a different kind of question," I said. "For Dad, it was always about saving everyone. Not just the victims. He had to try for the monsters, too."

"Weird," Carlos said.

"Not so weird," I said. "Maybe if someone had offered a hand to the monsters, they wouldn't have become monsters in the first place. You know?"

"I don't," Carlos said. "Maybe I've seen too many monsters." He settled his weapons belt a little more comfortably on his hips and wrapped himself up in his cloak again. "Or too many victims. I don't know."

Our steps crunched in the sleet, and between that and the rattle of more sleet and the crash of waves on the shore, I almost didn't hear his next words.

"About six months into the war," he said, "I was carrying pliers with me, so that I could take vampire teeth as trophies. That was how much I hated them."

I didn't say anything. Carlos, like a lot of the other young Wardens of the Council, had been baptized in fire. Harry had spoken of it once while doing his best to shield me from the war. He'd felt horrible leading a team of children, as he saw it, into a vicious conflict between the White Council and the Red Court:

*I feel like I'm putting them through a meat grinder. Even if they come home in one piece.*

"You hated them. And then they were gone," I said.

"Poof," Carlos said. "War over." He shook his head. "*Odium interruptus.* And then it was supposed to be back to business as usual again. Just supposed to move on. Only I never quite figured out how. And half the bunks in the barracks were empty."

"Part of you misses it," I said.

His lips tightened, though it wasn't a smile. "I miss the certainty," he said. "I miss how tight I was with the squad. The rest I can mostly do without." He glanced at me and then away. "The Wardens' job isn't always simple. Or clean. I've done things I'm not proud of."

"Haven't we all?" I said.

We walked in silence for a few steps. Then he said, "Once we get these kids clear, I want to kiss you again."

My tummy did a little happy cartwheel, and my heart sped up to keep it company. "Oh yeah? What if I don't want to?"

He gave me a very direct, very intense look. His eyes were dark and hot and bold.

"You want to," he said.

He wasn't wrong.

WE STOLE UP to the *Betsy Lee* under my best veil, moving quickly and quietly. We'd already worked out the plan. Carlos was going in first and was going to raise a hell of a racket and attract everyone's attention. My job was to stay veiled, grab the kids, and get them off the ship.

Then we'd kill things.

But halfway across the deck toward the door leading below, Carlos paused. He tilted his head to one side and narrowed his eyes. He glanced at me, lifting his brows in an unspoken question.

I paused, frowned at him, and then looked carefully around the deck. It was empty. The boat rolled and pitched with the waves, but there was no other motion. It was still and silent as a tomb. In fact . . .

It just *felt* empty, like an apartment with no furniture, like a school playground on the weekend.

Carlos suddenly moved faster, gliding to the stairs. He held up a hand, telling me to wait, and went down them in a rush. He reappeared within a minute.

"Empty," he reported. "There's no one down there."

"Dammit, something must have tipped them off," I said.

He nodded. "They've got eyes somewhere, all right."

I went back to the dock and then to where it met dry land. I couldn't see very well, but I murmured, "Akari," flicked my wrist, and created an orb of glacial green light in the air over my right shoulder. Green was a good color for this kind of work. The mortal eye can detect more shades of green than any other color on the spectrum.

I cast back and forth, but it took only a few seconds to find what I was after: a depression in the accumulating sleet, the marks of the passage of many feet. "Carlos," I said, and pointed at the ground. "Tracks."

He came over and squinted down. "Aren't these from when they came back to the boat the first time?"

"Can't be," I said. "Our tracks from an hour ago are gone. These were made after we left."

He lifted his eyebrows. "Seriously, Aragorn? Where'd you learn this stuff?"

"Mom taught me. She was scoutmaster for my brothers."

"And to think I wasted my youth learning magic," Carlos said. "Can you tell if the kids were with them?"

"Dammit, man. I'm a Faerie Princess, not a forensic analyst." I jerked my head to tell him to follow me, and we set out after our quarry.

The trail ended at a church.

It was a Russian Orthodox church, complete with a couple of onion domes, and the sign out front read HOLY ASCENSION OF OUR LORD CATHEDRAL. It was also creepy and ominous as hell in the freezing night. Odd blue-green light glowed within the windows of the sanctuary. I thought I saw a shadow move past a window, sinuous and smooth, like a cruising shark.

"Oh," Carlos said, stopping short. I could see calculations and connections forming behind his eyes. "Uh-oh."

"What-oh?"

"This just got worse."

"Why?"

He licked his lips nervously. "Uh. How much Lovecraft have you read?"

"I haven't kept track," I said. "Somewhere between zero and none. Should I have?"

"Probably," he said. "It's always the last thing a formally trained apprentice learns about."

"I have a funny feeling my training wasn't formal," I said.

"Yeah. Neither was Harry's. Have you heard of the Old Ones?"

"I don't think it's a very kind nickname for the Rolling Stones. They still put on a great show."

He nodded and squinted at me. "I kind of need you to put on your serious face now."

"That bad?" I asked.

"Maybe," he said. "They're . . . kind of a collection of entities. Really old, really powerful entities."

"What, like gods?" I asked.

"Like the things gods have nightmares about," he said.

"Outsiders."

He nodded. "Only they aren't *outside*. They're here. Caged, bound, and sleeping, but they're here."

"That seems kind of dangerous."

"Yes and no," he said. "They feed on psychic energy. On fear. On the collective subconscious awareness of them that exists within humanity."

I squinted at him. "Meaning what?"

"The more people who know about them and fear them, the more awake and more powerful they become," he said. "That's why the people who know about them don't talk about them much."

"What's that got to do with the price of beer in Unalaska?"

"One of the Old Ones is known as the Sleeper. It's said his tomb is somewhere under the Pacific. And that goddamned moron Lovecraft published *stories* and *easy-to-remember rhymes* about the thing." He shook his head. "The signal boost gave the Sleeper enough power to influence the world. It has a number of cults. People get . . . infested, I guess. Slowly go insane. Lose their humanity. Turn into something else."

I remembered the captain's open mouth and writhing tentacles and shivered. "So you think that's what is happening here? A Sleeper cult?"

"It's the Holy Ascension of Our Lord Cathedral," he pointed out. "That means something way different to a Sleeper cultist than it does to most folks. They aren't exactly making it difficult to suss out."

"Okay. So, how does that change anything about what we have to do tonight?"

He nodded toward the cathedral. "You feel that?"

"It's capital-C creepy," I said, and nodded.

"It's worse than that," he said. "It's holy ground. Consecrated to the Sleeper. We go in there, we won't be dealing with a bunch of 'roided-up fishermen with tentacle mouth. They'll have power. It's a nest of sorcerers in there."

"Oh," I said. "Ouch." I thought about it for a moment. "So, how does that change anything about what we have to do tonight?"

He bared his teeth. "Guess it doesn't."

"I guess it doesn't," I agreed.

"You know," he said, "I am pretty damned valorous."

"I know," I said.

"But I am not stupid. You're a Faerie Queen now, right?"

"Uh-huh, I guess," I said.

"Couldn't you whistle up a squad of ogres or something to help make this happen?"

I thought about it for a second and said, "Yeah, I could."

"Maybe something like that should happen?" he suggested.

I was quiet for a second before I said, "No."

"Uh-huh," he said, and nodded. "Why not?"

"In the first place, it would take time to get them here. In the second, this is Miksani territory, and the ogres would have to arrange payment for intruding and observe customs, and it would take even longer. And in the third place . . ."

I blinked. Oh. *That's* what Mab meant.

"What?" Carlos asked.

"This is my first showing. Everyone in Winter, every wicked and predatory thing in Faerie, is going to pay attention to it, and will interact with me based off what I do here. First impressions matter, and I'm not going to be a child who screams for help the first time she hits a bump in the road. I'm going to be the predator who freaking takes you apart if you cross her. I'm going to make sure I don't have to prove my strength to them over and over for the rest of this gig. So, you and I are going to go in there and handle it."

Carlos sniffed, then gave a short nod. "Right. Well. These people—they aren't human anymore. Something else moved into their bodies. There's nothing left to save. You get me?"

I got him. He meant that I could play hardball without fear of running afoul of the White Council. I squinted at the cathedral and said, "Okay. New plan."

HARRY WAS A big believer in kicking in the teeth of whoever you planned to fight. Granted, those kinds of tactics played to his strengths, and it wasn't always smart or possible—but it *was* always a way to seize the initiative and control the opening seconds of a conflict.

Granted, Harry would have used fire. And I'm pretty sure he wouldn't have pulled out a wand and prepared the One-Woman Rave spell I'd developed. And I'm absolutely certain that he wouldn't have taken a moment to start up DJ Molly C's Boom Box spell, which would play C&C Music Factory's "Gonna Make You Sweat (Everybody Dance Now)" loud enough to be heard in Anchorage.

But I did. I wanted loud noise that was totally out of place and as weird as possible to whatever supernatural critters were riding around inside the fishermen—and the creatures of the supernatural world aren't exactly pop-culture mavens. Plus, it was dance music from the '90s. Nobody thinks that stuff is normal.

Heavy bass and lead power chords started thumping against the windows. I turned loose the One-Woman Rave, and the air around me filled with a light-and-pyrotechnics show that would make Burning Man look like *Mister Rogers' Neighborhood*. My heart started pounding in fear and excitement and something disturbingly like lust as I crossed the last few feet to the cathedral's entrance.

And then, just as the song screamed, "Everybody dance now!" I leaned back, drew the power of Winter into my body, and kicked the big double doors off their hinges as if they'd been made of balsa and Scotch tape.

At which point I learned the real reason Harry keeps doing that.

It. Is. Awesome.

"Give me the music!" I screamed with the song, and walked straight in. I might have had some hip and shoulder action going in time with the beat.

Look, I hadn't been out dancing in a while, okay?

I crossed the little vestibule in a couple of steps and passed into the sanctuary in a thundercloud of rave lights and showers of multicolored sparks, music shaking the air. I got a good look at the fishermen as I came in.

All twenty of them were there, scattered around the sanctuary, though three, including the captain, were up on the altar, along with half a dozen Miksani children, aged about four through ten. Their wrists were bound together with one long length of rope, which cut cruelly into their wrists.

Everyone in the cathedral lifted a hand to shield their eyes as I came in. The cultists' mouths gaped open and tendrils emerged to begin thrashing the air.

I felt the surge of power coming, an ugly, greasy pressure in the air, and as it gathered, physical darkness swirled and surged around the fishermen. And then, like a stream of fouled water, it surged from each of the cultists to the captain, where his tentacles gathered it, whipping and writhing, and sent the enormous collective surge of negative energy flying directly at me.

It came fast, too fast to dodge, too intense to be stopped by any magic I could manage, and struck my solar plexus like an enormous, deadly spear.

Or, at least, that's what it looked like to them. I was actually about ten feet to the left, hidden behind my best veil while maintaining a glamour of my image. The bolt struck my little illusion, and the conflict of energies, combined with the difficulty of running the Rave and the Boom Box, made it too much to hold together. The image popped like a soap bubble, and the dark bolt tore through the flooring and foundation in the vestibule like a backhoe.

The captain froze for a second, unsure of what had just happened. I had no such moment of hesitation. I was already rushing down the leftmost aisle behind my veil, plastic-handled knife in hand. I reached the first of the tentacle-mouthed fishermen and, with a single flick, cut his throat.

I could barely hear the creature's sudden, high-pitched scream of pain over the thunder of the Boom Box, and I'd known it was coming. It didn't register on the other fishermen in the chaos, and I didn't slow down.

I killed three of them with my knife before one of the cultists saw what was happening and screamed, pointing.

Number four went down when he turned his head to look, but he writhed as he went down and I was splashed with blood.

Magically speaking, blood is significant in all kinds of ways. It carries a charge of magical energy inside it, for example, and can be used to direct a spell at a specific person from hundreds or thousands of miles away. This blood was stronger than mortal stuff and carried a heavier charge. The power in it flared into sparks as the blood hit my veil, and then it ripped a huge hole in it, and I was suddenly visible to the entire cult.

Another bolt of energy came my way, this one tossed by an individual cultist. It lacked the landscape-rearranging power of the first bolt, and I was lucky it did. I threw up a shield of enough strength to barely deflect it, and dove to the floor as others came winging my way, chewing chunks the size of my fist from the wall behind me.

From the floor I couldn't see much—but the cultists were howling and they had to be coming closer, sending their nearest members to rush me while the others kept me pinned down with their blasts of dark power. If I didn't move, and fast, I would be swarmed. Winter Queen or not, that wouldn't end well for me.

I let go of the remnants of the veil, crystallized a new spell in my mind, and gave it life. Then I hopped up and ran for the exit.

I also hopped up and ran down the nearest aisle of pews. I also hopped up and sprinted toward the altar. I also hopped up and started vaulting the pews diagonally, heading for the nearest fisherman. I also hopped up and backed up one step at a time, conjuring what looked like a heavy energy shield in front of me. I also hopped up and hurled a blast of deep blue energy at the captain. I also hopped up and . . .

Look, you get the idea: Thirteen Mollies started running everywhere.

Blasts of dark power ripped apart pews and tore holes in the walls and shattered panes of stained glass. Some of them struck home, disintegrating the images, but the others continued to move and duck and evade.

Meanwhile, I stayed low and scramble-crawled twenty feet into the concealment of the confessional. I had done what I meant to do: entirely occupy the cult's attention.

Carlos made his entrance in perfect silence. The wall behind the altar was made of dark wood, but it just . . . fell apart into freaking grains of matter in an oval six feet high and three across, revealing the young Warden on the other side.

Without ceremony, Carlos pointed at a cultist, muttered a word, and a beam of pale green light struck it in the back. The man-creature simply *dissolved* into a slurry of water and what looked like powdered charcoal. The young Warden didn't miss a beat. Before the first cultist was done falling to the floor, he drew his sword and ran it smoothly into the nape of another cultist's neck. The creature arched for a second and then dropped like a stone, his mouth moving in frantic, silent screaming motions.

The captain whirled on Carlos and unleashed a wave of dark energy the size of a riding lawn mower. The Warden dropped his sword, slid his back foot along the floor, and tensed into a crouch. His arms swept up in smooth, graceful symmetry and intercepted the energy, gathering it like some kind of enormous soap bubble.

It was a water-magic spell, Carlos's specialty. He rolled his arms in a wide circle, took a pair of pirouetting steps, and swept his arms out toward the captain, sending the dark spell roaring back at him. It hit the captain like a small truck, hurtling him off the stage and halfway down the sanctuary.

"Come on, kids," Carlos shouted. He recovered his sword and almost contemptuously deflected an incoming blast of cultist magic with it. "I'm taking you home!"

The little Miksani didn't have to be told twice. They got up, the larger children helping the smaller ones, and began hurrying awkwardly toward the escape route Carlos had created on the way in. He shielded them, backing step by deliberate step, calling up a shield of energy with his left hand, intercepting blasts of energy with it, or swatting them wide with his Warden's blade.

In a few seconds, he'd be out of the room, along with the Miksani children, leaving me with nothing but cultists. I tensed and began to gather my energy.

And then Clint's reddened, work-roughened, clammy-cold hand shot into the confessional and seized my throat. It caught me off guard, and the sudden pain as his fingers tightened and he shut off my air supply was indescribable. He lifted me and, without hesitating for a second, began to slam me left and right, against the walls of the confessional, each impact horribly heavy, with no more passion than a man beating the dust from a rug.

My head hit hardwood several times, stunning me. My knees went all loose and watery, and suddenly the Rave and the Boom Box were gone. The next thing I knew, I was being dragged by the neck toward the altar. Clint walked up onto it and threw me down on my back on the holy table. I blinked my eyes, trying to get them to focus, and realized that the cult was gathered all around me, a circle of tentacle-mouthed faces and dead eyes.

Carlos and the kids were gone.

*Good.*

"It isn't a mortal," Clint said, somehow speaking through the tentacles, albeit in a creepy, inhuman tone. "See? It's different. It doesn't belong here."

"Yes," the captain said.

"Kill it. It cost us our sacrifice."

"No," the captain said. "You are new to the mortal world. This creature's blood is more powerful than generations of the Miksani and their spawn." The tentacles thrashed more and more excitedly. "We can drain her and drain her. Blood more powerful than any we have spilled to pave the way for the Sleeper. Our Lord shall arise!" The captain's eyes met mine and there was nothing behind them, no soul, nothing even remotely human. "And he shall hunger. Perhaps . . ."

"Perhaps you should think about this," I said. I think my sibilants had gone slushy. "Walk right now. Leave this island and don't come back. It's the only chance you have to survive."

"What is survival next to the ascendance of our Lord?" the captain asked. "Bow to Him. Give yourself of your own will."

"You don't know who I am, do you, squid-for-brains?" I asked.

"Bow, child. For when He comes, His rage will be a perfect, hideous storm. He will drag you down to his prison and entomb you there. Forever silent. Forever in darkness. Forever in terrible cold."

"I am Lady Molly of Winter," I said in a silken voice.

The thrashing tentacles went abruptly still for a second. Then the captain started to shout something.

Before he could, I unleashed power from the heart of Winter into the cathedral, unrestrained, undirected, unshaped, and untamable. It rushed through me, flowed through me, both frozen agony and a pleasure more intense than any orgasm.

Ice exploded out from me in swords and spears, in scythes and daggers and pikes. In an instant, crystalline blades and points, a forest of them, slammed into being, expanding with blinding speed. Ice *filled* the cathedral, and whatever was in its way, living or otherwise, was pierced and slashed and shredded and then crushed against the sanctuary's stone walls with the force of a locomotive.

It was over in less than a second. Then there was only silence, broken here and there by the crackle and groan of perfectly clear ice. I could clearly see the cult through it. Broken, torn to pieces, crushed, their blood a brilliant scarlet as it melted whatever ice it touched— only to freeze into ruby crystals a moment later.

It took the captain, impaled against the cathedral ceiling, almost a minute to die.

And while he did, I lay on the holy table, laughing uncontrollably.

THE ICE PARTED for me, opening a corridor perhaps half an inch wider than my shoulders and the same distance higher than my head. I walked out slowly, dreamily, feeling deliciously detached from every-thing. I had to step over a hand on the way out. It twitched in flicker-ing little autonomic spasms. I noted idly that it probably should have bothered me more than it did.

Outside, I found Carlos and the Miksani children. They were star-ing at me in silence. The sleet made the only sound. Few lights glowed in windows. Unalaska was battened down against the storm, and other than us, not a creature was stirring.

I closed my eyes, lifted my face to the storm, and murmured, "Burn it down."

Carlos stepped past me without a word. I felt the stirrings of power as he focused his will into fire so hot that the air hissed and sizzled and spat as he brought it forth. A moment later, warmth glowed behind me, and the crackle and mutter of rising flames began.

As we walked away, one wall was already covered in a five-foot curtain of flame. By the time we got the children back to the fish mar-ket, the cathedral was a beacon that spread an eerie glow through the sleet and spray. A few lights had come on, and I could see dark figures and a couple of emergency vehicles near the pyre, but there would be no saving the place. It was set a bit apart from the rest of Unalaska, in any case. It would burn alone.

Cormorants had begun to circle us, their cries odd and muted in the dark, and the children looked up with uncertain smiles. When we reached the market and went in, Aluki and Nauja were waiting for us. Nauja let out a cry and rushed forward to embrace the smallest girl, a child who cried out, "Mama!" and threw her arms around the Miksani woman's neck.

Cormorants winged in from out of the night through the open door, assuming human form with effortless grace as they landed. Glad voices were raised around the children, and more parents were reunited with their lost little ones. There were more hugs and laughter and happy tears.

*That*, I thought, *should probably make me feel more than it does as well.*

Carlos watched it with a big, warm grin on his face. He shook some hands and nodded pleasantly and was hugged and clapped on the shoulder. As I watched him, I felt something finally. I was admiring his scars, the memory of his skill, his courage, and I had an absolutely soul-deep need to run my fingers over him.

No one came within five feet of me—at least, not until Aluki crossed the room from the bier where her husband still lay, and faced me.

"I assume you wish the tribute now," she said in a low voice.

I felt dark, bright eyes all over the room, focusing on me.

"I need rest and food," I said. "I will return when the storm breaks, if that is acceptable."

Aluki blinked and her head rocked back. "It . . . Yes. Of course, Lady Molly. Thank you for that."

I gave her a nod and turned toward the door. Just before leaving, I looked over my shoulder and asked, "Carlos? Are you coming with?"

"Ah," he said, and his smile changed several shades. "Why . . . why, yes, I am."

By the time we reached Carlos's hotel, the storm was raging.

And the weather had gotten worse, too.

Neither of us spoke as we reached his room, and he opened the door for me. It was a nice hotel, far nicer than I would have expected in such isolation. I walked in, dropping my coat to the floor behind me. It hit the ground with the squelching sound of wet cloth and crackles of thin ice breaking. Layers of shirts joined it as I kept walking into the room, until I was down to skin.

I felt his eyes on me the whole way. Then I turned slowly and smiled at him.

His expression was caught somewhere between awe and hunger. His dark eyes glittered brightly.

"You're soaked and frozen," I said quietly. "Get out of those clothes."

He nodded slowly and walked toward me. His cloak and coat and shirts joined mine. Carlos Ramirez had the muscles of a gymnast, and his body was marked here and there with scars. Strength. Prowess. I approved.

He stopped in front of me, down to his own jeans. Then he kept walking toward me until our bodies met, and he pressed me gently down to the bed behind us. My eyes closed as I let out a little groan when I felt the heat of his skin against my chest, and I flung myself into the kiss that came next like the world was about to vanish into a nuclear apocalypse.

The sudden explosion of desire that radiated out from him felt like sinking into a steaming-hot bath, and I reveled in it, my own ardor rising. My hands slid over his chest and shoulders, reached around to his back. He was all tight muscle, heat, and pure passion. His mouth wandered to my throat, then to my shoulders and breasts, and I let out groans of need, encouraging him.

*Molly,* said the voice of my better reason.

His mouth left me for a second as he pulled off my boots. I arched up to help him remove my jeans, and heard him kicking off his own. With an impatient growl, I sat up and ripped at his belt.

*Molly,* said reason again. *Hello?*

I flung the belt across the room, to tell reason to shut up, and tore at his jeans. I had never wanted anything so badly in my *life* as I wanted Carlos naked and pressed against me.

*This isn't you*, said reason.

I pushed his jeans down past his hips. God, he was beautiful. I took his hand and leaned back on the bed, drawing him with me. "Now," I said. My voice came out thick and husky. "No more waiting. Now."

He let out a groan as he kissed me again, and I *felt* him start to touch and then—

And then I was sitting on the floor of the shower, shuddering, hot water pouring down around me.

*Wait.*

*What?*

*What the hell?*

I looked down at the water. The drain stopper was down, and it was seven or eight inches deep.

And pink.

*Oh, God.*

I looked at my hands. My nails . . . my nails looked longer. Harder. And there was red under them.

What had just happened?

I stood up and left the shower, dripping wet, not bothering to stop for a towel. I hurried back out of the bathroom and stopped in the doorway, shocked.

The room had been wrecked. The mattress was against the far wall—and the door. It had been torn in half. The lamps were out, and the slice of light from the bathroom lights provided the only illumination in a stark column. What I could see of the furniture had been trashed. Part of the bed frame was broken.

And Carlos . . .

He lay on the floor, covered in blood. One of his legs was broken, the pointy bits of his shattered shin thrusting out from the skin. His face was swelling up beneath the blood, his eyes puffed closed. He was covered in claw marks, rakes that oozed blood. He lay at a strange angle, twitching in pain, one hand clutching with blind instinct at his back.

His injured back. His weakness.

I stared down at my hands in utter horror, at the blood beneath my nails.

I had done this.

I had used his weakness against him.

"Mab," I breathed. I started choking and sobbing. "Mab! Mab!"

Mab can appear in a thunderclap if she wants to. This entrance was much less dramatic. A light in the far corner of the room clicked on and revealed the Queen of Winter, seated calmly in the chair in the corner. She regarded me with distant, opalescent eyes and lifted a single eyebrow.

"What happened?" I asked. "What happened?"

Mab regarded Carlos with a calm countenance. "What will happen every time you attempt to be with a man," she replied.

I stared at her. "What?"

"Three Queens of Summer; three Queens of Winter," she said, that alien gaze returning to me. "Maiden, mother, and crone. You are the maiden, Lady Molly. And for you to be otherwise, to become a mother, would be to destroy the mantle of power you wear. The mantle protected itself—as it must."

"*What?*"

She tilted her head and stared at me. "It is all within Winter Law. I suggest you spend a few hours each day meditating on it in the future. In time you will gain an adequate understanding of your limits."

"How could you do this?" I demanded. The tears on my cheeks felt like streaks of hot wax. "How could you do this?"

"I did not," Mab said calmly. "You did."

"Dammit, you know what I mean!"

"You have been gifted with great and terrible power, young lady," Mab said in an arch tone. "Did you really think you could simply go about your life as if you were a mortal girl?"

"You could have warned me!"

"When I tried, you had no inclination to listen. Only to jest."

"You bitch," I said, shaking my head. "You could have told me. You horrible bitch." I turned to go back into the bathroom, to get towels and go to Carlos's aid.

When I turned, Mab was *right* behind me, and her nose all but pressed against mine. Her eyes were flickering through shades of color and bright with cold anger. Her voice came out in a velvet murmur more terrifying than any enraged shriek. "What did you say to me?"

I flinched back, suddenly filled with fear.

I couldn't meet her eyes.

I didn't speak.

After a moment, some of the tension went out of her. "Yes," she said, her voice calm again. "I could have told you. I elected to teach you. I trust this has made a significant first impression."

"I have to help him," I said. "Please step aside."

"That will not be necessary," Mab said. "He will not be in danger of dying for some hours. I have already dispatched word to the White Council. Their healers will arrive momentarily to care for him. You will leave at once."

"I can't just leave him like this," I said.

"That is exactly what you can do," Mab said. Her voice softened by a tiny fraction of a degree. "You are no longer what you were, child. You must adapt to your new world. If you do not, you will cause terrible suffering—not least of all to yourself." She tilted her head, as if listening, and said, "The storm is breaking. You have your duty."

I clenched my jaw and said, "I can't just leave him there alone."

Mab blinked once, as if digesting my words. "Why not?"

"Because . . . because it's not what decent people do."

"What has that to do with either of us?" she asked.

I shook my head. "No. I am *not* going to be like that."

Mab pursed her lips and exhaled slowly through her nose. "Stubborn. Like our Knight."

"Damned right I am," I said.

I'm not sure you can micro-roll your eyes. But Mab can. "Very well. I will sit with him until the wizards arrive."

I turned to regard Carlos's broken form lying on the floor. Then I hurried into enough clothes to be decent. I knelt over him and kissed his forehead. He made a soft moaning sound that tore something inside my chest.

"I'm sorry," I whispered. I kissed his head again. "I'm *so* sorry. I didn't know what would happen. I'm sorry."

"Time waits for no one, Lady Molly," Mab said. She had crossed the room to stand across from me over poor Carlos. "Not even the Queens of Faerie. Collect the tribute."

I gave him a last kiss on the forehead and rose to leave. But I paused at the door to consider, to consult Winter Law.

I had never really considered what the tribute *was*. But it was there in the law. I turned slowly and stared at Mab in horror.

"Their children," I whispered. "You want me to take their children."

"Yes."

"Their *children*," I said. "You can't."

"I won't. You will."

I shook my head. "But . . ."

"Lady Molly," Mab said gently. "Consider the Outer Gates."

I did.

Winter Law showed me a vivid image. An endless war fought at the far borders of reality. A war against the pitiless alien menace known simply as the Outsiders. A war fought by millions of Fae, to prevent the Outsiders from invading and destroying reality itself. A war so long and bitter that bones of the fallen were the topography of the landscape. It was why the Winter Court existed in the first place, why we were so aggressive, so savage, so filled with lust and the need to create more of our kind.

"You're filling me with a hunger I can never feed," I whispered.

"We cannot expect our people to bear a burden that we do not," Mab replied, her tone level, implacable. "You will learn to endure it."

"You want me to take *children*," I hissed.

"I am fighting a war," Mab said simply. "Fighting a war requires soldiers."

"But they're *children*. Children like my little brothers and sisters. And you want me to carry them *away*."

"Of course. It is the ideal time to learn, to be trained until they come into their strength and are ready to do battle," Mab said. "It is the only way to prepare them for what is to come. The only way to give them a chance to survive the duties I require of them."

"How long?" I asked through clenched teeth. "How long will they be gone?"

"Until they are no longer needed," Mab said.

"Until they're killed, you mean," I said. "They're never going back home."

"Your outrage is irrelevant," Mab said. Her voice was flat, calm, filled with undeniable logic. "I have condemned *millions* of the children of Winter to a life of violence and death in battle, because it *must* be done. If we fail in our duty, there will be no home to which they can return. There will be no mortal world, safe and whole for your brothers and sisters."

"But . . ." My protest trailed off weakly.

"If you have an alternative, I would be more than willing to consider it."

Silence stretched.

"I don't," I said quietly.

"Then do your duty," Mab said.

I opened the door and looked back at her. "I don't *yet*," I said, and I said it hard. "This isn't over."

Mab gave me the slow blink again. Then she inclined her head by a fraction of an inch, her expression pensive.

I turned and left the broken form of Carlos Ramirez behind me to steal away the Miksani's children.

And I couldn't stop crying.

# JURY DUTY

When you set out to write a wizard, there are a lot of issues you have to face: How does the magic work? Where did he get his power? What is the nature of magic in relation to the universe? How do people regard magic in that story world? And on and on and on. Those are pretty obvious questions. They make for some really fun and occasionally thought-provoking tales.

But as story devices, wizards also have some inherent problems with their popular perception: They are generally loner figures, living in some tower and only occasionally interacting with the world—which works great when the wizard is a supporting figure, and is complete garbage when it comes to having a wizard as a central character. Wizards have tremendous power—which is great when it's coming from a supporting character who has limitations that mean he can only occasionally do something. But, again, when casting a wizard as the central character, from a storytelling standpoint all of that power is a liability, not an asset. Protagonists have to be challenged, struggle, and grow, not just mow down everything that gets in their way with their Tenser's Mystic Inflammable Bulldozer spell.

So, I knew I was going to have to subvert some of these popular perceptions from the very get-go. To do that, I turned to a different set of archetypes: magicians. Short version, there are three archetypes of performing magicians: the dark and mysterious guy, the glitzy professional-showman guy, and the apparently incompetent buffoon. The popular perception of wizards definitely fits in that first category—but it ain't a simple trick to write dark and mysterious in a first-person protagonist. By its very nature, first-person viewpoint is incredibly intimate, and hiding things from the audience while using that viewpoint works against its deepest strength. So dark and mysterious was out. Glitzy was out, too, because I'm not sure Burt Wonderstone could carry a series.

So I basically went with option three, the buffoon. And the way I chose to do it was to make my protagonist a young, clumsy puppy of a wizard who was absolutely incompetent at real life, in this case reflected in how his magical powers disrupt modern technology. Once I knew I was doing that, it seemed clear that I had to go all in: While I needed him to be pretty savvy about matters pertaining to the wild side of life so that he could be good at his job, I wanted to make him into a character who was constantly challenged by the most mundane issues—paying his bills, fixing his car, dealing with his landlord, struggling with taxes and the DMV, and all the dumb stuff we grown-ups have to do, which, in our honest moments, we admit that we just hate doing and would much rather have some milk and a cookie and a nap.

This tale, set after the events of *Skin Game*, chronicles the latest clash between the mighty wizard Dresden and the dread forces of the Real World: in this case, a summons to jury duty.

"I don't believe it. They found me," I muttered grimly. I looked left and right, checking around me for lurking threats. "I don't know how, but they did it. I've been back in the world for less than a month, and they found me."

Will Borden, engineer and werewolf, set down a heavy box of books on the kitchen table and looked at me with concern. Then he came over and looked down at the letter in my hands before snorting. "Such a drama queen."

"I'm serious!" I said, and shook the letter. "I'm being hunted! By my own government!"

"It's a summons to jury duty, Harry," Will said. He opened the fridge and helped himself to a bottle of Mac's ale. He had to navigate around a few boxes to do it. I didn't think I'd had much out on the island, but it's amazing how many boxes it takes to hold not much. It had taken most of a day to ferry it all from the island into Molly's apartment in town. She rarely used the place these days and had given it to me to live in until I found my own digs.

"I don't like it," I said.

"Too bad," Will said. "You got it. Look, you probably won't be selected anyway."

"Summons," I said, glowering. "It's a freaking command. They want to see what a real summoning is, I could show them."

Will laughed at me. He was younger than me, shorter than average, and built like a linebacker. "How dare they intrude upon the solitude of the mighty wizard Dresden?"

"Nngh," I said, and tossed the paper onto the top of a box of unopened envelopes—my mail, which had accumulated for more than a year, most of it junk. Some of it had been at the post office. More had been set aside by the new owner of my old address, formerly Mrs. Spunkelcrief's boardinghouse, and now the Better Future Society. I hadn't been able to stomach asking the new owner for my mail, but Butters had gotten it for me.

"Maybe I won't show up," I said. I paused. "What happens if I don't show up?"

"You can be held in contempt of court or fined or jailed or something," Will said. He scratched his chin thoughtfully. "Now that I think about it, they actually leave it kind of vague, what's going to happen."

"Good threats are like that. Scarier when you can use your imagination."

"The government isn't the mob, Harry."

"Aren't they?" I asked. "Pay them money every year to protect you, and God help you if you don't."

Will rolled his eyes and got another bottle from the fridge. He opened it for me and passed it over. "Mac would kill you for drinking this cold, et cetera and so on."

"It's hot out," I said, and took a long pull. "Especially for this early in the year. And he would just give me that disappointed grunting sound. Damned government. Not like I don't have things to do."

"Is justice worth having?" Will asked.

I eyed him.

"Is it?"

"Mostly," I said. Warily.

"Well, that's why there's a legal system."

"What does justice have to do with the legal system?"

"Do you really want to tear it all apart and start over from 1776?" Will asked.

"Not particularly. I have books to read."

He spread his hands. "The courts aren't perfect," Will said, "but they can do okay a lot of the time." He reached into the box and picked up the summons. "And if you really think the courts aren't working, maybe you should do something about it. If only there was some way you could directly participate . . ."

I snatched the letter back from him with a scowl. "Think you're smart, huh?"

"You're kind of a solitary hunter by nature, Harry," Will said. "I'm more of a pack creature. We're smart about different things, that's all."

I read a little more. "There's a dress code, too?" I demanded.

Will covered up his mouth with his hand and coughed, but I could see that he was laughing at me.

"Well," I said firmly, "I am *not* wearing a tie."

Will lowered his hand, his expression carefully locked into sober agreement. "Viva la revolution."

So I WENT to court.

It meant a trek downtown to the Richard J. Daley Center court-house, whose name did little to inspire confidence in me that justice might indeed be done. Ah well. I wasn't here to create disorder. I was here to preserve disorder.

I went up to the seventeenth floor, turned in my card along with about a gazillion other people, none of whom seemed at all enthusiastic about being there. I got a cup of bad coffee and grimaced at it while waiting around for a while. Then a guy in a black muumuu showed up and recounted the plot of *My Cousin Vinny*.

Okay, it was a robe, and the guy was a judge, and he gave us a brief outline of the format of the trial system, but it's not nearly as entertaining to say it that way.

Then they started calling names. They said they only needed about half of us, and when they had been going for a while, I thought I was about to get lucky and get sent home, but then some clerk called my name, and I had to shuffle forward to join a file of other jurors.

There were lines and questions and a lot of waiting around. Long story short: I wound up sitting in the box seats in a Cook County courtroom as the wheels of justice started to grind for a guy named Hamilton Luther.

THE CASE WAS being handled by one of the new ADAs. I used to keep track of those people pretty closely, but then I was mostly dead for a while, and then living in exile, and my priorities shifted. When you live in a city with a reputation for political corruption as pervasive as Chicago's, and work in a business that sometimes treads close to the limit of the law (or twenty miles past it), it's wise to keep an eye on the public servants. Most of them were decent enough, I guess, by which I mean they were your basic politicians—they had just enough integrity to keep up appearances and appease political sponsors, and at the end of the day they had an agenda to pursue.

Once in a while, though, you got one who was thoroughly in someone's pocket. The outfit owned some of those types. The unions owned some others. The corporations had the rest.

The new kid was in his late twenties, clean-cut, thoroughly shaven, and looked a little distracted as he assembled notes and folders around him with the help of an attractive female assistant. His grey suit was tailored to him, maybe a little too well tailored for someone just out of law school, and his maroon tie was made of expensive silk that matched the kerchief tucked into his breast pocket. He had big ears and a large Adam's apple, and his expression was painfully earnest.

On the other side of the aisle, at the defendant's table, sat a study in contrast. He was a man in his fifties, and if he'd ever been in college it had been on a wrestling scholarship. He had shoulders like a bull moose, hunched with muscle, and his arms ended in fists the size of sledgehammer heads. The dark skin on his knuckles was white and lumpy with old scars, the kind you get in back-alley fistfights, not in a boxing ring. He had shaved his head. There was stubble around the edges but the top was shiny. He had a heavy brow, a nose that had been broken on a biannual basis, and his suit was cheap and ill-fitting. He had a couple of folders on the table with him, along with a pair of thick books. The man looked bleakly uneasy and kept flicking nervous glances across the aisle.

If that guy was a lawyer, I was an Ewok. But he sat alone.

So where was his public defender?

"All rise!" a large man in a uniform said in a voice pitched to carry. "Court is now in session, the Honorable Mavis Jefferson presiding."

Everyone stood up. After a second, so did I.

I guess you could say I'm not really a joiner.

The judge came in and settled down at her bench, and the rest of us sat, too. She was a blocky woman in her early sixties, with skin the color of coffee grounds and bags under her eyes that made me think of Spike the bulldog in those old cartoons. If you didn't look closely, you'd think she was bored out of her mind. She sat without moving much, her eyes half closed, scanning over a document on her own desk through a pair of reading glasses. There was something serpentine about her eyes, a suggestion of formidable, remorseless rationality. This was a woman who had seen a great deal, had been amused by very little of it, and who would not be easily made a fool. She finished scanning the document and glanced up at the defendant.

"Mr. Luther?" she said.

The bruiser in the bad suit rose. "Yes, ma'am."

"I see that you have taken it upon yourself to serve as your own defender," she said. Her tone was bored, entirely neutral. "While this is your right under the law, I strongly advise you to reconsider. Given the severity of the charges against you, I would think that a professional attorney would offer you a much more comprehensive and capable legal defense."

"Yes, ma'am," Luther said. "I thought that, too. But all the public defender wanted to do was plea bargain, ma'am. And I want to have my say."

"That, too, is your right," the judge said. For a second, I thought I saw a flicker of something like regret on her face, but it vanished into neutrality again almost instantly. Her tone took on the measured cadence of a cop reading formal Miranda rights. "If you go through with this, you will not be able to move for a mistrial based on the fact that you do not have adequate representation. This trial will proceed and its outcome will be binding. Do you understand this warning as I have stated it to you?"

"Yes, ma'am," Luther said. "Ain't no take-backsies. I want to represent myself, ma'am."

The judge nodded. "Then you may be seated." Luther sat. The judge turned toward the prosecutor and nodded to him. "Counselor." There was a pause about a second and a half long, and then she repeated, in a mildly annoyed tone, "Counselor?" Another impatient pause. "Counselor Tremont, am I interrupting you?"

The young ADA in the fine suit blinked, looked up from his notes, and hastily rose. "No, Your Honor, please excuse me. I'm ready to begin."

"Thank goodness," the judge said in a dry tone. "My granddaughter graduates from high school in three weeks. You may proceed."

Tremont flushed. "Um, yes. Thank you, Your Honor." The young man cleared his throat, adjusted his suit jacket, and walked over to face the jury box. He held up a glossy professional headshot of a handsome man in his thirties and showed it to us.

"Meet Curtis Black," Tremont said. "He was a stockbroker. He liked to go rock climbing on the weekends. He volunteered in a soup kitchen three weekends a month, and he once won an all-expenses-paid vacation to Florida by making a half-court shot during halftime at a Bulls game. He was well liked by his professional associates and had an extensive family and was owned by an Abyssinian cat named Purrple.

"You have doubtless noted my use of the past tense. *Was. Liked. Volunteered.* But I have to use the past tense, because one year ago, Curtis Black was brutally murdered in an alley in Wrigleyville near the corner of Southport and Grace. Mr. Black was bludgeoned to death with a bowling pin. His skull was smashed flat in the back, and the autopsy showed that it had been shattered into a dozen pieces, like plate glass."

Tremont took a moment to let the graphic description sink in. The room was very still.

"The state intends to prove," he said, "that the defendant, Hamilton Luther, murdered Mr. Black in cold blood. That he followed him into the alley, seized the bowling pin from a refuse bin, and struck him from behind, causing him to fall to the ground. That he then proceeded to continue beating Mr. Black's skull with twelve to fifteen heavy blows while Mr. Black lay stunned and helpless beneath him.

"This is a serious crime," Tremont continued. "But Mr. Luther has a long history of violent offenses. Forensic evidence will prove that Mr. Luther was at the crime scene, that he left his fingerprints on the weapon, and that the forensic profile of the attack matches his height and build closely. Eyewitnesses and security cameras witnessed him fleeing the alley shortly after Mr. Black entered it, the victim's blood literally on his hands. The evidence will prove Mr. Luther's guilt beyond any reasonable doubt and, in the end, you must find him guilty of this horrible crime. Thank you."

"Thank you, Counselor," the judge said, as Tremont returned to his seat. "Mr. Luther, you may present your opening statement."

Luther rose slowly. He glanced around the jury box, licked his lip nervously, and approached the jury.

"Ladies and—and gentlemen," he said, stammering a little. "I know I got a past. I did a dime in Stateville for putting a guy in the hospital. But that was my past. I ain't that man no more." He swallowed and gestured vaguely over his shoulder, toward Tremont. "This guy is going to tell you about all this CSI stuff that says I did it. But all those reports and pictures don't tell the whole story. They leave a lot of stuff out. I ain't a lawyer. But I'm gonna tell you the whole story. And then . . . then I'll see what you think about it, I guess." He hovered for a moment longer, awkwardly, then nodded and said, "Okay. I'm done."

"Thank you, Mr. Luther," the judge said. "You may return to your seat."

"Yes, ma'am," Luther said, and did so.

"Mr. Luther, you are charged with first-degree murder," the judge said, still in her rote-memory voice. "How do you plead?"

"I . . ." Luther looked down at some notes in front of him and then up again. "Not guilty, ma'am."

*Hell's bells.*

The full legal might of the state of Illinois was being thrown at Luther. The man seemed sincere enough. But apparently the only defense he had to offer was a story. A story from an ex-con, no less.

I wanted to hear him out. I knew all about being judged for things that were out of my control. But I was pretty sure Luther was going back to jail.

"Mr. Tremont," the judge said. "Is the prosecution ready to begin?"

"Yes, Your Honor," Tremont said.

"Very well," she said. "You may call your first witness."


TREMONT SPENT THE afternoon driving nails into Luther's coffin, thoroughly, methodically, and one at a time.

He did exactly what he said he would do. He brought out each case of physical evidence, point by point, and linked Luther undeniably to the scene of the crime. Luther had been photographed by a grainy black-and-white security camera coming out of the alley's far side, spattered in blood. His fingerprints were on the murder weapon, in the blood of the victim. The officer who arrested him had taken blood samples from his skin and clothing matching those of the victim. He additionally gave testimony of Luther's past criminal record, which had landed him in jail as a young man.

When given a chance to cross-examine, Luther shook his head, until he got to the testimony of the arresting officer, a black man in his late forties named Dwayne. He rose and asked the officer, "When you brung me in, was I injured?"

Officer Dwayne nodded. "You were banged up pretty good. Especially your head."

"Where at?" Luther asked.

Dwayne grunted. "Back of your head."

"Any other injuries on me?"

"You were one big bruise," Dwayne said.

"How big was the victim?" Luther asked.

"About five-four, maybe one fifty."

"Weight lifter or something?"

"Not so you'd notice," Dwayne said.

Luther nodded. "You known me awhile. How come?"

"I was the one who arrested you the first damn time."

"Officer," the judge said.

"Beg pardon, Your Honor," Dwayne said hurriedly.

"I remember that, too," Luther said. "In your experience, a businessman like that handle a guy like me?"

"Unless he's armed or got a lot of training, no."

"One more question," Luther said. He squinted at the officer and said, "You in my neighborhood ever since I got out. You ever think I'd be trouble again?"

"Objection," Tremont said. "He's asking for pure conjecture."

Luther frowned and said, "Beat cops deal with ex-cons on a regular basis professionally, ma'am. Figure that qualifies him as an expert opinion on potential, uh . . ." He consulted his notes and spoke in a careful, clear tone. "Recidivism."

The judge eyed Luther and said, toward Tremont, "Overruled. You may answer the question, Officer."

"No," Dwayne said. "I've seen you with your kids. I wouldn't have called you for it."

"In the arrest report," Luther said, "does it say what I kept asking the officers?"

Dwayne cleared his throat and looked down at a notepad in front of him. "Yeah. 'The suspect kept asking, *Where is she?* and *Is she all right?*"

"Who was I talking about?"

Officer Dwayne turned a page and cleared his throat. "'The suspect claimed that he only began the confrontation with the deceased after witnessing the man drag a female child, Latino, around the age of ten, into the alley,'" he read. "Subsequent investigation could not confirm the presence of any such person."

"How hard did they look?" Luther asked.

"I'm sorry?"

"You heard me," Luther said. "In your opinion, how hard did the investigating detectives look for a little girl who might clear an ex-con from being guilty of a murder of a big-shot businessman?"

"Objection."

"Overruled."

"I'm not a detective," Officer Dwayne said. "I can't speak to that. But I'm sure they followed departmental guidelines."

My finely honed crapometer, garnered during my days as a legitimate, licensed private investigator, went off. Cops were as thorough as they could be, but that wasn't always supremely thorough—that was why private investigators could stay in business in the first place. It was understandable: A city the size of Chicago has an enormous caseload, detectives are always buried in work, and the investigations get triaged pretty severely. The preponderance of evidence, absence of witnesses, and Luther's status as an ex-con would have made this case a slam dunk, a low priority—and, most of the time, the cops would have been right. Once the evidence was all taken and dissected and duly reported on, as far as the police were concerned, they had their man. And there was already a mountain of fresh justice waiting to be pursued on behalf of new victims. Even the most dedicated and sincere police detective could understandably have dropped the ball here.

"Sure," Luther said. He sat back down again and said, "I'm done."

The judge looked at the clock and asked, "Mr. Tremont, do you have any further witnesses?"

Tremont listened to something his assistant whispered and rose. "Your Honor, the prosecution rests."

"Then so will we," she said. "Mr. Luther, the defense can begin its case in the morning. I remind the jury that the details of this case are confidential and not to be discussed or disclosed. We will reconvene here at nine a.m."

"All rise," the bailiff said, and we did as the judge left the room.

I frowned as Luther was escorted out.

Something did not add up here.

If Luther had been a professional tough, a little guy like Curtis Black wouldn't have a prayer against him. I had been around enough tough guys to size Luther up. I wouldn't want to take him on in muscle-powered combat if I could avoid it, not even now with all the extra physical stuff the Winter Knight's mantle had given me. Doesn't matter how much you bench-press; some people are damned dangerous in a fight, and you're a fool to take unnecessary chances against them. Luther struck me as one of those men.

Also, Tremont was way too young a kid to be pulling a high-profile murder case like this one. This was the kind of flashy prosecution DAs loved to showboat. Killers brought to justice, the system working, that kind of thing. They certainly didn't hand the case off to some kid straight out of law school. Which meant that the old hands in Chicago thought that something about this case stunk to high heaven as well.

I didn't know the law really well, but I have a doctorate in the parts of Chicago that never showed up on the evening news. If Luther was telling the truth, then Curtis Black couldn't have been human.

Problem was, most humans didn't know that. Even if Luther was telling the truth about Black, he wasn't going to get a fair shake from Chicago's justice system. Hell's bells, the cop acquainted with him wasn't even giving him much. Nobody was going to go to bat for him.

Unless I did it.

He was a father. For his kids' sake, I wanted answers.

I glanced at the clock as I filed out with the rest of the jury. Nine tomorrow morning. That gave me just under sixteen hours to do what wizards do best.

I left, and began meddling.

"WELL?" I ASKED the rather large wolf after he had been casting around the alley for a while.

He gave me an irritated look. He sat, and after a few seconds, shimmered and resumed the form of Will Borden, crouched naked on the dirty concrete. "Harry, you are not helping."

"Did you find anything or not?" I asked.

"This isn't as easy as it looks," he said. "Look, man, when I'm wolf, I've got a wolf's sense of smell—but I don't have a wolf's freaking brain. I've been learning how to sort out signals from the noise, but it's freaking hard. I've been doing this since my freshman year, and I could follow a hot trail, but you're asking me to sift background. I don't even know if a real wolf could do it."

I looked around the alley where Luther had beaten Black to death with a bowling pin. It had been nearly a year to the day since the murder. There was nothing dramatic to suggest a man had died here, and the bloodstains had long since faded into unrecognizability with the rest of the grunge. We were far enough down the alley to be out of sight of the street except for a slim column of space that cars crossed in under a second. "Yeah, that was a long shot, anyway."

"You going to wizard up some information?"

"After this long, there's nothing left," I said. "Too many rains, too many sunrises. Not even Molly could get much."

"Then what are we going to do?"

"Get furry again. We might be here awhile."

He frowned. "Why?"

"I think the girl might come by in the next few hours."

"Why?"

I shrugged a shoulder. "Let's assume Luther's telling the truth."

"Sure."

"This guy grabs a little girl and drags her into the alley. Luther jumps him from behind and gets thrown into a wall. Fights him hard, and beats him to death with a bowling pin. What can we deduce?"

"That Black was stronger than normal and tougher than normal," Will said. "Some kind of supernatural."

I nodded. "A predator. Maybe a ghoul or something."

"Yeah. So?"

"So a predator, operating in the middle of a town? They don't tend to openly grab little girls off the street, because someone might see it happen."

"Like Luther."

"Like Luther. But this guy did. He didn't go after a transient sleeping in an abandoned building, or someone wandering down a dark alley to buy some drugs, a prostitute, any of the usual targets. He went with something dicier. He's going to do that, he's going to cut down on every random factor he can."

"You think he stalked her."

I nodded. "Stalked her, learned her pattern, and was waiting for her."

Will squinted up and down the alley. "Why do you think that?"

"It's how something from Winter would do it," I said. "How I would take someone in a busy part of town, if I had to."

"Well. That's not creepy or anything, Harry."

I showed my teeth. "Not much difference between wolves and sheepdogs, Will. You should know."

He nodded. "So, we wait here and see if she's still going by?"

"Figure if she still goes by here, she'll do it fast and she'll be worried. Should make her stand out."

"You know what else stands out on a busy Chicago street? A timber wolf."

"Thought of that," I said, and produced a roll of fabric from my duster's large pockets.

"You're kidding," Will said.

I smiled.

"And what's in the guitar case?"

I smiled wider.


A FEW MINUTES later, I was sitting on the sidewalk with my back against a building, an old secondhand guitar in my lap, the case open beside me with a handful of a change and an old wadded dollar bill in it. Will settled down beside me, wearing a service dog's jacket, resting his chin on his front paws. He made a little groaning sound.

"It'll be fine, boy."

Will narrowed his eyes.

"Just keep your nose open," I said, and started playing.

I started with the Johnny Cash version of "Hurt," which was pretty simple. I sang along with it. I'm not good, but I can hit the notes and keep the rhythm going, so it more or less worked out. I followed it up with "Behind Blue Eyes," which gets a little harder, and then "Only Happy When It Rains." Then I followed it up with "House of the Rising Sun," and completely mangled "Stairway to Heaven."

There wasn't a ton of foot traffic on a weekday evening on this street, not in a fairly brisk late March, but nobody really looked at me twice. I made about two and a half bucks in change the first hour. The life of a musician is not easy. A patrol car went by and a cop gave me the stink-eye, but he didn't stop and roust me. Maybe he had things to do.

The light started fading from the sky, and I was repeating my limited set for the fifth or sixth time when I started to think about giving up. The girl, if she was still following the same pattern, definitely wouldn't be running around town alone after it became fully dark.

I was singing about how you'd get the message by the time I'm through when Will suddenly lifted his head, his eyes focused.

I followed the direction of his gaze and spotted a girl of about the right age getting off of a bus. She started walking right away, down the street, though she stayed on the other side, directly toward the El station a block away.

"There we go," I said. "Kid walking a regular route alone gets jumped in Chicago, kid's probably using public transit, running on a schedule. Makes her real predictable. Perfect mark for a predator."

Will made a low growling sound.

"I think I'm kinda smart, yeah," I said to him. "Get her scent?"

Will nudged me with his shoulder and growled again.

I frowned and looked around until I spotted a rather large and rough-looking man descending from the bus at the last second before it left for the next stop. He started down the sidewalk, in pursuit of the girl. He wasn't maniacally focused on her or anything, but he wasn't moving like someone coming home tired after a day of work, either. I recognized his pace, his stance, his tension, just as Will had. He was a predator in covert pursuit of his prey.

Worse, he had a smartphone. His thumbs were rapping over it as he walked after the girl.

"Damn," I said. "Whoever Black was, he was connected. I'm on the creep. You stick with the girl."

Will gave me one brief, incredulous look.

"I'm six-nine and scarred; you're furry and cute. She's eleven— she's going to like you."

Will gave me a flat look, his gold eyes utterly unamused. On a wolf, that's unsettling.

"I don't know," I said. "Wag your tail and paw your nose or something. Go!"

I'll give Will this much: He knows when actions matter more than questions. He took off at once, vanishing into the oncoming evening.

Meanwhile, I put my guitar in the case, set it back into the alley, rose, and focused my will and my attention on the thug. Wizards and modern technology don't get on well, and nothing dies as fast as cell phones when a wizard means to shut them down. I gathered up enough power to get the job done without taking out the lights on the whole block, flicked a finger at the man pacing the girl, and murmured, "Hexus."

A wave of disruptive energy washed out across the street and over the man and his smartphone. There was a little flash of light and a shower of sparks from the phone, and the man flinched and dropped the device. Most people would have stared at it or looked wildly around. This guy did neither. He sank into a defensive crouch and started scanning his surroundings with wide eyes.

He knew he was being threatened, which meant he had some kind of idea that a wizard might be about. That meant he was no mere thug. He was clued in enough to the supernatural world to know the players and how they might operate. That meant he was elite muscle, and there were only so many players who he might be working for.

I checked the street, hurried through an opening in traffic, and went straight for him. He spotted me in under a second and ran without hesitation, both of which impressed me with his judgment—but he took off after the girl, which meant that he wasn't giving up, either. I swerved to pursue him, leapt, and pulled my knees up to my chin in the air, hitting the hood of a blue Buick with my hands as I flew over it, and came down still running.

We rounded a corner, and I understood what was happening.

The thug I was pursuing wasn't the grabber. He was just riding drag, making sure the girl didn't bolt back the way she came. I saw the girl ahead, being hurried into a doorway by three more men, and my guy poured it on when he saw them.

I slowed down a little, taking stock. The goons ahead had seen me coming behind their buddy, and hands were going into coats. I flung myself into the doorway of an office-supply store, now closed for the evening, and the thugs all hustled through their own door, without producing guns on the street.

Suited me. I had been hoping to get them somewhere out of the way, anyhow.

I waited until they were inside, gave them a five count, and then paced down the street. The door they'd gone through belonged to a small nightclub. A sign hanging on the door read CLOSED FOR REMODELING.

The door was locked.

It was also made of glass.

I smiled.

I HUFFED AND I puffed and I blew the door in with a pretty standard blast of telekinetic force. I tugged my sleeve up to reveal the shield bracelet I'd thrown together out of a strip of craft copper and carefully covered with the appropriate defensive runes and sigils. I channeled some of my will down into the bracelet, and the runes hissed to life, spilling out green-gold energy and the occasional random spark.

"All right, people!" I called into the club as I stepped through the door. "You know who I am. I'm here for the girl. Let her go, or, so help me God, I will bring this building down around your ears." I wouldn't, not while the girl was still in here, but they didn't know that.

There was silence for a long moment. And then music started playing from deeper inside the club. "Bad Romance" by Lady Gaga.

"Okay," I muttered. "Have it your way."

I advanced into the darkened club, my shield bracelet throwing out a faint haze of light from the runes—just enough to keep me from bumping into walls. I went through the entry hall, past a collection window where I supposed cover fees would be paid, to double doors that opened onto the bar and dance floor.

I raised my left arm as if wielding an actual shield, the bracelet glowing, and stepped forward into the club.

The little girl was sitting in a booth against the far wall. The four thugs were fanned out on either side of her, guns in hand but pointing at the floor. Sitting with the little girl in the booth was the ADA's pretty assistant. When I came through the door, she lifted a hand and clicked a remote, and Lady Gaga's voice cut off in the midst of wanting my bad romance.

"Far enough," the woman said. "It would be a shame if someone panicked and this situation devolved. Innocents could be hurt."

I stopped. "Who are you?" I asked.

"Tania Raith," she replied, and gave me a rather dizzying smile.

House Raith was the foremost house of the White Court of vampires. They were seducers, energy drainers, and occasionally a giant pain in the ass. The White Court was headed up by Lara Raith, the uncrowned queen of vampires, and one of the more dangerous persons I'd ever met. She wielded enormous influence in Chicago, maybe as much as the head of the Chicago outfit, Gentleman Johnnie Marcone, gangster lord of the mean streets.

I made damned sure to keep track of the thugs and precisely what they were doing with their hands as I spoke. "You know who I am. You know what I can do. Let her go."

She rolled her eyes and spun a finger through fine, straight black hair. "Why should I?"

"Because you know what happened the last time some vampires abducted a little girl and I decided to take her back."

Her smile faltered slightly. As it should have. When the bloodsucking Red Court had taken my daughter, I took her back—and murdered every single one of them in the process. The entire species.

I'm not a halfway kind of person.

"Lara likes you," Tania said. "So I'm going to give you a chance to walk out of here peacefully. This is a White Court matter."

I grunted. "Black was one of yours?"

"Gregor Malvora," she confirmed. "He was Malvora scum, but he was our scum. Lara can't allow the mortal buck who did it to go unpunished. Appearances. You understand."

"I understand that Gregor abducted a child. He did everything he could to frighten her, and then fed on her fear. If Luther hadn't killed him, what would he have done to the little girl?"

"Oh, I shudder to think," Tania replied. "But that is, after all, what they do."

"Not in my town," I said.

She lifted her eyebrows. "I believe Baron Marcone has a recognized claim on this city. Or am I mistaken?"

"I've got enough of a claim to make me tickled to dump you and your brute squad into the deepest part of Lake Michigan if you don't give me back the girl."

"I think I'll keep her for a day or two. Just until the trial is over. That will be best for everyone involved."

"You'll give her to me. Now."

"So that she can testify and exonerate Mr. Luther?" Tania asked. "I think not. I have no desire to harm this child, Dresden. But if you try to take her from me, I will, reluctantly, be forced to kill her."

The girl's lower lip trembled, and tears started rolling down her face. She didn't sob. She did it all in silence, as if desperate to draw no attention to herself.

*Yeah, okay.*

I wasn't going to stand here and leave a little kid to a vampire's tender mercies.

"Chicago is a mortal town," I said. "And mortal justice is going to be served."

"Oh, my God," Tania said, rolling her eyes. "Did you really just say that out loud? You sound like a comic book."

"Comic book," I said. "Let's see. Do I go for 'Hulk smash,' or 'It's clobberin' time'?"

Tania tensed, though she tried to hide it, and her voice came out in a rush. "Bit of a coincidence, don't you think, that Chicago's only professional wizard wound up on that jury?"

I tilted my head and frowned. She was right. In fact, the more I thought about it, the more this felt like a turf war. "Oh. Oh, I get it. Luther was one of Marcone's soldiers."

"So loyal he went to prison for ten years rather than inform on Marcone," Tania confirmed. "Or maybe just smart enough to know what would happen to him if he did. He went straight after he got out, but . . ."

"When he got in trouble, Marcone stood up for one of his own," I said. "He pulled strings to get me on the jury."

"Luther was getting nailed to a wall," Tania said. "Marcone controls crime, but Lara has a lot of say over the law these days. I suppose he thought someone like you might be the only chance Luther had. Gutsy of him, to try to make a cat's-paw of Harry Dresden. I hear you don't like that."

Dammit. Marcone had put me where there'd been a guy getting fast-tracked to an unjust sentence and known damned well how I would react. He could have asked me for help, but I'd have told him to take a flying . . . leap. And he'd have known that. So he set it up without me knowing.

Or hell. He and Mab had been in cahoots lately. Maybe he'd asked her to arrange it. This had her fingerprints all over it.

"Tania," I said. "It's hard for me to tell with vampires, but I'm guessing you're pretty new to this work."

She winked at me. "Let's just say that I'm old enough to know better and young enough not to care." She picked up a drink from the table. "This one is over, Dresden. You can't do anything here. You can't produce evidence in the trial—not as a juror. You can't get to Luther to tell him you found the little girl—and even if you could, you aren't taking her away from us. Not until it's too late. The girl is the only evidence that Black wasn't a poor victim, and I have her. This one is done. Marcone lost the round. I win." She winked at me. "What does Marcone mean to you? You don't owe him anything. Why not sit down, have a drink, help me celebrate?"

I stared at Tania for a minute. "No," I said quietly. "You just don't get it. This isn't about Lara and Marcone anymore. It's not even really about Luther." Then I looked at the little girl. "Honey," I asked, making sure my voice was a lot gentler. "Do you want to go home?"

She looked at me. She was cute enough for a kid her age, with caramel skin and big green eyes. She nodded very hesitantly, flinching as if she thought Tania might hit her.

"Okay," I said.

Tania was staring at me as though she couldn't quite grasp what was happening. But her voice was harder when she said, "Gentlemen? The wizard doesn't like the carrots. It's time for the stick."

To my right, from behind the bar, another four men rose. They were holding short-barreled shotguns. To my left, from the bathrooms, another four thugs appeared, clutching various long guns.

"I'll count to three," Tania said. "Boys, when I get to three, kill him."

Crap. They were flanking me. My shield was excellent, but it was not omnidirectional. No matter which way I turned it, one or more groups of thugs would have a shot at my unprotected back.

"One," Tania said, smiling. "Two."

"Comic book, huh?" I said. "Have it your way."

"Three," she chirped.

Guns swiveled to me. A dozen men took aim.

*"Hexus!"* I snarled, unleashing a wave of disruptive energy.

And every light in the place blew out in a shower of sparks, plunging the club into darkness.

Guns started going off, but only from the most confident or stupid gunmen, so I wasn't cut to ribbons. I was already moving. Hitting a moving target isn't easy, not even when it's fairly close. Hitting one in the dark is even harder. Hitting one moving in sporadic flashes of light is harder yet.

I got lucky, or none of them did—however you want to think of it—and I got to the thugs beside Tania in one piece.

One of them got off a shot at the sound, but I caught the round on my shield, and the resulting shower of sparks showed the men on my flanks that I was among their compatriots, and no one shot at my back. I knew Lara hired almost exclusively from former military, mostly Marines. Men like that don't shoot their buddies.

I dropped the shield and threw a punch at the guy in front of me. Ever since I'd started working for the Queen of Air and Darkness, I'd been stronger than the average wizard. Or the average champion weight lifter, for that matter, and I knew how to throw a punch. I connected with the man's jaw, hard, and shouted, "BAM!" as I did.

The thug reeled back, his legs going wobbly and useless as he ragdolled to the floor. I threw a stomping kick toward the belly of the guy next to him, shouting, "POW!" I hit him in the dark, somewhere more or less near his belly. His gun went off randomly as he was lifted off the floor and thrown ten feet back into a wall. He was trying to scream, breathlessly. I winced. I hadn't meant to hit him *there*, but those are the breaks.

I raised my shield again and dropped, just as the bad guys with shotguns realized that I didn't have any of their buddies standing near me. I trusted the shield and turned my face away from the blinding shower of green-gold sparks it sent flying up as buckshot hammered into it. The copper band got hot on my wrist, even as I flung my right hand out toward the group of goons by the bathroom and shouted, *"Forzare!"*

Raw telekinetic force hit three of them—one was the guy from the street, who again impressed me with his smarts by diving to one side, out of the wave of energy. As shotguns pounded my shield, he slid to a stop with an automatic braced in both hands, took a breath, and aimed carefully, only moving his finger to the trigger after he had his sights lined up on me.

*Crap.* To steal from Brust, no matter how turbo-charged the wizard, someone with brains, guts, and a .45 can seriously cramp his style.

Fortunately, I wasn't in this fight alone.

I'd been counting on Will to join in at the right moment, and he didn't let me down. Two hundred pounds of grey-brown timber wolf (wearing a service dog cape) hit the Smart Gunman at a full sprint, bowling him over. A flash of white fangs sent the gun flying.

Total elapsed time since I'd killed the lights? Maybe three and a half seconds.

Will threw himself into the guys I'd knocked around by the bathrooms, and I turned to discover that I'd been right about Tania. She was new to this kind of game. She'd been sitting there with a stunned look on her face at the abruptness of the violence.

I flung myself into the booth with her, getting as close as I could, wrapping my left arm around her neck hard enough to pull her head in against my body and still have my shield ready to stop more gunfire. But the Smart Gunman screamed, "Check fire! Check fire!" the second I did.

The shooting stopped. There was an abrupt silence in the club, which was filled with the sharp scent of gunpowder.

For a second, I felt a cool, sweet sensation flooding into me. I realized that Tania had slipped a hand beneath my shirt and was running her fingertips over my stomach.

If anyone ever tells you that being fed on by a vampire of the White Court is not a big deal, they're lying. It's Ecstasy and heroin and sex and chocolate all rolled into one, and that's just the foreplay.

So I stopped her by tightening my grip on her until it threatened to break her neck. Tania let out a little yelp and whipped her hand away from my skin.

I met the wide eyes of the little girl and said, "Hold on, honey. I'm going to take you home in just a second."

"You can't!" Tania said.

I scowled and flicked her skull with the forefinger of my free hand in annoyance. "Wow, you're new at this," I said, panting. Five seconds of combat is enough cardio to last a while. "How old are you, kid?"

"I'm twenty," she said, her teeth clenched with discomfort, "and I am *not* a child."

"Twenty," I said. "No wonder Lara sent a babysitter along with you."

Just then, the room flooded with green chemical light. I eyed the Smart Gunman, who had just fired up a chemical glow stick from a pocket. I nodded at him, holding it a moment, and said, "I'm Dresden."

He pushed himself up from the floor with his left arm, holding his right in close to his side. It bore long lacerations, and the blood looked black in the green light. He nodded back to me and said, warily, "Riley."

I twisted my upper body just enough to drag Tania around a little. She let out a squeaking sound. "Can you see the score here, Riley?"

He studied the room, wincing, and said, "Yeah. How you want to play it?"

"Guns down," I said. "Me, the wolf, the girl, and Miss Raith here will walk out. No one comes after us. Once we're on the street, I'll let her go."

He stared at me, and I could see the wheels turning. I didn't like that. The guy had been too capable to give him time to work something out.

"You boys just gave me a twenty-one-gun salute, and the front door to the club was broken open, Riley," I said. "Police response time around here is about four minutes. How long do you think it will take someone to call it in?"

Riley grimaced. "Give me your word."

"You have it," I said.

"Okay," he said. He looked around the room and said, "Stand down. We're going to let them leave."

"Damn you, Riley!" Tania snarled.

I pressed the still uncomfortably hot copper bracelet against her ear, and she yipped. "Come on, Miss Raith," I said. I stood up, keeping her head locked in my arm. She could have made a fight of it. White Court vampires can be unbelievably strong, if only in bursts. She didn't seem up for a physical fight, but I wasn't taking chances. I moved carefully and kept my balance, ready to move instantly if she tried anything.

"Come on, honey," I said to the little girl. I extended my free hand to her. "I'm going to take you home."

She stood up and reluctantly took my hand.

Will padded out of the shadows to walk on the other side of the girl, his teeth bared. On a wolf, that is an absolutely terrifying expression.

As I went by Riley, I asked, "Lara giving Tania here a lesson?"

"Something like that," he said. "You hurt her, things will have to get ugly."

"I get it," I said. "You'd have had me if I hadn't cheated."

"You aren't cheating, you aren't trying hard enough," he replied. "Another time, maybe."

"I hope not," I told him sincerely.

And I walked out with a vampire in a headlock and a little girl overlapped in the protective shadows of a wizard and a werewolf, while Lara Raith's soldiers looked on.

"YOUR HONOR," THE foreman of the jury said to the judge. She paused to turn to me and give me a deadly glare. "After two days of deliberation, the jury has been unable to reach a unanimous verdict in the case."

Luther, lonely at his table, blinked and sat up straighter, his eyes opening wider.

The assistant DA made an almost identical expression. Beside him, Tania sat staring stonily forward, with her hair combed over her singed ear.

The judge eyed the jury box with weary resignation, and her gaze settled on me.

"What?" I said, and folded my arms. "I believed him."

She rubbed at her eyes with one hand and said something beneath her breath. I listened closely, which is much closer than most people can, and thought I heard her mutter, "Goddamned supernatural assholes . . ."

She lifted her eyes again and spoke in that rote-repetition voice. "That being the case, I have no choice but to declare a mistrial. Mr. Tremont, the prosecution's office will need to notify me about whether the people mean to continue pursuing this case against the defendant."

I eyed Tania, smiling.

If the White Court tried to push this trial again, I could produce the girl, Maria, as a witness. Maria was currently being watched by a number of werewolves and wasn't going to go anywhere. If they continued pushing Luther, I could drag their ugliness out into the light—and if there was anything the White Court hated, it was looking ugly.

Tania gave me a sulking glance. Then she muttered something to Tremont, who blinked at her. They had a brief, heated discussion conducted entirely in whispers. Then Tremont looked back up at them. "Ah, Your Honor. The state would like to drop all charges."

"It would?" the judge asked. Then she rolled her eyes and said, "Of course it would. All right, people. Justice is served; court is adjourned."

She banged her gavel down halfheartedly and rose. We all stood up as she left the courtroom, and then we began filing out.

Luther sat there dazed as the bailiff approached and removed his handcuffs. Then he was buried by a pair of quietly squealing children who piled onto him, and were shortly joined by a woman with tears in her eyes. I heard him start laughing as he hugged them.

I left, because there was something in my eyes.

Outside, in the parking lot, someone approached me and I felt a tug at my sleeve. It took me a second to recognize the judge in her civilian clothes—a plain pair of slacks and a white shirt.

"Let me guess," she said. "Someone found the girl."

"The girl from what's-his-name's testimony?" I asked, guilelessly.

"And if the girl had gotten up in front of everyone and answered questions, it would have made things awkward for whoever was behind Black. Am I right?"

I scratched at my nose with one finger and said, "Maybe."

She snorted and turned to walk away. "Worst jurist ever."

"Thanks," I said.

She stopped and looked at me over her shoulder with a faint smile. "You're welcome."

I hung around long enough to see Luther, a free man, leaving the building with his family.

Maybe Will had been right.

Justice served.

Waldo Butters was never supposed to amount to much.

No, seriously. He was a throwaway character. I had a particularly gruesome morgue scene that I wanted to leaven with a little humor, so I more or less swiped the medical examiner from the movie *The Prophecy*, dyed his hair black and curly, made him a Jewish polkaphile, and had him start spreading levity.

A while later, I was writing a story that was going to have a pretty good dramatic high point, and was going to be filled with necromancers. I wanted it to be a particularly tough ride for Dresden, so I looked around for the perfect sidekick for this story—someone who would be thematically appropriate yet be able to do almost nothing to actually help Dresden in a fight. I had necromancers and animated corpses, and I had this goofy but highly intelligent medical examiner who had already been planted into the series. As a bonus, Waldo Butters was a newbie to the world of the supernatural, but was bright and could be counted on to ask smart questions—and since this book was going to be my first hardback, it was also going to be the Dresden Files' introduction to a slew of new readers, and Butters's questions would make it easy for them to get into the structure of the story world. Kind of made it a no-brainer that Butters needed to be the guy.

*But*, my brain said, as it does endlessly, *that's not quite enough, is it?* And so I looked at Butters and started making plans.

At the end of the day, the greatest power Harry has is in lifting up the people around him. As he has gone through his story, the people he trusts and has befriended have themselves grown in knowledge and in power. He's never really meant to do it, but this little community of people with brains, backbones, and good hearts has developed around him, and Butters is one of the foremost members of that community.

The little guy has grown a lot over the course of this story. He was entirely unexpected, and I just couldn't be more pleased with how his story is going. Here's a small but important piece of Butters's tale: his first day on the job as a Knight.

**M**y name is Waldo Butters, and I am a Jedi Knight, like my father before me.

Okay, so that isn't exactly, technically, in a completely legal sense true. I mean, my dad was actually a podiatrist. But I'm as close to the real deal as anyone is likely to ever see in this world. I'm an actual Knight, anyway. Or, at least, I was training to be one, when on a Thursday morning I first heard the Call.

Only I didn't hear it, exactly, technically, in a completely legal sense. . . . Look, maybe I should just tell the story.

OF ALL THE training Michael Carpenter had me doing, the cardio part was what I liked best. Then again, my main Pandora station plays only polka music, so what the heck do I know?

I ran along through the early-dawn light in Bucktown while the city began to wake up. The training belt around my waist tugged at my balance constantly and unpredictably. It was hooked to a bungee cord attaching me to Michael's bicycle, being pulled along behind me as I ran. Michael would swerve and brake randomly. Sometimes he'd hold the brake for several strides, and I'd have to shift to much more powerful strides to keep moving. It was demanding work. Constantly being forced to alter my balance meant that I could never fall into a nice, efficient rhythm and I had to pay attention to every single step.

The first several weeks, that had been a problem, but I was getting used to it now. Or, rather, I was getting used to it until I saw something impossible, forgot to pay attention, got pulled off-balance by my bungee cord, and crashed into a plastic recycling bin waiting by the side of the street.

Michael immediately came to a stop, swinging his stiff leg out like an improvised kickstand. He was action-hero-sized, moving toward his late fifties, and had his walking cane strapped to the backpack he wore. "Waldo?" he asked. "Are you all right?"

I stumbled upright again, panting. "I, uh." I peered down the street. "I'm not really sure."

Michael looked in the same direction I was, frowning. He pursed his lips thoughtfully.

"You don't see that, do you?" I asked.

"See what?"

I squinted. Took off my glasses. Cleaned them on a corner of my shirt that wasn't covered in sweat. Put them back on and checked again. It was still there. "If you could see it, you wouldn't have to ask that."

He nodded seriously. "Tell me what you see."

"That homeless guy on the bench?" I asked.

"Yes."

I took a breath and said, "There's a big yellow exclamation point floating over his head." After a brief pause, I added, "I'm not crazy. My mother had me tested."

Michael sat back a little on the bike's seat and rubbed at his beard pensively. He missed the reference. "Hmmm. Odd. Does that bring anything to mind for you, personally?"

I snorted. "Yeah, it's what every NPC in every MMORPG ever looks like when they have a quest to give you."

"There were a great many letters in that, and not much that I understood," he said soberly.

"Video games," I clarified. "When a game character has a quest for you, that's how the game shows you where the quest begins. A big floaty exclamation point over their heads. You go talk to them and that's how the quest starts."

Michael barked out a laugh and gave the sky a small smile and a shake of his head. "Well, then, Sir Waldo. You've just had your first Call."

"My what, now?"

"Your first Call to a quest, I suppose."

I blinked. "Uriel talks to the Knights through video-game symbolism?"

"As far as I know, Uriel talks in person. The Call comes from higher up."

"What?" I asked. "You mean, like . . . God? God speaks video game?"

"When the Almighty speaks to men, He always does it in voices they can understand," Michael said. "When I felt the Call, it was always a still, small voice that would come to me when I was in prayer or otherwise quiet. Sometimes I'd have a very strong impression of a name or a face, and a direction that I needed to go." He nodded toward the transient. "Apparently, you have been Called to help that man."

"Put like that, it does seem to be fairly obvious." I swallowed. "Um. I know we've been training pretty hard, but . . . am I really ready for this?"

He reached into the backpack, withdrew an old leather messenger bag from it, and offered it to me. "Let's find out."

I swallowed. Then I nodded and slung the bag over one shoulder. I reached into it and patted the old, worn wooden handle inside, and then walked over to the sleeping man. He wore an army-surplus field jacket and old Desert Storm–style khaki BDUs, and he had a beard that birds could have nested in. There wasn't much grey in it, but his skin was weathered enough to make it difficult to guess his age. Forty?

By the time I got within five feet of him, I could see that something was wrong. There was a lot of vomit on the slatted bench by the man's head and the ground beneath. One of his eyes was half open, dilated, and his breath rasped in and out.

"Hey," I said. "Hey, buddy. Can you hear me?"

No response.

I knelt down and took his wrist, feeling for his pulse. It was hard, because it was thready and irregular. "Hey," I said, gently. "Hey, man, can you hear me?"

He let out a little groan. I checked his other eye. The pupil was normal in that one.

I didn't enjoy the work of being an actual physician, professionally. I liked examining corpses for the state of Illinois. Corpses never lie to you, never give you opaque answers, never ask stupid questions, or ignore what you tell them they need to do. Corpses are simple.

And this guy, who wasn't nearly as old as I had thought when I walked up to him, was going to be one if he didn't get attention fast.

"Call nine-one-one," I said to Michael. "I think he's had a stroke, maybe an overdose. Either way, he's lucky he slept on his side or he'd have choked on his own vomit by now. He needs an ER."

Michael nodded once, hobbled a few feet away, and produced a cell phone from a leather case on his belt. He called and began speaking quietly.

"Okay, buddy," I said to the guy. "Hang in there. We're calling the good guys and they're going to help y—"

I don't even know what happened. One second he was lying there, a wheezy vegetable, and the next he was coming at me hard, his ragged-nailed hands grasping for my throat while he gurgled, "No hospital!"

A few months ago, I'd have gotten strangled right there.

But a few months ago, I hadn't been training in hand-to-hand with Michael's wife, Charity.

It takes several thousand repetitions of a motion to develop motor-memory pathways in the brain to the point where you can consider the motion a reflex. To that end, Charity, who was into jujitsu, had made me practice several different defenses a hundred times each, every day, for the past two months. She didn't practice by just going through a motion slowly and gradually speeding up, either. She just came at me like she meant to disassemble me, and if I didn't defend successfully it freaking hurt.

You learn fast in those circumstances—and one of the basic defenses she'd drilled into me had been against a simple front choke.

Both of my forearms snapped up, knocking the grasping hands away, even as I ducked my head and rolled my body to one side. He kept coming through the space where I'd been. His arm hit my face and sent my glasses spinning off me.

I fought down a decades-old panic as the world shifted from its usual shapes into sudden streaks and blurs of color.

Look. I wear some big, thick glasses. I'm not quite legally blind without them. I know, because after I gave my optometrist a very expensive bottle of whiskey, he told me so. But without them . . .

Without them, it's pretty tough to get anything done. Or see anything more than an arm's length away. Seriously. I'd once mistaken a dressmaker's mannequin for my girlfriend. Reading was all but impossible without them. *Reading*.

My great nightmare is to be stuck somewhere without them, trapped, peering at the sea of fuzzy things that couldn't possibly be identified. When I'd been a kid, the first thing the bullies did, always, was knock my glasses off. Always. It was like they'd all had a sixth sense or something.

Then they would start having fun with me. That wasn't a delight, either, but it was the not knowing what was coming that made it all worse.

Inside, that kid started screaming and wailing, but there was no time to indulge him. I had a problem to solve—and the Carpenters had given me the tools I needed to solve it.

For instance, they'd taught me that once things are this close, you don't really get a lot done with your eyes when it comes to fighting. It was all speed and reflex and knowing where the enemy was and what he was doing by feel. I was sloppy and it took me a second, but I managed to lock the bum's arm out straight. I kept it moving, got my body to twist at the right angle to put pressure on the shoulder joint, and brought him flat onto his face on the sidewalk with enough force to send stars flying into his vision and stun him.

It didn't stun him much. "No hospital!" he screamed, thrashing. I fought to control the fear that was running through me. He was operating with more strength than he should have been, but it didn't matter. Physics is physics, and his arm was one long lever that I had control of. He might have been bigger and stronger than me, and the way we were positioned that didn't matter in the least. He fought for a few more seconds and then the burst of frenzy began to peter out. "No hospital! No hospital." He shuddered and began to weep. His voice became a plea, rendered flat with despair. "No hospital. Please, please. No hospital."

Then he went limp and made slow, regular rasping sounds.

I eased off the pressure and gave him his arm back. It fell limply to the sidewalk as he cried. "Buddy," I said, "hey, it's going to be all right. I'm Waldo. What's your name?"

"Stan," he said in a hollow voice.

"Hey, Stan," I said. "Try not to worry. We're going to get you taken care of."

"You're killing me," he said. "You're killing me."

"Your pulse is erratic, your breathing is impaired, and your eyes are showing different levels of dilation, Stan. What are you on?"

"Nothing," he said. "You're killing me. Damn you."

In a few minutes, the ambulance arrived. A few seconds later, someone tapped the side of my chest with my glasses and I put them back on. I looked up at an EMT, a blocky black guy named Lamar. I knew him. He was a solid guy.

"Thanks, man," I said.

"You tackle this guy?" he asked. "Shoot. You ain't no bigger than a chicken dinner."

"But spicy," I said. I gave him everything I had about Stan, and they got him checked, loaded up, and ready to head out to the ER in under four minutes.

"Hey, Lamar," I said, as he was rolling the gurney.

"Yes, Examiner Mulder?"

"Scully was the ME," I complained. "How come no one calls me Examiner Scully?"

"'Cause you ain't a thinking man's tart," Lamar drawled. "What you need?"

"Where are you taking him?"

"St. Anthony's."

I nodded. "Is there anything, uh, odd happening over there lately?"

"Naw," Lamar said, scratching his chin. "Not that I seen. But it's only Tuesday."

"Do me a favor," I said. "Keep your eyes open."

"Hell, Butters," he said.

"Let me rephrase that," I said. "Let me know if you see anything odd. It might be important."

Lamar gave me a long look. I already had a reputation and history with supernatural weirdness, even before I met Harry Dresden and learned how scary the world really is. Lamar had gotten a few peeks at the Twilight Zone, too, over the years, and wanted nothing to do with it, because Lamar was pretty bright.

"We'll see," he said.

"Thanks," I said. We shook hands and he left.

Michael came to stand next to me as the ambulance pulled away.

"You hear that?" I asked him.

"Most of it."

"What do you think?"

He leaned on his cane and blew out a slow breath through his lips, frowning in thought.

"I think," he said finally, "that you're the Knight now, Waldo."

"Somehow, I just knew you were going to say that," I said. "It might be nothing. I mean, I suspect Stan was strung out on uppers and downers and God knows what else. And if some commuter had been the one to try to wake him, he might have strangled them. Maybe this was a low-level warm-up quest, you know? That might have been the whole thing right there."

"Maybe," Michael agreed, nodding. "What does your heart tell you?"

"My heart?" I asked. "I'm a doctor, Michael. My heart doesn't tell me anything. It's a muscle that pumps blood. My brain does all of that other stuff."

Michael smiled. "What does your heart tell you?"

I sighed. I mean, sure, it could have been something really simple and easy—mathematically, that was possible. But everything I'd seen about the supernatural world told me that the Knights of the Cross were only sent into matters of life and death. And, like it or not, when I'd decided to keep the Sword of Faith, I'd decided to get myself involved in situations that would be scary and dangerous—and necessary—without actually knowing exactly what was going on, or why I was being sent.

I wasn't really hero material. Even with my recent training, I was small and skinny and rumpled, and I'd never drunk from the fountain of youth. I was a mature, nerdy, Jewish medical examiner, not some kind of daring adventurer.

But I guess I was the guy who had been given the Sword, and Stan needed my help.

I nodded and said, "Let's head back to your place."

"Of course," Michael said. "What are you going to do?"

"Get the rest of my stuff," I said. "And then check up on Stan at St. Tony's. Better safe than sorry."


MICHAEL PULLED UP to the hospital in his solid, hardworking white pickup truck, and frowned. "God go with you, Waldo."

"You still don't like it, do you?" I asked him.

"The skull is a very dangerous object," he said. "It doesn't . . . understand love. It doesn't understand faith."

"That's what we're here for, right?" I asked him.

"It's not for me," Michael said, setting his jaw.

"You think I should take it on my first quest with me?" I asked.

"God Almighty, no," Michael said.

"Just keep an eye on it until I get back."

"If it fell into the wrong hands . . ."

"It won't be my problem, because I'll be all dead and stuff," I said. "Michael, give me a break. I don't need you rattling my confidence just now, right?"

He looked chagrined for a second and then nodded. "Of course. If you weren't the right person, the Sword wouldn't have come to you."

"Unless it was an honest accident."

Michael smiled. "I don't believe in accidents."

"I'd better get out. If God has any sense of humor at all, you're going to get rear-ended any second now," I said, and got out of the car. "I'll call you when I know something."

"God go with you," Michael said, and pulled away, leaving me standing on the curb alone.

Just me.

*Oy.*

I took a deep breath, tried to imagine myself about two feet taller than I actually was, and walked quickly into the hospital.

MOVING AROUND A hospital without being noticed is pretty easy. You just wear a doctor's white coat and scrubs and some comfortable shoes and walk like you know exactly where you're going.

It also helps to have a doctor's ID, and an actual MD, and to actually be a doctor who has sometimes worked there and to actually know exactly where you're going.

I'm a doctor, dammit, not a spy.

"Patterson," I said to a lanky ER nurse with a buzz cut and a lumberjack's beard. "How's my favorite druid?"

Patterson looked up at me from a form-field-filled computer screen and squinted. "Waldo Butters, aka I Put the *Pal* in the Paladin. Your guild stiffed our guild on a treasure roll two weeks ago."

I pushed my glasses up on my nose. "Yeah, I've been kind of busy. Haven't been online to keep the power gamers in check. My word, I'll have Andi look into it, and we'll make it up to you guys."

The nurse scowled at me, but let out a mollified grunt. "Hell are you doing down here? They kick you out of Corpsesicles 'R' Us?"

"Not yet," I said. Though they might, with as many times as I'd called in sick lately. I hadn't been sick. Just too bruised and sore to move right. "Look, I'm kind of here on something personal. Maybe you could help me out."

Patterson stared at me with unamused eyes. Not to get too much into the details, but HIPAA basically means that no one who wants to remain working in the medical field can share any patient information with anyone who isn't directly involved in that patient's care, unless the patient gives permission to do so. It's the kind of thing people get reflexively paranoid about. Also the kind of thing you have to ask a favor to get them to overlook.

"Why should I?" he asked.

"Because I have something you want," I said.

"What?"

I leaned a bit closer and looked up and down the hall theatrically before speaking in a lowered tone. "What about . . . a blue murloc egg?"

Patterson sat up ramrod straight and his eyes widened. "What?"

"You heard me," I said.

"Dude, don't even joke about it," he breathed. "You know it's the last one I need."

"Two thousand five was a very good year," I drawled. I reached into my pocket and produced a plastic card from my wallet. "Behold. One code for one blue murloc. The rarest pet in all the game can be thine." Patterson reached for the card with twitchy fingers, and I snapped it a bit farther away from him. "Do we have a deal?"

"It's legit?"

I dropped the drama voice. "Yeah, man, I was actually at the con. It's real—you have my word."

Patterson crowed and seized the card with absolutely Gollum-esque avarice. "Pleasure doing business with you, I Put the *Pal* In." He gestured for me to join him behind the desk, and rubbed his hands together in mock-epic greed. "What you need?"

That's the thing about knowing a lot of gamers. They do not necessarily count their riches with bank accounts. Not when there are virtual status symbols to acquire.

"Guy got admitted a couple of hours ago, ER, first name Stan," I said. "I sent him in with Reg Lamar, probable overdose. I want to see him."

Patterson started thumping on computer keys. "You sent him in?"

"Out jogging this morning, found him seizing," I said.

He stopped typing for a second and looked at me. Then he looked back at the monitor and said, "Someone's taking his character way too seriously."

"Nah, I just have too many corpsesicles already," I said.

"You're lucky it happened in the morning. We start getting busy come the afternoon."

I started to tell him that luck hadn't had anything to do with it, and felt myself shiver.

I mean, that's kind of a huge thing to think about, you know? That in all probability, luck really *hadn't* been involved. That God, or some version of God, who the Knights simply referred to as the Almighty, had knowingly arranged for me to be in the right place at the right time to help Stan—and that He (or She, or It—I mean I didn't want to get too presumptuous, all things considered, and how should I know?) had done so in such a way as to make it uniquely possible for me, personally, to go help Stan.

Could God, with all the majesty of the universe at his disposal, with the uncounted myriad of life forms to look after throughout practically uncountable galaxies, really be all that interested in one little drug addict? One little medical examiner, playing at being a hero?

Answer that question with a yes or a no, and tell me which is the more terrifying. I'm not sure I can.

I'd asked Michael the same question, more or less. He'd been of the opinion that God couldn't *not* be interested on a personal level. That He knew each and every one of us too well to be anything less than passionately involved in caring about our lives and our choices.

And, honestly, that seemed a little stalkery to me. I mean, bad enough when your mom is too interested in what you do. Do you really want God looking over your shoulder at every moment? Me, personally, that was too embarrassing to even consider.

In the end, I'd decided that whatever the Almighty might care about or not care about, He seemed to be interested in helping people who needed help, at least where the Knights of the Cross were concerned. So, okay. Fine. I could work with the Guy. But all these deep questions bothered me.

"Here he is, top of the list," Patterson said. "Oh, Stanley Bowers. Been in and out a lot lately. I think I know this guy. Addict. One of the worst I've seen. Got maybe a year left in him, if the weather isn't too bad. Got a sedative, saline, observation."

"How's he get the drugs?"

"Disability, and some kind of court settlement. Pretty much sticks it up his nose. Won't do rehab."

"Family?"

"Nah. We've looked."

"Damn," I said.

"You want to help guys like this," Patterson said. "But he doesn't want to help himself. You know? You can't save someone who don't want to be saved."

"Doesn't mean we can't try," I said. "Where is he?"

Patterson peered at the monitor and rattled the keys a couple more times. Then he said, "Huh. That's weird."

———

As a medical examiner, I don't spend a lot of time in pediatrics. Neither, as a rule, do adult junkies. But for some reason, Stan had been moved up with the kids.

I rode the elevator up, trying to look distracted and disinterested like a proper physician, most of whom were operating on not much sleep at least part of the time, but it was tough, because I was feeling something that I suspected was a deeper-than-usual anger.

Whatever had hurt Stan was bad enough. But now there were kids involved. And some things you just don't do. You know?

I walked briskly into pediatrics. There are a ton of pediatric physicians at St. Tony's, plus various pediatric specialists, consulting physicians, et cetera, et cetera. The floor was busy, its beds full, and the nurses had their plates full—and to make things worse, there were renovators at work on the floor. Plastic sheets hung from some of the walls, shutting parts of the floor off from the rest, and buckets and tools and sawhorses and materials were stacked up, blurry shapes just out of sight on the other side of the first layer of curtains.

Workmen, tagged with hospital tags and clearly utterly ignorant of the place's rhythms, were walking out, evidently headed to an early lunch break. One of them was flirting with a young nurse who obviously had a mile of work to do. It was kind of pandemonium, or what passes for it in an orderly hospital.

I confess that I took advantage of it. I breezed in without any trouble, swooped up an armful of charts, and kept moving as though I knew exactly where I was going, scanning the charts as I did.

I stepped into the first room where a girl, maybe eight or nine, was curled up into a fetal position on her side. She had a very pale little face, and hollows under her eyes as dark as tire marks on a city road. Her hair was brown and listless. I checked charts and found hers. Her name was Gabrielle. She twitched violently as she slept. Her breathing was unsteady, and she made constant sounds as she exhaled.

I'd never been a father, but I didn't have to be to know that little girl was in the grips of a nightmare. And given the medicine in her IV, she wasn't going to be able to get out of it.

I read the charts and they told me the story. Seven kids, plus Stan, were down with a remarkably similar set of symptoms. Paranoia, hysteria, insomnia, and a refusal to go to sleep due to horrible nightmares, especially anytime at night, necessitating chemical intervention.

Eight people.

Holy moly.

If that many people were down, and a Knight of the Cross had been sent to deal with it, even if that Knight was me, it meant that there was a supernatural predator of some kind at work. A genuine Grade A monster. That was all mine to deal with.

Just me.

I guess maybe this wasn't a beginner's quest.

I slipped out of the room and into the next one in the hall, and found Stan. He'd been restrained as well as being sedated, which, dammit, should not have been happening in his condition. He should have been on saline and close monitoring until his body had a chance to process whatever combination of street drugs he'd been on that nearly killed him. He was in the same condition as the little girl, or worse—out of it, obviously suffering from some terrible dream and unable to escape it. His pulse was thready, his breath erratic, and his monitoring equipment had been jiggered—it was showing numbers that could not possibly have matched up to his respiration and heartbeat.

Someone had done this to him.

"Jesus, Stan," I said. "I sent you into this. I'm sorry. I should have listened to you."

He didn't respond, though his head kind of twitched in my direction. There was something desperate in the little movement. I bit my lip and put my hand on his head. "Hang in there, buddy," I told him. "Whatever power is given to me, I'll use it to help you. I promise."

If whatever had done that to Stan and the kids found me snooping around, it would be happy to do exactly the same thing to me.

My heart started beating faster. It took me a second to realize that it was pounding in time with rapid footsteps coming down the hall. Women's heels. *Click, clack, click, clack*—firm and purposeful.

I had a couple of seconds to realize that my fear and the footsteps were connected, and then, just in case that hadn't been enough, an open square, maybe four by four feet, made of red light, appeared on the wall, evidently tracking the movement of something hostile coming down the hall toward the door to Stan's room.

I eyed the ceiling and muttered, "I get the point." I looked around the room and weighed my options as my terror increased, and then ratcheted up more, and I panicked. I stepped into the bathroom and shut the door until it was almost all the way closed, and held very still.

The monster stepped into sight. She wasn't much of a monster as they went—maybe five-four in the low heels, a woman of slender build with dark hair. She was of Asian extraction, and her name tag read DR. MIYAMUNE. Behind the thick, dark rims of her glasses, her eyes were absolutely crystalline blue.

As she came into the room, she paused, and her eyes swept back and forth, right past me. She didn't look old, maybe mid-thirties, like a doctor who had finished her internship and was a few years into a specialist's residency. Those blue eyes fastened hard on Stan, and suddenly she wasn't just a woman in a white lab coat anymore. She changed, right in front of me.

It wasn't a physical transformation. I mean, a camera wouldn't have shown you bupkes. This was something deeper, something intangible. Her posture changed slightly, from rigidly proper into a more relaxed, looser-limbed tension. Her eyes narrowed. It was her mouth that was worst. Her lips just sort of lifted away from her teeth. The expression was damned creepy, and I felt a little sick to my stomach.

*Monster* is a subjective word. But the thing that was hiding inside a human shape met the definition. I held absolutely still.

Miyamune stalked from one side of Stan's bed to the other, focused on him, then turned and paced back, like a restless lion at the zoo. For a moment she did nothing else, but Stan reacted. His soft sounds increased in pitch, and as they did her eyes seemed to brighten. She put one hand on the bed and ran it over his bedclothes, not actually touching him, dragging her fingertips along as she went, and Stan's breathing became ragged, desperate.

She was *feeding* on him. Maybe on his fear. Drawing the life out of him.

Stan was getting close.

Well.

Time to saddle up.

I moved one arm toward the bag at my side, cloth making a soft whisper as it slid across cloth.

And she *heard* it.

I had my fingertips on the smooth wooden hilt of *Fidelacchius* when her hand and arm smashed through the wooden bathroom door in a shower of splinters, seized me by the lab coat, and flung me out of the bathroom and into the opposite wall.

I couldn't believe the force of it. Miyamune's arm tore through the rest of the door as if the wood had been damp cardboard, ripping the sleeves of her coat and shirt to ribbons while leaving the skin beneath untouched. I dimly registered that I was up against a being with supernatural strength as I flew, relaxed, and hit the wall as flat as I could, my arms slapping back as if taking a fall in judo, one of the other things Charity had taught me.

It worked. I spread out the impact enough to keep it from shattering any bones, and came down on my feet, more or less, hand fumbling for my bag.

Miyamune stared at me for a second, facing me from the far side of the bed, over Stan's knees. Then, without taking her eyes from me, she reached behind her, as if she knew exactly where to move her arm, and calmly locked the hospital door.

Which did not, at all, send part of me into a gibbering panic. My hands shook so hard that I could barely feel the hilt of *Fidelacchius* as my fingers closed around it.

"One chance," I heard myself say, my voice a pale ghost of itself.

"Leave. Leave them. All of them. Do it now. And you have my word that you get to walk away alive."

Her mouth curled up in pure contempt at one corner. "And who is it you think you are, little man?"

"All you need to know is this," I said, and drew out the Sword.

There was a sound too musical to be called a shriek, too fierce and furious to be called a chord of music. From the old broken wooden hilt in my hand sprang a blade of light, three feet long and shining white. The sound of the blade's birth settled into a humming musical chord, something low and ominous.

Miyamune faced me without any reaction at all. The Sword's light reflected in two bright bars from her crystalline blue eyes—and the shadow that the Sword's light cast on the wall behind her was not shaped at all like her. It was something hulking, with a leonine mane and a writhing tendril of some kind whipping around its head. Her skin, too, became semitranslucent in the Sword's light, showing shapes that moved and shifted beneath the surface, some kind of grey-and-gold mush of colors, as if something far too large for it had been forced into Miyamune's tiny form.

"I make you an offer, little man," she said in calm reply. "Leave this place. Leave what is mine to me. I will permit you to spend the rest of your days exposed only to the nightmares you have created for yourself."

"Sorry, lady," I said. "I can't do that. Step away from that man."

I moved the Sword to emphasize my words. The chord bobbed and changed with the Sword's motion, rising to a higher, tenser pitch as it edged closer, and lowering again as it backed away.

The only other time I'd drawn the Sword in earnest, the guy I'd pulled it on had panicked.

Miyamune kicked Stan's bed at my legs.

She moved fast, but I'd been paranoid enough to sense the movement and dodge in the only direction that wouldn't have hemmed my movement in more, and it was the right way to move. I avoided the bed, shuffle-stepped forward with my feet dragging the floor just slightly, to make sure I wouldn't lift them and put them down on any-thing that would trip me, and swept the blade in a clean cut at her midsection.

Miyamune avoided the blow by an inch with a gracefully timed step back, and flung her clipboard at me with supernatural strength. It made an ugly hissing sound as it came, tearing bits off the papers that were on it. I barely got the Sword in the way, splitting the plastic clipboard as if it had been sliced with a laser cutter, sending a small cloud of chopped printer paper into the air. The pieces of clipboard flew past me and, from the sound of it, buried themselves, quivering, in the drywall.

One of her heels was coming along the floor in a leg sweep even before I had finished the defensive cut. I shifted my weight back, barely in time, and she kicked my forward leg hard enough to make it go numb—but didn't send me to the ground with the kick. I swept the Sword into a clumsy arc as I fought for my balance. It forced her to duck to one side instead of following up in my moment of vulnerability—directly toward Stan.

"No!" I said.

She seized his throat and her hand flexed. As quickly as that, Stan's labored breaths stopped completely as she closed off his windpipe.

That predator looked out of the doctor's face, and its blue eyes danced with amusement. "I'll kill him," she said. "One move, little man, and I will end his life."

"Don't," I breathed.

Her smile widened a little as she regarded the Sword, still hum-ming with the power of an angry chorus. Silence stretched.

"I was like you once," she said finally. Something ugly went through those blue eyes. "Struggling to protect them. What a fool I was."

"Yeah?" I asked. "Look, we don't have to be doing the combat thing. Be glad to talk with you about it. Coffee, maybe some nosh? What do you say?"

She sneered. "Do you think I care about your thoughts, little mortal?"

"How will you know if you never hear them?" I asked mildly.

Whatever I'd said, it was the wrong thing. Pure rage flared through her features. "So righteous," she spat. Then she looked me up and down and said, "I offer you a trade for his life."

"Um," I said. "I'm listening."

"Give me your glasses."

That made my heart all but stop.

Suddenly that scared ten-year-old kid inside me was screaming again.

"Give me," Miyamune purred, "your glasses. Or I kill him. Right now."

"If I do," I said quietly, "you walk away. You leave him alone."

"For as long as you live and breathe," Miyamune said.

I swallowed.

Stan was here because of me.

I took one hand off the Sword and reached up.

The world dissolved into a blur of vague color as I took off my glasses, and my stomach jumped and twitched in random spasms of pure, unfiltered, childhood fear.

I felt the glasses in my fingers, heavy and cool. Then I tossed them toward the last place it seemed like Miyamune had been standing. There was no sound of the glasses falling. She must have caught them silently.

A second later, there were crackling, popping sounds—and the sound of safety glass pattering to the floor in little squares like so many oversized grains of sugar.

"Little protector," Miyamune said a moment later. "I will make you suffer. I give you as long as it will take me to shoo the mortals from this floor. Then I will hunt you. I will feed on you. And in the end, I will take your life."

There was a clack as the door unlocked. Then it opened.

"Run," Miyamune said softly, "and others will die in your place."

Then the door closed again.

The whole time, her feet never made a sound on the floor. But I had that feeling, that certainty you have when you're standing in a room that isn't otherwise occupied.

My legs gave out and I found myself sitting helplessly on the floor next to Stan's bed as he whimpered in his nightmares. The light of the Sword went out when I hit the floor.

I sat with him in the blind gloom. I was breathing too fast and making sounds just like him.

"Yellow," answered a voice when I speed-dialed 1 on my cell phone, by touch. "Harry's Taxidermy. You snuff 'em, we'll stuff 'em."

"It's me," I said.

The levity vanished from his voice. "Butters? What's wrong?"

"I, uh," I said. "I . . ."

*I am the wrong person to be a Knight of the Cross*, is what I wanted to say. But instead I said, "What are you doing?"

"You just caught us. Getting set to take Maggie and Mouse to the zoo to meet mighty Moe," he replied, his voice holding gentle cheer. "Going to be a good time. You ever been to the zoo?"

"Not really an animal guy," I said.

"You should come along, maybe," he said.

I felt myself laugh weakly. "I can't. Working."

"Which hat you wearing?"

"The Jedi hat," I said.

"Oh," he said. He was quiet for a second, then exhaled slowly. "Guess they're starting you early. How bad?"

"It's bad," I said. "I . . . I might need help."

There was a long silence from the other end of the phone. It hissed and crackled with static. He was upset. Wizards play merry hell with electronics around them when they get emotional. Even on an old landline, nothing was a sure bet. Especially not around Harry Dresden.

"I won't come," he said quietly.

"What?" I asked. "Harry . . ."

"Michael told me something once that I thought was utter crap," he said. "But I'm going to tell it to you now."

"What?" I demanded.

"You're a Knight now, Butters. You're working for the freaking Almighty. And He won't give you a burden bigger than your shoulders can bear."

"Harry, He already *has*," I said. I didn't *say* it, honestly; I sort of gibbered it.

"Butters," he snapped.

I'd heard him use that tone of voice one other time. Exactly once. It had been in a basement, and zombies had been coming to kill us.

"Polka will never die," I breathed. It came out, smooth and automatic. It was kind of a mantra of mine.

"Good man," he said. "Tell me what's going on."

I did. I stuttered a lot. I stammered a lot.

"Wait," he said. "The thing's shadow. A lion's mane and a damned elephant's trunk?"

I thought of the thrashing tendril in the thing's shadow. "Yeah, uh, I guess it could have been."

"And it had blue eyes, didn't it?"

I hadn't gotten to that part yet. "Yeah," I said. "It did. They were crazy."

"Hell," he said. "It's a baka baku."

"What is *that*?" I asked. "I've never heard of that creature."

"Because it isn't real," he said. "Or it wasn't, until the nineties. I mean, there was a thing called a *baku* in Japanese lore, but it wasn't the same thing at all. Look, some company made a kid's stuffed toy, called it a dream-eater, said that it was a magical protector that ate bad dreams before children could have them. Came with a little book that explained the whole thing."

"I'm fighting a stuffed animal?" I asked. My leg pounded. There would be a huge bruise there for weeks where the thing had kicked me.

"Nah," he said. "Look, they were just making a toy, but they gave it to *kids*. Kids believing in things has freaking power. It either created the real ones or it gave access to something similar from the Nevernever that used that belief to create a place for itself in reality."

"Then why has it gone all Manson on these people?" I asked.

"Some laws are kind of universal. Like 'You are what you eat,'" the wizard told me. "You eat enough nightmares, sooner or later you turn into one. Now, instead of protecting people from nightmares, it uses them to inflict torment. Probably gets energy from it."

"Oh, fantastic," I said. "What can they do?"

"Listen carefully. This thing has laid a fear whammy on you, man."

"That stuff doesn't work on Knights," I said.

"Horse crap," Harry said. "Look, the Knights have power, but you have to choose to use it, man. You don't get any get-out-of-jail-free cards. What you get is the chance to fight when other people would get eaten. That thing has gotten into your head. It's scaring you to death. Just like those people around you. It's eating you."

"Harry, I can't *see*," I stammered.

And, I swear to God, he shifted to a nearly perfect imitation of Alec Guinness in the original movie. "Your eyes can deceive you," he said. "Don't trust them."

I barked out a laugh that felt like it was going to shatter something in my chest.

Or maybe actually did. Suddenly, I started to get my breath back.

"Butters," he said. "Look. I know it's hard. But there's one way you deal with fear."

"How?" I asked him.

"You stand up and you kick it in the fucking teeth," he said, and there was a quiet, certain power in his voice that had nothing to do with magic. "You've forgotten the most important thing a Knight needs to remember, Butters."

"What's that?" I breathed.

"Knights of the Cross aren't afraid of monsters," he said. "Monsters are afraid of you. Act like it. Commit to it, hard. And have faith."

Act like it. Commit. I could do those things.

Faith was harder. I'd never asked God to help me handle things before.

But I had faith in my friends.

One friend in particular.

"Got it," I said quietly. "I guess I better go, Harry. Got work to do."

"Good hunting, Knight."

"Thank you, wizard."


WHEN I OPENED the door, things had changed.

I'd taken a white sheet from Stan's bed, draped it over my shoulders, and tied two corners around my neck. On the part of the sheet that draped over my chest, I'd taken a first-aid sticker from a drawer of supplies beside the bed and stuck the red-cross symbol over my heart.

It wasn't like Sanya's or Michael's cloaks. But it would do.

More important, I'd put my headphones in my ears, plugged the jack into my phone, and blared "Weird Al" Yankovic's "NOW That's What I Call Polka!" at full volume on loop.

I could barely see. And I couldn't hear anything but my goofy, beautiful polka, one of the songs I knew perfectly at that, which was kind of the point.

In the hallway, I could feel the emptiness stretching out around me and the low fear in the air. The baka baku had run everyone off the floor—I could dimly see hollow yellow squares retreating, tracking the workmen and nurses and doctors all leaving the floor by the stairs and elevators, leaving it to just the two of us and the trapped, dreaming victims.

The fluorescent lights were all flickering and flashing as if they needed changing.

I didn't see the hostile red targeting carat.

But I didn't need it.

I went to the center of the hall, lifted the Sword to a high guard, and felt it ignite and change the way shadows fell on the hall. As

Yankovic translated popular music into polka in my ears, I shouted, "Baka baku! Betrayer of children! You have lost your path! Come and face me!"

And I closed my eyes and waited.

See, magic isn't really magic. I've spent a lot of time studying the theory, and I know that for a fact. I mean, it is magic, obviously, but it doesn't just happen in a giant vacuum, inexplicably creating miracles. Lots and lots of magic actually follows many of the physical laws of the universe. Energy can neither be created nor destroyed, for example.

If the baka baku was sending magical fear into people's brains, that fear had to be transmitted by something. It can't just appear magically—poof—in someone else's head. It's a kind of broadcast—a signal. And that means that, like other magical broadcasts, such as those used on the communicators I'd designed and built in the past, waves on the EM spectrum were the most likely culprits for those transmissions.

Using those things had a side effect of causing distortions in nearby cell phones. It was even more noticeable in headphones.

So I listened to one of my recent favorites and waited. My inner ten-year-old was screaming at me to run.

I told him to shut his mouth and let me work.

And, sure enough, about the time Al was singing about looking incredible in your granddad's clothes, I heard the sound distort suddenly in my left ear.

Moving quickly is not about effort. It isn't about making every muscle explode in an instant in an effort to be fast. It's about being relaxed, smooth, and certain. The instant I heard the distortion, my body just reacted, turning and sweeping the sword down, all in a single liquid motion.

I felt the Sword hit, and the blade's hum shifted to a triumphant note. I opened my eyes to see a shape about the size and same general coloring as Miyamune reeling back.

There was a much smaller, flesh-colored shape lying on the floor not far from my feet.

I tugged out the earphones and heard Miyamune let out a moan of pain, and the last of my fear fell away from me.

The baka baku bounced off the wall and fell, and I advanced on it, slow and steady.

The creature's huge, weird shadow spread onto the wall behind it, even as its human face stared up at me.

"Who *are* you?" the creature asked.

The words that came out of my mouth only sort of felt like my own. "*Ehyeh ašer ehyeh*," I said quietly.

The walls of the empty hallway quivered slightly as the words washed over them, even though I never once raised my voice.

The creature just gaped at me.

"Even now," I heard myself say, "it isn't too late for you to turn aside. To be forgiven."

I couldn't really see its expression—but I saw the gathering tension in its blurry form, felt the anger in the way it suddenly exhaled and came at me.

And the Sword of Faith swept down one last time and ended it.


WHEN MICHAEL PICKED me up from the hospital in his old white pickup late that night, I was exhausted.

He handed me my spare pair of glasses first thing and I put them on gratefully.

"Have to do something about that," I said. "Maybe sports goggles."

"Seems like a good idea," he said. "How's Stan?"

"He'll be fine," I said. "So will the kids."

"What was hurting them?"

"Something that should have been protecting them," I said quietly. I squinted out the window as he pulled away. "Just dissolved into nothing when I took it down."

"What's wrong?" he asked me, his deep voice gentle.

"I'm not sure I succeeded at this quest," I said. "I kept trying to reach out to the creature. To give it a chance to turn away."

"Sometimes they do," Michael said. "Mostly, they don't."

"It's just . . ." I said. "Killing is such a waste. What I did was necessary. But I'm not sure it was good."

"Killing rarely is," he said, "at least in my experience. Could you have done any differently?"

"Maybe?" I said. "I don't know. With what I knew at the time . . . I don't know."

"Would they all be alive if you had done differently? The children? Stan?"

I thought about it for a moment, and then shook my head. "I don't think so."

"Then be content, Sir Knight," he said.

"Didn't even have to get my hand cut off to get there," I said, and leaned my head against the truck's window.

I never knew it when I fell asleep, relaxed and unafraid.

# ZOO DAY

I never really meant for Harry to be a dad.

I mean, I knew what I was doing on a step-by-step basis. I knew that for *Changes*, I wanted to throw out an extinction-worthy threat from the bad guys, and a proportionate response from Dresden. For Harry, the ultimate motivation would be saving his own child—especially because of his own childhood experience as an orphan, where no one ever came to save him. And it was kind of baked into the cake of my unconscious assumptions that Harry would save his child, of course. Clumsy though the young wizard might be, and sloppy, and desperate, and uncoordinated, and I really feel like the word *collateral* needs to be worked into it somewhere, Dresden does tend to get the job done in the end.

But I never really paused to work through the implications of the fact that Harry would be pathologically devoted to being there for his kid, and that he was going to save her life. I could see both 2s, but I had never added them up to 4: Maggie was going to be there, a presence in the story moving forward, and he was definitely going to want to be involved with her. Which meant that my hardboiled, unlucky-in-love PI wizard was also going to be a parent.

Which, of course, changes absolutely everything about one's life. It restructures priorities in a way nothing else really can.

Which is something that is really, really contraindicated when you're writing a long-running series. You don't go majorly changing your main character without facing a loss of audience.

The easy, safe thing to do would have been to leave Maggie with the Carpenters, or shuffle her off into the Church's supernatural witness protection program—which seems like a quite wizardly thing to do, maybe even for the child's own good. But as I kept writing, I realized that I couldn't do that and still have Dresden be Dresden, either. He believes too much in what it means to be a parent, as shown in the Bigfoot short stories, and the payment he demands from River Shoulders.

So, at the end of the day, the character was a-gonna change, one way or another. I went with the way that felt most true to who he is as a human being.

Harry's a dad now. He might not know too much about it, but at least he has the jokes down.

**M**y name is Harry Dresden. I am possibly one of the more dangerous wizards alive, and I have never once spent a whole day as a dad.

My memories of my father are few and faded. He was a good man, and he was kind, but he died before I got into first grade. Sometimes I wonder whether the memories I have of him are mine or they're just the stories I've been retelling myself my whole life.

The point is, I don't really have much in the way of a personal role model to base my dad technique on. The man who mostly shaped me was a sadistic monster, and by the time my grandfather came along, Ebenezar wasn't parenting so much as enacting psychological damage control.

And besides, I'm pretty sure you don't dad a furious, sullen, magically powered teenage boy the same way you do a ten-year-old girl. Not only that, but I was pretty sure I'd never really spoken to a ten-year-old girl for any length of time. Nor had I ever been one.

I was completely in the woods here, and sure of only one thing:

I really, *really* wanted to get this right.

Maggie walked next to me, taking maybe three steps to every one of mine. She was a tiny child, in the lowest percentile for height and weight in every class she'd ever been in, with pale skin, dark hair, and absolutely enormous dark eyes. She was wearing purple pants and a beige T-shirt that bore an image echoing the original *Star Wars* poster, but done in the style of Edo-period samurai art, and her shoes flickered with little red lights when she walked.

Next to her paced a granite grey mountain of muscle and soft fur named Mouse. Mouse was a genuine Temple Guardian, a Foo dog. He weighed about two hundred and fifty pounds, and the length of his fur was something like a mane around his neck and shoulders. He wore a red nylon vest that declared him a service dog, and walked as carefully as if he were avoiding baby chicks with every step. Maggie kept one of her little hands buried in his mane and her eyes on the ground.

"So, you haven't been to the zoo before?" I asked.

Maggie shook her head and watched an elderly couple pass us on the sidewalk. She waited until they were several yards away before saying quietly, "Miss Molly tried to take me once, but there were too many people and too much sky, and I cried."

I nodded. My daughter had seen some bad things. They'd left their marks on her. "That's okay, you know."

"Miss Molly said that, too," Maggie said. "I was little then."

The spring afternoon sun peeked out from some clouds for a moment, and my shadow engulfed her and enough space for five or ten more of her. "That was probably it," I said. "But if you need to, we can leave whenever you like."

She looked up at me for a minute, her face thoughtful. She was the most beautiful child I'd ever seen, but everyone thinks that about their kid.

Maybe everyone is right.

"I want to see the gorillas," she said finally. "So does Mouse."

Mouse wagged his tail in agreement, and looked up at me with a doggy grin.

"Okay, then," I said, as we approached the entrance to the zoo. "Let's do that."

Maggie looked at me for a moment more and frowned before saying, "Are you nervous?"

"Why would I be nervous?" I asked.

She looked down and shrugged. "I don't know. I'm nervous. I haven't ever gone to the zoo with my dad before. What if I do it wrong?"

I felt a little jab in my chest and cleared my throat. *Smart kid.* "I'm pretty sure this isn't something you get right or wrong."

"What if . . . I don't know. What if I set something on fire?"

"Maybe we'll roast some marshmallows," I said.

She didn't laugh, and she kept her face down, but her cheeks rounded up with a smile. "You're weird."

"A little," I said. "Is that okay?"

"I don't know yet. I think." She stepped a little closer to Mouse. She could have ridden on his back and he wouldn't much notice her weight. "Did you really save the gorillas from a monster?"

"Yeah, pretty much," I said. It had been three hags, and I'd saved one gorilla from taking the fall for a murder one of them had perpetrated. A couple of people died. But that was a lot of dark and complicated conversation for my first dad-daughter outing.

Maggie nodded seriously. "So, you like animals. Like me."

"Yes, I do."

"Even dinosaurs?"

"Especially dinosaurs. And dino-dogs."

"Whuff," said Mouse, pleased.

I leaned across Maggie to ruffle his furry ears.

A group of noisy children in private-school uniforms came trooping by, and Maggie flinched and withdrew into herself until they'd passed. After that, she stared grimly at the busy entrance to the zoo, looking for all the world like someone a great deal older who badly needed a cup of coffee. Then she sighed, squared her shoulders, and said, "Okay. Let's see some animals."

So we did.

THERE WAS A spectacularly good showing from the animals in their various enclosures. The otters played with bombastic fervor. The tigers prowled back and forth at the very front of their pen. One of the polar bears stood up on his hind legs, and a sun bear enthusiastically tore apart a log just as we came walking up. I mean, if I hadn't known better, I would think they were putting on a show.

Maggie was enchanted, her little face stretching into one quiet smile after another, though she rarely stepped far enough away from the dog beside her to cease being in physical contact with him.

The lion actually roared, a sound that shook the air and sent a dozen people scurrying a few steps back. But not Maggie. Though she flinched whenever anyone walked too close to her, she regarded the lion with an intent gaze, as the beast finished his pronouncement and shook his mane with lazy majesty.

"Awesome," she said after, and her smile was a sunbeam.

"Yeah," I said, quietly. "Awesome."

The actual lion's roar had been a little too much. There was no way all the animals would be showing off like this without some kind of intervention, and I knew I hadn't done it. I eyed Mouse with some suspicion.

The dog noticed and dropped his jaws open into a guileless canine grin, panting happily and wagging his tail. I arched an eyebrow at him and shook my head. The beastie was full of incompletely understood yet helpful magic, but he couldn't play poker to save his life.

Get it? The dog. Playing poker. That's an art joke.

I may not know humor, but I know what I like.

We had just turned to head toward the gorilla house when my day started getting complicated.

I felt it at first as a series of flickering sensations against my fore-head. It reminded me of a moth fluttering against a lit wall—constant and random flutters, somehow conveying confusion, frustration, and fear. The hairs on the back of my neck stood up, and a quick check around showed me at least three different people who were suddenly perplexed that their electronic devices had started malfunctioning.

Magic was in the air—and it wasn't coming from me.

"Um. Dad?" Maggie asked me.

I eyed her. She was looking at me in mild confusion. Then I saw her eyes widen as she had some kind of realization, and she moved to stand with Mouse on one side of her and me on the other. "Is there something bad?"

I felt my shoulders tighten into iron bands. *Dammit.* This day was supposed to go smoothly—just dad-and-daughter time, where Maggie knew that she was the most important thing in the world to me.

God knew I'd been away from her long enough.

The last thing I needed was for her to think I took my job more seriously than I took her. But at the same time, wizarding work wasn't the kind of thing that came with regular hours. Or dental insurance. Also, there was the minor issue that the moral obligation to do the right thing didn't suddenly go away due to inconvenience.

"Maybe," I said. I looked at her. "Maybe nothing. I don't know. I need to look around and see what's going on. I need to put you in a safe spot before I do that."

Maggie stared at a spot in the middle distance, chewing on her lower lip. "It's important, isn't it?"

"Maybe," I said. I nodded toward the café that served the zoo. "How about we go get a booth and order some food? You and Mouse sit, and I'll go look around and be back before the food gets there."

Maggie's arms tightened around the dog's neck. She looked at him, then at me, and nodded her little chin firmly. "Yeah. I guess that's okay."

"How about it, Mouse?" I asked. "Can you behave yourself around food?"

My dog was staring out across the park, in what would have been considered a pensive expression had we all been cartoon characters. He made a noise in his chest that was part whine and part rumble.

"Trouble, boy?" I asked. It wasn't cliché dialogue. Mouse was better than me at sensing trouble coming, and had proved it on multiple occasions.

He stayed staring for a minute, then exhaled slowly and looked up at me. His ears perked up and he wagged his tail. I took that to mean that all was well. "All right," I said, and wagged my finger at him. "Be good."

"Whuff," Mouse said.

"He's always good," Maggie said, and kissed his ear. She had to lean down only a little to do it, and he lifted his head obligingly.

"Okay," I said.

We got seats in the restaurant, and I ordered some French fries and left Maggie with a twenty to pay for more if she needed it. I made sure she was comfortable, got Mouse settled in at her feet, and strode briskly outside, carefully opening my wizard's senses.

Magic is a living, breathing force, but nothing makes it stir and swirl as much as human beings, and especially human emotion. Based on what a given person is feeling and how strong an emotion they are experiencing, magic can quiver and pulse like the cover to a rock-concert speaker, vibrating hard against the senses of anyone born with the ability to sense it. More people have that than you'd think: folks who get unexpectedly creeped out in the woods, who sense that something seems particularly ominous about a darkened parking garage, who sometimes feel something in the air that grates against them and makes them abruptly cross the street for no particular reason—they're mostly gifted with sensitivity. If they trust their instincts, such senses can help them avoid no end of possible trouble.

For example, I could, with a little concentration, feel an intense and unpleasant sense of unease off to my right, along one of the park's paths. Even as I watched, I saw half a dozen people either swerve off to one side, apparently distracted by something else, or else simply change their minds and not follow the path. Their instincts were serving them well.

My instincts frequently roll their eyes at the decisions my brain makes. I walked firmly, directly, into the unpleasant energy and started looking for trouble.

I found it within fifty yards, in the shadiest part of the path, where the park's trees and bushes and the walls of the various buildings and enclosures hoarded a cluster of shadow that shouldn't have been quite as dim as it was.

A young man in a black hoodie stood in the shade, hands thrust deep into his pockets. The air around him pulsed with anger and a fear that was near panic. The air around him thrummed with tension and energy, far more of it than a vanilla mortal should be able to emit. He was slender, and though I could only see a bit of his face in profile, the acne was visible enough.

*Stars and stones.*

A warlock.

Magic sort of bursts onto the scene with most youngsters, who find themselves in possession of talents and powers that must seem as if they simply emerged from a beloved series of children's novels. Ideally, word of such gifts gets to the White Council, who dispatches someone to make sure the emerging talent receives training appropriate to prevent them from doing any harm with their powers.

The ideal was too rare, and getting rarer. As the population increased, more and more gifted children were emerging, and it was just possible that the group of three-hundred-year-olds who commanded the White Council were . . . somewhat slow to adapt to changing conditions among mortal kind. When a child fell through the (widening) cracks, their talents could emerge in frightening, even violent ways, often to such a degree that they were forced to flee their homes and communities. Those kids were then forced to cope with life alone and their emerging talents all at once.

A lot of them used their gifts in the worst ways. Unforgiveable ways. Kids like that were known as warlocks, and the Council dealt with them harshly and permanently.

I stared at the kid for a while.

I'd been that kid for a while.

Then I did something I don't do very often: I turned my back and walked away.

"WHAT WAS IT?" Maggie asked me when I got back. She looked nervous, and wiggled a bit in her seat.

I debated whether to play it down. She didn't need to be any more anxious than she already was. But . . . Enough time in the saddle as a wizard had taught me that there are bad repercussions when I keep people in my life in the dark, even when I'm only trying to protect them.

I looked down at her open, earnest face and her huge eyes.

*Yeah.*

I didn't need to start off my relationship with my daughter by repeating some of my classic mistakes.

"A warlock," I said quietly. "A young wizard whose power is not in control. Dangerous."

Her eyes widened. "Did you fight it?"

"Him," I said. "No."

"Why not?" she asked.

"Because most of the time, they never meant to do anything bad," I said. "They don't even understand what's happening to them. No one has warned them what will happen if they break the rules."

"That's not fair," Maggie said.

"No," I said. "But that doesn't make them any less dangerous."

"Can't you help?"

"Sometimes," I said very quietly. "I'm not sure."

She picked up a French fry and dipped it in a large mound of mustard. Not ketchup.

*What?*

She licked the mustard off the fry thoughtfully and then said, "But I'm here."

"Yeah," I said. "And you're more important to me."

She darted a look up at my eyes and smiled a little. Then she said, "They just get powers?"

I nodded. "Born to it, yeah."

She nodded again and asked, "Am I going to get powers?"

"Maybe," I said. "There's no way to know for sure."

"Weird," she said. She passed the French fry to Mouse, who snapped it up. She picked up another fry, dipped it in mustard, and began to repeat what was obviously a well-rehearsed cycle. "If I do, will you teach me stuff? So no one gets hurt?"

"If you want me to," I said.

She chewed her lip, looking intently at her fingers. "If . . . something happens to you, who is going to teach me?"

An invisible boxer socked me in the gut. "Nothing's going to happen to me," I said.

"It could," Maggie said quietly. For those two words, her voice sounded older. Way too old for the little body it came from. "And maybe there wouldn't be anyone. Maybe I'd be a warlock."

I took a deep breath. She'd seen her foster family murdered. Horribly. And maybe she'd seen even worse. She knew what the world could be like sometimes. She'd probably seen worse than that kid in the black hoodie.

"Maybe," I said.

"That could be me." She nodded to herself several times and took a deep breath, as if getting ready to hold it. Then she looked up at me. "I can eat more French fries. Mouse will keep me company."

"You sure?" I asked her. "It could . . . cut today kind of short."

"If someone needs your help, you help them," Maggie said simply. "Even when it's really hard. Miss Molly told me that about you."

Her eyes were searching, studying. I'll be damned if the kid wasn't assessing me warily, watching for my reaction. So young yet so cynical.

She must get it from her mother's side.

"Yeah," I said, feeling my face stretch into a smile. "Yeah. That's right."

I WENT BACK down the dark path, walking briskly. The thing about warlocks is that they really are damned dangerous. Without even knowing what they're doing, they can turn their wills to the pursuit of black magic, and that has a degenerative, addictive effect on their psyches. Warlocks, caught in the grip of black magic, did the kinds of things that give coroners and psychologists nightmares. They don't absolutely have to go completely off the rails, but most did. People in that frame of mind suddenly confronted by the White Council's Wardens rarely chose to put up their hands and come quietly.

I remembered when the Wardens had come for me. Scary guys. If I hadn't been so exhausted, I'd have been just one more warlock slain while resisting arrest.

Maybe this kid was a dangerous monster. The sheer malice radiating from him was convincing enough.

Or maybe he was just a terrified kid.

I walked up to him quietly, my footsteps audible, cleared my throat, and said, "Hi."

Hoodie turned to me, gave me half a glance, and snarled, "Get out of here."

There was the force of magic in his voice, subtle power that tugged at my ear, made me want to lift my foot, pivot, and go the other way.

It wasn't a very coherent compulsion. I waved it off with a defensive gesture of the fingers of my left hand. "Whoa, kid," I said. "Save it for the tourists. You and I need to talk."

That got his attention, pronto. His spine stiffened and he spun toward me on one heel, his shoulders tightening. He wasn't tall, maybe five-six, and his shoulders were almost comically narrow, hunched up like that.

I sidled up and leaned a hip on the railing a few feet out of arm's reach in front of him, crossing my arms. "When did it happen? Year ago? Year and a half?"

He had that wary poise of a wild animal, balanced and waiting to see which way would be the best to flee. His eyes were focused on the center of my chest. "Who are you?"

"Someone who had the same thing happen," I said. "One day, things changed, and everything got weird. I thought I was going insane. So did my teachers."

"You a cop?" the kid asked, his voice suddenly sharp.

"Kind of," I said.

"I didn't do nothin'," he said.

I barked out a quick laugh. "Wow, are you not good at this. People who are innocent don't have to walk around saying it."

His face reddened and darkened at the same time. "You'd better be careful, asshole."

"Or what?" I asked.

"Or something bad is going to happen to you."

"Nah," I said. "Won't turn out like that."

That ticked the kid off. His jaw clenched so hard that I thought he might crack some of his teeth. His fists clenched with audible popping sounds.

At the same time, the air grew thicker and tighter and more threatening, and there was a sudden rippling sensation against my skin, as if someone had abruptly torn a long strip out of the fabric of my blue jeans. Then there was a sound in the greenery, and my skin began to crawl on the back of my neck. I came on balance in an instant.

Remember those instincts I was talking about earlier? Mine were telling me that something dangerous had just come into the world.

The kid staggered suddenly and dropped to his knees, panting. Then his head came up, his eyes wide and everywhere. "Oh no," he breathed. "Oh no, no, no, no."

"Oh, for Pete's sake," I muttered, understanding what had happened.

The kid had a strong magical talent, and a gift for summoning. Magic is mostly in your head, and unfortunately for anyone who's got to deal with us, human beings' heads are murky, conflicted places. All kinds of things are going on in there, a lot of them under the surface, a lot of them not entirely in our own control.

Hoodie's subconscious had gathered up all that anger and fear he'd been feeling and sent it spiking out of him like a kind of spiritual beacon; a beacon that had attracted the attention of something from the spiritual world—something that had just crossed into the shadows of the walkway.

The spirit world is the home of an unlimited variety of supernatural beings—but I was going to take a wild guess and assume that this one wasn't a placid herbivore.

"Right here? In the park?" I demanded of the warlock in an aggrieved tone. "Hell's bells, kid."

Hoodie just stared at me with frightened, confused eyes. That spiritual dinner bell he'd just unconsciously rung had taken a lot out of him. "I didn't mean to. I never mean to!" Then his eyes widened. "You have to get out of here. Run!"

"First lesson," I said. I took a couple of steps back from the kid and peered around the thick greenery, relying more on my wizard's senses than on sight or hearing. "Running away from your problems rarely gets them solved."

"You don't get it," Hoodie babbled. "It's coming. It's coming for you."

"You don't get it, kid," I responded. "I—"

I had a second's warning, maybe a little more. It came through the greenery, staying in the heaviest shadow it could. It erupted from the dark and took Hoodie's legs out from under him as it went by. I had the flickering impression of a wolverine's squat, powerful legs; a head too wide to be anything from this world; a thrashing, scaled tail; and crocodilian teeth. It went through the kid and straight for me, bounding for my throat.

I was already moving as it came. I swept my arm up in a vertical line, fingers locked and rigid like claws as I channeled my will into them and barked, "Aparturum!"

My fingers peeled back reality as they swept up, tearing open the veil between the mortal world and the world of spirit. The berserk whatever-it-was from the Nevernever, the spirit world, let out an abrupt, abbreviated shriek of frustration as it hurtled directly into the opening, passing from the mortal world and back into the spirit realm again.

"*Instaurabos!*" I shouted, whipping my hand back down along the rend, this time inverting my will and sealing closed the opening before the vicious little thing could turn and leap back out again. I could feel the normality rushing back in to seal over the rend in the veil, and could faintly sense several thumping protestations from the hungry spirit creature as it found itself sealed away from the mortal world again.

After a few seconds, the shadows seemed less thick, and the sun emerged from behind the clouds, sending golden shafts streaming onto the path.

Hoodie lay on the ground where he'd fallen, staring up at me in silence, his mouth open.

I walked over to him and dropped down to squat on my heels, resting my hands on my knees. "As I was saying," I said. "You don't get it, kid. I'm the guy who is ready for it. I'm a wizard." I offered him my hand.

He took it, and we rose together. He pulled away from me quickly and scowled—but not precisely at me. "What do you want?"

"To talk," I said.

"What if I don't wanna talk to you?"

"Guess you don't have to."

That made him turn a shade warier. "I could just walk away?"

"Sure," I said. From this close, I could smell the kid. He needed a shower. His clothes didn't look like they'd been changed in a while. His shoes were too small and worn-out. I gestured toward where the demon he'd accidentally summoned had been banished. "But how's that been working out for you so far?"

"I'm fine," he said. His voice cracked when he said it. He looked away.

"Well. I'm not going to make you get help. You hungry?" I asked. As a conversational gambit went, it was a pretty solid one. Kids were hungry about ninety-five percent of the time.

"No," he lied, his tone sullen.

"There's a restaurant not two minutes from here. My daughter is there, with my dog, eating French fries. But I could just murder a burger right now. How about you?"

Hoodie didn't say anything. People had begun to resume using the pathway, and the everyday world began to reassert itself more firmly.

"Look, I kind of am a cop," I said, "just not for the usual stuff. For special things. Like today."

He shifted his weight warily.

"Tell you what," I said. "Let's eat. Maybe talk a little. You've got to be tired of dealing with this stuff on your own."

He bowed his head at that, so I couldn't see him tear up.

"I'm Harry," I said, and held out my hand.

He eyed my hand and then me, huffing out half of a laugh. "Wizard Harry. You're kidding."

"Nope," I said. I looked at him and lifted a speculative eyebrow.

"Oh, uh. Austin," Austin the warlock said. He might have been thirteen and a half.

"Hi, Austin," I said, as gently as I could. "It's nice to meet you. Hey, have you ever seen the gorillas here?"


HI. MY NAME is Maggie Dresden.

My dad is okay, I guess, but I wish he were a little more up on his monsters. It's not his fault, I'm pretty sure, on account of he's a grown-up, and grown-ups can be awfully dumb about some things. Mainly the creeps.

Grown-ups are about as thick as you can be when it comes to the creeps.

Normally, you didn't see a lot of them out on a summer day, but today they were everywhere. An elderly couple who had been taken by baglers walked by. I don't know if that's their actual name. Me and Mouse kind of made up our own as we went. But there were shrouds over their heads, like a couple of dirty old paper bags that you could kind of see through if you looked hard enough. Baglers weren't really all that dangerous as creeps went. I had a theory about them, that they just fed on the brain energy of people who talked about politics too much, and made them want to talk about politics more, because that's just about all that came out of their mouths. You just watch: First chance they get, baglered people start talking politics.

You'd think even grown-ups could be interesting with some kind of psychic monster eating their faces all the time, but you'd be wrong. So there you go.

"So, you haven't been to the zoo before?" my dad asked.

My dad was a pretty scary-looking guy if you didn't know him. He was bigger than anyone else I'd ever seen, with scars and dark hair and muscles. I mean, kind of long, stretchy muscles, but you could tell he was strong. Plus, he was a wizard. I mean, most people don't believe in magic and monsters, which just shows you that most people are pretty dumb. For a grown-up, he didn't seem too stupid. And he kind of liked me. You could tell sometimes when he talked or looked at me.

I liked that a lot.

I waited until the baglered couple were far enough away so that they wouldn't overhear us, just on general principle, before I said, "Miss Molly tried to take me once, but there were too many people and too much sky, and I cried."

I waited to see what he would think about that. My dad fights bad people and monsters professionally. I didn't want him to think I was a big chicken.

I mean, we were just getting to know each other. But sometimes, things get really, really loud, or really hectic and fast moving, and I just can't deal with anything. It helped to have Mouse with me. Mouse always understood when things were getting too big, and tried to make me feel better.

My dad seemed to think about his words for a minute before he said, "That's okay, you know."

"Miss Molly said that, too," I said. With that same little pause before she said it. I really didn't want him to think I was crazy. I wasn't crazy. It was just that sometimes it was really, really hard to keep from screaming and crying. I slowed down a little so that I could stand in his shadow, where it was darker and cooler. Summer in Chicago is hot. "I was little then."

"That was probably it," he said. I liked his voice. It rumbled in his chest, and sounded really nice. When he read to me, it sounded like that voice could go on, steady, all night long. "But if you need to, we can leave whenever you like."

I looked up at him. Did he really mean that? Because today was looking brighter and louder and shinier every minute. My ears were already itching with all the noises around us, until I wanted to just jam my fingers into them and close my eyes and shut out everything.

But today was my first day together with my dad. We'd never done that. The Carpenters had been really, really nice to me and given me a home. I loved them. But they weren't my dad.

I'm sure he would take me somewhere else if I asked him. But I didn't want him to think I was some little baby who couldn't even go to the zoo.

Mouse, walking next to me like always, walked a couple of inches closer, reassuring me. Out of the corner of my eye, I saw his jaw drop open in an encouraging doggy smile, and his tail thwacked against my back when he wagged it.

My dad was pretty strong. Maybe I could be strong, too.

"I want to see the gorillas," I said. "So does Mouse."

Mouse wagged his tail even harder and smiled up at my dad.

He smiled at me. The smile really changed how he looked. It made him look more like a dad, I think. "Okay, then," he said. "Let's do that."

He said it the same way that you hear soldiers say, "Begin operations," in the movies, and his eyes flicked about, checking all around us and into the nearest trees overhead in maybe a second, as if hunting for a monster to blow up. I'm pretty sure he didn't even realize he was doing it.

My dad has fought bad things for a long time. He's seen bad things happen to people. Miss Molly says that that kind of thing leaves wounds, but that you can't see them. Sort of like how grown-ups can't see the creeps. But she said he carried them without complaining or letting it stop him from helping people. Even when it was really, really hard.

Sort of like being around me.

I try to be a nice person. But when things get too big, it's hard to do anything very well. Other kids mostly stay away from me. Even when I can make friends, sometimes, they don't really understand.

Maybe he wouldn't understand, either. He already had a hard job. Maybe being my dad would be too hard.

"Are you nervous?" I heard myself ask.

He blinked at me. "Why would I be nervous?"

He was looking at me like he really liked me. I couldn't keep looking at him when he was like that. What if he changed his mind?

Things can change. So fast.

"I don't know," I said. "I'm nervous. I haven't ever gone to the zoo with my dad before. What if I do it wrong?"

He walked along next to me for a second, and then I felt his fingers brush against my hair gently. "I'm pretty sure this isn't something you get right or wrong."

Which would make sense, if I didn't have to worry about turning into a complete spaz if things got too big and loud. "What if . . . I don't know. What if I set something on fire?"

"Maybe we'll roast some marshmallows," he said.

Which was the kind of goofy thing you'd expect a grown-up to say, but it was nice to hear him say it. "You're weird."

Mouse leaned against me with a little huff of a breath that he used when he thought something was funny. He was clearly pleased, though I thought he was a little distracted, too. Must be because Dad was here, and he really, really liked Dad. Dad saved him from a monster when he was a tiny puppy, and then Mouse grew up and helped Dad fight monsters, and then Dad gave him to me to be my protector.

Mouse was good at that. The creeps mostly didn't bother me—and the particularly old and nasty underhide that had moved into the space beneath my bed had found out the hard way that you don't mess around with Maggie and Mouse Dresden.

Dad was talking to me about how he had saved a gorilla once, and was leaning over me to pet Mouse when we all but walked right into an entire tribe of haunts.

These had taken a bunch of kids, and you could see it in their eyes—they were entirely black, no color, no whites, no nothing. Just these hollow, empty spaces that were full of the kind of nothing that wanted to suck you into it and watch you spin helplessly and scream. The kids walked around like well-behaved children from a boarding school—but I saw their eyes, suddenly fastening onto me, maybe a dozen sets of them. The eyes stared at me, and they had a horrible power. I suddenly remembered my last nightmare, not just the details of what happened, but the way it made me feel when I was having it, and my legs got weak.

Dad was paying attention to Mouse and vice versa, and neither of them saw the way that the haunts all stared at me for a good second as they went by. I felt each gaze and knew what was happening.

The haunts were marking me for prey.

Oh, great. This was all I needed.

I folded my arms against my stomach and took slow, deep breaths that were supposed to help me not spaz out as much. My dad couldn't see the haunts. He couldn't really interact with them. But they were able to hurt him, and he wouldn't even know what was happening.

I was pretty sure that it was probably a terrible idea to go into the zoo with a bunch of hungry, hunting creeps. Haunts could be dangerous if you didn't know how to handle them—which was bad enough, all by itself.

I glanced up at him for a second. He was watching me with that concerned look adults get before they carry me off to a dark, quiet room. All I had to do was say something, and he'd do it. I'd be safe and it would be quiet.

And then that would be the end of our first real day together.

*Stupid haunts. Stupid, creeping haunts.*

I wasn't going to let them and their stupid faces ruin this for my dad.

I would deal with them myself.

———

But first, I would see a bunch of superawesome animals. I mean, Mouse was cheating, which he does all the time. He's a Foo dog, and he has a bunch of weird powers. Most of his powers generally relate to telling monsters to back off, and then they do it, but having him around makes everything a little easier. When Mouse is there, there's always a seat in the restaurant when you're hungry, and you get the good waiter. TV commercials always have the good movie trailers mixed in them. Cartoons show funnier episodes. If you go to a game, the people around you are always really nice. It doesn't work at school, because Mouse won't cheat there, but everywhere else he just makes things happen a lot nicer than they otherwise would.

Nobody seemed to notice it but me, but that was okay. Mouse was the only one to notice when I needed a big furry hug sometimes.

Mouse was using his powers to make the zoo more awesome. The animals were all being super cool. The otters were running and playing, and the monkeys were swinging and making noises, and even the lion roared for us while we were there.

If it hadn't been for the haunts, it would have been perfect.

They were following me. I mean, they weren't obvious about it or anything, but their group had split up into pairs and there were always a couple of them within thirty or forty yards, keeping track of me and staring.

Always, always staring.

That was what haunts did. They followed you, sometimes for days and days, and they stared and their empty eyes made you relive the bad things from your life. If they did it long enough, you'd just wind up in a ball on the ground—and when you got up, you'd have big black eyes and the haunt would be telling you what to do from then on.

I thought about telling my dad about them, but . . . he may have been nice and a wizard, but he was also a grown-up. If you started talking to grown-ups about things they couldn't see, let's just say that you didn't get to go chase fireflies near dark very often.

Besides.

What if he thought I was, you know? Broken. What if he didn't want a daughter who was all funny in the head?

So I kept quiet and close to Mouse. The haunts didn't dare get very close as long as he was there. Mouse could sort of see the creeps, if they got close enough and weren't careful to be super quiet and low-key. Even though he's an adult, he's a grown-up dog, and that makes him a lot like a kid. So far, they'd kept their distance to avoid his notice, and as long as they stayed that far back, their Scare Bear Stare couldn't do much more than make me grumpy—and the awesome factor in the zoo was kind of countering that.

Maybe today would go smoothly after all.

And then my dad's head shot up like Mouse when he smells lighter fluid at the Carpenter's house, and his eyes flicked around him like a big, hungry bear looking for something to tear into.

"Um. Dad?" I asked

He looked down at me, and he did not look like a dad. He looked like the hero of a revenge movie—tense and alert and maybe even a little angry.

*Oh.*

*Oh, wow.* There must have been a monster or something for him to look like that. I didn't see anything, but it seemed like a good idea to get between Mouse and my dad before asking, "Is there something bad?"

He looked away from me and the little muscles in his jaw jumped a bunch of times. I wasn't sure if maybe I'd made him angry. I didn't think so. I didn't think I'd done anything that he could get mad about.

But I didn't always realize it when I did.

"Maybe," he said, finally. He looked at me, and his face got softer for a minute. "Maybe nothing. I don't know. I need to look around and see what's going on. I need to put you in a safe spot before I do that."

Sometimes safe spots were nice and safe, and sometimes they were a room with a locked door. Did he think I was about to have an attack or something? Or maybe he was just being careful.

Grown-ups are always being careful.

But how could I be sure which it was?

"It's important, isn't it?" I said.

My dad couldn't have understood what I was asking. "Maybe," he said. He nodded toward the café that served the zoo. "How about we go get a booth and order some food. You and Mouse sit, and I'll go look around and be back before the food gets there."

I needed a big furry hug, and Mouse was right there. I hugged him and thought. If he was going to stay here instead of taking me somewhere, then he probably didn't think he had to take care of me. *So, you know. That's good*, I thought.

But it would leave me on my own, with creeps all over the place.

Well. That was my problem. And I'd have Mouse with me. Mouse always helped.

I looked up at my dad and nodded. "Yeah. I guess that's okay."

"How about it, Mouse?" he asked. "Can you behave yourself around food?"

Mouse was staring out across the park, like he was trying to see something hidden from him. I'm sure he knew the creeps were around, though he left them alone if they left me alone. He made a noise in his chest that was part whine and part rumble.

"Trouble, boy?" my dad asked.

See, my dad is pretty smart. Most grown-ups try to tell you about how limited dogs are and how smart they aren't. Mouse has been going to school with me since I was little, and he reads better than I do. If he thought there might be trouble, only a dummy would ignore him, and my dad wasn't a dummy.

Mouse stayed staring for a minute, then exhaled slowly and looked up at my dad. His ears perked up and he wagged his tail.

My dad took that to mean that all was well. "All right," he said, and wagged his finger at Mouse. "Be good."

"Whuff," Mouse said.

"He's always good," I said, and kissed his ear. "We're gonna have to handle these haunts while he's gone, Mouse," I whispered. "Real smooth, okay? He worries enough."

Mouse made a sound that I could feel in his neck but couldn't hear. I hugged him a little tighter and then let go.

"Okay," my dad said. He got us seats in the restaurant, which were miraculously open—*Good boy, Mouse.* He bought me some French fries and handed me a twenty-dollar bill. "To pay for the food if you need more."

"Okay," I said. I was pretty hungry, and the fries smelled good.

"Don't leave until I come back for you. Okay?"

I nodded, and he strode out. He should have had his coat. It would have been all swirly, like Batman. Jeans and an old *Battlestar Galactica* T-shirt just didn't make the same impression.

I'd eaten maybe three French fries when the chair across from me scraped on the floor, and the haunt sat down across from me.

It looked like a girl, maybe a year older and a lot bigger than me. She had blond hair and a nice school uniform and her eyes looked like outer space.

"No one likes you," the haunt said. "They make people be your partner at school."

Mouse growled, and the saltshaker on the table rattled a little.

I tried to ignore what the haunt said. They all did this. They stared at you and read all your terrible memories like they were a cartoon strip. Then they talked to you about them.

"No one likes you," the haunt repeated. "You're weird. You're different."

I felt Mouse gathering himself, but I couldn't let him act. As far as everyone standing around us knew, it would look like an absolutely giant dog attacking a little girl when she hadn't done anything to provoke it. That would be bad. So I put my foot on his head and pushed down as hard as I could. It barely made him move, but I felt him relax. Mouse is a pretty good dog.

"You're losing your mind," the haunt said. "No one wants to be your friend. No one wants to play with you. No one even wants to say your name."

I put more salt on my fries. Quite a bit of it, actually. Some of it fell into my other hand.

"You should be alone. Then no one would have to put up with you," said the haunt.

I looked up into its empty eyes and said, "I know what you are. I'm going to give you this one chance to go away and bother someone else. After that, things will get ugly."

"Don't you think you should be somewhere safe?" the haunt asked in a calm voice. "Somewhere you can't hurt yourself when you have a f—"

I interrupted it by throwing salt into its black, empty eyes.

Creeps in general don't like salt. Don't ask me why. That's how it is.

The haunt flinched back so hard that it fell out of the chair. It didn't make any sound, but the body it was occupying twitched and jerked randomly, the muscles all tight. I felt bad about that, a little. It wasn't this other girl's fault that the creeps got her. She probably didn't even know why she was doing and saying the things she was.

"You should wash your eyes out," I advised the haunt. "Someplace else."

The creep stood up, tears streaming down its expressionless face. It stared at me for a moment, eyes all red around the black, then hurried into the café's ladies' room.

Mouse let out another growl and rose, pacing restlessly around my chair.

"Hey," I said. "Settle. It's okay. They're in the Book. I know how to handle them."

Mouse made an unhappy noise. He'd read the Book, too. Molly had started it, back before she'd become a grown-up and forgotten it all, and her little brothers and sisters had added to it. Harry Carpenter, who was kind of my big brother, had passed it on to me when the underhide had come into the house.

Mouse knew what I had to do as well as I did. He just didn't like it.

"Maybe they'll leave me alone now," I said. "Come on. We need mustard."

I got mustard, which is the best, for my fries. We started eating them, and Mouse settled down a little. He has a very practical attitude about worry—he doesn't, when there is good food with people you love.

My dad came back in a couple minutes later, looking . . . older. He didn't seem like he was angry anymore, just really, really tired. He tried to smile at me but it wasn't a real smile.

"What was it?" I asked him.

Behind my dad, the door to the bathroom opened. The girl haunt came out, her face dripping with water she hadn't dried off. She gave me a dirty look, and the power of it brought up a smell, something from my darkest dreams. Kind of rotten and metallic, and I suddenly felt my stomach do swirly loops even though I was standing still.

Then the haunt walked out and just stood there, facing away from me.

The others began to drift closer to her, in ones and twos, until they all stood silently together in a circle, facing one another. Nobody talked. Maybe haunts just think at each other or something.

I ignored them and looked up at my dad, who looked thoughtful. "A warlock," he said quietly after a moment. "A young wizard whose power is not in control. Dangerous."

Miss Molly had told me about warlocks. They were awful. "Did you fight it?"

"Him," my dad said. "No."

"Why not?"

"Because most of the time, they never meant to do anything bad," he said. He didn't talk to me in a kid voice, like some grown-ups did. They sound different when they talk to children. My dad sounded like he did when he talked to anyone else. "They don't even understand what's happening to them. No one has warned them what will happen if they break the rules."

"That's not fair," I said.

"No," he answered, and he made the word sound sad. "But that doesn't make them any less dangerous."

"Can't you help?"

"Sometimes," he said very quietly. "I'm not sure."

I shared a French fry with Mouse, thinking. My dad always helped warlocks if he could. Miss Molly had been a warlock and my dad had helped her. I figured he'd be running to help this one, but . . .

"But I'm here," I said.

"Yeah," he said. "And you're more important to me."

That made me feel warm all over, hearing him say that. "They just get powers?"

He nodded. "Born to it, yeah."

Just like my dad and Miss Molly. And maybe me, someday. Or that's what Miss Molly told me. "Am I going to get powers?"

"Maybe," he said. "There's no way to know for sure." He sounded honest, like a teacher talking about George Washington. I tried to imagine him teaching a class, only maybe wearing like a teacher outfit. In my head, it was kind of easy to see him doing it, really.

"Weird," I said. I passed a fry to Mouse, who snapped it up, and got the next one. "If I do, will you teach me stuff? So no one gets hurt?"

"If you want me to," he said.

Which wasn't the same thing as if he said that he wanted to teach me. But he probably just meant that he wouldn't if I didn't want to learn. Like that would happen. Only maybe it could happen. That thought made my tummy flip and turn some more. "If . . . something happens to you, who is going to teach me?"

"Nothing's going to happen to me," he said.

"It could," I told him quietly. Because it could. His work was dangerous. "And maybe there wouldn't be anyone. Maybe I'd be a warlock."

He looked at me and took a deep breath. He was wondering about whether he should tell me the kid-safe version of the truth. "Maybe," he said, finally.

"That could be me." In the corner of my eye, I watched the circle of haunts regard one another, then turn as one to stare at me. Ugh. It just felt icky.

This warlock boy needed help. And I needed to deal with the haunts before they hurt me again, or maybe hurt someone else, like my dad. That was the right thing. Even though it would be really scary.

It's what my dad would do. I think. I mean, we'd just met, really.

"I can eat more French fries," I told him. "Mouse will keep me company."

He blinked at me as if surprised. "You sure?" he asked. "It could . . . cut today kind of short."

"If someone needs your help, you help them," I said. "Even when it's really hard. Miss Molly told me that about you."

Because what if Miss Molly had told me the kid-safe version of the truth about my dad? What if he wasn't as good as she said he was? What if he didn't want to take care of a daughter who had issues? Who was really hard to be around?

But he looked at me and then he smiled, and I suddenly felt warm inside, like I'd had all the hot French fries in the world.

"Yeah," he said, winking at me and rapping a fist cheerfully on the table. "Yeah. That's right."

MY DAD LEFT, and I told Mouse, "You know I have to do it like this. You can't come all the way."

He made a soft, distressed sound, and kissed my face with his big, sloppy tongue.

"Yick," I said, and rubbed my face in his fur. "I love you, too, Mouse."

He made a rumbling sound in his chest and sighed. He felt tense, his weight shifting, as though he was eager to go somewhere and do something. He wanted to help, but he couldn't.

I got up from the table and walked out of the café and straight up to the waiting haunts. I addressed the girl directly. "Hey, you. Space Face."

The haunts all stared at me with their empty eyes, and for a second it was like there were shadows writhing everywhere, people in pain. I ignored those images because otherwise I would have gotten really scared. Instead, I made eye contact with every haunt and then said, "You guys are the worst. Let's get this over with."

And I turned and started walking, Mouse at my side.

There was a confused moment of silence, and then the haunts started following me.

The Book is pretty specific about haunts. They feed on fear. That's why they dig up all the scary things from your past. It's like their mustard. They want you to marinate in fear, and then, when you're soaked and dripping in it, they move in and start eating you like some kind of gross bug. All the kids these haunts had taken? The invaders would eat them up from the inside, taking bites out of their minds, keeping them focused on fear. When they ate their fill, they would start looking for someone else to move into. The kid would wake up, like from a bad dream, but the Book said that the kids the haunts had gotten wouldn't ever be right again.

There were a dozen black-eyed kids walking along behind me. I wondered what it would be like to get chewed on by a dozen haunts at once.

Probably really scary. Like a nightmare you couldn't wake up from.

Anyway, the Book says that there's only one way to deal with fear, and only one way to deal with creatures who thrive on it.

You face them.

You go, alone, to the darkest and scariest place around, and you face them. It has to be alone, nothing but you and yourself facing the fear. It has to be scary, because you have to face the fear on its own ground.

Otherwise, the haunts just . . . follow you. Endlessly. Nibbling at you until you just collapse on the ground making *bibbly* noises.

Mouse walked alongside me, his head turned to face the haunts, the mane around his neck and shoulders bristling. He didn't growl, and his body language had changed to something grim and very serious.

It's never really hard to find a scary place; they're everywhere—it's just that grown-ups don't pay much attention to them. I found one right there in the zoo, and I had to go through only two gates marked EMPLOYEES ONLY to get there. By sheer coincidence, they'd been left unlocked.

*Good boy, Mouse.*

So it took me only a couple of minutes to walk down a utility staircase into the basement of the big cat exhibit, and from there to open the door to an old, old, old staircase made of stone and slick with water that went into the building's unlit subbasement.

At the top of the stairs, I turned to Mouse and said, "Don't be afraid. I got this."

I was kind of lying. Maybe I didn't have it. Maybe the Book was wrong. Maybe I'd have an attack. Maybe the haunts would just beat me up. There were enough of them.

Mouse seemed to sense my uncertainty. His expression shifted and he whirled to face the haunts following me, baring his teeth and letting out the kind of rumble you hear only from really old cars and maybe tractors.

The haunts drew up short. Their leader, the girl with the tear-streaked face, faced him and sneered.

"Guardian," she said. "You know the Law. We are within our rights."

Mouse growled lower and took slow steps forward, until he stood before the haunt, almost eye to eye. His fur did that thing where light comes from it, silvery blue sparkles that glitter across the very tips of the hairs.

If the haunt was impressed, it didn't show it. "I know the Law. As should you." It pointed a finger past him, at me. "That is my prey. Stand aside."

I really needed Mouse not to get involved. If he did, I couldn't break the haunt's empty-eyed pursuit.

"It's okay, boy," I said. "I got this."

Mouse looked at me, falling silent. Then he bowed his head down low to the ground for me. He prowled past the haunts—bumping a couple of them with his massive shoulders, enough to make them stagger—to the entrance we'd just come in, and settled down with an attitude of patience.

All the eyes turned toward me.

I took a deep breath and got my phone out of my pocket. I had it powered down, because I'd been hanging out with my dad, and wizards kill phones just by looking at them funny if they've got any electricity actually moving through them. Powered down, the phones seem to be okay. I turned it on, waited for the dumb little apple screen to go away, and then flipped on the light.

Then I walked down the stairs into the black, and the haunts came with me.

I got to a room at the bottom of the staircase. It was a big, open concrete space with a lot of dusty old machines. It smelled musty down there. It smelled awful. Shadows stretched everywhere, threatening. My light glittered off small eyes, close to the ground, outside of the actual area it lit. Rats, maybe.

The light was shaking a little. I was afraid.

That wasn't a good sign. If I was afraid and they hadn't even started on me, maybe I'd break. Maybe I'd just fall down and cry. Maybe they'd get me. Maybe I'd walk back up into the zoo with my eyes all black and my dad wouldn't even be able to see it. I'd just start freaking out and everyone would just think, you know, that I had gotten worse. And they'd have to put me someplace safe.

I shivered.

Then I turned around and faced the lead haunt.

Tear Streaks stood, like, six inches behind me. As I watched, her mouth twitched into this bow of bared teeth that resembled a smile about as much as Sue the Dinosaur's teeth at the museum. Her eyes gaped black, like a skull's sockets.

The other haunts slowly walked around us, until they stood all around me in a circle, close enough to reach out and touch me. Their eyes got darker, got absolutely huge, and then . . .

And then—

—I was standing in the kitchen of a house I recognized without remembering.

TV was on. It was *Sesame Street*, but the language was Spanish, which I'd been brought up speaking. I still spoke it, though it took me time to make my brain understand it, like shifting gears on a bicycle. Elmo was talking about letters.

I looked up and saw a very kind lady with dark hair whose name I couldn't remember. I'd been very little when I had lived with her. She was humming to herself and making cookies or something, and she paused to smile at me and tell me that I was a good girl.

Her husband came in, speaking in a tense voice. She dropped her spoon and then hurriedly set her mixing bowl aside and picked me up.

That was when the vampires came in. Shapes, not quite human, in black cloaks and coats and wrappings. They let out inhuman shrieks, bounding through the air, and I heard a gun go off just before the kind lady's husband screamed, and the air went all thick with the smell of metal, and the kind lady screamed and pressed me against her.

"I know," I said out loud in a firm voice. "The Red Court came for me. They killed the foster family who was taking care of me. It was awful."

The kitchen vanished abruptly, and I was standing, half-bent over with my hands on my knees, breathing hard. The light from my phone showed me a lot of patent leather shoes.

I looked up, angry, and said, "I didn't get hurt that day. Other people did. You'll have to do better than that."

Tear Streaks stared at me for a long moment and then said, "You're going to lose this family, too. You always lose them."

I started breathing harder. All my thoughts started going so fast that I couldn't steer them.

*Oh no.*

*Oh no, no.* I was having an attack.

Tear Streaks stepped closer to me, something eager in the way her body curled toward me a little. "Your father means well. But he's going to die. You've seen his scars. One day, he'll get unlucky or he'll be wrong, and he'll die. You'll be alone."

My chest was clenching up. I couldn't breathe. I heard myself making those stupid little-kid noises, and my eyes blurred over with tears. My heart felt like someone was hitting it with a hammer, *wham, wham, wham.*

"The Carpenters could die just like your first family. Horribly. Screaming. Because of you."

"Stop," I tried to say. I just heard sounds like, "Guk, guk, guk."

The haunt leaned closer. I felt other kids putting their hands on my shoulders, fingers rigid and just wrong.

"Your mother died because of you," the haunt said in that same tone. "Your father is going to die because of you."

I had fallen to my knees. Tear Streaks came with me.

"You selfish little monster," she said. "All those good people, dead because of you. You should just throw yourself into a hole. It would be better for them."

In the dark and cold, when you're tired and scared and can't talk or breathe, with creeps all around you, words like that sound true. And if that was true, then there was no reason not to agree with them. There was no reason not to just lie down and let the monsters have me. For a second, I wanted it. I wanted to just lie down and stop. The words seemed right.

They really did. They sounded true. They felt true.

But feeling true isn't the same as being true.

In fact, feelings don't have very much to do with the truth at all.

Monsters had killed my foster family. That was true.

My mother died on the mission to save me. That was true.

But all those people were dead because monsters had come and killed them. And that was the only reason.

Monsters a lot worse than the ones who now surrounded me. Grown-up monsters. Monsters I had survived.

I made myself breathe as the others started to talk. They all said horrible things to me.

And then it hit me: The Book was right.

A dozen of these creatures, and they had dared to select the smallest kid with the scariest things in her past that they could find. They hadn't tried to jump my dad or even a vanilla grown-up. They hadn't tried to eat Mouse. They'd come after the littlest, most vulnerable person around.

Because they were afraid.

And if they were afraid, then maybe that meant they couldn't be the scary ones.

"You know what I think?" I said suddenly and in a very clear voice.

The haunts fell into a shocked silence as I looked up at Tear Streaks. Her black eyes stared at mine, her mouth open, frozen in the middle of a sentence.

I narrowed my eyes at her. "I think maybe right now, I'm the scary one."

And then I turned off my phone so we were all in perfect darkness—and I threw back my head and laughed at them.

I haven't ever felt a laugh like that. It wasn't exactly a bubbly laugh, but there was a ferocious, lionlike, sunlit joy beneath it. It wasn't an angry sound, but it told them that I wasn't impressed with their black eyes and their bad dreams. I didn't try to be very loud, but the sound of it rang from the black stone walls, as true and clear as a bell.

And the haunts screamed.

Their screams didn't sound like pain exactly. They were each on one note, an absolutely pure tone that didn't waver around. None of them were notes that went with the others—it was just this horrible mash of sound, like a steam whistle on the cartoons, but without any of the happy, harmonious overtones a steam whistle carried. It sounded like when Molly or Harry walked into the room while the TV was on—sort of a shrieking, monotonous feedback.

And then, all at once, they went silent—and the only sound left was me giggling.

"Heh, heh, heh," I heard myself say. "Ahhhhh. Stupid creeps."

I turned my light back on. The kids were all lying on the floor, dazed. They were my age, more or less, and they started to sit up one at a time. Their eyes weren't black anymore. They were just eyes.

The haunts were gone.

It was just us kids.

"What happened?" asked a boy.

"Ow," Tear Streaks said, and started sniffling. "My eyes."

"Um," I said. I kept shining my light in everyone's eyes so that they wouldn't get a very good look at my face, and decided that it was probably simpler to go with the kid-safe version of events. "Gas leak. Come on. We should get out of here. It's very dangerous to stay."

It took a little cajoling, but I got everyone back out of the building and into the daylight. They all seemed very confused. Mouse was waiting right where I'd left him, and he walked very carefully next to me, each movement slow and deliberate, so that he didn't knock over any of the confused kids.

One of the boys was smart enough to go straight to a security guard and ask for help, and Mouse and I went the other way. I found myself smiling. I might have skipped a little.

Beating the monsters is kinda fun. I mean, it's awful when it's happening, but after it's over, it's better than video games.

Maybe that's crazy to feel that way. I guess I get it from my dad.

Mouse and I got back to the café, and I bought us victory fries. Mouse collapsed flat onto his tummy under the table in pure relief that I was all right, but that was okay. I leaned down a little extra to make sure he got his fries.

My dad came back about five minutes later, walking with a kid a few years bigger than me. He smiled at me, and I smiled back at him.

"Hey there, punkin," my dad said. "This is Austin. He hasn't ever seen the gorillas here, either. How about we get some food for everyone and then we'll go over there?"

"Okay, Dad," I said.

He blinked at that, and then he smiled so hard I thought he might break his face.

"Whuff," Mouse said, and wagged his tail.

MY NAME IS Mouse and I am a Good Dog. Everyone says so.

There are many wonderful people in my life, but the most important ones are My Friend Harry Dresden and his daughter, Maggie. I love them, and I love being with them, and I love going to the zoo.

I had never been to the zoo, but from what My Friend said, I just knew I was going to love it.

My Friend and Maggie both smelled very nervous, though they were trying not to show it. My Friend was worried he could not be a good father to a little girl, which was ridiculous—but if he wasn't worried about it, he wouldn't be the person he is. She was upset, too, but for different reasons. She was worried that she would have an Anxiety attack, and that then I would have to help her, and that her father would think she was weak and broken and not want to be her father. That, too, was ridiculous, but her life has not been an easy one.

They are both good people, and both often misunderstood by their fellow humans.

You humans have the potential to be the most wonderful beings there are—if you can get past all these enormous stupid spots you seem to have in your hearts. It's not your fault. You just don't know how to work your hearts right yet.

That's why there are dogs.

I think it's nice to know your purpose.

We rode in My Friend's car down to the zoo in the park. I used to get confused when we went to the park, but then I realized that humans had made many parks inside their city, not just one. I love parks. And they are one of the many reasons humans are good.

I walked carefully next to Maggie, and she held on to my mane or to the handle on my support-dog vest. Maggie says my vest is red. I don't know what that means, but it is her favorite, and that makes me happy. I was careful to wag my tail a little and smile as I walked. Humans are little and can be frightened very easily, so it is very important to show them that you want to be friends.

At least, until it is time to not be friends.

My Friend and Maggie walked together, talking. They were saying all kinds of words, but what they were really saying, over and over, was "I hope you like me." That was silly, to think that they would not love each other—but sometimes humans are slow to figure things out, because they are heart-stupid.

You are, too. That's okay. Just get a dog. Dogs can teach you all kinds of things about your heart.

I felt Maggie suddenly grow tense, and paused to look at her, one paw in the air. Her expression was intent and serious, and I knew there was one of those creatures she called creeps nearby. Creeps were serious business, a threat to children; adult humans could not seem to sense them at all. Even I could barely tell when one was nearby. I had to get close enough to jump on one to sense it properly, and even then I only saw shadows and smelled cold and hunger.

It was not my place to fight them. I knew that from my nose all the way in my tail, the same way I knew how to use the power that had been given me. It was my duty to defend and protect the home, and these creatures were meant to be a training ground for the young. Humans forgot them as they aged, but the lessons taught by facing such predators lasted for life. It was not my place to interfere in Maggie's learning.

Unless they came in the house, of course. That was simply unreasonable.

Two humans speaking angrily to each other smelled like old tobacco and mildew, and their voices hurt my ears a little. They were discussing the role of the United States in combating poverty, illiteracy, and terror in Central Africa, and were quite upset about it. They must have been baglered. They were no threat to anything but pleasant conversation.

But the group of a dozen schoolchildren who smelled like sick ferrets and had black shadows under their eyes were a different matter. They were being possessed by more creeps, haunts, by the smell of it, and could be a severe threat to Maggie's well-being. Not physically—

physically, they were only more children, and if the creeps chose to take their battle to the physical arena, the same law that bound my power would allow me to intervene. The true threat they represented was intangible and serious.

Maggie had not pointed them out to me. Perhaps she wished to ignore their presence on such an important day. That was a reasonable attitude. But slink-thief predators like haunts were not often reasonable. They marked her and began tracking her as we moved.

That could be a problem.

But . . . something was wrong. I knew it in my tail.

I focused my senses, trying to locate the threat that only my instincts insisted was near, but I could smell nothing. Human racket was drowning out the subtle sounds, as per usual in the city. There were scores of people walking through the park, and I could track no movement.

But there shouldn't have been so many creeps here, walking about in plain daylight. I had been expending energy for two days to help make this day smoother for My Friend and his little girl. Their first day together was important, and I had worked hard to make sure no malicious energy would interfere with it.

Perhaps simple ill fortune was at play, and things might otherwise have been much worse.

Or perhaps there was a force working against me.

My Friend leaned down to ruffle my ears and tell me how much he loved me, and my heart surged happily at the gesture.

Well. If something wanted to interfere with My Friend and Maggie's happiness, it would have to get past me.

That thought normally made me wag my tail.

But today, it sent a slow, cold chill up my spine.


"Hey," I said to the otters. (We were seeing the otters.) "Hi, guys!"

"Hi!" burbled an otter.

"Hi, hi!" said another.

"I'm tired," said a third, yawning.

The humans around us didn't notice the conversation, of course. Humans think you need your mouth to talk.

I wagged my tail at the otters so they would know I was friendly. "I'm Mouse, and this is the best little girl in the world. Could you guys please show off for her? She's never seen an otter before."

"Show off?" asked the first otter. "What's that?"

"Go play!" I said.

"Play!" shouted the first otter, and jumped on the third otter's head.

"Eeeep!" the third otter shouted. The first otter bounded off, and the other otters followed, into the water, out again, around and around a tree trunk, and then back into the water.

"Look, look!" Maggie said, tugging on My Friend's coat. "Hey, look!"

The otters ran behind some rocks, but before Maggie could even ask, My Friend had scooped her up and lifted her high so that she could follow the action. Maggie let out a rolling, bubbling giggle, fascinated, and the warmth between them sang of love and light.

I wagged my tail so hard that I had trouble standing up.

I spoke to the sun bear, who was sort of grumpy but who didn't mind tearing a section of log apart to show Maggie how strong sun bears were. The lionesses only rolled their eyes when I tried to talk them into a pouncing demonstration, but the lion was pleased to roar. The monkeys were as happy to play as the otters, and I didn't even have to ask the peacocks to show off their pretty feathers.

All in all, I did a good job, I thought.

*Good boy, Mouse.*

And then magic, dark and ugly, rippled through the air.

And under it was . . . energy. My kind of energy, but dark and hard and terrible, full of cold, merciless clarity.

I caught a scent: the far-off scent of something I could barely remember. It made me think of mountains and burning oil lamps and cold, bright sky.

My Friend had reacted to the black magic in the air. He was scanning the park, tense, the happy energy around him suddenly replaced with watchfulness and an unconsciously projected aura of confidence and power. My Friend is not to be taken lightly. He is not heart-stupid at all when it comes to defending those weaker than he is. He sensed a threat, a dark practitioner, and he was ready to confront it.

I had a dark feeling roll through me and make the soft spot of my throat itch. A magical threat, here today? My nose told me that the pack of haunt-ridden children was still trailing us, even if they were keeping a distance.

What were the odds of a threat unique to each of my family appearing? Especially when I'd been working energy to avoid this exact outcome?

Something was out there.

I felt the hairs on my spine try to rise. But my red support-dog vest hid them.

My Friend knew he had to assess the threat he sensed, and that was proper. But he was worried to leave Maggie alone. He trusted me, but no safety measures could ever be thorough enough for him to feel completely sure she would be all right. He was right. Nothing is truly safe in this world—and that being the case, why worry about threats that have not yet appeared? Far wiser to make what preparations one could, face trouble as it arose, and be happy in the meantime.

That might be the saddest part of human heart-stupidity: how much happiness you simply leave aside so that you have enough time to worry. I know sometimes I'm not very smart, but I don't see what's so interesting about worry.

My Friend spoke to me. He used many words, but what his heart said was, "I don't want to leave her even for a single second, but I trust you to protect my daughter while I am fighting evil."

I told him I would. He's learned enough to know how to hear me when I say that much. Then he took us to a place with food smells and got Maggie and me French fries to eat while he scouted out the threat.

Is My Friend awesome or what?

He got Maggie settled and then strode out, moving with purpose. I had to resist the urge to follow him, because when he did that it made me want to go with him and help. Instead, I sat by the French fries and watched them intently. You know. In case any villains were hiding inside and might be a threat to Maggie.

We'd only gotten to eat a few when one of the haunts simply walked up to our table and began to say mean things to Maggie.

No.

When one of the haunts was pushed to our table to confront Maggie.

This time, I sensed a change in the air. Someone was working energy against us.

Outside, partially concealed in some greenery, was a hulking, furry shape that looked like my shadow. I could sense that dark clarity flowing from it in a torrent, strong enough to push the creep toward Maggie, urging the creature to attack.

I felt myself begin to surge to my feet, a growl bubbling in my throat.

But Maggie put her foot on my head and pushed down.

Maggie was tiny, even for a human, even for one her age. She was a surprisingly tough-minded child, but she could not have stopped me from rising and running even if she'd been her father's size.

My Shadow faced me calmly, something arrogant and mocking in its stance, in the angle of its head. It was crouched like a hunter, ready to leap.

And it was trying to hurt my little girl.

But I couldn't leave her side. What if it pushed the haunt to break the rules and physically attack her and I wasn't close enough to intervene?

So I didn't advance on the threat. I stopped using my breath to growl and instead focused it into working energy, reaching out for light and softness to counter the black ice of My Shadow's malice.

The dark energy pushing the haunt rolled back from mine like fog before an oncoming car, and just then, Maggie threw a handful of salt into the haunt's face.

The haunt recoiled from the salt, more than from the pain the body it possessed suddenly experienced, and I directed energy toward it, urging it to back away. If the haunt left Maggie, I could deal with My Shadow directly and make it depart. I'd gotten its scent now, the smell of its hostile intent. I could follow it into, through, and out of every shadowy realm to which it could possibly flee.

The haunt retreated before Maggie's defiance and my breath, and I began to move, to eliminate the true threat before it could make another attempt on Maggie.

But the scent was . . . gone.

I sniffed again, harder. That wasn't right. I knew it in my tail.

But it was gone.

Impossibly, simply, gone.

*Huh.*

What in all the wide universe could do that?

My Shadow, it would seem.

When My Friend came back, he was tense, troubled, and quiet. That made me uneasy. I have seen him face many terrible things, and they rarely troubled his heart like that. A human, then. Monsters were not nearly the threat to him that other human beings had proved to be. He was in pain.

I would have gone to him, but my duty was to guard and protect Maggie, and she still was not safe—not with the haunts and My Shadow running around the zoo as if it was their own personal hunting preserve, and not with her Anxiety waiting to undo her if she didn't have me beside her. He was her father. His primary concern was to protect and nurture her, and I would help My Friend with anything. So I stayed by Maggie's side.

Also, she had French fries.

They spoke together some more. He told Maggie about warlocks and the dangers they posed. Maggie felt sad for the warlock, which I knew My Friend was feeling, too. But Maggie feared more than that— that he would not want to be her father. And he was afraid that she wouldn't want to be his daughter if he always had work to do.

I sat very still and breathed bright energy all around them. Their fears were foolish, but dangerous, this early in their relationship. If only so many things had not come up at once, and today of all day—

*Ah.*

That made more sense.

These encounters were not the result of chance, but malice.

My Shadow was attempting to disrupt the course of what should naturally be taking place—bonding between a father and his daughter.

I lay quietly, staying focused on working energy. It would not do to dwell on violent thoughts during that process. But while I did what I could for my family, I also pressed my teeth together, to be sure they were ready.

They were.

My Friend set out to save the warlock, of course. He had no idea that haunts even existed, much less that they were nearby. I would have preferred to go with him—warlocks were dangerous propositions, and I could have sized up the person for him, helped him understand whether compassion or resolution was the most important virtue to hold while facing the warlock. I could have warned him, protected him.

But only by leaving Maggie vulnerable to the circle of hungry haunts waiting outside the cafe.

Maggie waited for My Friend to stride out of sight before she stood up and turned to me. "You know I have to do it like this. You can't come all the way."

I had read the Book as much as she had. I knew the course it recommended to confront haunts, and its reasoning was eminently sound. Evil left unconfronted only grows stronger. But to do that, she would have to face them alone—entirely alone. I would not be able to defend her from the haunts and their terrible thoughts. She would have to face them, and while the proper course was always to confront evil, victory over it was never assured.

This was her path. She had to walk it on her own. But . . .

She could be hurt. Perhaps even destroyed.

My perfect Maggie, the best little girl in the world, could be lost to those who loved her.

I made a soft, distressed sound and kissed her face gently.

"Yick," she said, but she meant something else. She rubbed her little face in my fur. "I love you, too, Mouse."

My heart pounded hard as the simple, frail, devastating power of that love flowed into me.

I tried once again to tell her that I loved her in human speech, and again only made some random sounds. I sighed. She knew.

We walked out of the café together and straight up to the waiting haunts. Maggie had already intuited which was the leader of their pack, and she faced the little girl with her back straight and her eyes bright. "Hey, you. Space Face."

The haunts all stared at her with their empty eyes and felt the sudden surge of malicious power in the air as they drew up horrible memories from her time among the vicious, violent, and satisfactorily dead Red Court of vampires.

There were memories within her that could kill her, memories she didn't even know she had.

They came out only when she was sleeping.

I saw her begin to struggle with the images and then brush them aside in an act of will startling in its intensity. She clenched her jaw and turned in a slow circle. She was a head shorter than every other haunt-taken child there, but she made full eye contact with each and every one of them before speaking in a clear, calm voice. "You guys are the worst. Let's get this over with."

We turned together and headed for the nearest place of darkness and fear, and the haunts followed us.

On the way, my instincts warned me again. My Shadow was near.

Whatever this creature was, it was a master of remaining unscented and unseen. It would, I presumed, rely heavily on its abilities and be accustomed to being undetected by its prey. It had struck me as arrogant before, as poor a look as I had gotten. I decided to trust that instinct as well. So instead of going on guard, I only walked beside Maggie, as if I were entirely unaware of the threat.

Together we walked into a building that smelled of stale old predator scents, and inside found stairs that went down into darkness and fear sufficient to encourage the haunts to come out of their protective human shells and be destroyed.

If she could. They would do everything in their power to tear her heart into pieces and leave her vulnerable on the ground, meat to be taken.

At the top of the stairs, Maggie turned to me and said, "Don't be afraid. I got this."

My Maggie is clever and quick and brave, but she was also lying. She didn't know if she could do it.

But, then, if she had been certain, it wouldn't be an appropriate challenge for her.

Then I caught it again—the scent of black ice, the vibration of violent energy, rolling forward like mist around the haunts behind us. I could hear the dark whisper of thought behind that energy as well, enveloping the haunts like fog.

*Kill the child.*

I saw the haunts at the rear of the group, nearest the source of dark energy, begin to clench their fists and reach into their pockets for objects with which to hurt and tear.

Sudden rage filled me. My Shadow was a creature of evil the likes of which I had seldom faced. It was trying to get the haunts to violate natural Law, to physically attack a little girl. Certainly, if they did, I could intervene—but only by hurting innocent children who had committed no sin but to be unprepared to face spiritual threats they had likely never imagined.

My deepest growl rumbled from my chest and into the air with my breath, beginning the work of disrupting that dark energy and serving as a warning to the haunts at the same time.

The weight of small human bodies had begun to shift, but they settled back again at the sound of my growl. For a moment, I thought that they might break and leave Maggie in peace—but then their leader, the girl with the tear-streaked face, turned to me and sneered.

"Guardian," she said. "You know the Law. We are within our rights."

I growled lower. I needed to be closer to them to protect them from the influence of My Shadow. I took slow steps forward, growling out more of my breath, until I stood before the haunt, almost eye to eye. I was working energy in earnest now. Excess power skipped along the tips of my hairs in a glow of blue starlight, and the dark energy once more recoiled before light.

The haunt hadn't even realized what was happening. It thought I was trying to threaten it. "I know the Law. As should you," it said. It pointed the child's finger past me, at Maggie. "That is my prey. Stand aside."

I could send these creatures fleeing with a roar, but that would only scatter them. It wouldn't stop them from continuing their pursuit later.

"It's okay, boy," Maggie said. "I got this."

I looked at her, falling silent.

This child was about to walk into the darkness with a dozen predators, knowing full well the danger she faced—and knowing equally well that there was no promise that she would emerge victorious. Her heart was pounding, her eyes a little wide, but she stood with her feet planted and her expression set in stubborn calm.

Maggie was not heart-stupid at all when it came to courage. She had chosen to forge her own destiny in this meeting.

So be it.

I bowed my head down low to the ground in respect. I could, at least, be sure that nothing else disturbed her during her confrontation. I moved past the haunts, brushing excess energy gathered in my fur against several of the taken children who were still touched by darkness, wiping it away. I got to the doorway My Shadow must use if he wished to interfere, and settled down by it to wait.

Maggie stared at me for a moment more. Then she took her phone from her pocket and, without looking back, descended into the darkness.

The haunt-ridden children followed her down. The last shut the door behind them.

"You might as well come out," I said.

There was a moment of silence, and then in the darkness of the stairwell above me, something stirred and appeared at the landing.

My Shadow.

I huffed out an energetic breath, and it was like wind blowing away fog. The shadows and darkness lifted, and standing a single long leap from me was . . .

Me.

He was a celestial hound, just like I was, though his fur was streaked with broad bands of nearly black coloring. His mane, especially, was vast and dark, and it made him look threatening. He was leaner than I was, with more sharply defined muscle, and scars that showed through the fur in streaks of fine white. He showed every mark of having lived a difficult life.

"Brother," My Shadow growled.

I inhaled, and the scent of him filled my nose and brought out brilliant, simple images from when I had been small enough to fit in My Friend's pocket. Taken by figures in dark robes, male and female, from the monks of the monastery. They'd swept all of us, my brothers and sisters, away to a place of dark power, and surrounded us with cold stone, black enchantment, and watchful demons.

Until My Friend had come. He slipped in when the dark robes were briefly away. He fought the demons, and saved me and my brothers and sisters.

But he hadn't saved all of us.

The figures who had taken us had only left the others unguarded in order to take my siblings, the largest male and female, away. I had never scented my brother or my sister again.

Until now.

I tilted my head at My Shadow and then bowed it slightly and politely. "I hardly recognized you."

"We were puppies," he said.

"We grew up."

"I grew," he said. "You . . ." He lifted his lips from his fangs in a sign of contempt. "You merely ate."

"I like food," I said.

"You're fat."

"And very happy," I said. "Are you happy?"

He flashed his fangs again. "What does that question even mean?"

"Oh! I like philosophy as well," I told him. "Is that why you're here? To talk about the meaning of life?"

"I am here," he said, "to shape things to my will."

I growled at him, but gently. "Brother," I said, "that is not our purpose in this world."

"That is not the purpose we were given," he snarled. "What we were designed to do. We were made to be slaves."

"We were made to be dogs," I said, as gently as I could. "To love. To show others how to love. To be guardians. To be examples."

"You speak, but your words have no meaning," My Shadow said. "You're soft. But you at least chose your own path, rather than bowing to the will of our masters."

"Master Wong was very kind, I thought," I said.

"He was a fool," My Shadow said. "You stand across my path, brother. I cannot have that. Step aside, or I will kill you."

I felt my tail swish briefly across the floor and I yawned at him. "I believe I will make my voice heard before that matter is decided."

My Shadow bared his fangs and advanced a step, growling out a darkness that frothed and bubbled from his chops like black foam. "Hear me. Because you are my blood, I will give you one more chance. Leave these feeble mortals and come with me. There is great work that needs must be done. Your power could make the task much simpler."

"Needs must be done?" I asked. "Who talks like that? Honestly."

"Do not mock me," My Shadow snarled.

"An acquired habit. I can't imagine where I learned it," I replied. I rose slowly to my feet. "I meant only to be amusing. No disrespect was intended. I apologize for the confusion."

My Shadow glared at me, as if he could not quite decide how to reply.

I think perhaps that no one had ever apologized to him for anything before.

"Now hear me, brother," I said gently. "Cease your attempts to harm my humans. Depart this city. Do not come back."

"Or else?" he asked.

"There is nothing else," I replied calmly. "You will do these things. The only question is whether you will do them of your own will or if I must teach you how."

My Shadow considered that in stillness for a few heartbeats, staring. There was something rather unnerving about that. I suddenly remembered how I had never outwrestled my brother when we were small.

Of course, I was no longer small.

I steadied my breath, gathering power, muscles growing tenser.

Just then, there was a thump of magical energies colliding somewhere nearby. A fraction of a second later, there was a second thump, and instantly after a third, coming so fast and so close together that a human might only have sensed a single instance of colliding energy.

"I've been working energy on that warlock for days, brother," My Shadow said, his voice filled with satisfaction. "The demons attracted to his aura aren't particularly impressive. But, as it happens, the ground where your master is standing is precisely the wrong sort to allow him to manage them all. Fortune does not favor him this day."

I came to my feet, snarling, tongue lashing out between my teeth as I spoke to him. "What have you to do with My Friend?"

"Please," My Shadow said, contempt thick in his voice. "You are like the others, after all. His slave. I don't deal in such trivial matters. I care nothing for your broken wizard."

I narrowed my eyes. "The child."

"I find her future interesting," My Shadow said. "As do my associates."

"I won't let you hurt them."

"You cannot stop me," My Shadow said. "Choose, slave. Lose the wizard or lose the girl."

I tilted my head to one side and said, "I assume you never saw *The Dark Knight*."

That gave him pause. He tilted his head and said, "What?"

I lowered my head and let the growl billow up out of my chest. "You don't want to destroy one of them. You want both. You want me to run after one instead of doing what needs to be done."

"And what is that?" My Shadow asked, sneering.

I roared, breath and energy filling me, and shot forward and up the stairs toward him, the darkness of the hallway suddenly full of azure starlight.

My Shadow was not the sort to drop his guard, but he genuinely hadn't expected the fight to begin when it did. Which is not exactly the most honest way to approach a conflict. But, then, I was raised by a wizard. When it comes to fighting, I tend to cheat wherever possible.

I struck My Shadow's shoulder with my own. He was too quick to be overborne, but he slammed into the concrete wall behind him, sending a web of fine cracks out from the point of impact. The blow stunned him for part of a second, and I sank my fangs into the ruff of his mane. He twisted, and I didn't get hold of his throat—just fur and loose skin. But that was enough to let me clamp down and fling him into the door leading outside.

My Shadow hit the ground rolling, emerging into a sunken stairwell that led up to the ground level of the zoo. I flung myself at him again, but he slipped beneath me, and I slammed into the concrete of the stairwell wall. His claws raked my chest and belly and drew blood as he scrambled away and bounded up, hitting the vertical wall of the building once and then flinging himself out of the sunken stairwell entirely, his paws leaving traces of dark energy on the wall that quickly began to fade.

I summoned energy with my breath and left paw prints of azure starlight behind when I hit the wall at the same place and bounded after him.

I missed the leap, and my tummy hit the top of the concrete wall. I had to sink my claws into the ground outside and haul myself up with only my front paws, the back ones scrambling to get me out, and by the time I was, My Shadow was fifty yards away and accelerating.

Well. He was quite a bit, ah, sleeker than me. I told you, everyone says I am a Good Dog and that means treats. But perhaps I would make more time to exercise when this was settled.

I set out after him, and My Shadow darted off the paths and into the greenery of the park. There was precious little cover to hide him, but somehow there always seemed to be just enough of it to keep him all but invisible. Even as we ran, I could feel him begin to fade from my senses, and I redoubled my efforts, working energy to pour on speed and close the distance before he could lose me a second time.

I was soon on his heels, frustrating his efforts to conceal himself. I was about to seize his tail in my teeth when he gave up his energy work to hide himself and instead used it to fling himself up the trunk of a tree and out of reach, then bounded to the next trunk, zigzagging forward into more greenery. I followed him relentlessly, relying on the solid earth and the power of my breath to fuel my speed, and crashed into him again in the thicker brush, truly out of sight of anyone at the zoo.

It was, in fact, an excellent spot for a trap.

I had been so intent on the pursuit that I almost didn't sense the warlock's demons before their claws and fangs reached me. They were not large creatures, being perhaps a third my size—but they were equipped with hideously wide jaws and ripping claws, coupled with a squat and extremely powerful body. The nearest struck at my spine just above my tail with its jaws, and only a desperate roll kept it from getting hold of me. Instead, its teeth raked my haunch, slicing and burning with hot, bright pain.

The second demon simply clamped its wide jaws down on my right foreleg, all serrated sharpness and horrible pressure. I roared with pain and whirled to seek its throat—only to have My Shadow slam into my shoulder with his and send me sprawling.

The demons seized the opportunity with unearthly hunger, leaping onto me, fangs and claws tearing while I desperately tried to fend them off.

Worse, a third demon, driven by dark energy, bounded off into the brush.

"Good-bye, brother," My Shadow said, his voice thick with satisfaction. "Three demons would certainly have ended your wizard, but I suppose one will do—as long as fortune is on its side."

And he turned and vanished into the brush, already fading from my senses.

I roared, a sound not too unlike the roar the lion had made for us earlier in the day, except that my roar was full of bright energy. That energy, focused all in one place, smashed into the demons' false flesh like a sandblaster, stripping away the outer layers of the bodies they'd built from energy in order to walk in the mortal world. The impact shoved them back, and I used the brief opening to seize one by the throat and shake it in the ancient technique of my kind. I whipped it back and forth, once, twice, thrice. There was a satisfying sensation as I felt the demon's neck snap, and then suddenly the demon was gone and my mouth was full of transparent, flavorless gelatin—the ectoplasm the demon had used to build its mortal shell.

But the second demon leapt onto my back as I did. Claws sank into my shoulders and haunches as its lethal jaws snapped down at the back of my neck. Pure terror washed through me along with the primal sensations of pain.

I didn't give those jaws a chance to get hold of me. Instead I crashed out of the brush and flung my back against the nearest tree, smashing the demon into the trunk. I heard people scream and begin to run as, clear of My Shadow's clouding influence, they saw plainly what was happening.

*Uh-oh. Bad dog, Mouse.*

The demon let out a croaking scream at the impact but only clamped down tighter. So I slammed it against the tree again, dazing it. Then, harnessing energy in my breath once more, I bounded against one tree trunk, then another, then straight up into the air. Sometimes when My Friend and I went camping, I would do that and leap out over the lake, just to see how high I could get. My record was nearly twenty feet.

Of course, I hadn't been terrified then. This was more like thirty. And I came down on my back.

There was a crunching sound, and suddenly the claws were gone and my back was marinating in ectoplasm.

There was no time to enjoy the relief I felt at ending the threat to my own safety. My Shadow was still out there, still working, and I could not sense where he was. That was all right. I already knew where he was going. He was off to work energy against My Friend, to give the third demon the lethal advantage of surprise. All I needed to do was find My Friend and I would find My Shadow . . .

Unless.

My Shadow had been laboring to deceive me at every turn. Each of his actions had shown me something about him. He worked from the shadows, influencing events while remaining unseen. He had successfully provoked me into pursuing him by threatening the humans I loved, and led me into a trap that had come near to killing me, while exposing himself to the least amount of danger. He hadn't even tried to do battle with me until the numbers had turned and I was outnumbered three to one.

My Shadow would not hazard himself against a threat of the likes of My Friend unless he had no other choice. That was not his nature.

He would pursue the weaker target.

He was going after Maggie.

I turned to sprint back to her, hurtling down the walkways of the zoo like a grey and silver-blue comet, threading through humans, leaping over trash cans and benches, and generally behaving in a manner that would have earned a disapproving look from My Friend in any other circumstances.

I had no choice. My Shadow would return to Maggie, but he would do so while remaining hidden, following the trees and the plots of greenery through the park. My only chance of beating him to my little girl was to run a shorter distance, a straight line, and that meant doing it in the open.

As I ran, I tracked the third demon, closing in on the same general area where My Friend had gone to confront the warlock. There was nothing more I could do to help him. I would have to trust to fortune and the Almighty and Queen Mab and Odin and whatever other friendly Powers that might be watching that My Friend would, please, please, please be all right.

"*Aparturum!*" thundered My Friend in his spellcasting voice, from somewhere within several hundred yards, and I felt the distant surge of magical power. "*Instaurabos!*" he shouted again a second later, with a second surge, and the third demon simply vanished from my senses as neatly as if it had been popped into a jar.

My heart soared and my speed increased.

And when My Shadow reached the door down to the subbasement, I was there.

Waiting for him.

Teeth bared.

He came to a stop, staring at me. Both of us were breathing hard, but in a controlled fashion, gathering more energy as we did.

"Clever," he said.

"I have my moments," I replied.

"You're bleeding," my brother noted. "Weakened. I could kill you."

"By all means," I said, "please do."

He tilted his head at that.

"I am bleeding," I said, "and weaker than I could be, and tired from one fight already. Assuming near parity between us, you should have the advantage. But you don't. Because you forgot something."

"Oh?" My Shadow asked.

"I don't need to survive this scenario to succeed," I said.

He showed me his teeth in a sneer. "Do you expect me to think, fat, happy little brother, that you do not wish to survive?"

"Survival isn't enough," I said. "I wish to live. And I will best do that by taking you with me."

"If you can," he said.

"If I ignore my own survival, it gives me a great many options in a fight that I would not otherwise have, brother. Are you that confident of your strength?"

"If you can," he snarled.

"But whether or not I can isn't really the question, is it?" I noted. "The question is whether you believe me. The question is whether I am truly willing to sacrifice my life so that she may have hers." I rose and shook out my mane, causing motes of bright energy to fall like tiny stars. "I love that child. And if you take one step closer, I will gladly die to rip out your guts with my teeth."

My Shadow stood for a moment, staring.

"Why?" he said finally.

"Because she would do the same for me," I said.

We faced each other in silence.

"You're wrong about them," he said finally. "They don't care for you. Not really."

"One of us is wrong," I said. "Are you willing to die to find out which of us it is?"

He said nothing.

And then . . . laughter.

Laughter drifted up to us from the subbasement below. My Maggie raised her voice in laughter, straight from her belly, amused and warm and strong. Seconds later, the faint sounds of creeps, screaming in despair, rose to us.

My Shadow took in Maggie's victory for a moment and then his body language shifted, becoming less aggressive.

I didn't relax my stance. My brother moved indirectly. It was best to consider him dangerous at all times.

"Well," he rumbled. "It would seem the day is yours."

"It doesn't have to be," I said. "There's no reason it can't be your day as well. You should come with me. You have great power. You could do much good. You'd be welcome—and there would be French fries."

My Shadow only shook his head, his expression bleak. "How can so much ignorance fit inside so little skin?" He turned away and began to stalk off. "Good-bye, brother."

"Brother," I said, my voice hard.

He paused, cocking an ear without looking back.

"You didn't harm them. You are leaving. As I told you."

The hairs on his back went rigid.

"Remember the third part," I said. "Don't come back. Or we will answer that question together."

My Shadow answered me with a calm glance over his shoulder.

And then vanished back to where he'd come from.


MAGGIE LED THE freed children from the subbasement, and once we'd gotten them up into the sunlight, where the human authorities could take care of them, we hurried back over to the café. Working so much energy, combined with the exertion of fighting and running and getting hurt, had left me exhausted. My fur was fine enough to get into the cuts and stop the bleeding. My body would heal itself in a few days. I knew I would be all right—but I wanted nothing so much as to throw myself down on a nice cool spot of floor and nap.

But I was still on duty. So though I wanted very much to sleep, I sat beneath the table with my head up, guarding Maggie until My Friend returned.

He came in with the warlock, whose name was Austin. Austin had been so soaked in dark energy that I could practically see it smudged all over him like soot.

I sighed. I was tired, but there was work to do. I summoned more energy with my breath and shook hands with him while My Friend got everyone food. Then I settled down by his feet, breathing gentle energy over him, wiping away the darkness my brother had drawn over his eyes.

In the end, we all wound up in My Friend's car. I sat in the backseat with Austin, who had slumped against me and simply fallen asleep.

"What's going to happen to him, Dad?" Maggie asked.

My Friend smiled at her and patted her hand with his. His hand could have held four of hers. "We get him a good night's sleep, a bath—that kind of thing. Then, when he's ready, I'll go with him to go talk to his parents. I'll give him some basic lessons on how not to let his abilities get out of control, and after that we'll see what he wants to do."

"You're going to stand by him," Maggie said carefully. Though she really meant *by me*.

"Yes," My Friend said simply.

Maggie tightened her grip on his hand.

I was tired. But I leaned forward and gave him a kiss on the ear.

"Yick!" My Friend said, smiling. "Gross!"

But what he meant was, *Good Dog*.

A martial arts enthusiast whose résumé includes a long list of skills rendered obsolete at least two hundred years ago, #1 *New York Times* bestselling author **Jim Butcher** turned to writing as a career because anything else probably would have driven him insane. He lives mostly inside his own head so that he can write down the conversations of his imaginary friends, but his head can generally be found in the Rocky Mountains of Colorado. Jim is the author of the Dresden Files (*Skin Game*, *Cold Days*), the Codex Alera novels (*Furies of Calderon*, *Academ's Fury*), and the Cinder Spires series (*The Aeronaut's Windlass*).

---

CONNECT ONLINE

jim-butcher.com
facebook.com/author.jim.butcher
twitter.com/longshotauthor